Praise for *The Night Is Mine*

"An action-packed adventure. With a super-stud hero, a strong heroine, and a backdrop of the world of the Washington elite, it will grab readers from the first page."
—*RT Book Reviews*, 4 Stars

"A gripping, multilayered military romantic suspense."
—*USA Today Happy Ever After*

"Absolutely amazing… The romance and relationship blends seamlessly into the story line… A great first book for a new series, and I cannot wait for the next one."
—*Night Owl Reviews* Reviewer Top Pick, 5 Stars

"Buchman's hard-to-put-down novel, with its nonstop action, surprise villain, and story of forbidden love, will be a real treat for fans of military romantic suspense. Readers who enjoy Suzanne Brockmann, Vicki Hinze, and Merline Lovelace as well as those who like good romantic suspense, military or otherwise, will enjoy the first book in the Night Stalkers series."
—*Booklist* Starred Review

"Takes kick-ass to a whole new level… I was on the edge of my seat during every action scene. This is a must-read."
—*Fresh Fiction*

"Awesome, intriguing, powerful, and seductive."
—*BookLoons*

"The secrets, the suspense, and the romance just all rocked in every sense of the word."

—*Romancing the Book*

"Packed full of action, adventure, and romance."

—*Tyra's Book Addiction*

"Strong characters, a suspenseful plot, and fast pacing to make a very entertaining read."

—*Reviews by Martha's Bookshelf*

"Truly wonderful scenes that stole my breath and had my heart thudding heavily."

—*Where's My Muse?*

"A superbly well-rounded, seriously entertaining story."

—*Smitten with Reading*

"*The Night Is Mine* provides all the thrills of a great suspense novel and all the romance one could wish for."

—*TBQ's Book Palace*

"A multilayered story with a gripping plot and a strong cast of characters and sweet, tender scenes between the hero and heroine."

—*My Book Addiction and More*

"A breakout romantic suspense novel with thrilling action and a capable heroine."

—*Book Savvy Babe*

I OWN THE DAWN

THE NIGHT STALKERS

M.L. BUCHMAN

sourcebooks
casablanca

Published by Sourcebooks Casablanca, an imprint of Sourcebooks, Inc.
P.O. Box 4410, Naperville, Illinois 60567-4410
(630) 961-3900
FAX: (630) 961-2168
www.sourcebooks.com

Printed and bound in the United States of America
VP 10 9 8 7 6 5 4 3 2 1

To my stepdaughter,
for showing me more of my own heart
than I ever knew I had.

Thrust *n*.

The aerodynamic force produced by tilting a helicopter's rotor that provides a directional force to fly forward, sideways, or backward

Thrust *v*.

To drive toward a goal

Chapter 1

"THERE'S NO WAY YOU'RE ASSIGNING ME TO SOME girlie-chopper."

Kee Smith had to look a long way up to see herself reflected in the Major's mirrored shades. Well, let him look down into his own damn reflection in her shades and see how he liked it. All he'd see was himself shimmering in the desert heat and the helicopter he'd just rammed down through the dawn sky.

They stood in a baking soccer arena, which was now turned into a baking forward air base out in the middle of the baking desert in bloody baking Pakistan. Already, the tier upon tier of weathered concrete seating focused the blast of light on the bare dirt field like a magnifying glass.

No response. Crap!

Maybe she couldn't read the Major's eyes through those shades, but after six years in the U.S. Army, she could read his silence.

"Sir." *Damn. Screwin' up already, Kee.* She'd spent the last thirty-seven hours going from one lumpy flight to another to get into the theater of operations. Her reward, a dusty bivouac fifty miles from Afghanistan's brutal Hindu Kush mountains. That part didn't bother her. If President Matthews said the war was here, fine. She came here. But that her new commander turned out to be a stick-in-the-mud, protocol-bound dweeb… That she didn't like so much.

She was dirty, stank worse than after running a tenner with a field pack. Her butt was chapped from one too many hard racks. Sweat dripped down from her bandana in the desert heat. And there wasn't no way she'd done all that to get assigned to some girlie-chopper. She wanted to fly, damn it. Into the bloody fray, not away from it.

Major Chunk-o-Muscle cracked a smile without a single drop of friendly behind it. His flight suit showed rough wear that she knew from experience didn't happen overnight. The handle of his piece, a non-reg Sig Sauer P226, sweet, looked worn too. The silvery aluminum showing through the black anodizing. That took serious use. The hand resting loose beside it had a gold ring; she'd seen him slip it on after he climbed out of the chopper. Common practice. If you were downed, you didn't want anything shiny on you to attract attention.

Of course, the symbol on his finger had never stopped men from hitting on her before; built short and curvy, they all figured she was easy. They all found out fast just how wrong a man could be. Besides she wasn't into married ones, muscley or otherwise. The Army might choose her partners in the air, even if she didn't like its choices sometimes, but she sure as shooting chose hers on the ground.

"Oh, what's wrong with a girlie-chopper?" His deep voice practically laughing at her.

She shrugged her duffel off her shoulder and let it smack, creating a knee-high local brownout of its own in the dust-fine sand. She rested her aluminum rifle case on top of it. Dragging her hands through her jaw-length mop of hair didn't calm her one bit. She still looked dark and tousled in the Major's shades. Shit, didn't matter anyway. Go for it.

"Permission to speak candidly, sir?"

His half-amused nod really ticked her off.

"I fought too damn hard to get here to be slotted in with some cute little public relations fantasy you have in your head, sir. Sure I've heard of Major Beale, goddamn legend and all. But if I end up on her squad, I'll catch no end of flak and you'll be wasting both my time and the Army's. They didn't ship my butt to this forward air base, thirty miles into the middle of nowhere, to form a chick squad." That he'd even suggested it told her what kind of a commander he was and she wasn't looking forward to it.

"They shipped me here because the nastiest battle on the planet is happening just north in the Hindu Kush. I came to kick some serious ass, pardon, sir, not to be slotted by gender. I want, I deserve to be placed because I'm the best at what I do. I belong in a bird like that." Kee pointed over her shoulder without turning. She'd seen the distinctive T-shape of the beautiful chopper, the twin of the Major's own bird, reflected in his shades. The heavy rock 'n' roll beat of its rotors pounded against her diaphragm before she could hear it.

The Major didn't bother to glance up. "You ready to ride on that?"

"Damn straight."

Now he did look up, a smile impossibly softening his stony face. Mr. Chunk-o-Muscle was Major Handsome as well. Who'd have known with that permanent scowl. She turned to follow his gaze.

Falling down like a hammer out of the crystal blue

sky came her baby. A Black Hawk helicopter. And not just any Hawk. It was an MH-60L DAP. The Direct Action Penetrator was the nastiest gunship God ever put on Earth and only the best flew in her. Kee'd almost died of pleasure the first time she saw one. Actually she'd been about to die literally too.

She'd spent five long years bucking her way up from infantry to get aboard. It had taken her three of those to get into SOAR and another two to get through SOAR training. Now she was here, forward operations. She'd done it and now was facing a DAP Hawk. No man had ever made her feel this good.

And this sweet bird wasn't fooling around. Two massive weapons' pylons stuck out from either side of the midsection. On one side she had a rocket pod carrying nineteen birds and a 30 mm cannon just in case they wanted to go mastodon hunting. On the other pylon, another rocket pod and a rack of Hellfire anti-tank missiles, three of which were missing.

Unfriendlies lay pretty close around here. The surrounding town of five thousand people could be hiding anybody. The two crew chiefs still had their hands on the M134 miniguns peeking out of their shooting holes even while they were just a hundred feet up. The chopper was still exposed to the "friendlies" lurking in the town outside the stadium. The Hawk even had the midair refueling probe, which meant she went in way deep. Kee was down with that.

Only one group flew such a bird, SOAR. The Special Operations Aviation Regiment (airborne), the Army's 160th. The Night Stalkers. The baddest asses on the face of the sky. And she was here. She pinched her leg, on

the side away from Major Muscle-head. It stung. This
wasn't no dream. Wide awake. She'd done it.

They both turned away and covered their faces as a
brownout of dust washed across the field, adding another layer to her too-many hours of grime. Once the
bird hunkered down, and speech and vision were again
possible, she faced him.

"That." She cocked a thumb over her shoulder.
"Me." She thumped her chest with a fist. "Sir!" For
good measure.

"Done!" Again that hidden laugh. "If you can talk
your way past the pilot." He turned on his heel and disappeared into the heat shimmer.

So, all up to her, huh? Good. Didn't scare her none.

Kee yanked her duffel over her shoulder, grabbed her
rifle case, and tromped over to the DAP as her rotors
wound down and the dust and sand settled.

Respect. She'd give that a shot first. Respect with a
little help. Because, like a good soldier, she had more
than one weapon in her arsenal. She tossed down her duffel and the rifle case at the edge of the rotor sweep and
made sure her T-shirt lay smooth and tight on her skin
so that every muscle and curve showed. Pack 'n' rack.
Six-pack abs and a good solid rack for a chest. On clear
display. Her dusky skin, almond eyes, and single blond-
streak in dark hair had some kind of magic at knocking
men dead. Wasn't why she had it, but it worked.

She didn't tease, it wasn't her mode. If she offered,
she meant it and delivered. But having men's brains
switch off around her had its advantages. She wasn't
gonna be filing a letter of complaint with the chief people designer who'd wired men's brains to blow away

like dust in rotor wash whenever they were around her. It just amused her that it worked every damn time.

The pilot climbed down, leaned in to trade a joke with his crew chief, and then headed out from under the slowing rotors. He almost passed her by, but Kee snapped a sharp salute.

"At ease." No salute back.

Crap! Newbie mistake. She jerked her hand back to her side and couldn't help checking behind her, but Major Muscle was gone. She knew better, had been forward-deployed plenty to know better. In the field you never salute a superior officer. Sure way to tell a sniper who to target.

Kee dropped to parade rest, clenched her hands behind her back. Muscled arms and shoulders back focused men on a chest that wowed 'em all. Some civilian women thought they were hot, but there was nothing like a buffed-out soldier babe. And the civilians knew it, too. Wasn't a single civilian chick ever gave her a smile when she entered a bar.

"Sergeant Kee Smith. Best damn gunner you ever met. I want on your ship, sir."

The pilot peeled off his helmet, revealing blue-green eyes and an unruly wave of soft brown hair that she'd bet never stayed under control, no matter how long a woman played with it. He opened the front of his flight suit to reveal a sweaty tee on a slender frame.

"First Lieutenant Archibald Jeffrey Stevenson III at your service. And it's not my ship. You'll be wanting to converse with the Major." His voice so slow and smooth and refined, like a radio announcer on those classical stations.

Then he grinned at her, a saucy, funny grin. Started in his eyes and wandered down to his lips, ending up kind of lopsided. Not Handsome Mr. Major, but it made him look pretty damn cute. She couldn't help but notice that his long and lean had some nice muscle underneath, you'd expect no less from a SOAR.

The Lieutenant, however, didn't even have the decency to rake his eyes down her body. The Major hadn't been able to help studying her frame, she could tell despite the mirrored shades he wore like they'd been welded there. But this Lieutenant somehow managed. Either gay or self-control of steel-like strength. Came down to it, she'd be betting on the latter. What happened when that much self-control let go? Now that could be worth the price of the ticket to find out.

He moved off to her right, passing so close they almost brushed shoulders. He leaned in and whispered, "Good luck. You are going to need it. More than that nice chest, Sergeant."

"But it's a damn nice chest, isn't it, sir?" So he had noticed.

"Yes, ma'am, it is." And even though she didn't turn to look at him, she knew they were smiling together for that moment.

Lieutenant Archibald Jeffrey Stevenson III. What was this woman's Army coming to? Did he have any idea how ridiculous he sounded? Like those late-night movies when the only thing on was some British hoo-ha, everyone prancing around in long dresses. Hard to believe he even said "chest" with a voice like that. Though she'd liked the way he said it, as if it were a compliment, not a drool.

She spotted the oak leaves on the collar of the other pilot and set aside thoughts of long and lean lieutenants with wavy hair. The Major was still helmeted and chatting with the crew coming in to service his chopper. The Hawk'd been through some hard times. Tape patches showed more than a few hits on the fuselage; some of the panels had been replaced, and a couple of those had patched holes too. Now that they'd stopped spinning, she could see that one of the rotor blades was clearly newer than the other three, replaced after taking too much abuse. This bird had seen some heavy action. She moved in to check out the guns, worn hard but so immaculate you could eat off them. Her kind of weapon.

"Pretty, isn't she?" Some crewwoman's voice close beside her. SOAR had women in the ground personnel, but Kee was only the second woman to ever make the grade for flight operations. Sweet candy for sure. A serpent of coiled gray had been painted across the dusky green of the chopper. The colors so close in tone made it hard to see in places, which made it appear all the more dangerous. It wrapped around the gunner's lookout window and writhed across the pilot's door. Etched in his scales, the name of the bird. *Vengeance*. The serpent's head, striking forward along the nose of the chopper, sported mirrored shades. In the lenses, someone had even drawn a reflected explosion of an enemy going down hard.

"Better than sex." She rubbed a hand down the long barrel of the 30 mm cannon. "I can't believe that bastard Major wanted to slot me on the girlie-chopper. This is real flight."

"Don't like girlie-choppers?"

"Not one friggin' bit. I want this bad boy. I didn't come here to form no goddamn chick squad." She stepped forward to stare into the face of the rocket launcher. Seven fired. They'd been in some heat last night. She'd wager it hadn't turned out well for the bad guys. Night Stalkers ruled the dark.

Something kept dragging at her attention. She'd been trained to pay attention to the niggling feeling that something was out of place. Not right. It had saved her life more than once while pounding ground for the 10th Mountain Division.

Looking up, she spotted it.

"The rotor blades. They look different."

Kee could feel the maintenance chick, still behind her, focusing her attention upward.

"Thicker. Most can't see that. This is the first M-mod in the theater. The MH-60M upgrade adds twenty-five percent larger engines, needs a heavier blade."

Kee whistled in admiration. "She must haul ass across the sky."

"She does."

Kee glanced over at her new companion. "Kee Smith."

The first thing she noticed was the shoulder-length blond hair and the bluest eyes on the planet. Pretty, slender, perfect posture. Would fit in with Archibald Jeffrey Stevenson III just fine. Maybe they were hitched. Met in a frickin' hoity-toity fern bar somewhere on the Upper West Side. The woman dug a sparkler out of a pocket and slipped it on her left, though the Lieutenant's hand had been clean. Still, could be.

The second thing Kee noticed was the worn flight suit, the battered helmet under one arm, the scuffed-up

M9 Beretta at her hip, and the pair of major's oak leaves on the woman's lapels.

Kee's poker face clicked in a beat and a half too late. One woman had made it into SOAR before her. A friggin' legend. And not for spreading her legs to the top. A girl couldn't turn around without being compared to the one other woman flight-qualified in the whole regiment. That damn Major Muscle had tricked her. Tricked her into begging to get onto the girlie-chopper she so hadn't wanted. Who'd have guessed the girlie-bird would be a DAP Hawk?

Kee knew the woman's name even before she spoke in that refined voice of hers.

"Emily Beale."

―⁓―

"You for real?" Kee couldn't equate the tall slip of a blonde standing in the dust beside her with the legend. Real or not, no woman truly met SOAR standards before Kee'd come along. That was cold cash to your dealer on the street. There had to be another story here.

"Last I checked."

Kee managed to clamp her tongue between her teeth before she could put her foot any further down the rabbit hole. The legend told that the title of SOAR's number-one pilot belonged to the only woman flying in all five battalions. Kee also knew for a fact that officers lived to mess with lower ranks' minds.

SOAR pilots were as badass as the ground pounders they carted through the sky. Every hour a Special Forces guy trained, a SOAR flier trained. Green Berets didn't have nothing on a Night Stalker. And they couldn't fly.

The Delta operators, the D-boys, okay, they were something other. Even a SOAR couldn't keep up with them, but the crew for the 160th's helicopters sat at the pinnacle of the U.S. military's air power for a reason. They were the best. That meant being the toughest.

Major Beale was a total lightweight, all trim and slender. If you gave Kee a .50cal machine gun to cart around with a case of ammo, you'd be getting somewhere. But if you gave a little FN SCAR carbine to Ms. Major Beale, could she even pick it up?

Major and Major. Her brain went click, loud enough to be audible. Major Chunk-o-Muscle had smiled at the sky when this bird had swung into view. He had the shackle of gold on his left hand to match Beale's sparkler. Married her way to the top. Hey, whatever worked. Didn't mean she wanted to fly with the little Miss Hoity Girl. She'd never make her mark if they always kept her in the shadow of SOAR's only other woman.

But, damn, a berth on a DAP Hawk. Even with a girl pilot, she'd be aboard some serious hardware.

"Having trouble, Keiko Smith?"

"Don't call me that shit."

"What shit?" The curse sounded prissy coming out of that perfect face.

"Keiko. My mama may have named me after a stupid killer whale, but that don't make it my name. Name's Kee."

"Not unless you're fifteen years old. No one knew Keiko the Whale's name until he starred in the movie *Free Willy* in the mid-nineties. She named you in Japanese. It means blessed child. A—"

"Don't give a shit. And I'm not Japanese. I'm

American." Maybe half Japanese, or part Chinese or whatever, and half who-knew, for sure her mother didn't. Two days in transit, Kee really needed sleep. She wanted on this chopper so bad it hurt right down to her aching butt. Maybe the cute copilot she'd met earlier, Archibald something the flippin' Third, really flew the missions. Could Beale be a fake legend?

"Doesn't matter. The name is Kee. And how is it you know my name?"

The silence landed on her as oppressive as the heat. Fort Campbell, Kentucky, could be hot, but she was dyin' here. The heat off the bird burned into her brain. The first day in heat was always tough. The first day in heat and going on forty-eight hours with no shut-eye, that rated plain old harsh.

Only when a hand landed on her shoulder, hard, did she realize she was weaving. Soldiers didn't weave. She blinked her eyes several times to clear the fog and shrugged off the steadying hand even though it belonged to a major.

"Name's Kee, ma'am. Kee Smith." A name she'd taken the day she joined the Army, the day she'd re-invented herself. She staggered away, stumbled on her duffel and dragged it onto her shoulder. The rifle case, usually so light in her hands, weighed a ton.

Beaten. Again. She'd set her hopes so high. Five years of busting butt and she'd made it. SOAR. The 160th. She'd toughed it out. Survived. Faced down every man jerk on the way up who said women couldn't make the grade. Every crap sergeant who thought a woman only had one use in the world and then tried to demonstrate what that was.

First they hated you for being a woman, then for not giving out, and finally, most of all, for when you whupped their ass in public. Then this. SOAR had five battalions, and she'd ended up here. Even if Kee had the heart to climb over another obstacle, knowing that Major Muscle backed up his wife meant she never could. The Army'd stuck it up her backside but good this time.

"Sergeant Kee Smith!" Major Beale's voice snapped through the burning heat.

Kee stumbled to a halt, head hanging down and she couldn't drag it up. Right. As stick-in-the-mud as her hubby. She'd offered no "sir." No frickin' kowtow to the high master. She'd be cleaning out latrines until she died, a skill she already had too much undeserved practice in.

She managed to turn but didn't speak. If they were going to burn her down, she'd take it standing. Head up, shoulders back, and, screw Ms. Perfect Size Two, chest out.

Major Prissy-Butt Emily Beale of Hoity Toity Land still stood in front of her bird. A couple of armorers in their red vests were reloading the rocket pod. A fuel truck hovered nearby, waiting for the ordnance crew to clear.

Her arms were crossed, her purple helmet, unbelievable, with the rampant gold Pegasus, the winged horse of the Night Stalkers, dangled negligently from her fine-fingered hand. It had a bullet crease where a round had shot into the Kevlar, probably made the woman poop her pants. Or maybe she'd shot the helmet herself by accident. They stared at each other across a dozen paces of stamped earth.

Kee stood ready for ire, rage, dressing down. But the woman just stared. The smile that pulled up one corner of her mouth lit the eyes and changed her from pretty to magazine-ad beautiful. She was a knockout! No wonder she'd tripped Major Muscle. But the smile wasn't for Kee, but rather for some joke only the woman knew. Then, snap! The smile was gone. So gone, Kee couldn't even picture it in her mind's eye. Not on that face.

"I know your name because Major Henderson assigned you to me, Smith. And we're both going to have to learn to live with that."

The Major paused. Long enough for Kee to hear the unspoken second half of that sentence. Beale was most definitely not looking forward to figuring out how to live with her.

"You've got eleven hours and fourteen minutes to briefing, eleven hours and thirty-four to flight. Get some rack time. And lose the goddamn attitude." She turned away.

Kee wavered on her feet again, the duffel almost dragging her down to the dirt.

The Hawk. It filled her vision. They were letting her on a DAP.

—◊◊◊—

Archie watched Sergeant Kee Smith from where he lounged comfortably in the shade of Major Henderson's Black Hawk, just two birds away.

The tiny woman saluted Major Beale's back smartly. Enough spite to it that maybe she hoped a sniper was watching and would take out the Major. Then glanced around to make sure no one noticed.

Fooling yourself again, Archie.

But he didn't turn and leave. Couldn't. Sergeant Kee Smith. Almond eyes. Buffed out the way even most guys couldn't achieve, but a body that was all woman. Dark skin of the warmest shade the sun had ever kissed, like a permanent, perfect tan. Brown-black hair, with a single streak the color of a golden sun. It made for a saucy statement that lightened what would otherwise be a forbidding beauty.

With his usual luck she'd be a tramp or a prude or a lesbian, or just want to be his friend, if that.

He'd never found a way to speak to an attractive woman. Pretty, sure. But attractive, the ones who wrenched at his gut merely walking by, tied his tongue into a Gordian knot. Had he really commented on her chest? It was very nice, and rated somewhere between remarkable and spectacular on his own personal list. He had always been partial to well-chested women and that fact surprised him. It did seem rather crass after all, but true nonetheless. But there existed no First Lieutenant Archibald Stevenson III he knew who would actually say such a thing to a woman. Now he watched her from his bit of shade as if she could fulfill every prurient fantasy he'd harbored as a young boy.

Sergeant Kee Smith hadn't acted offended at his comment, but neither had she flaunted her body at the Major as she had for his enjoyment.

Still she stood facing the DAP Hawk, entranced despite Beale's departure. Some pixie-sized fairy of mythological origin reborn in this desert wilderness. Careful, Archie. It couldn't happen of course, he was an officer and she was enlisted. Quick road to a court martial.

However, that didn't stop a man from thinking thoughts. He knew himself too well. He could fall for a woman, dream of her from afar for months, and never take action. Never actually speak to her. Too much disappointment lay down that road, one he'd vowed never to walk again. He liked women, enjoyed being with them. But when someone hit the inner ring of his "attracted" button, he became a mute. Patricia in high school. Mary Ellen in college. Most recently, Lorenna, the medevac trainer, who he managed to never speak with directly during the entire two-week course.

Well, if any of those women had hit the inner target ring, Sergeant Smith had just whacked it with a bull's-eye shot. Despite her size, there was a force of nature, a power that wrapped and curled around her filling up far more space.

He'd wasted far too much of his life thinking about women who would never be his. He really should pay more attention to the ones who wanted to be with him, but they never bull's-eyed that button in his brain.

"What are you staring at, Bucko?"

"That's Lieutenant to you." His response was instinctive even as he blinked a couple times. Kee Smith stood right in front of him. His eyes had tracked her, even if his brain hadn't. And this time they were focused where no decent man's should be, on that delicious double curve where chest rolled into that mysterious crevasse between her—one more blink and he returned his eyes to her face.

"Nothing. Simply observing."

"Well, Lieutenant." Amazing that she could pile so much sarcasm into a single word. "Have you observed where my billet is, Lieutenant Professor, sir? I need some sack time."

Professor? The nickname that had nearly made him insane during Green Platoon training didn't bother him in the slightest at this moment. And that made for an interesting observation in itself.

"Professor?" She snapped her fingers in front of his face.

Now she'd think him a complete dolt.

"This way. I'd be glad to show you."

"No thanks, just point the way. I need to sleep, not wrestle off some guy."

That snapped him out of it. "Stow that, Sergeant!" Came out harsher than he intended. A little flirting, that is all she was doing, and he had shut her down hard. Very smooth.

She actually blushed and looked down. "Sorry, sir!"

About the cutest damn thing he'd ever seen, that a woman so clearly a primal force could blush. No longer trusting his tongue, he pointed at the small tent set aside as women's quarters.

"Thank you, sir." She headed away without a backward glance. No teasing sashay of the hips, no coquettish glance over the shoulder. Had his own thoughts misinterpreted her comment? Had she thought he was suggesting…? He'd never… But she wouldn't know that, so he was just another guy to her.

He watched the diminutive juggernaut heading for her target.

He headed for the showers, hoping his common sense would catch up with him somewhere along the way.

Chapter 2

"WHEN DID THE DESERT GET SO FRICKIN' COLD?" KEE cinched down the cuffs of her flight suit to cut any chance of airflow up her arms. Slick, fingerless gloves helped, but she had to huff on her fingertips to make sure they had feeling. Two hours cruising in the dark and all she had to show for it was a chill halfway to frostbite. She tapped her rifle case for the third time where she'd secured it against the bulkhead. Felt good to have it near her, even on a DAP Hawk where the chances of using it were close to—

A low laugh on the headset in her helmet, just a notch louder than the turbine whine and rotor thud that was part of a Hawk ride. She'd guess Staff Sergeant Big Bad John, her fellow crew chief. One serious piece of very large man with a deep boomer of a voice to match.

"At this altitude, we often experience a sixty-to-seventy-degree temperature swing day to night," Lieutenant Stevenson said. Okay, she didn't have their laughs sorted out yet. He didn't act put out by her earlier screwup so she did her best to stop kicking herself over it.

"Oh, really? Do tell, Professor, sir." She'd tagged him with it and he hadn't argued. Just started answering to it with those perfect manners of his.

"With the low moisture and thin air—"

"Less chatter." That was Queen Hoity, though Kee'd been smart enough to keep that tag to herself, sounding all put out. Clearly someone she'd rather have in Kee's seat had left the Black Hawk. Well, tough. Sergeant Kee Smith nursed the copilot-side gun now, right behind Professor Stevenson III's seat, and they wouldn't be prying her out anytime soon.

"And Smith?"

"Yes, ma'am?" She turned to look over her shoulder between the pilots' seats. Beale was looking straight at her with the night-vision goggles focused on her like the glowing green eyes of a ghoul. NVGs looked alien no matter how often you saw them.

"Show some goddamn respect unless you want to walk home." Major Beale's voice was far chillier than the high-altitude desert air.

Kee felt as if she'd just been kicked, again. Disrespecting a lieutenant. Twice. What had she been thinking?

"Yes, ma'am. Sorry, sir." And she focused back outside over her gun. How could she have been so stupid. Lieutenant Stevenson had seemed so… pleasant? Easygoing? But this was the Army and Major Beale had just made it clear exactly how she ran her chopper. This wasn't some forward infantry squad who didn't care how you acted as long as you shot straight. She was in regular Army now and had to keep reminding herself to act it.

Kee desperately sought something else to concentrate on other than her current failings, but not a damn thing was happening out there.

—⁂—

The slip of a girl moved quickly between one rock and the next. Twice the helicopter had passed near. As her parents had taught her, she'd never looked at them, never tried to see. Instead, she hid behind a rock, shifting to make sure she stayed hidden from view. "Flying Death could see in the dark," her parents had told her. Now they were gone, leaving a hole in her chest that was bigger than her heart, and she had to remember the lessons for herself without reminding.

She swallowed hard against an aching throat. She hadn't found water since last night. But she hadn't found food in four days. Her stomach was past growling. It simply hurt all the time.

Once the helicopter moved away, she edged forward again and peered around the rock. Some men had driven a pickup truck up here, high into the mountains, driven right by her. They had then parked it and walked away, hiding themselves out of sight. She watched for a long time, but no one moved near the truck. Maybe, just maybe, they had left some food or water there.

It was close enough to reach in a quick dash. She could get there, grab any food, and get away with no one the wiser.

Still in a squat, she raised to her toes, her bare feet aching against the cold rock.

Before she ran, she listened one last time.

The helicopter was returning. She eased back, resting her heels on the hard stone with a shiver. Again she must wait. Before they were gunned down, her parents had taught her how to wait.

She was very good at it.

Kee rubbed her eyes. Hours of night patrol and nothing to show for it. Tonight's briefing included line patrol of a no-fly zone. She hadn't latched into rumor central yet, but she'd bet something was going down elsewhere on the line. Real common to have a legman out to watch for a flanking maneuver. We push in one place, bad guys squeeze out in the other place.

Bet they pulled line watch a lot in this bird. Major Muscle being protective of his wife with his assignments and all. Kee'd just have to wait for the stray bad guy instead of the main action. Once she nailed a few, maybe Major Muscle would transfer her somewhere real.

Over chow before the preflight briefing she'd confirmed that Major Mark Henderson and Major Emily Beale had just tied the golden noose around their throats couple months back, stateside. Some big deal. Big John had said the President served as best man. When she'd asked president of what, he'd clammed up and given her a look like she was dumber than stupid. Well screw him, too. She'd been scratching her way through house-tall blackberry bushes on a ten-day training mission in the Washington State rain forest two months ago.

"Light up two o'clock low." Kee snapped it out before her mind consciously registered the sudden movement, then a bright splash of green streaked across her night vision. If she hadn't had the night-vision binoculars flipped down into position, she might not have seen anything at all before they were all dead.

She toggled off the safety. Her gun spun up and she had the spot tracked even as the chopper slammed down and sideways. The streak of green light, hot across her night vision, shot past where they'd just been. RPG. Nasty piece of hardware. Rocket-propelled grenade, cost less than her sidearm and excelled at taking out $40 million choppers. If they'd been fifty meters closer or she'd been a half second slower, they'd be hurting.

The harness that kept her strapped to her seat jerked against her shoulder and crotch as the Lieutenant stood the Hawk on her nose. The Professor was better than Kee'd guessed. Queen Hoity probably watching the instruments and crapping her pants. Sure, Beale was the legend, but Kee couldn't picture Major Hoity as a hard-ass pilot.

Archie wasn't running, he was dropping right down on their heads. A bit of that hidden steel coming out. Nice.

Kee considered letting the pilot know she had the target, had picked out a car-shaped heat signature clear in her night-vision gear to track as reference, twenty yards from the point she'd first spotted. But you were supposed to have the target you called without telling anyone. It was her job to have it wired. She did, so she kept her mouth shut. She just didn't have a line on the shooter yet.

It wouldn't take much to slip the 'copter around so Big John had the target instead of her, but the Lieutenant wasn't going there. Decent.

"Jeep?" Queen Hoity, not the Prof. Only conversation gonna happen at this point had to do with the target, not Mr. Bad Guy's choice of ride.

"It's..." Damn, which way was north? "...at ten o'clock. In the rocks beside the road. Two rotors out." About a hundred and change feet. You learned that pilots wanted all distances in the size of their rotor-blade sweep. Gave them comfort they weren't about to hit anything.

Jeep? Kee spared a glance. Squared-off hood, the green glow of the infrared heat signature well spread, bit heavy on passenger side. Jeep. Been cooling for more than half an hour, less than two. Beale knew her heat signatures at least. That was something.

"I don't see it. Bury them on my mark. Two, one—"

Kee never heard the "mark" as she unleashed the minigun on the point she'd picked out in the dark. Quick one-second bursts to save ammo, a hundred rounds of flying death in each volley tore at the rocks. The tracers lit the area enough that she could see where they must be hiding, a narrow crevice among the boulders.

The Professor swung the Hawk farther around, opening the target up for her. A searing flash somewhere down by Kee's feet announced a rocket was away. Two seconds later all hell broke loose as the Jeep disintegrated in a huge plume. More flash than just their rocket and the target's gas tank. Mr. Baddies had more explosives aboard the vehicle. Kee slapped the night vision aside as the Jeep's gasoline tank set off a secondary plume, bathing the area in blinding light. She could feel the heat blast on her face as they practically flew through the rising flames.

There, visible now that they'd come around, three men down and bloody, and a fourth with a launcher. Reloaded and headed back onto his shoulder.

She opened up and laid in hard. In the first second, the only man still standing was pinned to a boulder by her fire, the RPG launcher flailing out of control as the bullets tore him apart. Three seconds later she nailed something that didn't appreciate it and their hideout disappeared in the glare of another explosion.

Archie slammed the Hawk over and circled the other way.

"Check it, John." Ms. Hoity again.

For a second Kee felt the fighting heat rise. She didn't need checking. She'd nailed the bastards.

Then she remembered. Fresh eyes. Not blinded by rocket launches and muzzle glare.

One circle at hard gees, jamming her down into her seat. It blew the breath out of her. Though the Black Hawk laid so far over onto its right side that even aiming low, Kee could only see night sky. So, she'd watch the night sky for unfriendlies until landscape came back into view. Nothing up there but a couple stars. Moments ago the mountain night was covered with sheets of glittering stars. Yup, her night vision would be shot for another thirty seconds at least. Good call having the other crew chief check it out.

"Looks clean." John called out.

Damn straight. She'd done good.

With a hard snap the chopper leveled out and pummeled away from the site nose down.

"Hang on." That was definitely Big John.

Hang on. She didn't have any choice, harnessed in and hands clamped on the gun. So what the—

Her gut slammed one way as her body slammed the other. If her eyes could have bugged out of her head, they would have. Even with the warning, no way a year of training flights had prepared her for that move. And those trainers were brutal. The Professor had some serious moxie. And the souped-up MH-60M really packed a punch.

Turned around hard, the Hawk tipped nose down and roared back the way they'd just come.

She flipped the night-vision binoculars down in front

of her visor. Scan. Lean out and scan for any other nasties. If the Professor was really good, he'd fly exactly over the burning Jeep, so the flames didn't zap his gunners' night vision.

Give him another point. Kee caught only a bit of side glow from the fire. There, she could see where she'd set off the secondary explosion by nailing the shooters. Four bodies, maybe five, buncha pieces, hard to tell. Fifty feet, there lay...

"A single perp, plus one rotor, curled up, not spread-eagled." A spread-eagled stance, whether standing or prone, would indicate someone trying to steady themselves if directing a weapon. Curled up meant hurt or scared.

Usually.

The Hawk twisted on its tail again and slammed down. A kid. Gone fetal, wearing the white broadcloth of a poor villager less than five feet from the open door in front of Kee.

"Grab him."

Kee slapped her harness release, snapped a three-meter monkey line to her vest so that she couldn't get left behind, and jumped out. She snagged the kid as he tried to crawl away. Must weigh about ten ounces. She slid her hands down the body, chest a little rounded beneath the thin, cotton wrap. Girl not boy, and not as young as her size implied. No hidden hardware, hands empty, a hard grab found no weapon clenched between her legs and confirmed the gender. The girl batted at Kee's hands like moth wings.

Kee tossed her aboard and dove in behind as the Professor hammered the Hawk upward.

Only when she was securing their prisoner at the back of the bay did her brain register what her eyes had seen while she'd squatted over the girl.

The Professor leaning out his door, his FN SCAR carbine covering her, his NVGs down and bathing his face in a green glow. Above him, their backup team, a standard K Hawk, slewed into place with a hard hammer of blades, double-checking the area from on high.

If the Lieutenant was watching her, that meant Beale was piloting, had been piloting. So, the woman did know how to fly. To really fly.

And the Professor. He hadn't looked like an uptown wimp, but rather a guardian angel hovering over her.

As she clawed back to her post against the chopper's climb and harnessed in, she decided it made perfect sense that an angel in her world had the glowing eyes of night vision and stood ready to unleash hellfire from his hands.

Not too shabby, Professor.

Chapter 3

THE GIRL SAT ACROSS THE WOODEN TABLE FROM KEE IN the mess tent, shoveling it down as if she'd never seen food before. Someone had set her up with a mounded plate. Fries and sausage. Eggs and toast. Two pancakes and a hot dog complete with mustard, ketchup, and relish.

Some fliers wanted breakfast in the morning, some wanted dinner when they finished their night's flying. The girl was working her way through both.

Kee tried talking to her, but her Pashto sucked. Really sucked. Okay, beyond sucked. She could say "Thank you" two tries out of three. She had Los Angeles street Spanish, mostly too foul to use in public, picked up some Mandarin from the Chinese Tong gangs, learned Japanese and Korean after she'd joined the Army, but Pashto, Farsi, Urdu, Russian... nope.

She'd requested assignment to SOAR 5th Battalion because they were based out of Tacoma, Washington, and mostly worked the Pacific Rim stuff. She'd gotten that, but to a unit that was on loan to a mash-up force mucking out the 'Stani mountains. Army thinking.

"Has she spoken to anyone yet?" The Professor, though she'd keep that nickname to herself in the future, looked all cool with shower-slicked hair already drying into curly waves of sun-tipped mahogany. He had civvy shorts with a button-down shirt and sat down like at some fine dining table, setting his fork and knife

properly on his paper napkin beside his plate before sliding onto the wooden bench.

It was somehow easier to imagine him as a guardian
angel after seeing him in civilian clothes. His arms and
legs were the long lean muscle of a bicyclist or a cross-
country runner. Despite his thin frame, he looked tough.
Far tougher than his ever polite and reserved character
would imply.

"The kid?" He called her thoughts back from wherever they'd just wandered.

"Nada." Kee glanced at her. "The kid's mouth is
never empty anyway, so not much chance."

The Professor lit out with a line of something that
flowed all twisty and smooth as if he'd spoken it all his
life. Spoke what might be the same thing in two other
languages then shrugged.

The girl eyed him carefully as she took another slice
of toast, mashed it into her egg, and scooped both into
her mouth quickly, bulging her dark cheeks out like a
determined chipmunk. Those eyes, bright hazel in a
dark face beneath forest-brown hair, watched everyone.
Like a street kid terrified the food would vanish before
she could wolf it down. She ate even faster after the
Professor looked at her once more.

"Mission accomplished." Kee couldn't resist nee-
dling the man despite his rank. He was completely out of
place in a war. Though the image of being safely under
the protection of his avenging-angel mode slipped into
her thoughts again.

He grimaced. "Telling someone who's that hungry to
eat more slowly isn't likely to be effective. Even if she
understood me, which I doubt I achieved."

Kee looked at the girl's hollowed cheeks and whip-thin forearms where they stuck out of her wrap. That wasn't just a few missed meals.

"She'll figure it out in about two minutes."

"Figure out what?"

Kee poked at her own eggs. She was hungry enough after the long, cold night to wolf them down as well. Maybe if she ate slow, the kid might—

The girl's eyes widened in alarm.

"Too late. I'll get a rag."

Professor Archibald Jeffrey Stevenson III narrowed his eyes at her as she got up. She considered warning him to move, but decided against it.

Just as Kee returned, the girl's stomach rebelled. Her cheeks puffed for one more moment as she tried to fight her body's instincts, then she spewed half-chewed chunks of food all over the table, Kee's breakfast, and the Professor.

Kee slapped her hand over her mouth to suppress the laugh, not that it did much good. She handed the first cloth to the kid.

"Aww, I'm so sorry." She tossed another one to the Professor, his dignity clearly offended by being covered from mid-chest to thighs in hot dog pieces and lumps of soggy bread.

She turned to go fetch more serious cleanup tools. An orderly was already headed her way fully armed, so she aimed for the chow line to get two fresh plates. One egg and one piece of toast for the kid, and eggs, bacon, potatoes for herself.

The kid, once she'd wiped her face, came out clean. She'd almost gone haring off like a rabbit when Kee had squatted before her to wipe her face, but she put on a brave face and stuck it out. The Professor was gonna need another shower and a fresh set of civvies.

She slid the plate toward the kid, but stopped it half-way across the table.

"How do you say, 'slowly'?"

The Professor didn't look up from his attempts to remove the worst of the mess from his lap. "Which language?" He didn't sound at all happy.

"Like I'd have a clue."

At her acerbic tone, he stopped and looked at her. Glanced at the kid.

"*Medlenno. Ponyat?*"

The kid nodded and Kee finished shoving the plate across the table. Under Kee's watchful eye, the kid tore off only a small bit of bread, folded it around some scrambled egg, and may have even chewed it once or twice on the way down.

"Thanks, Professor. Wha—Sorry, Lieutenant. I'm sorry, sir." He shrugged noncommittally, letting her off the hook.

"Ask your question."

"What language was that, sir?"

"Russian for 'slowly.'"

"Not Farsi?"

"Afghani was the first one I tried. Then Pashto and Arabic. I don't know Tajik, Uzbek, or the dozen others kicking around this region. But I had an idea while she was covering me with her half-eaten breakfast." He wiped off the last of it with a damp cloth. The desert air was already drying his clothes. Still they'd need a good washing and he'd want another shower.

"Just as the common language of Southeast Asia is French for the oldest people and English for the next generation because of the Vietnam wars, in this region Russian is the lingua franca of war and commerce. Perhaps in another five years, if we're still in residence, we shall be privileged to bear witness to the next generation of war children speaking English."

He climbed to his feet, took a step toward the water station to wash his hands, hesitated, and turned back to her.

"And on the ground, and perhaps out of the Major's hearing, Professor doesn't bother me. Which I find to be a bit surprising, but true."

Big John dropped down a tray with a plate mounded high beside her, across from the Professor's spot. Then thudded onto the bench with a sigh of relief.

"Not you." He aimed a finger at John and headed off to wash up.

John looked after the Professor then at her. "What was that about?"

Kee poked her fork down until it hit food and brought whatever she'd stabbed up to her mouth. Her attention was all on Archibald Stevenson III. All that breeding had paid off. He hadn't raised his voice to the kid, never mind cuffed her upside the head. Hadn't even looked flustered as he'd dumped the worst of it into the orderly's bucket. She liked her men a little rough around the edges and seriously built. The Professor was reserved and the long-and-lean type, not her style at all. But "decent guy" looked damn good on him.

―――

The orderly swabbed the table, the bench, and even scooped up what had gone into the dirt. He headed off with Kee's nod for thanks.

"Are you gonna eat that?" Before she could respond, Big John snagged a piece of her bacon.

With a quick grab she secured his plate and half cocked it in his direction, the sausages almost tumbling off the lower edge.

"You gonna wear that?"

He laughed and handed the piece of bacon to the kid, who snatched it from his hand but managed to slow herself and nibble on one end.

Kee dropped his plate back to the table and took a piece of his toast in payback.

"Why Big Bad John?"

"Ask Crazy Tim." He waved a forkful of hash browns at a man sitting down next to the Professor's spot. He was short and dark-haired, part Latino in his broad face.

"You don't know the song? And they let you in the Army?" Crazy Tim's accent placed him as Puerto Rican, but it was mostly buried beneath a Southern smooth like good bourbon. He turned to Big John. "Don't they got standards no more?"

"Either way, they let her in." John's deep voice rumbled but remained absolutely neutral.

Kee couldn't tell if that was an intended insult or a compliment. She'd bet the former, but getting into a fight with a fellow crew chief on her first day wouldn't be such a good idea. Not that she hadn't done it before. But she'd resist, especially after the Major had reprimanded her during the flight.

"Because, he is big, he is bad, and he is John. Sure,

you could replace him with a tree trunk, which wouldn't smell so nasty, but it wouldn't be so big or so bad."

"And this pint-sized idiot," John aimed his fork again, "is Crazy Tim. And why Crazy you might ask…"

Tim leaned in, "Because I is one crazy-ass dude." He was also one built dude. A head shorter than the Professor or Big John and twice as wide, without an ounce of fat anywhere. He clearly worked out big-time and she was down with that. His tank top revealed a Night Stalker stallion with wings across his upper arm, like a lot of the guys wore. But instead of death riding on its back, there was a serpent with an improbably big nose on a human face.

"What's with the nose?"

"We're the 3rd Black Hawk Company of the 5th Battalion of the 160th Special Operations Aviation Regiment, airborne, commanded by Major Mark 'The Viper' Henderson, the baddest dude in the sky." Tim said it all in a single breath like a blessing. "You are flying with the Black Adders, if you can hack it. And the ultimate Black Adder…" He tapped the tattoo of the face with the tip of his knife. "Mr. Bean."

He flexed his shoulder, making Mr. Bean's nose even more prominent.

If Queen Hoity Beale could hack it, Kee knew the Black Adders had to be a cakewalk. The woman had become a legend, as a woman. Kee'd show them what a real woman could do. She'd spent the last two years in training and met some real stand-up fliers. But the training-team caliber sure wasn't carrying over to this pack of lame misfits.

"He's Crazy Tim because," the Professor returned to sit

beside the kid with a fresh plate of his own, "he was the first one to ask for it when Captain Beale formed a crew."

"What about you? How'd you end up stuck with her?" Kee winced at her own words. Here she was insulting the man. You didn't call a crewmate a wimp even if he flew on the girlie-ship. She gave it a day, maybe two before she found out how much of a laughingstock flying on the girlie-bird made her with the other crews. 'Course, the Professor flew with her, and there was no calling him a wimp once you got a good look.

John burst out laughing, showing a flash of his white teeth as he rocked his head back. The kid jumped a little, then slipped a hand half across the table.

Kee took a piece of bacon from John's plate along with another piece of toast and dropped them into her palm. "*Medlenno*."

The girl nodded and went back to eating.

"You got the wrong image, girlie. Captain, whoops, now Major Beale ain't someone you get stuck with, she's somebody you survive."

"If you are good enough." The Professor cut his bacon in pieces and ate it with his fork. The girl watched his actions with interest. Inspected her own plate, which lacked any silverware, Kee having forgotten, and went back to eating the piece of bacon in her hand. Kid was observant at least. Some brains.

"If you're good enough." Tim nodded all serious.

Kee wondered how long they'd keep teasing her. Sure, Beale'd proved she could fly, but the legend implied she could do it without a helicopter because she was so damn good.

A shadow crossed the entry to the tent. Major Muscle

"The Viper" and Major "Queen Hoity" coming in out of the sun. They moved in perfect harmony like they were wired at the hip, first to the chow line and then an open table in the corner.

"They always like that?"

John didn't even glance over. "Honeymoon."

"Do not be so sure, my big, bad friend." The Professor concentrated for a moment, his light eyes unfocused as he considered. "I've flown with her for seven years, you for half a year. Have you ever seen her look like that?"

"Honeymoon." John sounded like he was just being contrary for the fun of it.

"Honeymoon," she echoed, because she knew it would irritate the Professor. Kee handed the girl her juice and a piece of the Professor's French toast. Tim handed over a slice of apple.

The Lieutenant didn't even have the decency to sound huffed, just changed the subject.

"How'd you know?"

"Know what?"

The Professor's blue eyes, the color you could only find in the midst of spring watching new leaves against a blue sky, shifted from looking off into some inner space onto Kee, momentarily robbing her of the ability to speak. They were the kind of blue you could fly into forever, with just that elusive bit of green that came and went. And sharp. There was a real mind behind all that education and now it all focused on her. First time she'd wanted to squirm since hitting the base.

"The kid. How did you know she'd be sick?"

"Been there." She clamped her teeth shut fast enough to click her teeth together.

No past.

Her first rule of survival. She had no past before the Army. No starving kid from the streets barfing in the soup line when her stomach rebelled at a second serving. No Dumpster diving. No begging for change to buy one of the hard-boiled eggs the local booze merchant kept in the jar on the counter for the alkies. None of that.

She looked away until she caught herself, then she met his eyes directly. How in the world had this man done that? Seven years in the Army, no one ever slipped around her guard and into her past.

There was no way he would get another word out of her, guardian angel or no. Mr. Archibald Jeffrey Stevenson III had probably never been hungry in his life. *Ooo. We've missed teatime, Mummy. I'm simply famished.*

He opened his mouth, then apparently thought better of it.

Decent of him, damned decent. Kee almost blushed about the harsh thought she'd had just the moment before. Something else she never did.

His eyes traveled to Crazy Tim but found no refuge there. Then he spotted the girl, who had finally stopped eating and nursed her apple juice wrapped in both hands. Kee looked over as well.

Fine fingers, callused from work, from a hard life, but still slender. Whip thin. A narrow face with well-defined lips and those bright, watching eyes. Pretty, even without being cleaned up. Skin about as dark as Kee's, but with a different cast. Kee's tone looked like a white woman with a severely awesome tan. The girl's skin looked like someone had mixed a bit of black into an umber-brown paint.

The Prof rattled off at her in more of that rough roll that must be Russian.

Kee glanced at Big John who just shrugged.

"Don't have Russian. Vietnamese, my mom taught me, some Vietnamese and some French. She married an Okie farmer who speaks nothing but American. I take after Pops. He was even bigger than me."

Kee tried to picture it. It was hard to imagine how John even fit in the helicopter. Then his dad was bigger?

"I studied Bhasa and Thai, bits and pieces of other Asians, some French." John dug into his breakfast, but you could see him keeping his ear on the Professor's conversation with the kid.

Just like all Special Forces operators, everyone in SOAR was a polyglot. Any team could cover a dozen languages between them, even in a four-seat bird like the DAP Hawk. One of the first things you learned about your companions.

Tim shrugged when she looked his way. "Spanish, Portuguese, Dutch."

"Yeah, and sometimes he even comes out with some English."

The kid answered the Professor slowly, searching for words.

After more back and forth, he turned back to them.

"I was concerned that perhaps we'd killed her father last night."

Kee swallowed hard, felt the eggs stick in her throat. Hadn't thought of that.

"But we dodged that particular bullet. She was on her own. I think she was trying to steal food or water from the Jeep while we kept its owners busy. It's a good thing she didn't get there before our arrival. The doc ought to check her out anyway."

Kee's gut twisted. He was right, of course. Poor kid.

"Where's her village?" She forced out the words as normally as she could.

He and the kid did another couple rounds of halting communication. He shrugged and turned back to his eggs.

"She doesn't appear to know. To her it was just 'home.' Her Russian is even worse than mine. Whatever her native tongue may be, it's unknown to me. Three 'homes' have been 'taken,' probably bombed out of existence. She might have told me the name of one, I'm not sure. I am not even sure which country she is from. 'Mountains' is all I can understand. And walking. She keeps repeating that. I expect she's walked a long ways."

"What's her name? Never mind." She waved him off.

Kee folded her hands on the table and focused on the kid's eyes. The girl flinched back, an instinct too familiar. Kee held steady and waited for her to relax a notch or two.

She made as if her first and index fingers were legs and walked them across the table. "Walk."

Kee made ready to repeat it, but the kid nodded quickly. "Wak. Wall-ke. Wallkk. Walk." That fast and the kid had a completely foreign sound. She walked her own fingers across the table and repeated the words several times, nodding as she went. Kid was smart and had a good ear.

When she stopped, Kee pointed to herself. "Kee." Then she pointed to the girl.

None of that stupid back-and-forth. Kee could see

in her eyes that she got it right away. But didn't want to answer.

Kee refolded her hands and waited. Gave the girl the space to make up her own mind.

Again the Professor readied himself to speak, but caught himself. Not bad. Clearly he had some feeling for what the kid might be going through. She could definitely get to like this guy.

A couple more fliers came in. Easy to spot. Those who flew walked differently, taller maybe. One of them slapped Crazy Tim on top of his head as he went by. They both laughed. A good laugh, easy. Must be the crew from Tim's chopper.

Big John leaned in. "That's Master Sergeant Dusty James from The Viper's bird."

She didn't look away. She waited. The girl's eyes didn't stray even as the new crew settled just down the table beyond Tim and Big John.

When all of the men had turned to talk to their buddies, the girl leaned forward and whispered. "Dilyana."

Kee nodded. There was power in names, and the girl had just trusted hers to Kee.

Chapter 4

KEE WATCHED THE TOWN TAKE SHAPE AS THEY FLEW in from a long night. A long night of nothing. More exhausting than after the adrenaline letdown of last night's skirmish. She was just worn and looking forward to ten hours in the rack, and then a good run. Or maybe Big John could point her to some iron. He and Tim clearly did a lot of lifting so there must be a weight set around somewhere even in a camp this size.

But first, rack time. Wouldn't even be interested in a quick roll in the sheets. Not even if there was someone as cute as the Professor who wasn't her commanding officer. Weird that he kept coming to mind. She must be even more exhausted than she'd thought.

Kee was wrecked, plain and simple. One part of her body remained on Fort Campbell, Kentucky, time. Another part thought it should be awake during the daytime, but Night Stalkers lived in a flipped-clock world, sleeping in the heat of the day, flying at night. Most of her simply whimpered and wanted to stop.

As they circled down in the predawn darkness, she checked the town that sprawled around three sides of the white oval of the soccer stadium they used as a base. The fourth side nothing but desert scrub. Bati was cubes of mud-brick houses, most of them one-room sized, jumbled together as if someone had dumped a big bag of dice on the ground and then shoved them together until most of them were square with the donkey-wide streets. The town never wandered more than a few hundred yards from the narrow river, but stretched for a mile along its banks, finally turning into a scatter of houses in the distance. A long narrow strip of hand-irrigated green, then nothing but sheep and goat pasture.

The town was just waking as the dawn light reached across the sky. The food stalls in the central open market had the slow but purposeful movements of people setting up to start the day. The heat signature of the cow dung fires showed as soft spots of green in her night-vision goggles. Soon, any farmers and merchants who didn't have a wife at home to cook for them would wander through the market for their breakfast. A couple of goatherds were already opening rough corrals at the edge of town and guiding their flocks out to seek forage. It smelled of cool night, not yet given way to the hot dust of day.

Part of her training overrode her exhaustion. Friendlies weren't always friendly. So, she kept her hands on her gun for the first time since they'd taken off, aimed at the sky, but hands on. Eyes scanning the sleeping town for unexpected movement. Not that you ever saw the shooter who nailed you.

None of the Pakistanis wanted them there, not the ones terrified of the Afghan conflict spilling into their country, nor the ones secretly supplying that war. But when Uzbekistan closed its air bases to U.S. forces in 2005, logistics became an issue. Pakistan and Tajikistan were supplying arms into the area. The Afghan forces, the Taliban, and the insurgents had decided these impossible mountains would be their primary battleground.

The war had settled in the Hindu Kush mountains of northeast Afghanistan.

Since the mountains were too high for helicopters to work well, the Army had cut an aid deal including the soccer stadium to get them in close enough to attack quickly when needed. Also, long flights at altitude burned too much fuel. So here they were, perched on the edge of a village that would just as soon they were dead, in a country that would never admit they were there. Real comfortable feeling.

The soccer stadium, abandoned when a Taliban raid had killed all of the soccer players as false idols, waited for them like a cupped hand. Any buildings within a hundred feet, clearly there had only been a few, were long since removed. Sentries perched along the top tier of the bleachers and watched the perimeter. They showed up in her night vision as a string of wide-spaced green pearls.

At one end of the field, a pair of the massive, twin-rotor Chinook helicopters squatted and glowered like street gang leaders. Big and lumpy, and far more dangerous than they looked. The heavy lifters of the team.

The two-seater Little Birds, the street runners of the gang, clustered around midfield telling each other nasty little stories of quick insertion, quick fire, quick getaway. They were the wasps, they stung and were gone before you could smack 'em.

The far end of the field was Black Hawk home turf. Four troop movers, one cross-configured as a CSAR—Combat Search and Rescue—Hawk, and Major Muscle's DAP Hawk with a space for theirs, the two hammers of the outfit.

The sidelines were owned by the Special Forces operators that SOAR made a living delivering wherever they wanted to go. One sideline was packed the whole way down with Airborne Rangers and the other with Green Berets, about fifty each. Tough, swaggering, and dangerous as could be.

A small company of D-boys owned a small section of the curving end zone. Not even dawn yet and they were out doing calisthenics. Fifteen guys sprinting up and down the bleachers. Delta Force and their support crew, everyone trained even if they weren't field qualified. Maybe ten actual operators here, hard to tell with D-boys since none of them ever spoke.

Even Green Berets went quiet whenever a D-boy walked by. A lot of them had applied, but Delta Force was just as picky as SOAR. Maybe even more so, which was hard to imagine.

Kee watched them sprint up and down one more time before Major Hoity had circled their chopper into their spot of the lineup, just out-of-bounds beside where the goal had stood.

She locked down her weapon, shut off her comm, and made sure her harness was draped flight-ready. Setting her helmet on the gunner's seat, she stepped down, landing flat-footed and raising a small cloud of dust.

She waved off the red, the crewman in the red vest identifying his role on the ordnance squad. "Didn't get to fire a single lousy shot."

He nodded and went to check for himself anyway.

Too exhausted to even growl, she headed for her tent. The Professor had it right yesterday. Get out of flight gear into civvies first, then food, then rack time. Maybe skip the food.

The tent set up for women sported four cots, yet she always slept alone. The three women who shared it with her kicked into action during the day, a mechanic, a clerk, and a who-knew. They sacked out while she flew. And Major Hoity slept with Major Muscle. 'Nuff said there. They'd each found a way to get some regular action. More power to 'em. She even envied them a bit.

She didn't bother hitting a light, the predawn filtered through the thick canvas enough to navigate. Second on the right was hers. She dropped down onto it to kick off her boots.

A high squeal launched her back to her feet. She dove and rolled away, coming up with her M9 in one hand and a flashlight from her thigh pouch in the other.

The kid. Curled up with both arms over her head and one dark eye peeking out, caught wide in the flashlight beam.

Kee lowered her pistol and reset the safety. She closed her eyes for a long moment, wishing she could erase the fear, the terror on the girl's face.

Once she could breathe normally, she holstered her weapon and hit the switch on the camp light hanging from the central tent pole.

The girl had lowered her arms from protecting her head to hugging her knees, holding herself tightly as if she were going to blow apart in a cloud of dust if she didn't clamp down hard enough.

Kee took one more breath to make sure her voice sounded steady.

"Dilyana. What are you doing here?"

The girl watched her.

"Right. No English. Have you—No. Did they—Crap!" She didn't need this. Not now.

The girl's eyes were still bigger than dinner plates in her thin face.

Kee sighed.

"Food?" She rubbed her belly. "Hungry?"

———

All Dilyana could see was the black-circle opening at the front of The Kee's gun. Even though she'd put it away, it still loomed before her, dark and bottomless. Just as it had looked when her parents were shot and she'd been left to walk away.

The Kee—it must be a title, she was an elder after all—was making motions that seemed familiar. The nice man eating bacon with his metal tools. Her stomach growled loudly the instant she connected The Kee's motion to food.

"*Ha!*" She nodded her head vigorously, hoping that was the right gesture.

"Ha?"

How to tell her such a simple word? Dilyana pretended to eat, though even pretending the metal-tool motion made her feel clumsy. She'd never used them, and she knew she was getting it wrong. But she then patted her stomach, smiled and nodded, and repeated herself, "*Ha!*"

"*Ha.*" The Kee said it simply. "Yes."

"Yes?" The sound sat easily on Dilyana's tongue. It felt right there. "Yes."

"*Ha.*"

Then The Kee pulled off her shirt. Except for a band of cloth over her breasts, all of her skin was exposed from her pants to the top of her head.

Dilyana hid her head between her knees. It wasn't right. She couldn't look up.

It sounded like The Kee growled like an angry animal. Then she heard cloth moving.

She stayed that way until The Kee made a noise, a quieter one.

Dilyana peeked.

She now wore a new shirt, but still the same pants.

The Kee held out a hand for Dilyana to take. She avoided the hand, climbed off the other side of the bed, and sidled past The Kee toward the door of the tent. The last time The Kee had touched her, she'd grabbed and poked and thrown her on the hard metal floor of the helicopter. Better to stay near the nice man.

Archie was barely paying even half attention to Big John's latest tale, told between attacks on his breakfast.

Archie hadn't touched his own plate yet. It didn't feel proper, starting to eat before everyone sat down. He shook his head at that and deliberately picked up his knife and fork, waiting as if he still sat in his parents' formal dining room. All the timing of seating, setting napkins, and allowing his mother or the frequent guest to take the first bite.

In the desert. On an Army base. Who in the world would he be waiting for here?

He knew exactly who when he spotted Dilya slipping up to the chow line. Three steps behind came Sergeant

Kee Smith. She'd hypnotized him, at least that was his current theory. To not stare at her ranked near impossible. To not watch the easy smiles that crossed her lips but so rarely touched those cautious eyes simply couldn't be done.

And then the next moment when the wall crashed into place and Kee Smith disappeared behind the shield of U.S. Army Sergeant. All except those dark, dark eyes.

She fascinated him beyond all reason.

It was a safe enough fascination, because he knew himself. He'd screw it up long before anything could come of it, even if he wasn't an officer and she enlisted.

So he allowed himself to watch the incongruous gentleness that the warrior shared with the child.

—∿∿—

Kee followed the kid to the chow line. She couldn't even change her clothes in her own tent because of the kid. This was insane.

The girl started heaping her plate the instant she hit the line and almost flipped it to the ground when Kee touched her arm.

"*Medlenno*." Great. Her entire vocabulary with the kid had been reduced to a single word. No, two. "*Medlenno, ha*? *Medlenno*, Dilyana."

"Dilya." A sharp whisper.

Kee'd called the girl by her full name in the tent two or three times, but she got the message. In public, Dilya.

"Not Yani? Or Yana?"

The girl shook her head sharply, suddenly sad, looking down. Okay, forbidden ground. Parents' nickname probably, meaning a good chance they'd been decent folks.

"*Medlenno*, Dilya." Then she imitated the girl barfing up her last breakfast, with a smile and laugh to let her know it was okay.

Kee did it again, holding the back of her hand against her mouth with her fingertips touching and pointing outward. Then bursting apart as she made a ralphing sound.

"*Medlenno*."

A laugh. She actually got a laugh from the kid.

"*Asta*." Dilya nodded to confirm her understanding.

The word for being sick?

"*Asta-asta*."

No, didn't sound right. Word sounds often matched meaning in the languages she'd learned. And "sick" didn't fit the repeated pattern, but "slowly, slowly" might.

"*Asta-asta*." Kee dragged out each word making it slow and steady.

The girl nodded.

Okay, up to three words, even if two of them meant "slowly," a private name, and a public name. Progress.

She guided them over to Big John and the Professor who'd beaten them in. Dilya circled wide around John but settled in comfortable as could be next to the Professor. They looked awfully sweet together. This left Kee and John rubbing shoulders again. Wouldn't mind that much, but they were on the same crew. Though while she liked Big John's serious brawn, her mind was watching out of the corner of her eye. Watching Archie lean in to shape Dilya's fingers around a fork.

Same-crew fraternization never worked, not even when it was rank to rank. Big John was a grade up, so no way anyway. Cross-squad was tricky, but it could be done. Civilians were best. Even if they couldn't hack a warrior-chick long term, no matter how much they thought of themselves, civilians were always good for a tumble or two. She'd bet there'd be a real lack of local talent in the town pub, if there were a town pub, and if she weren't likely to be shot for walking into it. Security briefing had been clear. Don't go into town unarmed, and not in a squad less than four strong. From ankles to hair covered for a woman. Knees to shoulders for a guy. Great.

Kee spotted the medic she'd dumped Dilya on yesterday. She headed over, nodding to the Professor to keep an eye on their charge.

Not a word needed, he was in full sync.

It was a smooth feeling, as if she'd known him half her life. As if they'd run in the same gang long enough to be solid. Real solid. Completely familiar. She glanced back. Between one blink and the next he transformed back into the handsome pilot she barely knew but completely trusted, leaning over to tease the little girl. The images stayed overlapped in her brain as she turned to face the medic.

"Chief Medic Ray Mackenzie?"

"Mac will do. What can I do for you, Smith?"

"Kee." They shook. Hard to resist doing the full-on bone-cruncher most guys expected, but he was a medic and you don't mess with their hands. Still he cranked down a bit and she gave back as good as she got.

With a nod toward the seat opposite, he set down his own food.

"What can I do for you, Kee?"

"Like to ask about Dilya." She sat down.

"Dilya? Oh, the Uzbek kid."

"Uzbek?"

"Uzbekistan, about three hundred miles that way." He pointed north toward the mountains.

"She came through that?" On the Pakistan side of the border, the Hindu Kush mountains would kill you. On the other side, the Afghan war doubled the hazard. Neither was a place you entered and expected to live. To pass through both? What did that take?

"Must have. Though you were about halfway there when you picked her up. She has no other language but the bit of Russian."

"You speak Uzbek? Uzbeki? Whatever."

He dug in a pocket for a moment and tossed her a thin volume little bigger than the palm of her hand.

O'zbek–English Phrase Book.

"Great. What do I do with this?"

Mac looked at her and shrugged. "Extra copy. Give it back when you're done with it."

"Thought I was done when I gave her to you." She flipped the pages but they were a blur, none of the words made sense at the moment, not even the English ones. She didn't want the kid.

Mac shook his head and cut a chunk out of his pancakes. "I'm just medical. I checked her out, she didn't like it much. Eleven or twelve, I'm guessing. Intact. Nothing broken. No real bruises either, banged shin and other kid stuff. Serious calluses on her feet, girl's walked a long way without shoes. Other than borderline starvation like every other kid within five hundred miles, she's fine. We're forward operations here, so there isn't any liaison or community service to deal with her. Makes her your problem. Give her food and get her gone."

"Gone to where?"

"Refugee camp about fifty miles that way." He pointed his pancake-laden fork south instead of north this time before filling his mouth. The look on his face was a little sour. She felt a chill up her spine that had nothing to do with the temperature. She'd wager the camp deserved that grimace.

"Major Beale." Kee stepped up and snapped to attention in front of her commander where she sat with her husband over their breakfast. Resisted the salute. She didn't expect a lot of help here, but Beale was her CO. Next place to go and you don't ever skip the chain of command. Ever. That's one she'd learned more than a few times the hard way.

"At ease, Smith. What's on your mind?"

She dropped into parade rest.

"Dilya, ma'am."

"Dilya?"

"The girl we picked up. Rescued."

The two of them turned to look at the tiny girl sitting beside the tall Professor, who appeared to be teasing her at the moment, making Dilya laugh. At least most of her food was still on the plate. "*Asta-asta*, Dilya."

"She okay?"

"Yes, ma'am. Medical checked her out."

"Good. That's done." Major Chunk-o-Muscle Henderson went back to his breakfast, but Major Beale watched Kee a moment longer.

"I think that perhaps you should sit with us a moment, Sergeant Smith."

"Thank you, ma'am. Sir." She didn't relax when she sat, but remained bolt upright. Even so, she was inches shorter than either of these two perfect specimens of the human species. Their kids were gonna be stunners.

Focus, Kee.

"I'm worried about what's to become of her, ma'am. Medical suggested a Coalition Forces refugee camp south of here."

"Jali. Big one. Twenty or thirty thousand last I heard. Does she have any family?"

"Unknown. We think she was trying to steal food from that RPG team we deep-sixed the other night. A couple meters closer to that jeep and she wouldn't be here now. I'm guessing that she and her family walked over the Hindu Kush from Uzbekistan. Maybe got lost. Eleven years old and alone." Kee managed to keep her voice steady. She knew how that felt. Knew it far too well.

Major Henderson stopped eating and Major Beale paled.

"Damn!" He whispered it quietly. "Poor kid."

"Medical pronounced her okay and she's bright, just starving and lost. They dumped her back in my lap and I don't know what to do with her, ma'am."

"That camp is full of Afghanis." Beale looked toward the kid again.

Henderson picked up the unfinished thought without the slightest break, like one person speaking with two voices. "Probably not a lot of love lost with the Uzbek. Uzbekistan provided part of the invading Russian forces for years. But she'd be better in that camp than with the villagers here."

The three of them sat there in silence. Beale stared off into space for a moment then looked at her husband.

Some silent communication happened so fast Kee barely saw the flicker across the Major's eyes as he made his decision.

He shrugged. "Should only take an hour. We'll brief at 1800, which will give you an hour and a half before I need you on the line."

Beale nodded and turned to Kee. Just raised an eyebrow in a perfect arch.

Kee sat frozen in place, she'd never seen anything like it. Not even squadmates who'd served multiple tours in the same company communicated so effortlessly. Beale and Henderson had a harmony between them that Kee could feel. Even if she didn't believe in it.

She jerked to her feet, jarring the table, and nodded her thanks before heading off.

She couldn't begrudge the kid the hour and a half of sleep Kee'd just lost in the deal. It wasn't as if they were doing her any favor.

Chapter 5

ARCHIE STARED DOWN THROUGH THE PLEXIGLAS wind-shield that wrapped from behind and over his head, around the console, and ended near his feet. He usually appreciated the panoramic view, except when it let him see all the people shooting up at him. Or now.

They'd lifted from Bati, a quiet village of five thousand with a hundred-odd Special Forces operatives and a dozen helicopters camped in their abandoned soccer stadium. Twenty minutes by chopper they had done more than passed over fifty miles of arid, rolling landscape of grays and browns. They had crossed into another world.

Jali refugee camp sprawled across miles, and Archie hated it more each time he saw it. He leaned forward as if the extra few inches would let him see more clearly out the windshield of the chopper.

At first glance, the camp looked like a giant spider sprawled across the face of the desert. A dark central body made of tents and a vast mass of humanity. The legs, too many of them, long streams of people. People moving away from the camp, fast. Something was very wrong.

As they flew closer, he could see that the camp below them roiled in chaos. Solid rivers of seething humanity surged from the camp without appearing to ease the tight packing of those still within the camp's perimeter. Neat lines of large tents funneled the shoving crowds into narrow pathways. Even as he watched, a tent collapsed and part of the crowd surged over it as others struggled to escape from beneath the heavy canvas.

Archie scanned the skies, but the late afternoon blue shone clear to the horizon. If there was any gunfire going on in the camp, he couldn't see the telltale flashes. He double-checked the console. Radar showed clear. The infrared FLIR couldn't see anything in the afternoon heat, which was about the same as human body temperature, but neither did it show any hot sparks of weapons discharge.

He reported his findings to the Major in a single word, "*Niente*." Nothing. After flying together for almost a decade, they rarely spoke more than a word. Didn't really need even that very often.

People were streaming out of every gate, clearly overrunning every guard station. A line of official vehicles roared campward along the main road, and he could almost hear the horns blaring. The crowds parted like a river on either side of the vehicles. Troops at the gates were trying to stem the flow with little luck, but reinforcements were pouring in. After a moment, he spotted a concentration of troop carriers by the main gate. He pointed, and with a nod, the Major landed near them, hovering long enough to let the downblast of the rotors clear the people out of a landing space for them.

Kee climbed down and had tucked Dilya close under her arm by the time Archie joined them. The girl tried to stand tall, but he could see the shivers that periodically shook her shoulders like a leaf. Not much taller, Kee was a tower of strength beside the little girl, but looked little more stable for all that.

Major Beale and Big John stayed in the chopper with the rotors spinning at about half. That kept the curious and the desperate at bay. And if that didn't, Big John had unslung his carbine and glowered out at the world from the center of the cargo bay, a massive and evil-looking bulk in the shadows.

Archie unslung his SCAR carbine and did his best to dangle it casually from his hand, while Kee's remained strapped across her chest. He unfolded the stock, making the thing look even nastier. People backed away from them, leaving as wide a path as the pressure of humanity allowed. He took station on Dilya's other side as they headed toward the cluster of vehicles.

"Who's in charge?" Kee shouted at the first soldier with a ranking on his collar. Red beret, British, one pip on his collar, a second lieutenant. Archie could barely hear her over the seething ocean of twenty thousand people all in a panic. The man pointed toward a Hummer flying the red, white, and blue Union Jack of Britain and a dozen men gathered close about.

Once they were closer, Kee pointed to a man in close conference with two others. "He has the most noise on his collar."

Indeed, two pips and a crown. They moved up close behind him.

"Sir?"

The man glanced at her and looked back at the map spread over the hood of his vehicle, dismissing her as useless. Before she could grab his arm and find herself in real trouble, Archie stepped in.

"Begging your pardon, Colonel, sir." He snapped a sharp salute and held it.

The Colonel looked irritated, but at least acknowledged him with that flat-handed, palm out British salute that they used, even in the field.

"First Lieutenant Archibald Stevenson III of U.S. Army 160th SOAR, 5th Battalion." He dropped to parade rest. He checked to ascertain that Kee wasn't about to attack the Colonel for ignoring her. The man wasn't being sexist, he was busy. With Kee in full flight gear, the Colonel probably didn't even know she was female.

"SOAR?"

"Yes, sir."

"What can I do for you? We're a little busy."

He nodded toward Dilya, now cowering against Kee.

"Refugee, Uzbekistani. Picked her up the other night."

"Well, you can't bring her here. Afghanis would kill her on sight, if they didn't have enough problems of their own."

"What is going on here?" The noise surged to cover his question then washed back to a mere roar. It was a good choice that he'd kept his helmet in place simply for the sound protection.

"Local militia came in to do some recruiting." The Colonel pointed to the map indicating an area about two-thirds of the way across the camp.

"Typical problem around here. A few dozen fanatics start stirring up a rumpus, and twenty thousand who've lost their homes flee in panic. All in terrified belief that the war has reached out to shred their lives yet again. Happens every few months, takes a day or two to put the place back together, with everyone a day or two closer to starving. We have it handled."

One of his lieutenants tapped his arm for attention.

The volume escalated and they all turned in time to see a human wave surging in their direction.

The Colonel shouted over his shoulder, "You can leave her with the Corporal over there." He indicated with a quick nod. "God help her."

He turned away to his people and roared in a voice loud enough to carry to the dozen troopers station around his Hummer, "Ready arms." Every trooper took his carbine off safety and propped it against his shoulder. Archie couldn't believe he'd do it.

"No!" Kee's cry was drowned out by the next order.

"Into the ground, fire!"

At the roar of gunfire, the surge broke and the hundreds of starving refugees turned and drove back into the crowd, searching for a different escape from the driving pressure of the myriad souls behind them.

Smart. Shooting into the ground. Couldn't fire into the air or their bullets could kill someone a mile away and they'd never know.

Archie scanned the crowd, spotted the Corporal with the clipboard talking to a couple of families so newly arrived that they didn't know running away at the moment might be a better choice. He looked at the vast array of tents, row upon row of people praying that they were anywhere else.

Then he looked at Kee and Dilya. The woman and the girl from opposite sides of the world holding on to each other.

Would they be surprised to know that their expressions were the same? The narrow girl in white and the sloe-eyed warrior. Both stared at the camp with a mix of horror and fear. A stillness about them told him they were past shock and well along the road to numb. No motion.

"Come on. We're leaving." He leaned in and shouted to be heard.

Nothing.

Kee turned to him with desperation written wide on her face. Her mouth worked, but nothing came out.

"Now. Move, soldier." He had to shout to be heard as the mob surged once more in their direction despite the leading edge struggling to stay clear of the guns. The Brits unleashed another volley of shots into the ground. Kee and Dilya each jumped as if they'd been the targets.

Kee looked at Dilya and back to him, shaking her head. She mouthed over the noise, "No."

"Both of you. Back to the chopper!" He knew his shout couldn't be heard this time. He grabbed both of their shoulders, turned them as one, and gave them a sharp shove.

They stumbled, but in a moment they were running. He was hard pressed to keep up as he kept turning to check behind. But the Brits appeared to be back in control for another few minutes.

As soon as he'd buckled his harness, he turned to check that the women were strapped in. Kee was huddled by the rear cargo net, her vest's harness clip snapped to the net. Dilya wrapped tightly against her despite the harness and gear Kee wore strapped across her body. Kee holding on just as hard. No force could pry the pair apart. Close enough.

"Get us out of here, Major."

They were airborne before he'd finished speaking.

He glanced back once they were clear to make sure everyone was safe.

John remained out of his seat, his monkey harness snapped into a ceiling loop, moving from open cargo door to open cargo door as he tried to cover both sides of the craft with his carbine rifle.

Kee held the girl on her lap and the pain wracked her face. Odd, she appeared so strong, yet she came apart over a native orphan girl. Not that he didn't feel sympathy. Not that he didn't wish he could solve the problem. But he'd never suspected Kee had such an open heart. All that bravado and posturing, pierced by a young girl.

He had been drawn to the Sergeant the first instant she had stood there by the chopper, her hair glinting in the sunlight, her stance proud and fearless. He hadn't even noticed her tight T-shirt and amazing body at first. It was her eyes, a straight punch to his gut.

He could feel Emily watching him as he turned back. She'd caught how long his attention had been diverted to watch Kee, even if he hadn't.

"Let's go." Pointless remark, since they were already gone, Jali camp fading quickly into the afternoon's heat shimmer.

Emily cocked her head ever so slightly without turning to face him, a nod toward her rank insignia. Reminding him of his own.

He shrugged. Yes, he knew.

Archie turned his attention back to scanning the terrain and the skies. Checking their course and their fuel.

He tried to picture the milling crowd, panicked by the gunshots and also by the abrupt departure of their helicopter. The crowd stirred and swirled in circles leading nowhere. Nowhere for them to go but the desert. Nothing but miles and miles of dry, arid desert.

But all he saw were the warrior and the little girl.

Chapter 6

MAJOR BEALE HADN'T SAID A WORD ON THE FLIGHT BACK.

Not a word until immediately after they landed back at the stadium. She stopped in front of Kee as their fuel was topped off by the ground crew.

"You can either shove her out the front gate or you're responsible for her until the next humanitarian mission comes through."

"When's that?" Kee glanced around. Felt a pinch between her shoulders as if they were already coming behind her.

Major Beale did the screwiest thing. Always so damn military, she turned up the bottom of her foot and inspected it as if the Red Cross might be hiding there. Shaded her eyes and looked straight up at the sky for a half-dozen heartbeats, long enough for Kee to glance skyward herself. Squatted down to look beneath her helicopter.

Then she shrugged and went to check on the crew topping off the tanks.

Did the woman have a sense of humor?

They hit the flight line a half hour late.

Kee had tried to apologize and been brushed off in the hustle to get moving. Settling Dilya back on Kee's cot for the night had taken longer than it should. The phrase book hadn't helped when Kee couldn't focus her eyes, couldn't shake the awful image of that camp. Finally, she'd pushed Dilya onto the cot, pulled the blanket over the still shaking girl, and walked out.

She'd had to pause in the darkness outside the tent and work on her own breathing. The pressure of that place. No L.A. mission ever stank so of fear. No halfway house had been so panicked. More noise than a full-on street riot, cops and all. Worse than a firefight in the Colombian jungle. But she was late and broke herself loose of the nightmare that threatened to overwhelm her and bolted for the chopper.

The silence of the night was deafening. Tonight their mission profile was backup. Big surprise. The pair of big, double-rotored Chinook helicopters were taking a couple teams of Rangers and Green Berets in to deal with an import problem. Arms were flowing across the borders to the militias. They didn't know from where, but tonight they hoped to know where the arms were ending up. If all went well, they'd capture the weapons and be able to start tracing back to the source of the flow.

Their flight profile placed them in a high-circling station, twenty miles from the target. Five minutes out in case the ground op went bad. Midair refueling every three hours to keep the tanks topped up for action. Too high to bother manning the guns. They just sat and waited.

The silence ate at her. Ate at her from the inside. She'd let the commander down twice in twenty-four hours. Not getting Dilya dealt with, and being late for a mission. Didn't matter if she was a real legend or a fake one, Major Beale had been square with her and Kee owed her. Kee didn't like owing anybody.

"Major, I just wanted to say—"

"Are you quitting on me, Smith?" The major's voice was sharp over the open intercom. Any possibility of humor nowhere on the radar.

"Night Stalkers Don't Quit." Kee replied without thinking. That's one of the reasons she'd wanted to join in the first place. It was more than their motto, it was their first rule of life. SOAR fliers never quit. She never quit.

Beale swiveled in her seat until she was staring back at Kee between the two pilot seats. Even in the dim instrument glow of the night-flight cabin, Kee could see Beale's face. A way she hadn't seen it before. Not pretty, nor with that rare open smile that lit her up. Her face was the dead serious of a seasoned SOAR flight commander.

"You quitting on that little girl?"

Kee gritted her teeth and glared back at Beale, eye to eye.

"Night Stalkers Don't Quit!"

"Right. Until you do, we don't have a problem." Beale turned back to her console.

Big Bad John flashed one of his broad smiles at her.

"Told you so," he mouthed.

Right. Major Beale was someone you survived.

She gave him the finger.

He laughed silently and gave it back.

In harmony, they both turned back to stare out into the dark and wait.

—∿∿—

Dilya squatted and watched the sky. Familiar but not. She knew the stars. Jawza the twins. Asad the lion. Her friends shone down on her.

It was when she looked to the Earth that the world became strange and unfamiliar. A few helicopters were scattered across the field, but many had left at sunset, flying into the night.

The elder with the strange name, The Kee. Was it her name or her title? It sounded like an ax on hard firewood or the cry of an angry eagle cheated of its prey. She had attacked Dilya. Attacked her, dragged her onto the helicopter, but then given her food. The next day, The Kee had taken her to the city of fear, walking forward when everyone else ran away. Didn't she understand danger? Couldn't she smell it?

Why had they gone there? To exchange a salute and then to run away? She could make no sense of that. Dilya had held on tight because she didn't want to be left there by accident. No safety there. Nowhere to hide. Everyone desperate. Nowhere to steal food, because they wouldn't have any.

And back on the helicopter, the elder had held her tight. So tightly it hurt. But it hurt good as well. Held her so hard, The Kee'd squeezed out Dilya's first tears since she'd lost her parents. They had burned on her cheeks.

Now she sat on the highest row of the stadium, near one of the guards, but not too near, and looked at the friendly sky. She fingered the bread roll she'd hidden in her sleeve but decided to save it. For two days they had fed her. Maybe, if they came back down from the night sky, they would feed her again.

Chapter 7

KEE SPOTTED WHILE BIG BAD JOHN BENCHED. CRAZY Tim curled some free weights. They'd led her to the iron stash way at the back of the parts-and-supplies tent. But that was cool. Three benches and enough weights to satisfy even the strongest grunt.

Mr. Big Bad was only jamming his weight, but when he passed twenty reps, Kee knew he was serious. At thirty, he started blowing wind. At forty, she braced to catch a drop. At fifty, he grunted hard and managed to slot the bar back into the hooks without assistance.

"Good for a warm-up." His voice pretty steady, considering how his body must be sizzling. His statement ignored the fact that they'd been working their program for over half an hour in a companionable enough silence.

"You're in my way." She shed a fair stack of iron off the bar to get down to her own weight. She considered matching him one for one. Fifty reps, she might pull it off. But it wasn't her usual workout. Full body weight was for building raw power. She'd learned on the street that power didn't really count that much past a certain point, what mattered were endurance and speed. Her training goal had always been to outlast everyone around her.

She dumped another forty pounds on the ground.

John offered a sneer. Tim watched but didn't say a word.

She ignored them both.

At twenty reps she felt the burn start in. Nice and smooth. She kept the bar clanking up and down at about twice the rate John had used, her standard second and a half per rep.

At forty, she found the groove and settled in to do some work.

At eighty, the sweat was running down her cheeks.

At a hundred, she clanged it back into hooks.

John stood in spot position but hadn't even bothered to brace for a serious catch. Of course he was strong enough, he could probably snag her bar one-handed.

"You've done this before." Was all the praise he offered. It felt good.

She sat on the bench and knocked back half a bottle of water before checking on Dilya. The girl crouched on the floor playing with a piece of string she'd scrounged up somewhere. She'd tied it into a loop and was playing some sort of a game, flipping it back and forth over her fingers to create different designs.

"So, Mr. Big Bad." Kee studied the tattoo revealed right over his heart when he'd peeled his shirt to mop his face. A winged Pegasus with laser-vision eyes. The flying horse emblem of the Night Stalkers.

"Major Beale? The legend is for real?" She hadn't intended it to be a question. Her mind had put a scoffing tone on it, but some survival instinct had turned it into a merely derisive question.

He shook his head, picked up a pair of forty-pounders, and started doing some forearm work. "Don't get it, do you?"

"So I'm slow." She wasn't. But the Major was

something other. None of it fit. She should be having tea with her girlfriends before going shopping at Saks Fifth Ave., two kids off with the nanny, husband off to Wall Street.

"She comes from people." John would know what she meant. "People" were somebody. Money, power, luxury. Not street. Not Average Joe or Jane. Not Kee Smith.

Crazy Tim dropped the bar he'd been curling. Dropped it hard. Stepping over it, he left without even looking back.

"No clue, Smith. No damn clue."

She wasn't shut down so easy.

"You're saying she tweaked some noses when she went Army?"

"West Point. And I repeat, you have no clue."

"Heard that." She'd met enough officers whose only claim to fame was graduating from the Point. Didn't make you a soldier. "So, you gonna make me guess?"

He switched from reverse curls to flyaways. Made his muscles stand out so nice, she'd always liked that particular rep. But this time, rather than any interest, she found herself comparing them to Archie's runner's build. Favorably on the Professor's side of the scale. That was new.

She waited Big John out.

At fifty reps he swung 'em down and dropped the weights back on the rack. He toweled his face and chest before reaching for his shirt, which he threw over his shoulder.

He leaned in until their faces were a foot apart. In the blink of an eye, the workout buddy disappeared and was replaced by a staff sergeant of the SOAR 5th Battalion.

"A couple months back, Major Emily Beale earned the Silver Star, third highest combat decoration of the military, fetching a D-boy colonel out of a hellhole perched a thousand feet up a sheer cliff. Made me wanna crap my pants. Me!" He thumped a fist against the flying horse on his chest.

"We took over two hundred rounds in the twelve seconds she saved his life. And if the towel heads had been decent shots, we'd have taken ten times that many. A friggin' sheet of lead was raining down and she just sat there, holding the chopper three feet from rotor to cliff on two sides crammed up this narrow-ass ravine and waited for him for the longest twelve seconds of my life.

"She is the best pilot you will ever fly with, even Henderson says so. You strolled into the most coveted berth in all of SOAR because you're a woman. Crazy Tim…" He jabbed a finger in the direction the man had gone… "He got shoved aside to make room for you. You can't believe how hard that man is working every time he even talks to you without going nuts. His gettin' moved to Henderson's bird, because Henderson's gunner took a round, is the only reason he ain't beating your ass every damned day. And if you cross Major Beale, if you so much as let her down one tiny inch, I will pound the shit out of whatever she leaves of your carcass. Then Crazy Tim will start in. Clear?"

Kee's mind struggled to shift against the hammerblow of his sudden rage and disdain, not that she'd let it show. She'd answer his anger the same way she always did. With anger burning up from deep inside, a deep well roiling with a heat and fury she understood all too well.

She shoved up from the bench until they stood toe to

toe. She craned up her neck to stare at him. She'd been through too damn much to get here.

"I earned that seat, Mr. Big Bad. I didn't stroll in. Clear? I'm the best gunner you've ever seen."

"Words, Smith. Prove 'em!"

"If we stopped flying back patrols, I would."

Chapter 8

FORWARD PATROL. ABOUT TIME. KEE ALMOST SKIPPED chow after briefing to go and check over her gun and the rest of the chopper's armament. She wanted to do the preflight check now, even though it would be over an hour early.

She forced herself to go find Dilya. The little girl was asleep in her cot, curled up in the tight ball she always slept in. She looked so small that Kee could almost imagine picking her up and putting the girl in her pocket to keep safe.

Kee had to shake Dilya awake, and she dragged her feet all the way to the mess tent and through the chow line. Kee could feel her own nerves climbing toward that high, steady plane of a pending mission. She always felt calmer when they were headed into a storm. What drove her crazy was all the sitting still in between.

"Sergeant Smith?"

"Yes, sir." The Professor's tone set her back on her military heels for a moment. She'd been trading firefight stories with Crazy Tim, trying to make up a bit for pissing him off. She only belatedly realized that Lieutenant Stevenson had called her name twice. Had she forgotten something?

He tipped his head toward Dilya, who drooped beside him, no other word fit her look. She drooped. The hamburger on her plate had only a single bite out of it. And she hadn't taken any fries or salad. Up until now, her appetite hadn't slacked for a moment in the four days since they'd rescued her.

"Dilya?" The girl looked up at her. Her eyes half closed. Sweat stood out on her forehead.

Sick. What was the word for sick? Kee groped in her pocket, but the phrase book was back on her cot.

She imitated throwing up. Placed the back of her hand against her mouth, making the ralphing sound that had once bought the girl's laughter.

"Dilya, *ha*?"

Dilya nodded her head, then pushing her food aside, laid her head on the table.

Before Kee could do more than rise to her feet, Archie scooped up the little girl.

"Go find Mackenzie. I'll take her to the hospital tent."

She found Mac coming out of the showers and dragged him to the med tent half dressed.

———✺———

It took Mac about thirty seconds. He pressed his fingers down on Dilya's lower right abdomen.

Dilya groaned.

He released his fingers quickly and she cried out.

"Appendicitis. Pretty advanced. Hid it like an animal might. Had a golden retriever named Jasper, never knew he was hurting until one day he just stopped running after tennis balls. He was dead two days later."

Kee grabbed the side of the gurney. "Dead?"

"Yeah, cancer. Riddled with it. Nothing we could

do." He poked at Dilya's abdomen while he talked, eliciting varying whimpers that cut at Kee until she wanted to scream for him to stop.

"Loved that dog." He said it as calmly as if he were talking about the last magazine he'd read.

"I think it's intact, but I need to do this right away. She's hid her pain to this point, that's a strong kid." He stroked a hand over her hair as she lay there with her eyes closed, sweat running off her forehead.

Big John came in. "How's the kid? Hey, not looking so good there, short stuff."

"Appendicitis."

"You got it covered, Mac?"

"Yeah, I think so. Haven't ever done it on a kid, but I don't like the idea of transporting her this far advanced."

"Good, 'cause we're outta here. They moved the op up."

"Op?" This time Kee's grip on the gurney wasn't enough, and she sat abruptly on one of the nearby chairs. "Op?"

She couldn't fly. Not with Dilya in surgery. She had to—What? She couldn't think.

When she looked at Big John, he raised his hands palm out, no part of it.

Archie had stood quietly in the background through all this. Now he looked at her. He kept his gaze on her when he finally spoke. "How long, Mac?"

"Don't know until I get in there. The surgery itself should be under an hour. I'll roust Jeremy, knock out the girl. If all goes well, we could be done in three hours including pre- and post-op. Complications if the appendix bursts could get us to six." He left the tent.

Again that silent gaze of assessment, a question she couldn't answer. She couldn't leave, even if she had to.

Archie nodded to her. "I'll talk to the Majors and see if we can get cover personnel for this flight."

She nodded her head without speaking, it was all she could do. She tried to say "thank you." Swallowed hard several times to clear her throat.

By the time she managed, she sat alone with the little girl nearly lost in the great expanse of the gurney.

Chapter 9

DILYA HAD COME THROUGH CLEAN IN THREE HOURS flat and was resting well.

Kee leaned back in a metal chair placed beside the cot in the recovery tent, close enough for Dilya to touch her if she woke. The chair dug at her back.

She should have flown.

She knew it.

Archie knew it.

Even John knew it.

But she'd stayed.

She'd stayed for Dilya, but Dilya wasn't a Night Stalker. The girl needed her, but had she? Mac and Jeremy had prepped her for surgery while Kee held her hand.

Once Dilya was out, there was nothing for Kee to do except feel guilty and worry. She didn't even know who'd flown in her place. Or had the mission scrubbed? Probably not. No one had come in to check on her.

"Smith!"

She snapped her eyes open just in time to catch the yellow case with a large red cross on it that Mackenzie heaved in her direction. It thudded against her with a body blow almost knocking her backwards out of the chair.

"Hustle!" With two more cases under one arm, he grabbed a fold-up stretcher under the other and was gone out the door.

As she struggled to her feet, Kee glanced at Dilya. The child still slept.

Kee ran after the medic.

—◦◦◦—

Mac didn't react when Kee trotted up beside him. He simply stood on the landing field and watched the northern sky.

It took a moment for her to place where they were. Exactly where she'd stood while facing down Major Henderson one week earlier. Staring at the empty space where Beale would be landing her helicopter.

This time, the chief medic was meeting the helicopter at night.

Kee's vision tunneled as she too turned to watch the north sky, seeking the green of cockpit glow against the unmoving stars. No running lights to attract attention, of course; Major Beale's bird, *Vengeance*, would be hard to spot.

Someone hurt. On her chopper. Hurt, and she hadn't been there. Hurt because she hadn't been there. She tasted blood where she bit her lower lip.

Please not… who? How do you pray for one of your crewmates to be safe when that would cost another? When it should have been her?

Again, she felt the heavy thud internally before she heard the rotor beat against the air. Coming in hard and fast.

Kee didn't cover her face or turn from the pounding dust kicked up by the rotor wash. The chopper flared hard, dumping speed right at the margins of safety, but the last six inches were as gentle as could be.

Mac was aboard before the wheels were fully down.

Someone flicked on the cargo bay's white lights and the chopper's interior glared in red, the red of blood. It was all over her seat, Big John's flight suit was mottled with it, the deck awash. And the body stretched out in the middle of the bay was coated with it.

Bandages were everywhere. Two IVs were clipped to the ceiling, their tubes snaking down to the crewman lying on the deck.

"We can't move him, yet. Smith, give me the red case, open to the second level."

Kee grabbed it, set it beside him as he knelt in the bay.

Without looking, he reached back and grabbed a massive pair of shears. In moments, the flight suit was cut away. Large rounds had punched right through the crewman's body armor, leaving his torso a pattern of bloody holes.

"Light. I need light." Someone pointed a hand flood down.

Kee barely recognized him. He was a gunner on one of the Chinooks. Jeff somebody. She didn't even know his name and he was dying. Dying in her place.

Her stomach started to heave.

"You can be sick later. Blue case, get me four clamps." Mackenzie had his hand out. She found it and slapped them into his hand one by one.

No one spoke other than Mac. "John, pressure here. Smith, another IV, it's labeled saline. Check his tag for blood type." It had to be wiped clean of blood to be read, and Kee'd gone sprinting for the hospital's small blood fridge.

Other soldiers came and went. Jeremy arrived and

Kee was moved aside, slowly but inexorably pushed back until she stood outside the chopper.

Outside looking in.

Her guts now heaved uncontrollably. She puked until she thought to see her stomach come up and splat out on the sand before her.

When she was done and drained and there was no more in her, a movement attracted her vision. Someone dangled a cloth near her face.

"I don't get sick." Despite the evidence inches in front of her. The words burned in her throat.

She spat again and took the cloth. Wiped at her mouth and hands and knees where she'd squatted in her own bile.

When she looked up, the helicopter was empty. The interior light still on, but no body, no medics or nurses, just a sheen of red.

Kee didn't need to look to her right to know her benefactor. Didn't need to look to see the accusation in Archie's eyes. She should have been there. She belonged on that bloody floor, not Jeff of no last name.

Archie stood beside her in silence until her breathing settled. She could feel him, though she couldn't see. Only the glitter of bright light off wet blood.

Finally, a mere whisper she barely heard in the silence of the night.

"I know it's wrong, but I am glad it wasn't you."

When at last she looked over, she was alone.

She climbed to her feet and went to find buckets, water, and a scrub brush.

Chapter 10

EMILY BEALE FOUND SERGEANT KEE SMITH SITTING on the lip of the chopper's cargo door, her feet hanging out but not touching the ground. Her clothing looked stiff and uncomfortable, caked with brown stains that had started out red. Her head hanging down. Her hair a knotted halo around her face.

The Hawk shone in the morning light. Emily would wager that not one single stain of blood, which marked Kee so darkly, remained on the Hawk itself. The ground team reported that she'd threatened murder when they'd showed up to do the cleanup themselves.

The girl presented a puzzle. A top gunner, she'd turned in range statistics like few in the history of SOAR. Her ratings were universally high as a soldier. She earned top marks, even from the commanders who had thrown her in lockup for fighting. She had struggled even harder than Emily had to get here, climbed over unbelievable hurdles that her file only hinted at.

The girl would die for her team. Nearly had several times. But the teams never lasted. Somehow they always shattered around the Sergeant. A lot died because she led teams into the fray past where any sane squad leader would venture. This drive she could identify with, having done it a few times herself.

But some of Kee's teams had simply broken down, been disbanded and reorganized by their commanders.

Report after report included the line, "If she weren't such a dedicated and skilled soldier…"

Could she trust Sergeant Kee Smith?

Trust her with the lives of Emily's crew on the line?

Emily had taken her reluctantly. Was it because she was a woman? No, she'd liked the idea of a team of women showing men exactly what they were made of. It was the Sergeant's history of being a trouble spot that worried her. Yet this woman had consistently driven herself to the outer limits the military allowed. Always farthest forward, and her units, while they lasted, had incredibly low casualty rates for where they had gone.

Smith should have been in the bird. She'd proven on the first flight how fast her reactions were. No one dodged an RPG when it was that close, but Kee's warning had saved all their lives. The girl's nervous system ran at a different speed than the rest of humanity. Tonight, might she have been fast enough, had she been there?

The attack had come without warning, a dozen rounds fired out of the night from a goat's perch high on a cliff. In truth, Emily held little doubt that had Sergeant Kee Smith been at the portside gun, she would be the one entering the fifth hour of surgery, not Jeff Carlisle. Mac insisted Jeff had climbed out of the woods, but there was still a long road to discover if he'd ever again be physically fit for active duty. Assuming he wanted it. He was SOAR, so he probably would. SOAR soldiers didn't know how to quit, even when they had every right and reason to do so.

Emily moved to stand before the Sergeant.

Kee slowly raised her head until she looked at Emily.

Her eyes were dark hollows, her normally sun-kissed complexion gray with exhaustion.

"Are you quitting on me, Smith?"

Kee blinked once, slowly, as if waking from a dream.

"Night. Stalkers. Don't. Quit." She ground it out from a throat raspy with exhaustion. But the eyes had fire in them. Whatever drove Kee Smith still shone brightly.

Emily didn't know at what moment she made her decision, but she completed the ritual.

"Right. Until you do, we don't have a problem."

She turned and walked away, unable to face the pain in the young woman's eyes.

Chapter 11

TWO NIGHTS LATER, KEE STILL HADN'T SPOKEN TO anyone other than Dilya. The girl's sunny attitude had bounced back in a day, and she returned to her habit of eating like a horse. Conversations died when Kee entered the mess tent, so she ate her meals quietly with Dilya in recovery. Sergeant Jeff Carlisle had been shipped to a stateside hospital for rest and recoup with a good prognosis.

Usually only she and Dilya were in the hospital tent. Kee made herself scarce whenever the girl had a visitor, which was surprisingly often. Especially considering none of her visitors spoke even the few words of Uzbek Kee had mastered.

Big John had brought a doll, but who knew where he'd found one on a forward air base. It wasn't a big success, maybe it looked a bit too real for Dilya. She took it but set it aside as soon as John left. Then she reached out to turn it so that it faced the canvas side of the tent. Finally the girl draped a towel over it.

The stuffed orange cat that Archie dug up, however, was a huge success. Dilya hugged it tightly and tried to sit up to do the same to Archie. But a sharp wince of pain dropped her back against her pillow and instead earned a brush of his hand through her hair. And a smile.

Kee could get hooked on watching the Lieutenant's crazy smile. And when Dilya giggled at her cat and began trying out names for it, his smile slid into a lop-sided grin that had no place on his well-bred face. But it absolutely belonged there. She wondered how it would feel to have that smile aimed in her direction.

Kee'd tried to leave when he arrived, but stopped a few beds away to stand in the shadows and watch them. The Lieutenant had said he was glad it hadn't been her. Another man had been wounded in her place, and for some reason this well-bred, well-educated man had been glad it wasn't her life's blood pumped all over the chopper.

Boston money. So far above her, she couldn't make any sense of it. Men like him never noticed women like her. And she ignored them. But twice, as she lingered back in the shadows, the Lieutenant turned his sky-blue eyes on her. She could detect no reprimand nor question. He simply looked and saw her far more clearly than any man she'd ever met before.

He left without offering her any words, though he'd spent some effort teasing the girl in broken Russian.

The visitors tapered off, it seemed half the camp had come through, and Dilya finally slept. Kee sat in the stiff metal chair beside the bed, watching the perfect peace of a sleeping girl. She finally rested her forehead against the sheets and just concentrated on breathing. On remembering how to breathe.

A slight movement, and Dilya patted Kee's head.

Kee didn't move, didn't dare. Only one person had ever dared touch her that way. Had ever thought to. An agony of memories washed over her and she did her best to tamp them down, hard. And focus only on the small, gentle fingers brushing through her hair.

Dilya fell back asleep with her fingers tangled in Kee's hair. They stayed that way for a long time.

——⁓——

Tonight Kee was flying again. The first time in three days. The first time since Dilya's surgery.

The mission profile sounded easy enough. Her old unit, the 10th Mountain, was pushing a three-pronged foot patrol into three villages.

By the plan, her crew was backup. The 101st was offering primary cover with their Apaches. Except they weren't. Some rear commander had pulled them back when the firefight got too hot.

Two squads were in it deep when the call went out for backup. Chief Warrant Clay had his pair of transport Hawks packed solid with a ten-man squad of Rangers each, ready to drop in for support. But he couldn't get 'em down. The incessant ground fire had already wounded two of the Rangers while they were still in the choppers.

It was up to Emily's DAP Hawk to make a place for Clay to land.

They hammered over a ridge and Major Beale's call sounded over the headset.

"Steel!"

"We Deal In Steel!" was the unofficial motto of the DAP Hawks. They brought more firepower to the fight than any other chopper in history.

"Steel!" She and John echoed as they opened up with their miniguns.

The good guys had infrared reflective flags and buttons on their uniforms. The helicopter's FLIR lit them up, making it easy for Kee to spot friendlies in her night-vision goggles. And the array of figures without beacons numbered near enough a hundred, against the three, eight-man squads of Americans trying to secure the LZ.

She raked the hillside with her minigun. A blazing snake arced forth from her gun. Every fifth bullet was a brilliant tracer so she could see exactly where it was headed. No real lag from firing to impact as they were only a few hundred feet up and the muzzle velocity over two thousand feet per second. But the chopper weaved and dodged, making even the short line of tracers appear to swirl and whip as Kee held it steady for a moment on target after target. Her body, trained to pure instinct, compensated her aim for the Major's pitch and roll without thought.

"Ground reports mortars." The Professor reported matter-of-factly. "They have no read on the direction. But if I were a mortar crew, I'd set up behind that ridge at ten o'clock."

Kee looked out at the ridge. What distinguished this from any other? Who knew what had passed through the Professor's brain to make that judgment. The one at seven o'clock looked the same, as did the one they'd just overflown and that now loomed on John's side of the aircraft.

Mortars sucked for ground troops. They hid out of sight and lobbed their charges up into the air to fall from above. A forward spotter could tell them where to adjust their aim. Ground pounders had no recourse to fight back. No one to fire at, except the well-hidden spotter who did his best not to be found.

Major Beale didn't hesitate, she clearly trusted the

Professor's estimate completely. She also didn't turn
to climb over the ridge, they broke the crest sideways,
offering Kee the best chance of seeing the weapon em-
placement. She wished the Major had gone the other way
and given Big John the shot. Not put her on the spot.

A rattle of small-caliber machine gun fire rang
against the Hawk. Nothing like the caliber that had
nailed Jeff Carlisle, but still she twitched. Before they
passed over the shooter's position, a round or two spat-
tered against her shin armor. They hit like hammer-
blows despite having punched through the ship's side
plating first. No sharp pain of a through-shot, probably
just be black and blue. No time to check. And the heat
roared back into her blood. They weren't going to do to
her what they did to Jeff two nights ago. It just wasn't
gonna happen.

The Major held steady over the ridge as Kee scanned
for the mortar. Big John's minigun burped out a couple
hundred rounds. That was probably the end of the machine gun nest. Either way, that was just an irritant. It
was the mortar that was killing ground troops or would
be real soon. That's what counted.

Kee scanned over and back. "C'mon, buddy boy!
You lying sack! You're here somewhere."

On the verge of calling, "No joy," and declaring the
Professor's guess wrong, she saw it.

A flicker. A heat trail across her night vision. At least
a hint of one. Going straight up.

"Circle left! Circle left!"

Without hesitation the bird laid over. Almost.
Almost. There.

Kee unleashed her gun, walked its tracer-lit whip of

brilliant green across her night-vision gear right into a deep crevice.

Half a second later a pair of rockets launched from the chopper's side pods and tore a new hole in the mountainside right where Kee'd been firing. The Professor had taken his cue from her aim and pounded the daylights out of them. No time to double-check, no need either. The explosion kept going as the mortar charges cooked off, destroying everything in the area.

"We're gonna have to call you the Magic Man, Lieutenant!"

Her only response was a grunt as the Major jammed them back toward the ridge and they pulled a few gees.

Ten seconds later they were back in the fray, making a hole for Clay's birds to drop their load of troops.

"Come on, where are you?" Kee kept looking for the spotter in between other cleanup shots.

"Watch the peak five hundred yards to the west." Archie's voice sounded soft but clear in her headset.

Kee didn't even know she'd spoken her question aloud. But he'd been dead-on with locating the mortar crew, so she kept glancing there each time she had a moment.

Finally she spotted a man crawling out from under a boulder that had shielded him from discovery. It cheered her immensely when she deep-sixed the mortar team's spotter.

"You are the Magic Man!"

His tone was dry over the headset. "I think I preferred 'Professor.'"

An hour later they were a mile out cleaning up strays.

The 10th Mountain was back to doing what they did,

tearing up a village looking for an arms depot. Clay had reloaded his Rangers and dropped them on the backside of the village to keep the baddies from squeezing out as the 10th pushed in. Fighting insurgents foot by foot, but at least no one was battering them from impenetrable positions up the mountainside.

The 101st still hadn't released their Apaches, bet that was chapping someone's behind.

Kee changed over to her fifth belt of ammo. She'd never burned through so much ammo in a week, never mind an hour. Her gun was smoking hot, but she wasn't melting barrels yet, and Kee hoped she never would. That kinda firefight didn't make for likely survival of the chopper.

Major Beale had kept them in the center of the fray as the Hawk bounced and shifted over the brutal mountains of the Hindu Kush throughout the night. They'd given every baddy who thought he'd hunkered down hard enough, deep enough, a rude shock.

The vertical slashes of shattered rock soared vertically to impossible heights and heavy trees clung to the upper slopes, though the valleys below were bone dry. She'd walked and fought on those hills with the 10th Mountain and now couldn't believe it. It was the most rugged ground she'd ever seen, and the locals had been fighting back and forth across it for centuries. Without helicopters.

Suddenly the Hawk pulled a hard left. Her stomach hadn't noticed the extreme limits of control that the Major used throughout the firefight. Big John had been right. To fly with the woman wasn't a bad gig at all.

And there was no way she'd quit. She'd never again miss a flight.

They turned down the valley and climbed high enough for safety as they headed home. Kee fired a short burst into the mountainside to make sure the new belt was tracking well then let the gun drop against the stops.

Someone must have finally released the 101st Apaches now that the fight was over and the morning light hinted at the eastern horizon. She couldn't wait for the next time she ran into their pilots back at some cozy, safe air base with AC and iced Coca Cola. She was gonna smoke their behinds.

With the dirty work done, Beale's Hawk headed home.

And Kee felt that she once again belonged in her seat. Almost.

Chapter 12

ARCHIE SAT ON THE SECOND BENCH UP FROM THE soccer field, not far from the chow tent, and held out his hands. Dilya knelt beside him as she wrapped a loop of string over them. He knew Cat's Cradle well enough but was a little surprised that she did.

He waited for instructions to pick up the opposite loops with his forefingers. With long, fine fingers as quick as darts, she snagged the crossed strings between thumb and forefinger and scooped them under and through. When she pulled her hands apart, a new string design appeared.

He continued his sham of acting slow to catch on, forcing her to walk him through each of his steps slowly. With a huff at one of his dropped strings, she unleashed a rattle of Uzbek at him.

He smiled and methodically reset the starting figure, looking at her to check that he had done it correctly.

And they were off again.

It was comfortable with her. No words needed. Only with Major Beale had he ever felt as comfortable. While their families didn't know each other, their backgrounds were similar enough that they knew of each other. His father a high-end sailboat builder and his mother a government consultant in Boston. Her father was the director of the FBI, but she was fairly closemouthed about that, as you'd expect. Her mother was a Washington socialite who Emily claimed didn't know what to do with herself now that her only child had married. At least they were on a level.

They'd studied together at West Point and fought together for so long since that there was no question of anything between them. He could simply relax around her, as much as anyone did around Emily Beale.

This time Archie acknowledged remembering the fourth figure, much to Dilya's hand-clapping delight.

But any friendship with the Major was tempered more by their differences than connected by any similarities. His default entry into Army flying versus Emily's full-charge attack. The Major's belief that rules were to be shattered versus his own efforts to be adroit and skilled within the guidelines of operations. Her intense attractiveness to and comfort with the opposite sex. She spoke guy-speak better than most men. His complete ineptness with any woman.

Dilya decided they knew Cat's Cradle well enough for now and started him on a new figure, one he quickly recognized as Apache Door. *Wonder what it is in your language, little one?*

He knew certain figures were universal, but Dilya was Uzbek, a mostly Muslim people. Who had taught the girl representational images? Perhaps a Russian soldier. Would her parents be upset if they knew? Were her parents still alive somewhere to care?

Kee pounded down her last lap around the field. She'd sign over her next paycheck if she could run cross-country rather than chasing stupid little circles around and around and around inside the stadium. But getting picked off by some random goatherd with a thirty-year-old AK-47 didn't hit high on her list of good-time ideas.

Around lap ten, a couple of the Rangers set camp chairs along the track. They popped water bottles and watched her go by. They tried hooting and casting insults about lap fifteen.

"Baby girl flier. Can't even get into combat. Gotta stay all safe in the air."

"Runs like a man with boobs."

"Runs like a boob who just needs a good man."

She considered stopping and pounding one particular sergeant into a bloody pulp, but didn't want to give them the satisfaction. And telling them she'd done a ground tour with the 10th Mountain still wouldn't impress them. Rangers were convinced only those who'd hacked their way through Airborne training counted. Maybe. Maybe not. They weren't the kings of the hill either. She'd been there and done that. Airborne and Ranger were only two of the steps before you could even apply to SOAR.

Then there were the Delta operators doing some elaborate drill she couldn't make out. They ignored her completely each time she passed near their camp by the far goal.

By lap twenty, she decided that if it was a show they wanted, it was a show they'd get.

It was a new trick for Kee. She'd been in lockup a dozen times for settling arguments with her fists. Of course, she'd always looked much better than the guys locked up in the next cell over. "Self-defense" kept her out of some of it, until a little trainer lady named Trisha

O'Malley had pounded the shit out of her for falling to the guys' levels.

The woman was unbeatable, and Kee'd gone back and been trounced by her a dozen more times trying to learn. She'd learned plenty, especially that First Sergeant Trisha O'Malley truly was unbeatable in hand-to-hand combat. But she'd also learned to ignore guys who were just too damn stupid to understand that Sergeant Kee Smith wasn't all that far behind her.

Now she'd simply run them into the ground. Lap thirty, about eight miles in the blistering heat, they got bored and drifted away looking for a new plaything. One that reacted and twitched. By lap forty, ten miles down, they were nowhere to be seen.

She did a trot lap and a walk lap just to ease back down, though she was still dripping when she passed through the chow tent and knocked back a couple bottles of water and two salt pills. She stepped out beneath the shadow of the extended entry flap hoping to catch some edge of a breeze.

And then she saw Dilyana and the Professor. Sitting shoulder to shoulder on the second row of the bleachers, laughing.

Dilyana hadn't laughed with Kee but the one time. And that had been when Kee'd imitated Dilya puking on the Professor. The girl smiled sometimes, pretty easily in fact. When Kee wasn't flying or working out, the kid hung by her side like a leech. It had bugged her at first, but the kid was so damn sweet about it. And Kee was so relieved to see her up and around after the surgery that she wasn't about to complain. But they didn't laugh together.

The hard part had been the work with the phrase book. Sections on shopping, dining, and lodging did little to help in a wartime environment. She'd yet to pin down where Dilya's parents were.

"Walk." Dilyana's definitive word whenever Kee tried to dig into her past. Kid was strong as a gazelle, but would always find the shortest route across camp, climbing and crossing through helicopter cargo bays rather walking around. And she sat down the instant she arrived. Sick to death of walking. Or perhaps she'd learned the critical warrior lesson to conserve energy at every chance, so you had it aplenty when it hit the fan and you had to be somewhere else fast.

Piece by piece Kee put Dilyana's story together, word by word. Many times outside the scope of the little phrase book. They playacted to communicate the word "hide." That one became almost as popular as "walk."

The morning that Kee came up with "dead" by imitating the crack of a bullet as it zipped by your ear with its tiny sonic boom and then falling over with her eyes closed, Dilyana had screamed. That had been a real pain to fix. The girl wouldn't even speak until the evening and had spent the day curled up in a tight little ball on Kee's cot. Kee had finally climbed in with her and held her close through her precious downtime. Afraid that the little girl would never speak to her again, Kee hadn't slept a wink.

She had tried to imagine why she cared. In the street gangs she'd made a point of not caring. You were tough or you were dead. If you got attached to someone, then a cop shot him down while he was trying to get some dough for his next fix. Or your best girl, who always watched your back, suddenly flipped out and became a coke whore, or got busted into rehab or juvie. Kee had only broken her rule once and regretted it to this day.

But Dilya had opened a crack in Kee's armor, and she couldn't figure out how to close it back up. Standing here, watching the girl giggle as the Professor once again dropped a string from his fingers, Kee knew she was screwed. This eleven-year-old pipsqueak had gotten to her.

When she'd been a ground pounder in the regular army, Kee learned that the squad was her team. Knew it to the core. But ninety-nine times out of a hundred, they were all guys. All had their own agenda.

Actually, the girls always had their own agenda, too. The women were always afraid, once they latched onto some jerk, that another woman was gonna steal him. With such a misbalance in genders, being a warrior woman looking for a man in the U.S. Army was like being in a carnival shooting gallery with an M134 minigun. You couldn't miss, so why would you poach?

All the women either hung with each other and looked weak for not mixing, or they were tough as hell and didn't hang with each other because they got tired of being called lesbians. Kee found it best to never hang with anybody except for training, workouts, and sex.

The only one in this woman's Army she couldn't figure was the Major. Emily Beale really flew, the Professor only the copilot. Only. That meant he lived for navigation, armament other than the miniguns, systems status of the chopper, and tactical advice for the pilot. And backup flier if his pilot was hurt. Pilot and copilot in a DAP Hawk was a crazy symbiosis that only the very best could make work. Kee should have known that from the beginning.

No question that Beale flew. And Kee had ridden enough birds to know that few pilots were so smooth or quick. She wondered if half the legend might be true. Big John had insisted that the Major had earned that Silver Star fair and square.

The woman didn't fit any of Kee's patterns. She'd been absolutely standup about Dilyana. Another major point in Kee's book. And about Kee's failure to fly. That had shocked Kee to the core. She'd let down the team, failed in her sworn duty, and Major Beale had let her back aboard. Once. Kee knew there would be no second chance.

But independence wasn't easy. Nobody really spoke to her, though Big John had loosened up a little. Keeping Jeff alive on the flight back had both shaken him and built up his confidence once it was clear Jeff had survived because of him.

Dilyana laughed in the sunlight with the Professor.

And Kee Smith stood in the shadows of the chow tent, alone.

Separate. Outside their circle of laughter.

Dilyana had woken trembling in the middle of their downtime and had taken the book from Kee's pocket. She had lain there tight against Kee, studying and studying for an hour or more, while Kee pretended to sleep, wished she could sleep. At length the girl closed the book and snuggled a little closer to Kee.

When she spoke in the darkness of the tent, Kee could feel the words vibrating her body as well as her ears. Whispers. Whispers driven home with the force of a cannon.

"Mother. Father. Walk. Walk. Walk. Hide. Hide. Hide. Cold. Walk. Walk. Walk." Then silence, then she made the cracking sound of a passing bullet. Twice.

A sound you could only make correctly if you'd heard a hundred of them go by close enough to have had your name on them. But they found the person behind you. When she'd still been infantry, everyone would sit around bored out of their skulls in the quiet between the adrenaline rush of one firefight and the next. One pastime, the grunts would take turns trying to imitate the tiny, sonic-boom crack beside your ear.

The more you heard, the better your imitation. You learned to break it down. The timbre of the initial snap, the shrick of the whistle while it passed within a couple inches, the Doppler drop-off as it moved on. And that dreadful wait, hoping it hit rock or dirt with a sharp slap rather than turning into a silent moment and then the cry of a gut-shot guy who was supposed to have your backside.

Dilyana's imitation was near perfect.

"Dead. Family dead. Home dead." And then she'd wept. And Kee had held her. Held her more tightly than when they'd returned from the refugee camp. More tightly than she'd ever held anyone before. Like she'd often imagined a father would hold on to her, if her mother had known who he was. Or dreamed her mother would, even once, instead of dying a dose at a time.

On her first leave from the Army, Kee had looked for her mother but not found her. Even the Street didn't know where she'd gone. The Street had finally swallowed her mother whole and left nothing behind.

They were all of them lost. The Professor and

Dilyana with their string figures. Kee herself. Lost in the shadows.

———— ∞ ————

Archie had watched Kee run. Counted every lap, struggling to hide his distraction from the little girl. He was charmed by Dilya as if she were one of his nieces. There wasn't a bone in the child's body that didn't radiate joy. And it shone ten times as brightly knowing even a little of what the girl had survived.

Kee didn't radiate joy, she radiated pure power in its truest form. She ran the track like a mythical cross between the fleet-footed Hermes, messenger to the Greek gods, and a B-2 bomber. She plowed ten miles around the track, moving as strongly the last lap as she had the first. A feat most men couldn't achieve, especially in the midday heat. No wonder she scared the hell out of him. Granted, every woman scared the hell out of him, but in Kee Smith he'd unearthed that finest of treasures, the essence. The true definition. The ideal upon which all of the other women were based.

And when she finished her run, she approached them through the shadows of the tent, ultimately stopping out of Dilya's sight. He watched her watch him and Dilya playing. What did she see when she looked at him? Gangly Archibald Stevenson III.

And now she stood unmoving in the shadows, staring at him. Glaring at him perhaps? Wasn't he supposed to enjoy his time with Dilya? He'd certainly been terrified enough when Dilya fell ill. Had he somehow handled it wrong in Kee's eyes?

Did she think him less of a man for playing with

a child? Would it help to know that halfway through her run he had gone to the Rangers' commander and informed him that if his men ever again harassed one of Beale's crew, they'd never set foot on a 5th Battalion SOAR bird again? Would she think him less or more of a man if she knew that all he had thought of since the first moment they'd met was one Sergeant Kee Smith? And not just her amazing physique.

Even if she wouldn't admit it, he knew better. He didn't know how, but he would place a long-odds wager on the first horse race at Saratoga Springs that there were greater depths to Kee Smith than the average male perceived. More than her amazing body and her right-left punch of attitude. Perhaps more than she knew herself.

Dilya looked up to see where his attention had strayed. Her sharp eyes picked Kee out of the shadow. She left the string hanging between his hands, halfway between two figures, grabbed up the stuffed cat he'd given her, and sprinted across the burning sand toward Kee.

The string game they had been playing for almost an hour now hung lifeless and snarled about his fingers.

The girl launched herself at Kee, who caught her in a fierce hug.

And as Kee spun Dilya about until her feet lifted from the ground, she moved from shadow to sunlight. And in the direct light he could see a look on Kee's face, not of joy, though that was present, but of sadness. Almost terror. She was holding the girl so tight, he half feared Kee would hurt her. Then Kee plopped her down and, with a friendly slap on her butt, sent the girl scooting off for the chow line.

Archie watched himself, with more than a little

surprise, rise to his feet and move to stand beside Kee. They both looked into the tent's shadows where the little girl dodged around Big John's bulk to grab a sandwich.

"She loves you."

Kee jumped as if he'd electrocuted her. Why did he never do anything right?

Kee looked up at him, her eyes wide. The terror back tenfold in those deep, dark eyes. A terror so deep he could imagine no method powerful enough to wash it away.

Kee's voice was a whisper. "You're good with her. You're a good man, Professor."

Now it was his turn to be surprised. It was an assessment that few had offered outside his sister and Major Emily Beale.

"Thank you for Dilya's sake." She hooked a finger in the collar of his T-shirt and pulled him down.

"This," she kissed one cheek, "is for your kindness. This," she kissed the other, "is for saving me when I blanked at that awful refugee camp." And "This," she kissed him softly on the lips.

This.

Archie had never tasted anything like Kee Smith's kiss. She was the scent of a dusky sunset and the taste of abandon. He didn't know what to do. As all the devils and gods were his witnesses, he didn't know. He stood riveted in place by the lips of a woman who barely stood to his shoulder.

When she moved back, just an inch, he almost stumbled forward onto her. Her almond eyes were wide, as wide as they had been moments before, but there was no terror.

No. If he had to define that particular expression, he'd be forced to identify it as wonder. And then, impossibly, a deep blush roared up her face.

Had he a mirror handy, he would define his own expression as shock. This pint-sized warrior, more beautiful than the most perfect windup doll, had decided to turn his entire world on its ear.

When he blinked and shook his head to clear his thoughts, to clear the mesmerizing trace of warmth that lingered on his lips, Kee no longer stood before him. How long had he been standing in the sun?

Crazy Tim slapped him on the shoulder with a resounding buffet that sent him staggering into the tent. "You're daydreaming again, Arch."

His fingers were still tangled up in string.

———

Dilyana sat at the table and ate her food. Bit into the two pieces of hot bread filled with cheese, crisp cooked meat, and a thick slice of a red fruit she'd never seen before. She still found it hard to eat slowly, but it was so important to The Kee, she pretended to trust her meal would not be taken from her before she had finished. Made believe they wouldn't all be dead in minutes. And for days now it had been true. She could feel her defenses relaxing. She hadn't stolen food in two days, though she had some hidden beneath The Kee's bed that she checked each night as soon as they all flew away into the stars.

She pretended to be amused when the big man with a voice as big as thunder pretended to throw up on someone else. She could see it was expected, that he'd done it for her. So she smiled then rolled her eyes. He looked pleased.

But what she watched was The Kee and the String Man. He was as long and thin as the string they played with. Clearly, he too had been teasing her with pretending to not know the game. He had made it fun, so she let him believe that she didn't see what he was doing. Her mother would have liked him for being kind to her child.

Dilyana liked him too. Trusted him. He hadn't hit her when she was sick on him. And hadn't treated her like a baby either. He treated her as a friend might, even though he was so old. She hadn't had a friend in a long time.

Now he and The Kee stood talking in the shadows. Dilya could still feel where The Kee had wrapped her arms around Dilya so tightly and swung her about. Held her as if she were important. As if she mattered.

She watched The Kee reach up to the String Man and kiss him on each cheek and once on the lips. At that moment, they both changed.

Dilyana could remember her parents kissing. Sometimes quickly, and sometimes, when they thought Dilya wasn't watching, much longer. In the dark of the night, Dilya had watched them through the slitted eyes of pretended sleep as they had done even more. Removing each other's clothes beneath the blanket and moving silently together in the night. Dilya loved the memory, because they always looked so happy. Even when they'd been frightened and lost, they had held each other close.

She had to blink hard to clear her eyes so that she could watch them change.

Would The Kee and the String Man do this?

Now the String Man stood like a statue, not touching The Kee. And The Kee moved from him, slow at first, then very quickly to the food line.

She sat silently across from Dilyana and ate her food quietly. Ate as if she were alone at the table and no one else sat near.

The man with a horse painted into the skin of his arm slapped the String Man, waking him from his standing sleep. He turned, looking into the tent straight at The Kee's back. Stood and watched for a handful of heart-beats, then turned and disappeared into the glaring sun.

Maybe they were going to become a mother and father.

Dilyana bit into her sandwich. The question was, would that be good for her or bad? After making sure no one watched, she slid a round orange-colored fruit into her sleeve. Better to have something set aside in case she had to run again.

Chapter 13

ARCHIE WAITED WITH JOHN AND TIM NEAR THE EXIT from the soccer stadium. He noted the couple of Rangers behind sandbag emplacements, appearing relaxed but keeping an eye out. A double line of very new concrete pilings fifty feet from the entrance made sure no truck bombs could enter this way. The original line at twenty-five feet made sure that a second truck following wouldn't get through either.

Crazy Tim was doing what he always did, describing a trivial event in such a way that you were fascinated despite yourself. Today he was telling how Major Henderson had been tracking some baddies last night and spooked a six-point buck instead. They'd chased it over the hills, and Henderson had put a single shot from the 30 mm M230 cannon through its head at two thousand yards. The fact that the shot was completely impossible didn't really matter when the headless deer, cleaned and dressed by the Major, had been unloaded from the chopper and carried to the chow tent for the cooks to play with. The animal had certainly felt no pain.

Archie offered a scoffing laugh when expected. An easy laugh that choked in his suddenly dry throat. A vision walked toward them. The girl and the woman.

The girl, a slip of wind, wrapped in a plain white *hijab*. Skirt, overdress, and head scarf, leaving her merry face and bright eyes to shine forth.

And the woman. A long skirt of the palest blue. A long-sleeved blouse of flowing black cotton. A gray scarf the color of a winter sky slipping off her hair and onto her shoulders. Sergeant Kee Smith glared at him, her eyes narrowed and her mouth in a grim line.

John and Tim, finally catching his distraction, turned to see.

Catcalls and whistles. "Smith, you are hot!"

"Like to see you wearin' that when we fly."

"This is so unfair!" Kee brushed her hands down the skirts as if she were brushing mud off a tank.

"Oh, it's working for us!"

"Damn, girl, we're gonna make that your new required camp uniform."

Archie couldn't speak, couldn't face her, but couldn't take his eyes from the vision. He'd known the woman was there. Couldn't miss that about Kee Smith. She radiated female from every pore of her being. But the clothing, far more modest than anything she wore in camp, revealed a feminine side she never showed.

He bowed to her. He didn't know what else to do.

Her eyes, narrowed even further, then a small crinkle at the corners gave her away. She almost smiled before she caught herself, but she looked a little lighter when she turned to face her hecklers.

"Just don't mess with me, boys." She lifted her blouse from her side to reveal her M9. A tweak of her skirt revealed a backup piece in an ankle holster and the lower part of a calf-sheath for her knife.

They applauded. Archie couldn't even offer that. The woman and the warrior mixed before him. Neither elf nor fairy as he'd first thought her. She was absolutely and uniquely herself, which was the headiest tonic of all.

To cover his confusion, he bent down before Dilya and offered a perch on his back. The girl scrambled up and threw her arms around his neck in a choke hold as he hooked his arms under her knees.

Together, they turned and headed out of the stadium and into the town.

———ᴧᴧᴧ———

Kee pulled at her scarf for the thirtieth time, it simply wouldn't stay put. And when it fell to her shoulders, the looks she received from the locals shifted from sour to actively hostile.

Dilya pulled on her hand, indicating she should bend down. The girl did something that with a fold, a tug, and a quick slip of her hands, cool on Kee's skin, tucked the ends in neatly.

Kee stood and it felt different. Felt right for the first time. She turned her head right and left. Slightly limited her peripheral vision, but not badly. She smoothed her hand down Dilya's hair, only to realize the girl's head was uncovered. Scanning the street calmed her. While the women all had their hair covered, half the girls racing about the market had lost control of their scarves. She pulled Dilya's back up anyway.

She searched for the guys. Even in the few moments they'd knelt together, the market had shifted, flowed, changed shape. Bati was a small enough town to only have one market that everyone could reach easily on foot. And it was big enough for that market to be packed and teeming.

She stood by the nut vendor. A twist of paper in her hand warm with roasted nuts. Toasted cinnamon teased at her nose. Dilya fished another from the wrapper and led them forward. The men, who had been staring at a line of skinned and hung sheep covered with flies while she made her purchase, were nowhere to be seen.

The crowd was close, the open aisles narrowed by carts and tables shoved farther to the center than they should be. Yet, people flowed back and forth without contact or jostling. Not even the little that occurred in any American city when the sidewalks were busy. A man here would never think of taking advantage of the crowd to brush against a woman not his wife. There was no blast of male cologne offering a knockout punch. Even the wealthier women of the town understood the most feminine perfume was a fresh-bathed female.

She'd expected to be overpowered by the stench of unwashed bodies. Instead it was the bite of sizzling spices from a Biryani stall serving mutton over rice, the cool wash of sun-warmed eggplant at a vegetable merchant, the tickle in her nose as they passed the pepper merchant.

The noise was constant, steady, and wholly unlike any she'd experienced before. Everyone talked at once and at length. Voices echoed off the tall mud-brick walls, bright, cheerful, laughing. Apparently only bargaining was done quietly; all other conversations were boisterous and sounded full of humor. And over it all, the cries of merchants, announcing their wares, who could easily be heard on the far side of the river.

Despite the briefings, she felt safer here than in most American city crowds. Her nerves were on alert, but no panic signals slid down them. They revealed a personal politeness not spoiled by the tourist-as-target mentality so many more-visited cities suffered. Here the social dynamics were easier, simpler.

There also wasn't that second layer that most Americans couldn't or didn't choose to see. The layer where Kee and those like her had lived their childhoods. There were no rich in Bati, but neither did the poorest live in that thin world of desperation.

The crowd divided itself in only one way, and it did that instantly. Both sexes might be wearing the ubiquitous *hijab* of loose pants and a knee-length overshirt. But men either revealed their black, black hair or wore small circular caps. Women wore shawls over their hair. Most were solid colored, spreading down over their shoulders. But occasionally a head stood out in a beautiful piece of weaving. She'd have to find a stall that sold those.

The crowd shifted and parted and remerged.

Now she stood past the butcher, past the packed sweet stall. A bright orange twist of sugared bread in Dilya's hand. Had she paid? Even as the market shifted again, Kee remembered handing over a brass two-rupee coin. The sweets vendor nowhere in sight, she once again stood with the guys. Hard to miss them: Big John and Archie towered above most in the crowd, Tim was wide-shouldered enough to command his own space. But the native men, while slight, were also taller than Kee, the cause of her frequent immersion, though the guys had never been more than ten feet away.

The guys were… she laughed.

Archie turned to flash her a smile. He reached out, grabbed her hand, and pulled her into the group. His hand, warm and strong and so damn sure of itself, made her feel more a woman than the dress and blouse.

An elderly man, fifty or maybe ninety, she didn't know how to tell. His face lined, his hair gray, his smile lacked several teeth. But his eyes were clear and his grin bright with amusement as he spoke.

"This camel," he snagged a blue-harnessed snout and pulled it close for them to inspect, "she is my sweetheart." His English was heavily accented, but clear.

"She will cross a thousand miles with no complaint… and bite me in behind when I turn my back for one beat of heart. See her teeth. Very strong."

He pinched the animal's nostrils, and her upper lip curled upward revealing wide, yellow teeth, each the size of Kee's thumb.

"My behind. Many marks." He patted her muzzle affectionately.

She let herself drift past the brilliant colors of the dye merchant's piled bowls. Powders of red, blue, magenta, and yellow, painfully bright in the sun, seemed to fill that whole area of the market with color. The walls brighter, the air fresher. A tiny scale, a scoop, and plastic bags the merchant carefully filled with the colors of the rainbow once the price had been agreed on. People still dyed their own cloth here.

The market shifted again in its slow-fast way, and Kee spotted a shawl merchant. She dug in her heels against the gentle but irresistible flow of humanity and managed to stop. Dilya remained by her left side as effortlessly as she had the whole time. She'd clearly grown up navigating these markets. But Kee felt a pull on her right hand.

It was only as he emerged from the flow to stop beside her that she realized the Professor hadn't released her hand since the camel vendor. It felt as natural as if it had always been there. She glanced up at him.

"You had a following of young men. My pretending that you are claimed has caused them to disperse."

"Maybe I didn't want them to disperse. I could use a young man or two. Rub them together and start a fire or something." She glanced around and spotted a few still watching her from farther back into the crowd. Nothing inspiring.

She turned back to the stall, leaving her hand in the Professor's protection. As amused with herself as with him. She'd never in her life walked hand in hand with a boy. A bit late in life to discover she liked the feeling, even if it was just for pretend.

The shawl merchant displayed a wide variety. Mostly the solid colors for everyday wear, but from small hooks up the trimmed tree branches that supported his awning dangled scarves of ornate handwork. Several attracted her attention, but as she reached out, Dilyana stopped her.

She looked down and the girl shook her head. Were they religious scarves, or was it forbidden to touch something you hadn't purchased?

Dilya pointed.

The merchant followed her finger even as Kee's eyes tracked across. A pack rested against the wall behind the merchant. A dozen scarves peeked from the open top. She knew what Dilya had spotted the moment she saw it, so did the merchant. He reached over and selected the third one down, a midnight-blue cloth. Upon the surface of the night sky were scattered stars of silver and gold. A thin moon shone from a corner. He laid the cloth over Kee's raised arm so that she could see the colors against the back of her exposed hand.

A trim of palest green brought her skin to light.

It was nighttime. Mystical and dark, yet alive with light. The very vaults of Heaven had been brought to life. Trimmed in the green of hope, of new life.

No mere cloth, it was artistry. And the colors hadn't been painted, the piece had somehow been woven from many-colored threads. It should be in a museum, not worn on the head.

Once again, Dilyana pulled her down.

As Kee knelt on one knee, Dilya pushed her current scarf down to her shoulders. In moments, she had the new one in place.

The merchant held up a hand mirror little bigger than a postcard. Kee could barely see where the scarf crossed her forehead, but it was right. A Night Stalker. Dilya had found the perfect Night Stalker scarf for her. And, Kee didn't mind admitting to herself, she looked pretty damn cute in it.

"What do you think, Professor?"

She turned her head left and right for him to see.

"Professor?" She snapped her fingers to get him to stop that weird, focused thing he did.

"It, uh, looks great on you."

She turned away, then glanced back sidelong. He'd slid back into that staring mode of his. She almost wanted to sashay her hips. Her breasts had stopped men in their tracks before, but never loose-fitting colorful clothes and a head scarf.

"I'll take it." She reached for her money. Dilya stopped her.

With all the practice of a wise crone, she faced the merchant and raised an eyebrow.

He said something.

Kee was grinding away at the words when Archie leaned in.

"A thousand lira, about ten dollars."

It would cost a hundred in the states. Minimum. A real deal.

Dilya shook her head and indicated Kee should kneel once more. Dilya started untucking it.

"No, Dilya," Kee whispered. "I want it—"

The girl squinched her face up, clearly telling Kee to shut up and let a professional do her job.

The merchant cleared his throat.

Dilya left the scarf half-tied and turned slowly to look up at the man.

He spoke.

"Eight hundred," the Professor whispered.

Dilya glanced up at him.

He flashed her ten fingers, then folded down two of them.

Dilya looked up to the heavens in exasperation and held up two fingers as if it were an order being issued by a general.

The merchant glanced at Kee and Archie, then folded his arms and squarely faced Dilya. He knew who he was dealing with and that she didn't speak his language.

Kee had done her share and more of wheeling and dealing in her youth and since, but Dilya was a pro. Raised to it by her mother and her culture.

She began fingering other scarves of obviously lower quality, as if searching for a more affordable bargain.

The merchant held up five fingers.

Dilya cocked her head thoughtfully before indicating Kee should kneel again. This time, the girl didn't remove her scarf, but pulled at it back into place, fussing as if checking the fit of a formless piece of cloth. Then rubbed it between her fingers to test the fabric's quality. With a small turn, Dilya blocked her own right hand from the merchant's view. She held up three fingers then pointed at the pocket she knew Kee kept her spending money in. Kee slid three hundred-rupee notes into Dilya's hand.

Without turning, the girl held the three notes out to the merchant. Then, after a moment, looked at him in surprise, as if shocked to find the money still in her hand.

The two of them held the tableau for at least ten seconds before he burst out laughing. Bent forward and held his sides until he managed, with a quickly gulped breath, to regain his composure. He solemnly took the three bills from her and nodded his head politely.

Dilya barely acknowledged the nod. They were turning away when the merchant reached into the scarves burying his table and pulled out a simple one, solid color with plain trim. The body of the exact green that trimmed Kee's masterpiece, with a trim of the same midnight blue.

Kee saw Dilyana's eyes light up. Maybe she could pay back the merchant for some of his loss on her own scarf. She didn't like using a child to take advantage.

Dilyana took a breath, blanked her face, raised her chin, and turned to the man. But she'd have a real challenge, no one had missed her initial delight. She held up a single forefinger.

Then she bent it down at the knuckle. One half.

The merchant laughed. With a shake, he unfurled the scarf. Leaning over the table, he secured it over Dilyana's hair with a practiced twist and shooed them all away from his table.

Thunderstruck, Dilyana reached up a tentative hand to touch it. To stroke it.

How could Kee thank him? Money would be wrong. She started to reach across the table, but the Professor stopped her before she started.

He reached across and clasped the man's hand firmly. They exchanged manly nods that apparently crossed every culture. Then they merged into the flow and were drawn forward again.

"He couldn't touch you. You are not his wife. It is forbidden."

Dilya led them this time, straight to a kebab stall.

"The girl is hollow."

As they exited the constant flow of the market to stop at the food stall, Kee noticed.

The Professor once again held her hand.

She didn't find herself complaining.

—⁓—

When Kee headed to bed, she found Dilyana sitting cross-legged on the cot. Across her lap lay the green and blue scarf the merchant had given her that morning.

She stroked it until it lay without fold or wrinkle. A sea of color overflowing her lap.

Kee watched as the girl reached out tentative fingers

to stroke the cloth. To rub her knuckles across its fine-woven surface.

Kee knew the gesture. Knew it from her own past. The first new clothes she'd ever received had been a pair of sneakers Dave Bailey had stolen for her when she was twelve, just about Dilya's age. Bright red Converse. White laces, eyelets, and side rubber. She'd been mesmerized just as Dilya was now. And he'd earned her first real kiss as a reward.

Was the scarf Dilya's first-ever new clothes?

It was. Kee knew it.

Well, one other thing she knew for certain.

It wouldn't be the girl's last.

Chapter 14

"LEAVE?" KEE ALMOST CHOKED ON HER GLASS OF MILK.

"Yes!" Big John slapped his tray down beside her. "The 10th Mountain, with a little help from the 160th because we are so friggin' awesome—"

He raised a high five that she slapped more out of habit than enthusiasm.

"Cut a serious swath through the bad guys with that op the other night. They captured and cleared ammo dumps in all three villages as well as a midnight mule-train of inbound resupply from our supposed allies here in Pakistan. We hang for a week to make sure it stays quiet, then we get ten days stateside."

Crazy Tim dropped down beside Archie. "Suuuweeet! We bad!" He and Big John high-fived across the table with a smack loud enough to really sting.

"They are also experiencing," Archie said as he began unloading his tray onto the table, "month three of a drought and therefore money is very tight."

Dilya inspected the Professor's dishes on the bare table, actually ran a finger over her plastic tray and then over the table. After looking at the tip of her finger, she checked that everyone else kept their plates on their trays and decided that's what she'd do, too.

Kee did her best to hide the smile at what the girl was learning and deciding. Both the tray and the table were probably cleaner than any surface she'd ever eaten from before.

"They're in desperate times. What little they have will be used to purchase food," Archie continued. "It will take some time to save sufficient funds for enough ammunition to stage another assault. Might remain quiet for a couple months, which would allow our troops to perform some significant cleanup with a minimum of pain."

"What're you supposed to do with ten days leave?" Kee poked at the venison Hungarian goulash the sadistic cook had made. The taste was excellent, not gamey at all, but it scorched going down. A hot and hearty meal while it was still half a jillion degrees outside and at least a quarter jillion inside.

"Goin' stateside, see my dad, and tie on a good one together," Big John offered. "Work on this old GTO I'm rebuilding. See if Darlene or Maggie or Jennifer ain't hitched yet and might wanna do a little dancing. Oh, yeah. Suuuweeet!" Another resounding cross-table high five.

Dilya tried reaching across the table to get a high five from Big John. He offered a gentle slap as Archie leaned out of the way to give her more room. Didn't have the loud pop the guys achieved, but Dilya seemed very pleased.

"I'm gonna go home, and Ma and I, we're gonna cook." Crazy Tim made stirring motions with his hands. "Cook for the whole family."

"You cook?" Kee managed to put a decent scoff in her voice without choking on all these happy family images.

"Not as good as the Major, but yeah."

"The Major cooks?"

Everyone at the table turned to stare at her.

"What?"

"Don't you ever watch the news?"

"Only if there isn't something better on." Which would be anything. She used to watch the tube every chance as a kid and dream about living in the worlds they showed. But now that she'd escaped the streets and knew better, she'd stopped watching. On top of that, she got so sick of the American news. Fashion and celebrities over war she could understand, but there was a whole world of politics and economics outside the U.S. border that they completely ignored. Censorship by omission on an amazing scale.

Car breaks down on the Brooklyn Bridge got more coverage than the 2nd Infantry gutting a key insurgent stronghold and four Americans going home in body bags. If asked to name the top alliances around the globe, how many would get past NAFTA and NATO? Would anyone even know about the G8 if it weren't for those idiots who had rioted in Seattle? Certainly not through the American news. ASEAN, the AU, and the SCO wouldn't be on any American news map and they were huge powers.

"Major Beale cooks like a demoness." Crazy Tim made a wide gesture that Archie ducked out of practice. "CNN came out and did a piece on her that got world play. Ended up at the White House kitchen to protect the First Lady. Personally saved the Commander-in-Chief's life. Any of this soundin' familiar? What rabbit hole you been hidin' in?"

Kee blinked. It was all she could do. She'd heard the story. Seen the tape of the flights. One with an injured pilot and one with an injured chopper. Hell, either one they should've plummeted out of the sky like a brick and augered a hole halfway to China. Kee recalled that the pilot had been shot in the helmet and the arm, too.

She remembered the crease she'd seen that first day in the Major's helmet. She'd landed the helicopter after being shot in the head. And it was the most amazing flying she'd ever seen, though she hadn't connected that the pilot was Major Beale.

"She cooks, too," was all Kee managed.

Even though she wasn't a pilot, she'd seen the tapes of those two flights dozens of times. All the chopper pilots in the room going silent and moving closer every time the tapes were played, never tiring of it. Half of them working phantom controls as if trying to figure out what she'd done to stay aloft in a crippled chopper. The woman really could fly like that. No put-on.

That meant she really had earned the Silver Star. And she cooked. Kee could heat an MRE, maybe cook pasta if the pressure really came on, but half the time that turned out as a single chunk of gluey crap. Was there anything the woman couldn't do? When Big John said that the best man at the Majors' wedding had been the President, did he mean of the United States?

"Yeah," Tim continued as if she hadn't just been hit by a bunker-buster bomb. "She cooked for us a lot during the winter when the Hindu Kush was snowed in and it all went quiet up there. We've been a bit busy lately."

Kee nodded since she certainly couldn't speak yet.

"My family owns a restaurant chain. We're in D.C., Baltimore, and Philadelphia so far. 'Paulo's Island.' The best."

Kee managed a whistle. Or tried to between lips gone dry. She'd eaten there twice. Amazing food. Pretty high end, too. Both times glad the date was paying. And she'd taken Crazy Tim for street. Wasn't anyone who they seemed?

"So what's with the Army?" She managed to find her voice. "Why not cooking?"

Tim shrugged and dug into his goulash. "Dad was in Desert Storm, his dad in 'Nam, his in WWII. Part of what we do, cook for the troops. I signed up for my two years as a cook, but Army thinking put me in the air. Got hooked. Stayed in and worked my way to SOAR. No going back now. Open my own place when I retire."

No one ever mentioned that they were in the most dangerous occupation on the planet and SOAR wasn't a one-tour gig. It was a career slot at any level. Survival that long was maybe a sixty-forty bet. Maybe as good as eighty-twenty, but no one ever took that kind of money in a combat zone. It simply wasn't talked about, just part of the price you paid.

When she turned her questioning look on Archie, he shrugged.

"I was considering flying to the Aviano, Italy, air base, then taking a train over to the Amalfi coast. Perhaps renting a boat and doing a little cruising. What are your plans?" He had that puppy-dog look in his eyes again. How was she supposed to read that?

No way was he hooked after one little kiss and holding her hand in the market. And he hadn't offered another kiss when they'd returned from the market. She wouldn't have minded testing again to see if the heat remained, that sharp initial shock that had radiated from the briefest brush of lips. Officer and enlisted, better that he hadn't offered the temptation. But a part of her wanted to know why not. Wanted to know pretty badly.

Maybe she'd been too distracted as she and Dilya had been making a game of being coy behind their new scarves, taking turns peeking and hiding from each other around the edge. She hadn't missed Archie's hand until they were already back at camp and he'd departed for his quarters. Besides, absolutely no way was she messing around with an officer, especially not in her crew. Double threat.

Even now, sitting at the table, she could feel the heat of that moment-long kiss. No way was she going to tell how it had knocked her socks off. A kiss always meant sex to come, fast and rough and exactly the way she liked it. His kiss had been so gentle she'd barely felt it, at least not on her lips. Her toes, however, had curled up like a happy cat's and her body, instead of switching to full auto-fire, had gone all quiet.

The same way that his hand in hers felt safe. Just quiet and safe. Something she never felt around men. Voracious maybe, but not quiet and safe.

"I…" She had nowhere to go. The Army was her home. For leave, she typically stayed on the base, went out to movies and restaurants, picked up some local entertainment for a night or two between the sheets.

Dilyana watched her. Had followed the conversation as it batted around the table a couple times, understanding next to nothing of course, but surely keying in that something interesting was afoot and Kee wasn't as happy as everyone else.

"I can't leave Dilya. We'll just stay here." She gave

the girl a smile, thankful for the excuse of such an easy solution. "We'll be fine."

Big John and Crazy Tim looked puzzled. Of course they would. Chance to go stateside to family and friends. Let's see, Kee could go down Dog Alley and see if Hank still ran the meth shop out of the bakery's basement, or up to the Boulevard to see if Celia had another abortion yet because her pimp kept her too stoned to remember to take the pill. Not so much.

She smiled at them, reached across, and squeezed Dilya's hand for a moment, getting a smile and a return squeeze.

"No papers. She can't cross borders. We'll have a good time."

Archie shook his head. "They want the crew to decompress. The Major won't like it."

"I won't like what?"

Major Emily Beale set her tray down beside Dilya. The little girl looked up at her, not with fear, Kee was glad to see. She'd been pretty jumpy the first few days, except around the Professor. Calmer, steadier now as she started to relax around the rest of the crew.

"Where are you going for leave?" Kee dove for a subject change. Not much of a shift, but at least the focus would be elsewhere.

"Mark has this crazy idea that I want to go ride horses on his parents' ranch in Montana. Camping and fishing too, if you can imagine." Her smile belied her slightly sarcastic tone. "As long as he guts the fish, it should be okay."

She took a chunk of the crusty white bread, dipped it in her goulash, and tore off a bite with those perfect teeth of hers.

"What won't I like?" The woman didn't miss anything.

Dilyana turned from the Major to inspect her own bowl of food. Glancing back, she imitated the process of dunking the bread and biting it off. She waited for the Major to do it again and did her best to get the timing and motion the same.

The Major ran a hand over Dilya's head and down her long, dark hair to acknowledge the girl's attention without looking away from Kee.

"I'm going to stay here for leave. Don't have any-where to go." She bit her tongue hard. She'd never meant to say that. Especially not in front of Archie.

The attention of the others, which had mercifully begun to drift away, now snapped back. In addition to Crazy Tim and Mr. Big Bad, Dusty James and Lieutenant Richardson from Henderson's bird were looking at her oddly from their places farther down the table. And Mr. Professor Puppy-Dog was back in Archie's eyes.

"Uh, Dilya can't leave anyway. And I don't have anyone else to dump her on." That sounded bitter, even on her own tongue. "Anyone to leave her with." Not much better. "I don't want to leave her."

The Major's eyes, which had darkened for a moment, cleared as Kee crawled out of her verbal hole.

"Is that last the most accurate?"

Kee nodded. "I just wouldn't trust anyone else with her."

"She that much trouble?"

"No, ma'am. But no one cares about her like—" Kee had to bite it off again. She couldn't believe what she'd been about to say. She'd gotten through life by being very careful not to care about anyone other than Kee Smith.

The Major dipped a spoon into her venison goulash. Dilya had clearly been torn between waiting to imitate the Major and her own hunger. With the sudden release, she attacked her dinner. After a few spoonfuls she looked sheepishly at Kee.

"Dilya know. *Asta-asta*." And she slowed down but kept at it.

"I'd given that some thought. Hoped you might feel that way." The Major wiped her mouth neatly on her napkin. Dilya dropped her spoon and mirrored.

Her gesture had been a little too dainty and had left a splash along her chin. Kee took her own napkin, reached across the table, and scrubbed Dilya's entire face in a single playful sweep that both teased and gave Kee the chance to clear the missed spot. Dilya batted at Kee's hands and giggled. Not quite a laugh, but good.

"Are you willing to keep taking care of her?"

"I'm sure not taking her to any refugee camp like Jali." That Kee was absolutely clear about.

"What about family?" The Major kept her blue eyes locked on Kee. Dilya caught on that there was something important going on and it was probably about her. She slowed her eating further, but didn't stop, and once again began following the words back and forth. Kee could see the scared rabbit coming back to the surface. It still took very little for the survival instinct of the feral girl she'd first met to resurface. Kee knew from personal experience it would be years before that would go away, and it never left completely.

The rest of the table followed the conversation in silence. No way to make this private.

"From what I've been able to find out, her parents are

gone. After three villages were blown out from beneath them, they tried to cross the mountains. I'm guessing they were Uzbek living in Afghanistan and trying to get home. Got lost, really lost in the mountains, ending up where we found her near Asmar. They appear to have been noncombatants. My best guess is, mother and father dead from stray fire."

Dilya made the kwaa-ping noise of a round snapping by your ear so accurately that everyone at the table jumped, including the Major. Right, "mother," "father," and "dead" were in Dilya's limited vocabulary. Poor kid. Lousy way to start learning a new language. Her food now sat before her completely forgotten.

Kee was the first to recover her voice. "If she has other family, she doesn't know about it. She has nowhere to go. Something we have in common."

Again, unintentional truth. Kept happening around the Major. Kee had no shields around the woman. She'd never have said that to a male commander or one of the guys, but the Major somehow drew it out of her.

And Archie watched her. No disappointment. No dismissal. All she saw was sympathy and pity. Well, she didn't need anyone's pity.

Kee had met lots of grunts for whom the Army was the only escape from the street. Fewer as she climbed, though. Airborne, Special Forces, Green Beret, SOAR, each level had weeded out another group. Being street tough didn't cut it here. Dedicated wasn't enough either.

You had to want it so bad it became an obsession. And you had to be way smarter than the average bear. Anyone at this level packed an extra language or three, survival training, and a lot of other useful knowledge.

Kee could fix and fire anything from an M9 Baretta to a Hellfire missile. That was her specialty, things that go bang. But she could also take apart most of a helicopter and might figure out how to get it back in the air despite not having all the replacement parts. If you were down and no medics were around, she could get you stabilized so you survived until medevac. And while comm wasn't her specialty, she could get in touch if she had to with whatever kind of radio wasn't shot up including Morse code with an infrared beacon.

Now, sitting with the Major's crew, she sat with the very best, the very smartest. The Professor wasn't a weakling any more than Crazy Tim was a slacker. She'd earned the right to sit at this table. Be damned if she cared that she didn't have some pretty little home and goddamn picket fence somewhere, some hot car or herd of horses just waiting for her. Some family that—

"Smith."

"Yes, Major?"

Beale held her gaze steady, as if she could read where Kee had just gone. Somewhere hard and cold where she stood alone. To a place she thought she'd left behind, but clearly hadn't.

"It will take Chief Medic Mackenzie about a week to draw up special papers for Dilya. We can't get her cleared as a U.S. citizen without full adoption, but we can get her a friendly foreign pass. She'd be able to travel, but the paperwork requires a single sponsor willing to be completely responsible for all actions of the minor in question. Are you—"

"Yes, ma'am!" Kee didn't have to think. Didn't need the question to know the answer. "One hundred percent!"

The Major barely nodded, then dipped her spoon back into her dinner.

Dilya reached up a tentative hand to the Major's white-blond hair. First, she felt a strand, playing with it a moment, testing the texture. Blond hair, especially such a light blond, must be a mystery to the girl. Then she stroked a hand down the Major's hair exactly as the Major had done with her.

But her eyes were watching Kee. A look of absolute trust Kee knew she didn't deserve or want.

Chapter 15

"ROGER, HEAVY 1. ADDER 4 COMING IN."

Kee braced herself. Even anticipating what Major Beale was about to do didn't prepare her body for the sudden shift. In moments, Kee faced straight down, the helicopter on its side to get maximum speed. The g-forces rushed the blood toward her feet, even though she hung facedown in her harness. Her stomach told her a hard turn was happening at the same time, and it would be her side of the chopper that lined up with trouble.

They passed over the massive twin-rotor Chinook helicopter hovering with its tail ramp dipped into the river. A dozen Delta operators were launching a pair of Zodiac inflatable boats off the back ramp five miles above Naopari. The baddies dug in there would never expect a water assault, not in a mile-high desert. A recon team had reported the river navigable, if you were insane. Well below a D-boy's threshold of worry.

The Chinook was taking sporadic fire that normally would have been handled by the ramp gunner, but he wasn't in position because the boats were launching. And he'd make too much noise anyway with his big M240. Also, whoever was potshotting remained very well hidden.

"Remember, quiet." Beale's voice sounded over the intercom. Without the element of surprise, the D-boys would never be able to slip into Naopari, waterborne or otherwise.

The Professor would be doing his best to jam every frequency except the one they were using to stop any local spotters from reporting in. But that was dicey at best and couldn't be depended on for very long. And a blast from the minigun would make a concussive buzz-saw burst that would echo the five miles down the narrow, twisting valley. The deluge of supersonic rounds announcing loud and clear that death was coming. Far louder than the rotor noise from the helicopters, unmasking their presence more effectively than any called-in field report.

But where a minigun would be noticed, a few well-placed rounds would blend in with the general shooting already in progress among the steep hills. A squad from 10th Mountain, 3rd Company was running a rock-killing op just a couple miles the other side of the town. No enemy, just making noise to offer a distraction.

Kee struggled against the g-force as she locked the minigun in place and opened the rifle case she'd clipped to the bulkhead before her first flight on the bird. First time she'd had a need. No one had commented and only John had tried to open it. She'd let him try by pretending not to notice. But, not knowing the combination, he'd given up.

In under five seconds, by the time the Major had stabilized the chopper to a right-side-up hover, Kee had the Heckler and Koch MSG90-A1 out, the night-vision scope clipped onto the rail, and a ten-round magazine slapped in place with a round in the chamber. The same sniper rifle used by the FBI's Hostage Rescue Team.

She wound the strap around her forearm and braced herself in the gunner's chair. She turned on the night scope and began searching the hills.

"Nice toy, Smith." Mr. Big Bad sounded admiring. She didn't need admiring. She needed a spotter. But she'd make do without.

He'd unbuckled from his seat and snapped the ten-foot tether of a monkey harness to his vest. He came to stare over her shoulder. She was about to smack him when he whispered over the headset, "Four o'clock high. Notch between two boulders with a ledge above. Don't even see how he got in there. Long way. Call it two hundred and fifty meters."

She inspected it for a moment. Three fifty. At least he'd found the hidey-hole.

"Take me right," she whispered into her helmet's microphone.

Beale pulled up the nose until the chopper was slipping backward. Sniper's right, not pilot's right. And Beale nailed it first try. Of course.

"Got it. Hold."

"Wind twenty-four knots from down-valley." Archie's whisper had her adjusting her aim two full dots along the horizontal crosshair in the scope at this range. A big enough correction, she'd have missed without it. He knew what she'd needed and fed it to her right when she needed it.

She had the weapon dialed in at three hundred meters. She lined up right along the crosshair, already set to compensate for the fall of the bullet due to gravity while traveling from her gun to the shooter. She raised half a dot in the scope's view to get the extra fifty meters.

The chopper froze in place. She did her best to cushion out the vibration of the turbines and beating blades with her elbow on her knee. The hidden shooter raised his barrel to aim at them, exposing his face. The green image of the night-vision scope so perfect, she could see the darkness of his eye sockets in the outline of his face. She released her held breath slowly.

Then, in that quiet moment between one heartbeat and the next, Kee pulled the trigger.

Not much muzzle bang or flash with the suppressor. The round went through the exact centerline of his forehead, perhaps an inch lower than she'd intended. Three hundred and seventy-five meters or perhaps helicopter bounce. Either way the face disappeared. Another face popped up in the hole. She raised the crosshair to the dot, waited for her heartbeat, and dead-centered that one. Then she waited fifteen long seconds, counting her heartbeats, one per second. No one else appeared.

"Two down. All quiet."

"Roger." Was all Major Beale said before moving off.

Kee finally understood, finally knew how good the Major was, every inch of rank earned the hard way. First woman in SOAR. She'd probably had it ten times harder than Kee, but she'd done it. That "Roger" from Major Emily Beale rated as perhaps the highest praise Kee'd ever received.

John gripped her hard on the shoulder and shook her as easily as a leaf for a moment. She slapped his hand hard in thanks.

Damn straight she deserved to be aboard. And it was a privilege, too.

Chapter 16

KEE SPOTTED DILYANA WAITING FOR THEIR CHOPPER AS they set down. The girl stood back as the ordnance and fuel teams did their thing. Waited while the four of them reset the chopper to flight ready. They probably wouldn't be flying again before leave, but that didn't mean they left the bird sloppy. Helmets on seats, night vision plugged in for recharging, harnesses flipped back for quick entry.

Kee sat on the chopper's deck in the open cargo door and patted the place beside her. Dilyana scampered forward and sat. Both of them with legs short enough that they could swing easily above the sand. After a quick hug, Kee made ready to disassemble and clean the H&K sniper rifle.

Major Beale stopped by for a moment, ruffled Dilya's hair. Dilya popped up to her feet on the cargo deck, making her almost eye to eye with the tall Major. She reached out to ruffle the Major's hair before giggling and dropping back down to her butt. Beale shook her head like a wild animal, then, with a practiced flick, all her hair fell in place as if she'd just primped for an hour.

Dilya did the same thing and ended up lost behind a curtain of dark curls. The Major slid surprisingly gentle fingers into the fray and spread the girl's hair open, then holding Dilya's cheeks, kissed her on top of the head.

"Were we ever so beautiful?"

Kee had come to terms with being short and built. But if she'd ever in her own secret thoughts wished for one thing, it was to look like Emily Beale. And to have that perfect confidence.

"No, ma'am. Not even close."

The Major nodded to the rifle. "Never shot one of those."

"I'd be glad to show you, ma'am."

"Some other time." For half a moment Kee found herself wishing to have her own hair patted and a kiss placed atop her head for safekeeping. And the Major was gone into the predawn dark. No "job well done." No "where did you learn…" She'd complimented Kee exactly as a top commander would, by not commenting.

The red vest of an ordnance dude stopped in front of them.

"I could do that for you."

Kiss her atop the head? She'd lost her mind. Clearly.

A red. Offering to clean her rifle. Get your brain together, Kee. In shorts and Army boots, little enough need around here for the full flame-retardant suits he'd have worn on a carrier. Though the purple-clad fuelies, grapes, still suited up in full gear.

She looked at him, trying to decide if he was just being a helpful red or really wanted to get his hands on such a cool toy as her H&K. She'd bet more on the latter, but no one touched her sniper rifle. The rifle had cost three months pay, the night scope a fourth, and the custom work most of another. The Army had offered her an M24, nice enough in its own way, but to her eye the H&K shone like a star in comparison.

"No thanks, I got it." She started breaking it down.

He looked disappointed. "Need any rounds?"

She could reach over to the minigun and peel off two rounds without standing up, but he looked so cute and helpful. She held up two fingers and the guy was gone at a run to his stock truck. In moments he was back with two rounds. She'd nearly clicked them in the magazine before she noticed, M118LRs.

She looked up again and nodded her thanks. This was one of the moments she loved the Army. She'd always assumed she'd be forced to resupply with standard rounds now that she was in the field, and this red had just handed her the long-range specials designed specifically for sniper rifles. Made a big difference past five hundred meters. With nine percent more power, they made a thousand meters at least possible, if not dead on. Near enough two-thirds of a mile. Hope she'd never need to depend on pulling that off, even with the LR cartridges. For that kind of work you needed the Barrett.

"Thanks, but I still clean my own weapon."

He laughed. "Figured you would. You ever need more, let me know."

She nodded and he was gone leaving no name behind.

—⁕—

Dilyana ran her finger down the gun's barrel that stuck out of the piece The Kee had taken off the rifle and then set it down between them. It was cold, colder than a high mountain stream. It felt liquid, it was so smooth, but her finger wasn't wet when she took it away. The Kee took a cloth and began working on the trigger and handle.

"The Kee *qilmoq* dead?"

The Kee set the parts in her lap and fished out the

phrase book. Dilya tried not to sigh while she waited. The Kee always stopped and took the time. Dilya knew from experience how few grown-ups cared what a child had to say. She had tried studying the little book, but the words were hard and the writing strange.

Her father had insisted that his daughter learn to read and write. Her mother hadn't been happy, and both of her parents had made her promise to hide her knowledge. When they had lived in villages, they had practiced in the dark. She and her father whispering together, his face a bare outline in the starlight, as they traced letters upon each other's palms until she knew each one as a friend. During the day her father treated her as all fathers treated all female children, without notice. But night was their special time. Her heart came alive in the dark.

The Kee made a sound that Dilya knew she made when she was unhappy. She held the small book open in her hands. Dilya looked at the page and read: *Qilmoq* —to make. "Makee."

"Make."

"The Kee make dead?" Dilya tapped the rifle again to make sure she was being clear.

Another deep sigh, then, "Yes."

"*Ha*." She was tired of not hearing her own language. The Kee nodded. "*Ha*. Kee *qilmoq* dead."

She said it like a name. Maybe she was Kee and not The Kee. But it wasn't right to call her that, not an elder. She would use it as a title. That felt better.

Her hands began to reach and pluck at the air, like she did when she was seeking words. Trying to catch them before they escaped.

But Dilya had questions. Questions she didn't want turned aside so she spoke quickly.

"The Kee *qilmoq* mother father dead?" It wasn't quite right. She'd seen the white man who had shot her parents as she had huddled beside them. Her real question, did that man and The Kee work together? But it was the best she could do until she learned more language.

She watched The Kee's eyes. Eyes almost the same color as her own. Her mother had taught her that truth lay in the eyes.

Kee looked as if she'd been slapped. Her narrow eyes now so wide, Dilya leaned away. Kee grabbed the edge of the helicopter's floor on either side of her own knees and squeezed until her knuckles turned white. She opened her mouth and closed it again. Finally shaking her head once, hard enough to hurt. "No!"

She saw the truth as Kee stared at the ground past her toes. Her weapon forgotten in pieces on the floor of the helicopter.

The Kee flinched as Dilya pulled the phrase book from Kee's pocket. She had to make sure she asked her next question right. She'd gotten faster at looking for the words. It only took her a little time to find what she wanted.

"*Kishi*." She pointed to make sure Kee understood.

"People?"

Not how she would have guessed, *pee-op-l-ee*, but the sounds were there.

"People make Dilya mother and father dead."

"*Ha*."

"Not The Kee."

Again the head shake. "Not The Kee."

"The Kee make people dead. People who make mother father dead?"

The Kee swung to face her. She bit her lip, but Dilya watched the eyes. They changed as she watched. First they were far away, "watching ghosts" her mother called it. Then slowly the eyes narrowed, grew darker. The mouth narrowed. Firmer. Stronger.

She nodded once, "*Ha!*"

Dilyana crawled into her lap. Wanted to be there. She liked this Kee. Trusted she would kill her parents' killers. She'd seen that The Kee didn't lie.

Gently at first, The Kee held her. Then tighter and tighter until Dilya could feel herself folding up into a smaller person. These hugs had scared her at first, thinking The Kee would hurt her. Now they made her feel safe.

Dilyana managed to peek into the book as The Kee held her. Held her so tight that she believed for a moment The Kee might even find her parents' killers. There was the word she needed.

"Good."

Archie had stood riveted through the whole thing. Stood outside the other cargo door and watched them through the bay of the Black Hawk.

Seen the Major be so tender, though it proved difficult to equate the gentle woman with the ball-buster pilot he thought he knew so well.

He had heard the heartbreaking question, seen it slam into Kee. And the final benediction from a child, "Good." The impossible blessing to go forth and kill.

He had done enough shooting to know that snipers were different. Thought differently. Felt differently. Infantry shot toward their attackers. If they hit them, a lot of luck or a lot of bullets had gone by. When a pilot took them out, when he'd gunned down that mortar crew, not that Kee had left him much to kill, they were ciphers, bad guys.

A sniper fought personally. The finger of death. Choosing who died next and then looking them in the face before and after taking them down. That Kee could be so strong was beyond imagining, he knew he couldn't do the same.

For Kee, if there were any way she could find the killers, and he and she knew there wasn't a chance, it would be very personal. And he'd bet on Kee not hesitating for a single second.

Kee held the girl still. Kissed her atop the head and kept whispering, "I'll try. I promise."

He could watch no longer. He stepped onto the helicopter. If Kee noticed the slight shift on the shock absorbers, she didn't indicate it. Kneeling behind her, he could see Dilya's head tucked against Kee's shoulder, disassembled bits of a $10,000 rifle set aside and forgotten.

He didn't know why, but he wrapped his arms around woman and girl both.

Kee didn't startle, didn't flinch. She leaned back into his shoulder, hard.

He did the only thing he could think to do, he kissed her on top of her head.

The way she hid her face against his chest told him that maybe for once he'd done something right.

Chapter 17

KEE WOKE SLOWLY. THE SUN POKED THROUGH THE Black Hawk's cargo bay door in streamers cut thin by the heavy armament hanging from the pylons outside the door. It lit the drab steel of the cargo bay with a magical light, drawing patterns on her clothes and on Dilya's hair. The girl slept curled in Kee's arms. When parked on the ground, the Hawk offered enough of a visual shield to make them feel alone, isolated from the rest of the world. Safe.

As she went to move, she realized that her head was cushioned on someone's shoulder. His arm draped negligently over her shoulder. She knew the hands. Without having to remember them from the predawn light. Long, gentle hands she'd spotted on Archibald Jeffrey Stevenson III the first time she'd met him exiting the DAP Hawk on her arrival just three weeks ago.

Hands that had embraced her while she wept. Not outside, she hadn't ever shed a tear, but inside, where no one else could see. Hands that had rubbed her shoulders while Dilya slept. Hands that had held her when, finally exhausted, she had slept as well.

She raised her head enough to look into his sleepy eyes without waking Dilya. Blue eyes, still misty with the morning light. She slid her hand up behind his neck and pulled his face down to hers.

There. As their lips met, the shock she remembered

rippled through her. It hadn't been her imagination. She teased her lips against his, reveling in the lazy feel as his half-lidded eyes slid closed. He cradled her head with one of those nice, long hands.

Then he woke up. Fully awake.

If she'd expected him to pull back, curl back into Mr. Uncertain Timid Professor, she was gladly mistaken.

His eyes came open and he attacked her lips. Attacked them with such skill that they were soon sparring with their tongues, tasting each other as deeply as they could.

She fisted her hand tightly in his mahogany-and-sun hair. Every bit as soft as she'd imagined, hoped. She held his kiss hard against hers. His hand on her shoulder slid right down inside the neck of her T-shirt and under her sports bra. She arched into his clench and moaned against his teeth.

Then she felt it.

Dilya stirred, still curled in Kee's other arm.

Archie must have felt it too, for he cut his kiss but didn't move. Cupping her with his hands, head and breast, their lips both frozen in mid-attack.

From an inch away, she stared up into his blue eyes as he stared down into hers.

Without releasing her fist from his hair, she slowly eased the pressure and they both backed off enough to turn their heads.

Dilya woke slowly, stretching like a happy lap cat. Then she rolled out from under Kee's other arm, jumped from the helicopter, and turned to look at them.

"Breakfast." Of course she'd learned the names of the meals very quickly. "*Shoshish*."

Then a flash of white teeth and she was gone.

The two of them remained frozen, slowly turning back to look at each other. Her fist in his hair, his hand down her shirt.

She whispered with what little breath she could gather, "*Shoshish* means 'hurry.' She likes that word. Almost as much as breakfast, lunch, and dinner."

"Then we must not keep her majesty waiting."

"No, we mustn't."

She dragged his face back to hers and ravaged his mouth for one long aching moment more as he clenched her breast almost to the point of pain that so many men never understood, but instead Archie made her feel tightly held, hugely desired.

They broke apart and burst into laughter.

He used those long legs to step down to the ground. She slapped the subassemblies of her H&K back together, pushed in the two retaining pins and, shoving it into the carry case, locked it away. She'd finish cleaning it after breakfast.

Archie took her hand to help her jump down from the chopper.

She looked around, no one was watching. She dragged his face down for one more kiss, her whole body went taut and liquid at the same time, as if she'd run a 10K, then slept sixteen hours in a luxury hotel instead of having flown a chilly, high-altitude mission and slept three hours on hard metal plate.

"Damn, Professor. Where did you learn to kiss like that?"

"Learned it thinking about what I'd like to do to you." His smile started with his eyes first, then found its way down to his mouth and lit his whole face with that goofy grin. Really charming.

"Tell me more." The heat didn't rise to her face, but it certainly rippled through her body.

"Come to Aviano with me tomorrow. We'll go sailing together."

"I've got Dilya…"

"You have to bring her. I'd be sorry if you didn't." And he meant it. Despite the heat and lust they had been sharing moments before, he would be sorry if Dilya weren't with them. The man kept slipping past her barriers. Though with her body still humming from his brief manhandling, she found it difficult to complain.

In perfect harmony, just far enough apart not to be obvious, though she could feel the sizzle across the gap between them, they set out toward the chow tent. Dilya would already be sitting in her spot across from Mr. Big Bad John, a mound of food heaped on her plate. Crazy Tim telling some story, mostly with wide and hazardous gestures, trying to get her bright laughter to sound forth.

Chapter 18

DILYA HAD NEVER RIDDEN IN AN AIRPLANE, A TRAIN, OR any vehicle except for a few quick trips in a Black Hawk.

Kee had spent exhausting hours trying to sift through the girl's alternating excitement and fear as the whole crew piled into one of Clay's transport Hawks for a quick lift to Peshawar. Once she'd understood it wasn't back to the refugee camp and that Kee was staying with her, Dilya enjoyed that. She and Big John stuck their heads out the door as far as their safety harnesses allowed and watched the desert rush by. Out of Peshawar, a C-130 was heading for Incirlik, Turkey, so they'd grabbed it.

There they split up, most of the crew catching a 737 headed for Frankfurt then a connection to New York. The C-130 continued to Aviano after a four-hour lay-over mostly spent trying to teach Dilya how to play Ping-Pong, a game for which she showed much affinity, if little interest in the rules.

By the time they reboarded the plane, Kee and Archie were as exhausted from laughing as she had been the prior night from the full-on emotional churn. Mercifully, they all slept on the long grind to Italy.

When Kee awoke, Dilyana was gone. She slapped Archie awake and they both scrambled to their feet. He ran aft as she bolted forward, checking the foremost of the three fully rigged Humvees that filled most of the plane's cargo bay, Archie checking the other two.

Not finding the girl anywhere on the cargo deck, Kee scrambled up the ladder to the flight deck.

There Dilya sat, calm as could be, strapped into a jump seat and jabbering away to the pilots in Uzbek, and them replying in English. Clearly neither understood the other, and none of them cared.

Kee turned back to catch her breath and waved an all-okay to Archie as soon as he looked up at her. He put his hand to his heart and pretended to release a huge breath. She knew exactly how he felt.

The high-speed rail to Genoa unnerved Dilya far more than the planes. The fields and towns flashing by at helicopter speed inches outside the window proved much more alarming than flying at thirty thousand feet.

Also, she drew attention with her *hijab* of plain white linen. It had looked fine in camp. The white trousers, overdress to her calves, and a head scarf that spent more time around her shoulders than over her hair. On the train, she stood out among the civilians as a small, dirty urchin.

"People are eyeing her like she's Abu Omar." Captured by the CIA, taken to Aviano and turned over to the U.S. Air Force, then given to the Egyptians. There held and tortured for four years as a terror merchant with no concrete proof and finally let go. No one's finest hour.

"First step off the train, clothing store."

—∿—

Dilya showed no interest in revealing her legs. She ended up with boy's trousers paired with a pretty, high-collared dress of strong colors that barely reached her knees, despite her repeated attempts to pull it down. The traditional heavy-cotton scarf—she never wore the blue and green one except on special occasions—was happily traded off for shiny swatches of brightly colored, tissue-thin scarves. She owned five or six before they escaped the store.

Underwear was fine, a training bra wasn't. Sandals made the grade, but not sneakers or socks. Kee bought her a bathing suit just in case, but had to guess at the size as Kee knew there was no way Dilya would try it on.

"Are you buying something for me?" the Professor whispered in her ear, his breath tickling, his hands sliding onto her hips.

"We're in a women's store."

"I know that." Then he blushed the most amazing pink. She'd never had a man blush when asking her to buy erotic clothes before. She'd never obliged. Never liked them much. The one time she'd tried lace, it itched. Didn't make her feel the least bit sexy.

"Go buy Dilya an ice cream."

He scooted out, his ears still sunburn bright.

She made a few selections. She knew what she'd look full-on knockout in, but the Professor still wore his favorite button-down shirt at the moment.

Now it was Kee's turn to feel uncomfortable about the mode of transport.

"A sailboat?"

"What did you think people sailed on?" The Professor jumped aboard, scooped Dilya under her arms, and swung the happily squealing girl from dock to deck.

She'd been shocked enough at the sight of a harborful of water, Kee couldn't wait until the girl saw the ocean… But from a sailboat?

"I thought people sailed on a yacht? You know, a thing with a motor."

He scoffed and waved a hand dismissively at a very comfortable-looking, two-decked powerboat floating nearby. "This has a motor, but if we're lucky, we won't use it much."

"If we're lucky… But it's…"

"As long as a Black Hawk from nose to tail rotor and almost twice as wide."

"Black Hawks don't float."

"This does."

Then Archie reached up and tried to scoop her up as he'd scooped Dilya. She caught his thumbs and twisted them outward and back forcing him to drop to his knees and lean forward to ease the pressure.

"Well, if you're going to beg me from your knees, maybe I'll consider it." She let him go and stepped aboard. The boat bobbed and twitched sideways in a totally unfamiliar way.

It wasn't the water that bothered her. She'd aced the Navy's underwater egress class for surviving a helicopter crash at sea. She wasn't a SEAL, but she could navigate a small boat silently through a night-shrouded harbor better than your average Sue, Jane, or Mary. Small boats were for getting there and getting back. Ships were different. It made sense to land on a ship, tie down your chopper, and call it a night. Not boats.

She'd flown for six months as a gunner with the PJs. Pararescue jumpers were as nuts as D-boys. Scrambling out of perfectly safe helicopters in live-fire combat areas to fetch the wounded, okay she could see doing that. But these guys also jumped out into fifty-foot, hurricane-driven waves big enough to smack around a destroyer in order to haul three idiots off a twenty-five-foot sailboat.

At least with a power craft, the PJs could usually be lowered to the deck with a hoist. But sailboats had all those masts and wires in the way, making them accessible only to swimmers. There was something wrong about them. And now she stood on the deck of one. Two masts. Dozens of ropes and wires. Booms and pulleys. And a lively rocking that had nothing to do with being the size of a nice, safe Black Hawk.

Dilya had trotted end to end of the deck a half dozen times before she ran down below to inspect everything there. Then, with a squeak, shot back on deck.

Kee rushed to her side just as two heads popped up from below. She didn't need to be told who the elderly couple were, though they looked as surprised as she did.

A glance at the Professor confirmed her guess, but not in the way she expected. He positively lit up.

"Mom! Dad!" He rushed over and fell into happy hugs as they emerged onto the deck.

Dilya wrapped her arms around Kee's waist, and she welcomed the comfort as the trio expressed their mutual surprise and delight. Family as a good thing, it still didn't make any sense to her. And any illusions Kee'd built of quiet nights curled in the Professor's bunk were washed overboard. But she'd be fine. She had Dilya. If they found a quiet cove, she'd teach the girl to swim.

From the babble it rapidly became clear that at least

this wasn't a setup. Good thing, or she'd have to skin Lieutenant Stevenson the Third alive.

"You told us you were taking leave in Aviano." His father's voice was deep and friendly. "We knew you'd be on a sailboat, so we called the usual charter company and there you were. We flew over. And here you are. Hope that's okay." The man stood as tall as his son, but much broader of shoulder. He was a big man with a full head of hair on its way past white, headed toward silver.

"An absolutely fantastic surprise!"

Another round of hugs.

Kee looked down at Dilya. The girl stood comfortably against her. Other than the initial surprise, she appeared okay with the situation. Though she did hold on to Kee pretty tightly, that could be her normal shyness.

"And who is this?"

Archie turned, and though it was hard to tell in the bright sun, he appeared to blush quite thoroughly. Ashamed of her? Great. Just what she needed. She could feel the heat rise, but kept it tightly in check.

"These are my friends. Kee Smith and Dilya. Beatrice and Archibald Jeffrey Stevenson the Second." At least his lame-ass embarrassment never touched his voice.

"Steve and Betty." The man held out a hand. The spitting image of his son. No question where the Professor'd gotten his good looks or his wavy tousle of hair. From his mother, the wide, blue eyes, the sophisticated nose, and slight build. Not as tall as her husband, but still several inches over Kee.

"Uh, hi." Not her best, but Steve's handshake was solid, if not Army strong. No test either, though he raised an eyebrow for a moment and kept her hand in his.

"Military?" He knew strength when he felt it.

"She is a sergeant on Major Beale's helicopter."

The man assessed her a moment longer, added another good solid shake of her hand before letting go. "You keeping our boy safe?"

"Doing my best, sir."

"Steve."

"Doing my best." On about a dozen fronts at once.

Betty's shake was as light as you'd expect, and as brief. Her eyes inspected Kee and Dilya quickly, returning several times to Dilya. Looking for relationship? Disliking the dark skin on both of them? No real smile. There was trouble. Real trouble. Mama bear ready to throw any mere street punk overboard if she made eyes at her son. How would she take it if Kee told her that twenty-four hours earlier her precious son had his hand down Kee's shirt despite being a superior officer? Tempting.

Then the woman knelt in front of Dilya.

"And who do we have here?" She held out a hand to Dilya but waited for Dilya to reach out. Maybe she'd judged the woman too quickly.

Dilya looked up at her and Kee nodded.

Dilya held out a hand but clearly didn't know what to do with it. Betty covered the confusion by taking the slight, dark hand in both of her equally slender, light ones. Kee wished she'd thought to bring a camera. Just those hands holding for a moment, top of Boston society and Uzbekistani orphan refugee. How much farther apart could you get?

"And what do they call you?"

Dilya knew the word "name," but Mrs. Stevenson hadn't used it.

"Her name's Dilya."

"Dilya. I'm called Betty."

"Calledbetty." Dilya clearly didn't separate the two, just memorized the sounds.

Mrs. Stevenson, thinking her job done, rose to her feet. Apparently the Professor had missed it, too. She wasn't so sure that Mr. Stevenson II had missed it; he appeared to be fighting a smile. Kee decided to leave it alone and see where it led.

Where it led. Now the changing situation came clear in her mind. Archie had talked about sailing down the coast, port hopping. Except now it would be done with his parents aboard. When it had been a lazy couple cruising with a kid, mismatched though they were, light, medium, and dark, but okay together.

Kee could see that picture, now blown away.

The new picture formed of a happy family reunion and two unwanted outsiders. Uncomfortable questions. Heavy disapproval from mom, a constant upstream battle. She didn't need this shit and it definitely was not her idea of a vacation.

"Archie," she tried to keep her voice bright. "Thanks for showing us the boat, but I think Dilya and I will take a train down the coast. Maybe see Rome or Florence." *Or anywhere except stuck on a sixty-foot-long floating hazard with your parents.*

She turned to go, keeping a hand on Dilya's shoulders so they'd move together, but the Professor stopped her with a hand on her arm. A quick glare didn't dislodge it. Brave man. First alarm in his eyes, then, in mere moments, understanding. Smart, too.

"No, Kee. Really. It will be okay. Please stay."

Dilya knew something was up. Searched the faces around her, finally landing on Kee's. She held tighter for a moment. Whatever Kee did, this child would trust her. Now why did that scare her more than facing Calledbetty?

The mother just watched her steadily. No hint of welcome. No warmth anywhere.

Archie's father reached out and touched his wife's arm in a calming gesture. "Do stay. We become much less terrifying after the first day. We're just so glad to see our boy. Maybe we should be the ones to go ashore?"

The question was half to his wife and half to his son. Clearly his son had learned his manners straight from the source. She could like this man even if she wouldn't want to face his wife in a dark alley.

"There's no need. You're right. It will be okay." Kee dragged out each word.

"Are you sure?"

Dilya had been so excited a moment before, running up and down the length of the boat.

Kee squeezed Dilya's shoulder to her for a moment and released her held breath slowly. Then, in that quiet moment between one heartbeat and the next, Kee nodded her head.

This time at the wrong end of the shot. Which she suspected would hit its target all too soon.

And she wished she'd purchased a one-piece rather than a bikini after Archie had left the store.

Chapter 19

"Cinque Terre. Five Towns." Archie pointed down the coast at little clusters of buildings perched along the magnificent green cliffs. "We will stop here for a day or two. You will love this place."

Kee had yet to find anything to love. The first night, while still at the dock in Genoa, lack of sleep had finally smacked her down on a long bench at the dining table. She'd woken fourteen hours later, stiff, sore, and far too hot from the blanket someone had tossed over her. The only blessing, Dilya had been equally exhausted and slept as long.

Now they'd spent a long day rolling over waves in a motion her body didn't like, flinging her against hard surfaces without warning. The boat was fast and light on its feet, but she couldn't predict what it would do from one moment to the next.

The other dance, the one with the Professor's mother, also proved unrelenting.

"She hates me."

"It is not personal."

Kee didn't bother answering that. She pulled her shirt more tightly around her. The sun was hot, but she hadn't been able to feel warm all day.

"No. I'm serious. She's hated every girl I ever brought home, or rather that brought herself to my house with me in tow. I was never good with girls, and Mom hated them all."

"Great. Your mom hates me, and you're embarrassed to be seen with someone like me. If it wasn't for Dilya and your dad, I'd have abandoned ship hours ago and swum to shore."

Archie did something with the ship's wheel and pulled on a sail's rope when it began to make flapping sounds.

"What makes you think I'm embarrassed by you?"

She looked out to sea. She really couldn't do this. Blinked hard against the wind stinging her eyes.

"Kee?"

Cinque Terre better have a train or plane, because she was on the first one out.

"Kee?" The light touch on her shoulder was too much. She slapped it aside, hard enough to bruise.

"On the chopper I was fine. Good enough for you to put your hand down my shirt and kiss me like…" She choked on the words. Hated herself for them catching in her throat. "Kissed me like you meant it."

"I did."

She shoved him hard against the chest so he fell against the back of the bench.

"Then…" She waved a helpless hand to where she'd been standing when his parents put in their appearance. "Then you see me in front of your upper-crust parents and you want nothing to do with me."

"Where did you get that idea?"

"You blushed, you jerk. Blushed to be discovered by your parents with someone… someone like me. Dilya and me, we're the outcasts, but we know it. We're survivors. We can take anything the Street hands out. I know how to handle myself there. But for one lousy little moment, you made me think you wanted me as much as my body. And it felt so good." Her eyes burned, be damned if she gave in to the pain.

"It felt so good to have someone want me like that. I won't accept less. I deserve that. I deserve that and better."

She stood and moved quickly to where Dilya lay at the bow of the boat and watched the water rush by beneath her. They hadn't been able to budge her since the moment they rounded the breakwater and the Mediterranean had spread out before them.

All Kee could see were the distant towns. Maybe an hour at their present speed. An hour to land. Then what? In nine days they'd be back on the Hawk, separated by the thickness of his seat back and a thin sheet of the Kevlar armor that wrapped around most of the pilots' positions. A transfer? Damn no! She'd barely arrived. Could she switch choppers with Crazy Tim? Get him back on Beale's Hawk and she move on Henderson's. But then she'd be letting the Major down. Why had it all made sense two days ago? No wonder there was a goddamn rule against fraternization. It was all screwed up and they hadn't even done anything yet.

Dilya laughed aloud and pulled on Kee's hand to get her attention. The girl's gaze remained riveted over the bow. The moment Kee looked down, a dolphin leapt clear of the water in a glistening flash and, diving over the bow wave, disappeared back into the blue-green sea. Then she spotted another. Two of them dancing and playing back and forth across the slicing bow.

That was the answer. Hang on, and then she and Dilya would be clear and the two of them could go play.

—◦◦◦—

Stupid train. It hadn't come soon enough.

Kee could see the clock at the impossibly quaint Monterosso train station. No redemption by train for twenty more minutes, and her time had run out. The Professor's mother had come searching. Archie must have sent them all out into the streets searching for her. To bring back the truant girl who was supposed to warm his bed. Well, to hell with him and his high-class parents.

She continued working on the string figure of Jacob's Ladder with Dilya. They'd figured out a way to short-cut one step and they were closing in on shortcutting a second. Maybe if she didn't look up, the woman would go away.

No such luck.

Beatrice Stevenson came their way. Kee kept her head down, but Dilya looked up and offered a cautious smile. If Dilya was brave enough to greet the woman, she'd look stupid and petty for not doing the same.

Soft blond hair. None of the beauty of her son or Major Beale, just an average-looking, well-tended woman. White slacks with perfect creases up the front. A cream silk blouse. Sandals that probably cost more than a week of Army pay.

"May I sit?"

Kee shrugged but couldn't bring herself to speak.

She did her best to return to the game as the woman sat on the bench beyond Dilya. College kids with backpacks walked around, joked, took pictures of each other standing by the tracks, swigging American sodas and eating Snickers bars, and looking not the least bit anxious about the train's failure to arrive ahead of schedule.

Hard to believe they were within a couple years of her age. They came from another planet.

"I've never found it easy."

"What?" Kee asked without intending to.

"I wasn't home for most of Archie's childhood. My family's business kept me on the road. He and his father are very close, but I…"

The woman seemed to run out of steam.

Something in her attitude finally drew Kee's full attention. The woman wasn't angry, she was sorry about something. She was sad.

Kee fished out some Italian pocket change for Dilya and pointed toward the newsstand with a fair spread of candy in plain view. Making her choice would keep the girl out of trouble for several minutes at least.

Now she sat partly turned toward Betty Stevenson with several feet of empty bench between them. And she waited.

Betty took a deep breath. A hard breath. A painful one. Kee knew what it looked like when a woman was reaching deep. Knew the pain, and felt her own anger easing.

"I became vice president of my family's business, Blair Research, when Archie was five. I was president before he was ten. CEO when he went to college. His father's a good man and a fine sailboat builder. Even though I could support us ten times over, he chose to work. He has twenty employees, but always made time for Archie. At his shop, if nowhere else. The two of them love their sailboats. Steve understands the burden when my father left the business to me, but I could never bridge the gap to Archie. Oh, he loves me. I know that.

But neither he nor his sister, Becky, know what to do with me."

The woman inhaled deeply, "No more than I know what to do with either of them." Her spine stiffening as she sat more erect and gazed off into the distance.

Kee heard it, too. The low ground thrum of a train rolling along tracks, still far enough off to be more felt than heard. But coming now. Time suddenly urgent. Betty turned to face Kee directly. Those blue eyes staring into hers.

"I just wanted to ask you to stay. I never know what to say to the few girls he's brought home. I don't know what to say to you. But whatever passed between you two has devastated him as clearly as I see it has hurt you. You appear to be a sensible young woman. Your care for the orphan girl, Archie told me her story, is a wonder to see. You give so much love so spontaneously, so easily. A skill I lack completely."

The train now rattled down the tunnel loudly enough for the backpackers to pop their heads up and grow even more animated.

"If not for him, can you come back for me? I don't want my son to think I drove you off. He is out looking for you right now, but can't imagine that you'd just leave. It isn't in him, he's too nice a boy. I knew where I'd go, so I understood where you went. I've thought of doing it a thousand times, but then where would I be? Still with myself."

The train rattled and rolled into the station, and Dilya returned with a bright blue-wrapped candy bar labeled Ferrara. The white nougat was half gone, and her smile was huge at the newly discovered flavor.

Backpackers spouting a dozen languages milled about.

Somewhere in all that, Betty Blair Stevenson slipped away.

Dilya plopped down on the bench and inspected Kee as the train emptied and filled, but appeared to be fine watching the world go by with those wide, brown eyes.

Kee gave love so easily?

Chapter 20

In the cockpit, Archie jumped to his feet and cracked his head on the underside of the main boom. He doubled over, clamping his hands over the sharp pain radiating outward, creating sparks of light in his tightly closed eyes.

"Shit! Shit! Shit!"

He stumbled over something. Heard his father give a surprised laugh, but he squinted his eyes open enough to move out of the cockpit, where they'd been sitting in pained silence over a glass of wine, and up onto the deck. Where the safety lines had been dropped, he jumped down to the pier and almost pitched over into the water on the far side.

Blinking furiously he stumbled to a halt at the head of the finger pier. He touched his head and checked his hand briefly, no blood. It only felt that way. He put his hand back atop his aching head.

Kee and Dilya stood side by side at the head of the finger pier. Kee with her plain black civilian's backpack slung over one shoulder and Dilya with her luminescent orange-and-green eyesore that she'd chosen herself.

He opened his mouth. And closed it. Opened it again. Fish out of water. Head stinging so badly, he couldn't think straight.

"I never… I wasn't… I'm… a complete idiot." He hadn't meant to say that last part out loud. He turned away as Kee watched him. Turned back. Unflinching, no reaction. Nothing to be read in those dark, dark eyes.

"I…" He glanced over his shoulder, but his parents were mercifully most of a boat length away and clearly doing their best not to watch or listen to the only drama going on in the area.

Still the blank stare. Dilya as quiet and sober, mirroring Kee's mood. What was he supposed to do with these two women? Give him a helicopter and a whole line of power-mad warlords with RPGs any day of the week.

"I…" He lowered his voice to a whisper. "I wasn't ever embarrassed by you."

"What then?" He wasn't facing a hurt woman as he'd thought. He was facing a sergeant who'd spent five years facing down men much tougher than him. Every single shield in place, far stronger than Kevlar body armor.

"I…" He really needed to find another pronoun to start his sentences. "I was embarrassed that my parents could somehow see all of the things I'd hoped to do with you."

"To me or with me?"

"With you. I've never… There's not been…"

She held up a hand to stop him, and he shut his mouth because he didn't know what else to do.

"You're at a loss for words."

"I'm what?" What on Earth was she critiquing his language usage for?

"You always have the right words. You never do that. Are you that flustered by me?"

He opened his mouth and she held up her hand again. He closed it.

"Just nod yes or no."

He nodded yes emphatically. The bursts of light in his eyes from the pain had him squeezing them closed for a moment and holding the top of his head again.

She tipped her head to one side and then the other as she inspected him. Dilya mimicked the move with sidelong glances to see if she was getting it right. *Nailed it on the first try, little one.*

"Okay."

"Okay?"

"Yes."

"Okay what?"

"Okay, I'll give you another chance. But don't f—" Kee looked down at Dilya. "Don't mess up again."

"I will," he managed.

"Try or mess it up?" This time a smile cracked that terrifying facade.

"Both." He hung his head in frustration at his own pitiful failings outside the helicopter context.

Then she laughed and it ranked as the finest sound he had ever heard. She had the greatest laugh. It came from the gut and passed straight through her heart.

"I'll bet you do both as well."

―∿―

Kee didn't intend to spend the night with Dilya. Archie's parents slept in the aft cabin, reached from main cabin below but actually behind the cockpit at the stern of the boat. Except for a narrow hallway, they might as well have been on another craft entirely.

Dilya had fallen in love with a tiny cabin to the left of the stairs. She'd spent the whole evening after dinner playing quietly in here while the adults sat around the main cabin, sipping tea and eating cookies Steve had brought aboard. Slowly getting to know each other.

"Pilot's berth," Archie had informed Kee. It wasn't all that much bigger than the Professor and Major Beale's cockpit on the Hawk, but it was elegant in its simplicity. A wide single bunk with triangular-bottomed drawers. It took Kee a moment to realize they couldn't be squared off because they would hit the outside of the boat.

Then she peeked out one of the three, metal-clad circular windows and made a horrifying discovery. The water outside the boat came above her waist as she stood in the cabin. If she lay down, she'd actually be sleeping below the water's surface.

Turning deliberately away, she watched as Dilya happily demonstrated the room's other features. A trim little desk with a fold-down chair. A reading light and a fair collection of novels in English, French, German, and Italian. Rigged for tourists. She'd have to dig up a couple of kids' books in English next time she went ashore. What she'd taken to be a small closet turned out to have a flush toilet, with a foot pedal, a long handle to one side, and a set of instructions that were graphically clear if somewhat complicated.

When she'd gone to join the other adults in the main cabin, Dilya had kept hold of her hand and pulled her down to sit beside her on the bed.

She opened a small drawer in the desk. And pulled out two sheets of paper with pencil drawings on them. Faces. Very well-drawn faces.

Kee prepared herself to make admiring sounds, but stopped herself as she really looked at the faces. Dark expressions, foreboding eyes. One big and square, the other darker, narrow and spare. She wouldn't want to meet either one.

She glanced at Dilya.

"*Kishi*. People," she pointed at the drawings, "make mother father dead. The Kee *qilmoq* dead."

Kee stared at the two faces. Dilya had seen her parents' killers. Seen them well enough to draw these pictures. They were clear enough that if they were matched with the right men, there would be no question.

"*Ha*." If she ever met them, she wouldn't hesitate. "The Kee *qilmoq* dead," she promised.

Dilyana snuggled close against her. Kee folded the pictures carefully and slipped them into her pocket. There was no chance she'd find those faces among the millions in Afghanistan, but she'd watch.

The girl held on tightly even as sleep dragged at her eyes. She'd probably never slept alone, except for several terrifying nights beneath the stars before they'd found her on that mountainside. She'd certainly never had her own private room.

Kee'd stretch out with her until she fell asleep. Then maybe she'd go find Archie, or maybe she'd find another cabin as small and cozy as Dilya's and sleep there.

Chapter 21

ARCHIE SLID THE BLANKET OVER THEM AS GENTLY AS he could and turned off the light, wincing at the loud click from the reading lamp's light switch. But neither of them stirred.

By the moonlight coming in the portholes, he watched the two of them curled together. Closer than any mother and daughter would sleep. Just as they'd slept on the helicopter, where he'd watched them for hours in the dawn light.

Dilya curled with her back against Kee. Kee's arm draped protectively about the girl's waist, her chin just touching the top of Dilya's dark hair. Kee's anomalous blond streak catching the light in her dark brown hair. He wanted to play with that little streak of hair, separate it out until every single strand of light had been sorted from the dark.

Part of him wanted to wish Dilya anywhere else and Kee awake and as ravenous as she'd been that morning on the chopper, but he couldn't. The girl belonged in the woman's arms. The tragedy of Dilya's losses could never be repaired, but somehow he knew in a way he didn't understand that Kee could never have her past repaired either. Unless they could do it together. Dilya and Kee were meant to be together.

Shutting the small door as quietly as he could, he stood in the open space of the main cabin that was galley on one side, seating on the other. But the boat's true living space was up in the cockpit, especially in the warm Mediterranean evening.

He'd tried to give his parents the wide queen-size bed in the master cabin, but they had refused. Tonight there'd be no sleep for him there alone.

So he went on deck to watch the stars.

His mother sat, her legs tucked up under a lap blanket, reading a book on her e-reader, the light just reaching far enough to light her smile when she looked up at him. Then hidden in darkness when she turned it off.

She patted the seat beside her and he slid in, draping an arm behind her along the back of the bench seat. Not touching, but comfortable together in the silence.

At this hour the harbor lazed at peace. Most of the town lay shrouded in warm summer darkness and sleep. Streetlights were mostly off and only low footlights shone along the docks. Other than the gentle lap of water and the soft ting of wire rigging tapping on aluminum masts, night rested as gently over them as the blanket he'd placed over Kee and Dilya.

"You care about her a great deal."

"I barely know her."

"You care about her a great deal." The first had been a rhetorical statement, the second bald fact.

"Yes."

"What's her background?"

"Mom." He did not want to get into it with her.

"Archie, look at me."

He did. Her hair a shimmer in the moonlight. Her face prettier, friendlier. In the soft night, the two forehead creases just above her nose reflecting her intense personality were hidden.

"You are a man grown now, and you make your own choices. I'm not asking as your mother. I'm asking as someone who cares for you and sees you with a new friend I'm finding I can respect. She may be the strongest woman I've ever met, and far more approachable than Emily Beale. She is a woman who wears her heart on her sleeve. And she cares about you very much."

The Major was an amazing woman, but his mother was right. Major Emily Beale kept her emotions in tight reserve. She kept her secrets to herself along with her thoughts. One of the stories around camp told that the two Majors never spoke to each other. They often held hands, but everyone agreed they were operating on some strange level of intuition or telepathy that required few if any words.

If there was no mission, they often sat together high in the soccer stadium's bleachers as the sun set. In the fading light they were seen to speak quietly, nestled close on the deep tiers that were both seat and footrest for the next row. Or they'd make love after full dark, as Archie discovered accidentally while testing some new night-vision gear.

"Kee is different. She's right in your face. As likely to insult you as—"

"Kiss you?"

"Yes." He could feel the heat rushing to his face. He rushed for a subject change.

"She is the best gunner I have ever seen. She never wastes a round or misses a target."

"She flies with you? Into battle?"

"Yes. I told you."

"I know. I know. But I find it hard enough to picture you doing it. I'm finding it near impossible to picture such a pretty and caring girl riding into such danger and shooting people. I'm not judging what you do, I understand that it's important. I simply can't picture her doing it."

"I wish you could. She's..." Archie searched for the right word. Pictured her as he'd glanced back around his seat and seen in the night. A sniper rifle at her shoulder unleashing judgment, juxtaposed with the woman curled up down below with a little girl in her arms. "Magnificent."

They sat together watching the night. What did he know of Kee Smith?

"She never speaks of her past."

Chapter 22

KEE LAY ON THE SAND IN THE COVE JUST A FEW MILES north of Quercianella, wherever that was. Italy was all she knew. West coast of.

Dilya worked industriously on a sand castle near the water line, trying to copy the one perched atop the cliff above the cove. The fluted square tower collapsed several times and was erased several times more before the girl was content and moved on to the high walls. Her stuffed, orange cat, wearing a small blue scarf of her own, watched the entire operation from atop on overturned plastic pail safely on the landward side of the castle.

Dilya had consented to wear the one-piece bathing suit but refused to show her legs. They'd compromised with a lightweight pair of cotton trousers that even now clung near transparently to her legs with seawater and sand. The scarf that refused to stay on her shoulders, a transparent bit of lemon yellow today, lay tucked under the corner of Kee's towel.

The first swimming lesson had barely been needed. Dilya must have learned to swim in rivers, or perhaps crossing them. The water's warmth had brought a startled expression of joy that had turned into hours of swimming along the beach. All she really needed to know was to stay close to the shore and that sand was far more comfortable underfoot than high-mountain riverbeds.

A shadow crossed between Kee and the sun, and stopped there. The baking heat cut off like a knife, letting the slow breeze cool her deliciously.

She opened one eye and saw that her shadow came from a tall, thin silhouette backed by a radiant splash of sunlight. Again the image of the Professor as her protecting angel came to mind. No glowing eyes this time, no SCAR carbine, but a different side of the same coin.

Outlined in the sun, Kee could see the soldier fitness. Strong thighs of a serious runner, trim waist, and an upward taper of muscles to shoulders well defined in the sun, even on his slender frame. Archie stood, not like a man watching her, but more like a man paralyzed.

"You look incredible." He had apparently been making a similar assessment. And reached a similar conclusion.

"You like the chest?" Her bikini left as little to the imagination as possible. A combination of thin material and not much of it. Dilya had been horrified. Kee felt great. She'd never before so flaunted herself for a man.

"And many other things."

She patted the sand close beside her.

He spread his bright towel of giant sunflowers about three feet away.

As he dropped toward it, she snagged a corner and pulled it until their towels overlapped. Already past the tipping point, all he could do was twist so that he hit the towel instead of the beach.

With a carefully timed roll she ended up between his arms. She caught his weight so that he didn't slam into her, but lay on top of her from toes to chest.

"So, do you like the chest?"

"Kee, people will see."

She teased a kiss across his lips. "I'm not going to screw you on the beach in broad daylight."

When he tried to raise his head to look, she caught it in both hands and dragged him back to her.

She'd seen Dilya look up as she tripped the Professor, then return to her sand-castling. But there were a dozen other boats anchored in the cove, and somewhere along the strand strolled the Professor's parents.

"Besides. We have an audience."

He relaxed against her at last in a slow, nestling motion until they fit body to body most incredibly. She'd been with men as tall, and even lying down it had been awkward, always craning her neck up until it ached. Impossibly, Archie just fit.

"Now answer the question, soldier."

Together they looked down between them, where her breasts mounded against his chest.

"Yes. I like that very much."

Then he hit her with that kiss of his, and all she could do was wrap herself around him and hold on. Hold on as waves of heat much hotter than the sun scorched her skin. He tasted of sea salt and stability. Of promise and need. He tasted of hope and she couldn't get enough of that.

He trailed the kisses down her cheek and to her neck. She made to stop him—there was only so far she was willing to go in broad daylight on a public beach—but he stopped himself with his kiss on her shoulder and his nose nestled at the base of her neck. He inhaled, breathed her in until she could feel his whole body expand in her embrace.

At long last he exhaled a sigh of pure contentment.

"That spot. I could never get enough of that spot. You smell amazing there."

Kee ran a hand up into his hair and stared at the sky.

"What's different about you, Professor?"

"I'm busy here." He began nuzzling her neck.

Not that she'd expected an answer. She'd known about sex ever since watching her mother work a trick in exchange for a fix. From watching girls ply their trade on the Boulevard, though she never had. There wasn't much privacy on the Street, sex in all its forms occurred in every dark alley, against any handy light post or Dumpster.

She slammed the image aside, hard. Glad Archie couldn't read her thoughts. Shame flushed her skin, but she wasn't going to let it control her. She hadn't then and she wouldn't now.

When she'd started choosing her partners, she'd discovered that sex had many good points as well. It could be fun, relaxing, and a good contest.

But the Professor brought a level of focus and concentration to his kisses that she'd never encountered, and some needy part of her desperately wanted to explore further.

When the heat of the sun grew too much, before their sweat went from romantic to soaking, he levered himself to her side. He kept his head on her shoulder, not positioned to stare down at her breasts, but so that he lay inside the curl of her arm, his back touching her from ribs to hip. He wrapped both hands around her arm and held on as if he'd never let her go.

"It isn't me."

"What isn't?" Her brain was slow and lazy with the heat: the sun's and Archie's.

"It isn't me that's different."

"Then what is it? How do you make me feel the way you do? Answer that one, Professor."

He kissed the inside of her arm before propping himself up on his elbows to stare down at her.

"Easy. You're what's different, unique. I've never met anyone like you. All beauty and joy and mystery. Who are you?"

"Sergeant Kee Smith. Gunner."

"That isn't what I—I didn't—You know I didn't mean that."

He lost word choice not only when he was flustered, but also when he became irritated. Damn he was cute.

"I don't have a past before the Army. Not one that matters to anyone, especially to me."

When she closed her eyes, Archie went silent and began toying with her hair. She did her best to concentrate on the images of the day, this was a day she wanted to remember. Sailing into the quiet harbor. A leisurely breakfast aboard, an oddly accommodating Betty Stevenson, as if she'd been replaced somewhere in the night with a happier person. Or at least a more approachable one.

The two of them had talked long past finishing their meal on the boat this morning. Betty had an immense knowledge of the geopolitical landscape, a world of political giants Kee had always been intrigued by, but understood only on the surface. Betty knew the real news. As shy as she might be, she lit up once she understood Kee was truly interested in her area of expertise.

She'd described how the superpowers were no longer individual nations. Except for perhaps China. Even for the United States, a nation's power lay more and more in its alliances. Many were mostly about trading, NAFTA, ASEAN, the EU, and others. But there were military and governance players as well. NATO now faced the Shanghai Cooperation Organization and found itself humbled. Directly representing a third of the people and half of the military and economic force of the planet, the SCO had shifted the politics of the planet in under ten years.

Kee had felt momentarily adrift when the men had broken up the conversation, suggesting they go ashore for some beach time. She'd looked back at Betty, but she'd already pulled back into her shell. Though she'd offered Kee a brief smile before going below to gather her beach gear.

And then Kee'd gone swimming with Dilya. She couldn't recall the last time she'd so forgotten the past and future and dwelt so thoroughly in the moment. Nor if she'd ever let her guard down so completely.

That was her present to herself, a perfect day. As varied and impossible to imagine as it might have been a week ago, somehow she'd been planted in this marvelous, magical day.

Archie kept fooling with her hair. Tugging on it a little. Running his fingers through it. She knew the feeling, remembered it from her past. Snapped her eyes open to see the blond streak wrapped around the Professor's finger, not one single dark strand mixed with it.

Oh God! The past crashed in on her like a hammer blow right past all of her armor.

She jerked upright. Ignored the sharp pain when he didn't let go fast enough. Launched to her feet and was a dozen steps down the beach toward Dilya before her first conscious thought. And that cut her knees out from beneath her and she landed hard at the edge of surf.

The stark contrast of these last few days with the week before she joined the Army was irreconcilable. Two different people on two different planets. Two worlds farther apart than hers and the Professor's.

Hands rested on her shoulders from behind. His hands. She twisted to pull away. Almost succeeded, despite their anchoring strength, he had far more power than he typically used. She prepared to fight free, until smaller hands rested on her knee.

As much by instinct as affection, she reached out to pull Dilyana to her. Held the child hard. Held her and did her best not to think of her own past as she buried her face in the girl's salt-sweet hair.

"Kee?" Archie moved to kneel beside her and wrapped an arm around her shoulders.

She wanted to dig in, burrow under. One thing she knew, no way was she going to weep on him. An action taken once that would never be repeated. Her barriers had to stay in place. It was far too dangerous for her to let someone that close again. Memories that could destroy her life. She'd keep her past separate with all she had.

"Did I do something wrong? I'm—"

She shook her head to stop him.

There was a tug on her hair. On that same exact spot.

She opened her eyes, ready to bat him aside, but his hands were accounted for, in clear view. Dilya's fine fingers teased at the stripe shining gold in the sun, standing out even more against Dilya's dark skin.

A wave rolled in and tickled at Kee's knees before sliding away, leaving air bubbles to pop up from under the smooth, dark sand.

She had dyed that specific shade of yellow-gold in a streak there so that she'd never forget. It had elicited a thousand compliments, which was senseless if you knew why it was there. Not that she'd ever told a soul.

It was there for all to see. That was its purpose. And she didn't want to hide anything from Archie, in any way. Which shocked the hell out of her. She swallowed hard against the panic soaring through her.

Dilya continued to twist the strand about to catch the sunlight. Comparing it to her own dark locks. Kee could feel the gently shifting tug as Dilya began braiding the little strand. Holding the girl close, perhaps Kee could release that piece of her past. Or at least a small part of it. She pictured a different time, a different place. A place as dark as this sea was bright, as dirty as this sandy shore shone clean beneath the blue sky.

"Her name was Anna. I never knew her last name. On the street you keep your name close. Knew her three years, an eternity in our world, but I never knew her full name. How's that for a twisted way to live? We were as close as you could be there. Trusted each other to have each other's back." It was as if someone else was speaking. The dull monotone of a past Kee, one she no longer connected to. Now that she'd decided to speak, she found no emotion, just the words.

"Then one day a drive-by took her out. One second at my shoulder, the next bleeding out on the filthy concrete. I returned fire. I was already a good shot back then, I'd run for a while with a gang run by a Desert

Storm sergeant. He made sure we could all shoot. I was good, and he'd taught me more than the others. A lot more. I took out all three assholes in the car then sparked the gas tank. Four shots with a Glock that Billy had scrounged for me. It never did Anna any good, though."

She looked out to sea, but all she could see was the dark night and Anna's blood, black on the cracked pavement. "Two of the shooters were wanted on a cop-killer rap, so the prosecutor offered self-defense, provided I joined the Army and got off the street. Judge accepted and I was inducted that afternoon."

"This," she ran a finger down the lock now being braided in Dilya's deft fingers, "I did before I reported in the next morning. It's the closest I can get to her hair color. The only friend I ever had."

Archie didn't move away. Didn't flinch. She waited for the shift of a man wanting to get away, but too polite to show it. Not Archie. He remained solidly shoulder to shoulder, watching the sea as she did.

"I'm so sorry, Kee. No kid deserves that. No one should have to live through that kind of life."

Dilya found a short piece of string in one of her pockets, she constantly collected them, and tied off the braid.

In unison, they looked down at the girl in Kee's lap. Dilya's life had been hard as well. She'd seen her parents die partly of starvation and finally of bullets.

Pleased with her handiwork, the girl scampered off to defend her sand castle from the incoming tide.

Kee and the Professor remained kneeling together, watching the gentle waves beat on the sand. Watching and waiting for Kee to come back from the past to the world of light. To make that long passage back that she had faced a thousand nights.

It was a long journey in the dark. A long journey even in the daylight.

But this was the first time she hadn't faced it alone.

Chapter 23

DILYA HAD STAYED CLOSE ALL AFTERNOON, KNOWING Kee had been upset. It helped. The little munchkin had cheered her up, given her back some of the feeling she'd had about this day. Archie had stayed close as well, making it clear he cared more about her now than who she'd been then. A limit she'd not be testing any further.

Then Betty and Steve had insisted they climb the cliffs up to the Castello Sonnino for wine tasting, a tour of the castle, and dinner in the sunlit evening.

Dilya had been thrilled at the outing, insisting that she and Kee wear their complementary head scarves. Kee felt very flirty in the flowered sundress that Dilya had picked out for her to wear, a splash of tiny blossoms on a field of blue almost as dark as her scarf and a bright belt. The cut of Kee's dress was low above and high below, it would have been risqué if it hadn't been so cute. She didn't quite anticipate the fashion challenge of climbing into the skiff from the deck of the boat, but she managed and they were all soon headed to the castle.

At the chance to compare the tower to her sand creation long since washed away by the sea, Dilya scampered about the battlements and up the tower at an unimaginable pace. Kee finally let her run loose.

Betty slipped a hand through Kee's arm as they wandered about the gardens overflowing with color. Narrow paths of crushed stone wound through the plantings with no particular direction in mind. Kee knew roses, which she saw, and daisies, which she didn't, but for the most part they were a mystery. June flowers rather than September flowers.

The men soon landed on a shaded bench and fell to talking sailboats. She could hear Archie's interest as his father started describing changes he'd made to a chine that apparently had hardness and a waist that had narrowness rather than slenderness. Their voices faded as she and Betty moved off to inspect budding roses of dark yellow-orange and something shockingly blue alongside.

"Is everything okay?"

"Why shouldn't it be?" Kee looked over, but Betty kept her attention on the flowers.

Kee bit her lip and ordered herself to stop being a bitch.

"Yes. It's fine. A beautiful day."

"You looked... upset. When we returned from our walk."

Wonderful. Well, there was no way she would be telling that story again, once in a lifetime had proved enough.

"Just some old memories. Hard to shed those sometimes."

Betty nodded and they headed once again along the winding path. Dilya shot through the gardens, headed for a stone stairway leading up the face of the far wall. The long silences that punctuated their conversation didn't feel awkward, rather they made comfortable moments to wrap around your thoughts.

"I know what you mean," Betty offered, "though not exactly what you mean, of course."

Kee now knew where Archie had learned his quiet

and reserve. His patience with the chaos that had punctuated her first weeks on the crew. Now if only she could make any sense of what he saw in her. Clearly attracted, but he kept staring into her eyes and not at her body. Yet another new experience she couldn't unravel.

"Not because of Archie?" Betty asked.

"No. Your son is…" A wonderful young man? A red-hot-lipped man? She didn't know yet if he might be a latent sexual genius. What could she say to his mother?

"A good man." It was the best she could offer, but true. Archibald Stevenson III, a very good man. Raised to the same gentleness that his mother exhibited. An odd mix for a warrior. One of the best chopper pilots and tacticians on the planet, flying left seat on one of SOAR's DAP Hawks made that a given for sure, but he wasn't ego-ridden.

"You raised your son well."

"His father did."

"No." Kee stopped and Betty, taking one more step, was forced by their still linked arms to turn and face her. "No, he is his mother's son in so many ways."

As if she had conjured him with her words, Archie and his father came striding up the path. They moved at an easy mosey, but they were two very handsome and very purposeful men.

Betty squeezed Kee's arm and met her gaze for a moment before taking her husband's offered arm. Clearly they shared the same thought. And maybe they were becoming friends.

Kee slid her hand around Archie's elbow and appreciated the solid feel of muscle, the solid feel that described the man so well.

—ww—

To Kee, wine came in three flavors: white, red, and bubbly. But all three Stevensons kept going on about the Cinque Terre's fragility, legs, concentration, and a dozen other meaningless phrases. Kee did find the wine very easy to drink with dinner, but never finished the second glass. They were on vacation, but the habits were ingrained. Archie was equally fastidious, sharing a smile with Kee as his parents became more and more jovial somewhere in the second bottle.

The dinner was a wonder of fresh seafood and local garden produce, everything except a few spices came from within ten miles of the castle, they were proudly informed. Finally they reached the fresh fruit and whipped cream served with yet more wine, needing yet more comments about how the Sciacchetrà matched the fruit. She couldn't tell the two wines apart, they were both just white to her.

Dilya drank half a glass of well-watered wine with dinner, but still it brought a glow to her cheeks and a droop to her eyes.

She rode quietly on Kee's, then Archie's back as they worked their way back down the cliffs to the beach and out to the boat. The Stevensons each toted a couple bottles of wine in neat cloth bags bearing the Sonnino crest, crowned golden lion rampant on a blue field. Make a good patch for a fighting unit.

Dilya was asleep before Kee tucked her in, but still she sat with the girl for a few minutes. She could feel the boat quieting as Betty and Steve drifted to their cabin. The Professor waited. Kee could feel it. Not impatient, but knowing she would come. The girl didn't even squirm as Kee tucked in the blanket and slipped out.

She hesitated, standing near where the main mast punched down through the cabin ceiling and landed on the cabin floor. She laid her hand on the aluminum shaft, almost as big around as her own waist. Strength. A solid foundation to hold aloft the sixty-foot pole above deck.

Kee shook off the image. This was just sex. With a commanding officer. An action she'd never take, but they were on vacation, the first one of her life. That had to count for something, even if it wasn't supposed to.

And this was just sex.

—◆—

Archie watched her enter the room. He'd debated a dozen times about lying on top of the covers or beneath, clothed or partially or not, light on or not, would she even come to him or not.

Naked beneath the covers, he couldn't catch his breath as the dark silhouette stood framed in the cabin door for a long moment before entering. She slipped out of the sundress that had shown her like a fresh rose all through dinner. Without hesitation, she stripped until only the Night Stalker scarf was wrapped over her shoulders. The tails hanging down between her bare breasts.

In moments she wrapped herself around him and his brain blanked.

Her skin was everywhere, in his hands, his mouth, frozen in time on the tip of his tongue until she moaned with a timeless sound from the depths of her soul.

Her mouth ravaged wherever it went. His mouth, his

own breast, a pulling and tugging sensation he'd never imagined. Was that what a woman felt?

Down to nibble on the soft skin of his inner thigh as she wrapped a gentle hand around him.

He tried to speak. Tried to give voice to the wonder. But then she'd renew her attack and all he managed to emit was a low groan ripped from his gut.

He finally found enough purchase and sanity to flip her onto her back. The covers were long gone, they were dressed only in moonlight. Her breasts rose magnificent, proud, dusky. He attacked. She kept pulling him in tighter. Past where he'd ever gone. Past any reasonable point of pain. She drove her chest up to his mouth with the same fierce energy she did everything

When neither of them could stand it a moment longer, she rolled him onto his back. He reached for a condom, which she took from his fumbling fingers. She rolled it over him agonizingly slowly, almost driving him over the edge.

Then she sat up and bumped her head on the low ceiling, the bottom-side of the deck. She placed her hands palm up on the padded surface and shoved herself down on him with such a sudden force he could feel the mattress bowing beneath him. Enveloping him. Transporting him.

He cupped her magnificent breasts, and she leaned into him so that he supported her weight on his greedy palms. They rode each other, slowly, hard and fast, held, frozen to stillness on the edge of release, slowly, so slowly again until in near madness he drove up, she drove down, and they exploded with the heat of rocket fire scorching through his body and his brain.

Hands jammed to the ceiling, she kept him pinned in place as their bodies shuddered. Paused. Shuddered again. Wracking them both as they gasped for breath.

When the sparks faded from his eyes, he looked up to see Kee's eyes were still closed. He ran his hands from breasts to hips, then back up to her shoulders, and pulled her forward.

Reluctantly she released her clenched arms from where they jammed against the ceiling. She went to roll aside, but he pulled her straight down until she lay upon his chest. Ran his hand over her hair until her head was tucked beneath his chin. Held his heart to hers as he felt her breathing slow.

He tried to speak, tried to find some way to describe something he had never experienced, imagined, or even dreamed existed.

Sensing his intent, Kee slid a hand over his lips to silence them. So, he kissed her fingers rather than give voice to a miracle for which he'd never find the words.

She pulled her hand back as he stroked her hair.

He cradled her as her breathing slowed. Slowed and steadied into a sweet rhythm like a sixteenth-century Marenzio madrigal.

His mother had been wrong, he did far more than care about her.

He held her close as his own breathing aligned with hers and he slept.

—⁓—

Kee lay in Archie's arms, her eyes wide open, staring at the night.

She couldn't move her body if the entire Taliban

pounded on the cabin door. Numb. Sated in a way she'd never experienced. Relaxed beyond reason. Beyond possibility. Beyond everything except, regrettably, rational thought.

The Professor had offered heat for her heat. And passion for her passion. But he'd offered so much more.

She'd tried to push him into causing pain. Pain that would chase away the feelings building from that dark place she never went to. Tried to make him do things that would make her feel he was just using her. That's where she felt safe, in the ravaging of the beast she always unleashed from men's bodies. Familiar territory.

But he didn't. At first, he'd offered gentle. And when she'd refused, demanding more, he hadn't driven her to pain. He'd ridden her right off the peak of the purest, cleanest pleasure that had ever run through her body. More powerful than a rifle shot, he'd blown right past her inner walls and spread light everywhere he went.

Spread light into corners she'd locked away and never intended to see again. Spread hope that had failed too many times for her to trust.

Nothing but herself. She'd never again trust anyone but herself. Her own skills. Her own abilities. Between one minute and the next, one second and the next, it could all be blown away. If she were dead, she'd be done and wouldn't care. But while she lived, no one could be allowed that close, for at any instant they too could be swept aside like Anna.

Archie, no, the Professor. More distant. More formal. Safer. Lieutenant Stevenson… too far. That didn't feel right after the joy they had just shared. The Professor lay still and warm beneath her. His breathing settled. His hands lax, one resting across her back, the other twined in her hair. She reached up to move the hand from her head and discovered Dilya's braid had survived and now wound between his fingers even as he slept.

He probably lay beneath her, dreaming of how safe he'd made her feel.

She slipped her hand between her cheek and his chest.

He couldn't be more wrong.

A hand to catch the tears so they wouldn't fall on his breast and wake him.

So that no one would know about the pain.

So that no one would know about the fear.

The fear of having something so precious to lose.

Chapter 24

SHE WOKE TANGLED IN THE SHEETS. ARCHIE MUST have found them sometime in the night. He'd proved happily insatiable and thankfully quiet. Her body felt worn and lose. When he'd woken, she'd focused on the sex, a safe choice. Focused on the sensation, having rebuilt her walls back in place.

Archie claimed only modest experience, but he found several unique and highly entertaining ways to drive her over the top and down into the shuddering rotor wash behind. She'd done her best to return the favor, including raiding the pantry for a monstrous slice of apple tart. She'd ended up with some in her hair and more down her front when she'd attacked him mid-forkful, but having him lave her clean with his tongue had been worth it.

Now the light streamed into the cabin.

It took only moments to discover she was alone on the boat, everyone else gone ashore. She spotted Dilya once again sand-castling, Archie crouched close by, digging out a moat. The elder Stevensons in side-by-side chairs, reading.

Kee took a quick shower and grabbed some breakfast. For lack of a better solution, she tossed sneakers, a towel, sunglasses, and her pager in a waterproof bag along with a bottle of water. She pulled on light shorts and a sports bra. At the last moment, she tossed in Archie's favorite white dress shirt, then jumped over the side to swim ashore. SOAR fliers were never on leave without their pagers, hard to believe she'd forgotten yesterday, but Archie had his so they'd been covered. Still, it felt better having her own.

She tried doing the sexy goddess rising from the ocean waves thing, but Archie was so intent on his moat that he missed the whole thing. His father didn't, offering a sheepish smile when his wife elbowed him.

Archie's morning kiss tasted of sea salt. "Sorry, I meant to watch for you so I could row out, but I, um," he looked down at the fortified moat he'd constructed, "found myself somewhat sidetracked."

She patted his cheek to let him know it was okay.

Dilya barely looked up from her detailed reproduction of the castle grounds done in shells and tiny stones. The girl's visual memory was astonishing. Kee squatted to admire winding paths of packed wet sand. Stones for bushes, shells for hedges, Kee could trace where she and Betty had strolled the gardens.

Along the back wall of the castle a little line of shells created a hidden corner. A corner that, once discovered, she and Archie had taken advantage of. She'd expected a quick kiss and some heavy petting as the perfect appetizer to fire up her appetite. Instead, Archie had opted to slip off her sandals and give her, of all things, a foot massage. She shivered at the mere memory.

Even as she watched, Dilya built a little bench behind the hedgerows with a tiny scrap of driftwood. Then on it she placed two bits of twig, very suggestive of two humans in each other's arms.

She glanced quickly at the girl, who didn't look up. But Kee could swear the little twerp was smiling. She knew that any attempt to change Dilya's masterpiece would not be well received. *Just walk away, Smith*. That was the best advice.

She pulled on sneakers and shades. Tossed her pager and the water bottle in a small fanny pack. Then she kept an eye on Archie as she slowly extracted his dress shirt and pulled it on. That snagged his attention but good. A small wave attacked his moat wall and almost knocked him right over onto the sand castle.

With the sleeves rolled up to her elbows, the shirt hung loose down to mid-thigh. She left the front un-buttoned so that it hid and revealed her running togs with each step she took. Out of the corner of her eye she caught Betty's smile. Archie had gone past his zombie state and over to the greedy sex-demon she'd met last night. Clearly she'd been right about the look knocking his socks off. Even when he wasn't wearing any.

"Want some company?" He kept his voice surpris-ingly even for a man having trouble with the arrange-ment of his shorts as his body reacted.

"Sure. Dilya. Dilya!" She had to call twice to get the girl's attention. Kee pointed at the two of them and made running motions, then pointed at Dilya and the elderly Stevensons. Steve had some fat paperback with a sailing ship and a cannon on the front, Betty with her e-reader.

"Dilya stay close Calledbetty." Nothing had broken the girl of her belief that was Betty Stevenson's proper name. "Dilya know. No swim if no Kee." Then she turned back to her shell gardens. Kee, summarily dis-missed, stumbled back for a moment, unsure what to do.

Calledbetty insisted she was fine watching the girl.

Kee shook her head at how attached she'd become,

and they were off. *Have to watch that more carefully, too*. Between Dilyana and the Professor, she was fighting on two fronts now. Though she appeared to have acquired an ally in Calledbetty. Last night, Betty's tongue loosened by a fair amount of wine, a very pleasant and immensely intelligent woman had once again emerged, one with fascinating insights into almost every topic that came up.

Kee and Archie trotted slowly up the cliff, still warming up. Kee led them around the back of the castle rather than up the main road. The narrow coastal road hugged the cliffs and was filled with suicidal Italian drivers. Behind the Castello, a narrow road she'd scoped out yesterday wound up into the hills. They climbed several hundred meters in the first mile. Surprised farmers and goat herders, not used to a runner in nothing but gym shorts, a sports bra, and shades, Archie's shirt streaming out behind her, waved belatedly at them as she and Archie charged up the empty one-lane.

When the road ran out, they hopped a crumbling stone fence in unison and kept going. A flock of sheep startled and swirled away like so much dust caught below a chopper's rotor. Two counter-rotating whorls of stampeding sheep as they blasted through the gap in the middle.

Two fields over, they began climbing again and picked up another road. When it split four ways, Kee chose the least used and leaned into it.

"Where are we going?" Archie huffed out.

"Somewhere I can screw your brains out. If you can keep up with me."

He laughed, "I can fly pretty damn fast," and made to push ahead.

"Not as fast as I can shoot." She pulled even.

In moments they were at a full run over the Italian hills. The road twisted and turned through low trees, and the kilometers rolled away beneath their running shoes. When they hit a high pass with a deep valley ahead, she cut abruptly right. Not many men could keep up with her, but Archie was right in step.

"At least when I shoot..." he puffed in between breaths. "I'm shooting big guns."

"Just like a guy," Kee did her best to keep her voice steady against the need for air, "to think that size matters."

Kee planted both hands atop a fence post and swung her legs over the board fence in a side vault. Archie, who'd been taken by surprise at her move, hurdled it clean with his long legs and they were again running even.

Open field running, tall grass slapping against her bare legs.

"I'm always looking forward. Looking forward to those legs wrapped around me."

"You also need to see what's around you, cowboy." Her minigun was for side and aft work. His weaponry lay mostly in line with the helicopter's nose. The rest of the field of fire was up to her and John. "Got to focus everywhere."

"Breasts, too. I can do that."

No question he could. She veered around a boulder. "My most dazzling weapons."

"No." He gasped for air. "That's your eyes."

Damn the man, he kept knocking the wind out of her.

A steep slope took any remaining wind she might have used to egg him on. Instead, she kicked into a hard sprint. Finally she gained a lead on him.

She beat Archie to the hill's crest by half a dozen strides. Already had her water bottle out of her fanny pack when he hit the peak. Chalk one up for the girls' team. Both gasping for breath, they crossed back and forth across the grassy bluff, walking off what had to be at least eight kilometers and over a thousand meters of climbing up the rolling hills.

From the look, they were on the highest point around. The countryside rolled away in all directions. Trees and vineyards, cattle and sheep. Little towns tucked on the cliffs above cultivated terraces. Darker lines of shrubs and trees marking where streams slid through, headed for the sea. And off in the distance, so bright that it was painful to view, so hazy it looked like a dream, hung the Mediterranean.

All shocking in its normalcy. She'd been forward deployed for just three weeks, and already this world felt foreign. Not foreign in that they ran across Italian soil. But foreign in that the only guns within a dozen klicks or more were used strictly for varmint or deer hunting. It felt wrong. Exposed. Which gave her an idea.

"Hey, Night Stalker!"

"What?"

"One thing you need to know about. I mean running in the daylight and all."

"Yeah?"

She'd managed to maneuver her back-and-forth stride so that she passed close by him.

"Leaves a Night Stalker all exposed." She grabbed the waistband of his shorts and jerked them down around his knees. Caught in mid-stride, he almost face-planted at the unexpected constraint.

He struggled and weaved and managed to remain upright. His butt hanging out in the wind.

She peeled off his shirt and her sports bra as one and tossed them at his feet. His effort to catch them proved too much and he went to his knees.

"I didn't." He gasped and tried to move his feet back together, reach for his shorts, and not fall over the rest of the way all at the same time. "Bring any—"

Kee reached into her fanny pack and waved a string of condoms in the air. A long string.

The Professor, being a wise man, gave up on the shorts.

Hot, sweaty, gasping, they came together like a pair of steam engines. Unstoppable, hungry, devouring.

In moments they were naked but for their sneakers beneath the midday sun, cushioned by the deep grass and pounding away at each other. Last night had been no illusion. Their bodies responded to each other so hard and strong that by the time they were both done, by the time they'd ridden each other right up into the sky, they collapsed spent in each other's arms.

"Now we have to. Run back." Archie's tone was as dry as her throat. Their breathing still ragged from the workout they'd just had in the high grass.

"Frankly, I highly doubt if I can stand."

Kee laughed. One of the benefits of sex for her, it acted like a supercharger. The girls' team chalks up another one. Right now she could run twice as far as they'd come already.

They tried lying together, but the view remained hidden by the hill's grassy crown, and the grass itself, so soft a moment before, now prickled and poked. They finally ended up sitting on their clothes, leaning back to back and looking out at the world in opposite directions, letting the sun and the wind wash their bodies clean.

"What is it about you, Kee Smith?"

"I'm sexually gifted."

"No, you're a damned sexual goddess! But that's not what I mean."

She had to admit, the sex was beyond anything she'd ever experienced, but she didn't have to admit it out loud.

"Can you explain it?"

"I don't have a clue what you're on about, Professor."

He harrumphed, a grunt more felt through her back than heard through her ears.

She lay her head back on his shoulder, and he tipped his cheek atop her head. Comfortable. Too comfortable, but she didn't want to move.

"Mom said she couldn't picture such a pretty and pleasant girl flying around killing people."

"Your mom is a civilian. She could never understand why we do what we do."

"Actually, she was a chief supply officer in Saigon for two years. Air Force. Two bad years right near the end of the war. That's how I got started in flying, hoping she'd notice me."

Kee swallowed hard.

"You're never quite what I expect, Professor. Not you or your family."

"What do you mean?"

She gave it a moment for the picture to come clear.

"Nah, you'd just get all mad or offended."

"I'm not much given to such reactions."

He wasn't. Another point in the damn man's favor.

She kept liking him more all the time, and if that kept up, he'd make her plenty angry. She had no problem connecting to that particular emotion. Gotten her in trouble often enough, too.

"Go ahead. Lay it on me."

"Thought I just did."

He slid a hand back to find one of hers. She went to move it away but ended up with her fingers wound around his instead. She almost raised her head to see how that had happened, but leaning against the Professor proved too comfortable.

"When I picture your family…" She closed her eyes and it appeared exactly as in the movies. "Big house, security hedge hiding an old stone wall, family all at leisure. Laughing over dinner. Getting wound up over whose wife was getting it on with the country club golf pro. At least a cook and housekeeper, if not more.

"You've got money. Real money. Old Boston money. But the picture doesn't hold together in my head. Your dad's hands show the calluses from building wooden sailboats. And your mom never speaks, but she doesn't miss a thing. She loves you so much, it almost hurts to watch."

"You're kidding." His head popped upright and turned a bit as if he could turn to face her, though they still leaned back against back.

Kee released his hand and turned to face him. The breeze suddenly cool across her bare shoulder blades.

"How can you not know that? I would kill for what you have, and you don't even know it's there. It's written in everything she does. Did you know that she's the one who found me and got me back to the boat?"

"Mom? I wondered why you came back, but I was so thankful, I didn't want to spoil it by asking." Archie watched her eyes. Not her bare breasts. Nor the rest of her bare body he'd been so happily plundering moments before. He watched her eyes and listened intently. Concentrating. Intent. Now why was that more arousing than the wrestle they'd just had in the tall grass?

She slid around to straddle his lap and slowly worked her hips against him. His body hadn't recovered enough yet, but it was thinking about it. His hands definitely had, digging deep into shoulder muscles.

"She sees you." She arched back against the pleasure of his fingers. "She may have done a tour in 'Nam and run a big, fancy corporation. But she sees you. That is one very smart woman who loves you more than she knows how to say."

She nibbled on his shoulder for the taste of it. The Professor was fresh and warm, and the heat of the run and the sex and the sun made him taste very male. Far more than she'd expect from a long, lean rich boy.

"Funny, she said somewhat the same thing about you."

"What?" Kee could feel herself going all lazy and liquid as she worked her chest slowly back and forth across his magnificent torso.

"She said you wear your heart on your sleeve. That's a direct quote. And you do. I knew that was true the moment I saw you, but I lacked the proper words. Why can I see it on you and not on my own mother?"

He slowly tipped her onto her back, nuzzling down between her breasts. But rather than attacking them, he laid his ear on her heart.

"That's a great sound."

"What?"

"The beating of that heart you wear on your sleeve."

Kee had no response. Her own heart, the one thing she kept so carefully guarded she sometimes wondered if it still existed. In the dark of the night, she was often left to wonder if it too had died with Anna.

And Archie claimed he could see it like a goddamn shoulder patch.

She'd have to be more careful about that, too.

She didn't want it. Didn't want her heart out in the world. She lifted his head and rolled enough that one of her breasts brushed over his lips.

Kee led him until she knew he'd forgotten about her heart and only thought of her body.

If only she could do the same for herself.

Chapter 25

KEE'D SET OFF AT A GOOD CLIP, BUT ARCHIE WASN'T there. She slowed to little better than a jog trot as they worked their way back over the hills and fields toward the ocean.

The Professor wasn't hurting. Without a pack, this was an easy run for a SOAR pilot, especially for a Black Adder. Major Henderson's company, Kee was pleased to be discovering, always worked harder, flew longer, and posted seriously high successful completion ratios in a regiment that valued that above all else.

So, if he wasn't tapped… He had his thinking face on. His body ran along, but he wasn't paying it much attention.

"Okay, before you joined the Army is an out-of-bounds topic. Understood. So, how did you end up in SOAR?"

"How did you?"

"I asked first."

"I'm a girl, I can change the subject anytime I want."

"I'm your superior officer and that's purest drivel."

Kee reached for the waistband of his shorts. If there'd been a ditch, he'd have veered into it trying to get away from her.

"Cheater."

"Cheapskate."

"Cheapskate?"

"Sure." Kee kept the pace and let Archie catch back

up to her. "I give you gooood sex, Masser Stevenson, and you won't even let me change the subject in exchange."

"I don't keep a score sheet."

"I do."

Archie ran in silence.

Kee could feel that silence. Feel it clamp down between them.

"Sorry. Things like that keep coming out shitty around you. I really don't mean it that way."

Archie ran a little farther, though it felt as if the pressure had eased off.

"It sounds that way. It really does, Kee. It stings like hell when you do that."

"Sorry."

The silence continued. They plodded along in one of the slowest half kilometers she'd probably ever turned. Up to her to break it. She was about to open her mouth when he forgave her enough to do it himself.

"So what do you want to know?" Archie'd even given her the lead. Damn him for being decent.

"Why SOAR?" Kee considered phrasing it nicely, but it just wasn't in her. She couldn't resist the dig at the Professor's perfect manners. Digging at all that wealth. All those options he'd been raised to take for granted.

"Why didn't you marry Muffy or Pinkie and pop out a couple of perfect Harvard girls? Why fly a DAP Hawk alongside Major Emily Beale?"

"I ended up at West Point. I wanted my mom to notice me, but I didn't want to follow right in her footsteps either. I was a total loss at the Point. Sure, I had brains enough to nail the classroom. Additionally, building wooden boats is hard work, so I was strong. Getting into Army shape only took time and focus."

His words came slower as they trotted up a long slope. This time, the sheep that had spun aside barely broke from their grazing to inspect the passersby. Certified inside those furry heads as "not wolf," they were soon ignored.

"But I never fit in. I tried to be smarter, which was easy, but that only increased the heat from my classmates. I tried being stronger, but my physique doesn't go that way." He waved at his long, lean frame. "I'm not built the way you are."

Kee put on her best streetwalker tone and grabbed her breasts. "Hey, no one's built the way I am."

That earned a grin, but not much of one.

"Emily Beale was a year ahead. She was already a legend by the time I came along. Every woman's athletic record, and several of the men's, were hers. She outran, out-studied, out-survived everyone. Junior year she finished her senior coursework. Senior year she spent one on one with some of the best instructors the Point could offer. Tactics, strategy, leadership. Everyone knew she was someone special."

The Professor inspected the sky in a long silence broken only by the rhythm of their feet slapping the road. A lone hawk pinwheeled overhead.

"Actually, those classes were two on one. She picked me out of the crowd in my second month, first year. With her watching over me, I'd have graduated anywhere other than the Point in three years. My junior year I did my junior coursework and joined in her tutoring sessions at the same time. Double duty. After that, senior year was a cakewalk.

"Special Forces, Airborne, Rangers, Fort Rucker flight school. She paved every inch of the way, I followed right behind."

"But how did she break the barrier at SOAR?" Kee'd never unraveled that one. "The first woman. Special Forces isn't big on that."

When they reached the stone wall they'd first vaulted, Archie stopped and sat down on it.

Kee sat a few feet from him and took a hit off her water bottle.

"My mother told you she took over her father's company."

"Sure. Blair something."

"Blair Research. A government think tank. Very small. Very elite. Most of her staff is made up of retired generals, Secretaries of State and Defense, even a former President. When BR speaks, everyone right up to the President listens very carefully. On Emily's side, her dad is the Director of the FBI."

"Whoa!" Kee couldn't think of anything more intelligent to say. She'd stumbled into an enclave of overachievers even more driven than herself. Of course, they'd started with a damn sight more potential than she had.

"Between them they pointed out the loss to SOAR if they didn't take Emily Beale on board. When she went, she insisted on me as her copilot."

"Did you two ever—" Kee clamped down on her tongue and felt dirty. "Sorry. I'm so sorry, Archie. I'm just a heartless bitch inside. None of my business."

She folded her hands over her knees and stared down at them. How could that come out of her mouth? She just called him the Major's boy toy. She'd as much as stated that he didn't have the skills on his own, negating his years of experience and training. SOAR wasn't a free ride for anyone.

"Sorry." A nightmare. She kept stumbling into a nightmare around Archie.

She'd just crossed way past any line. She rose and turned away without looking up. There'd be no forgiving that. Now she'd need to find a reassignment.

His hand caught her by the upper arm.

She braced for the blow. Eyes closed. Head turned. Just as she'd seen the whores take it when their pimp taught them a lesson.

It didn't come.

And didn't come.

She finally opened her eyes and glanced at him sidelong.

He sat and watched her. No anger. No sign of any emotion. He just watched.

"Kee." He nodded to the wall. "Sit down."

She did as he ordered.

"Now—you're going to tell me who hurt you so badly."

Chapter 26

KEE COULDN'T FIND THE ENGINE START ON HER BRAIN.

Archie sat calm as could be and waited on the stone wall. The light breeze left her with a chill despite the warm smell of grass in the summer sun.

"I'd take someone down who said I got on that Hawk because I slept with you. It's the hardest thing I've ever done in my life, getting on that bird. How can you not hate me?"

Archie smiled a little. Not humor, more as if he were considering whether or not he held an emotion inside that he didn't know about.

"Keeping up with Emily Beale is the hardest thing I've ever done, and I've been doing it for ten years now. But I did it, Kee. Whether you believe it or not, I know it. I know to the core that I'm the one who did it. Sure, Emily picked me out of the crowd and drove my ass into the ground. But I'm the one who stood out from the crowd, and at West Point that is a seriously high-class crowd.

"And I kept up. Did better at a few things. Not many, but a few. She can outfly anyone, even Henderson. But I can outgun her, especially in high-speed situations. I have a better strategic feel for what the enemy is doing before they do it. She is the master of the tactical situation, how to take out the key pin. I know what to do to keep the enemy from placing that pin in the first place."

Kee kept her mouth shut.

"So, Kee, what I want to know is why you of all people would say what you just did? You fought just as hard to get where you are, or you wouldn't be here. Maybe harder, considering your background. Henderson picked you out of the crowd. Convinced Emily you were good enough, and trust me, being her husband probably made that task harder rather than easier. Emily doesn't believe in favoritism."

"Considering my background?" Kee didn't know if she should strike out, run away, or weep.

He nodded. He didn't apologize. He didn't redefine. He was asking on the level. Speaking plain truth.

Kee didn't know if that was something she was ready to do with this man. Not with any man, or woman, but Archie had a hold on her that she didn't like. And she'd slapped at him, hard. That required repayment. She didn't like being in debt to anyone.

A wave of panic washed over her, and she tried to let it flow by as she'd been trained. But it didn't. It left her stranded high and dry.

One thing was clear, she owed him truth. Plain truth.

—∞—

"The first DAP Hawk I ever saw was on night patrol." Kee knew it was a cheat, but she'd answer the easier question first. "We were in it and it was ugly. Trying to get Americans to safety in the midst of that Nigerian coup a couple years back."

She picked at some of the moss on the stone wall. It didn't let go, clinging tight to the ancient weathered rock.

Archie sat in silence, nursing his water bottle, the perfect audience.

"We were pinned down outside some U.S. contractor's office building, grand term for two stories of aging mud and mortar. My squad, what was left of them, was the only thing keeping several dozen civilian Americans alive and breathing.

"Out of nowhere, a DAP Hawk appeared like it had been teleported. Inside of twenty seconds, the gun emplacements that had pinned us for twelve hours were gone. Four Little Birds appeared from the four points of the compass. A full SEAL team fast-roped down, hit the ground, cleared, and secured the entire block. One minute later, probably to the second, six Pave Hawks were on the street and all the civilians were being loaded. I'd never seen coordination like that."

She closed her eyes and pictured it. "All hell is breaking loose and this SEAL commander strolls over to our hidey-hole, as if it were a sunny day here in Italy and not 2 a.m. in Hell. He leans into our dug-in position calm as could be with a full-blown firefight raging at either end of the street and says, 'Y'all want a ride?'"

Kee opened her eyes and looked at Archie. "I'm alive today because of those guys. We were down and on the way out. Most of our squad was hit." She pulled aside one tail of his shirt and pointed to the front-and-back scar below her rib cage where a round had passed through, missing vital organs by millimeters and miracles.

Archie traced a finger across it gently, as if he could wipe the past from her side.

"That's when I set my sights higher than becoming a regular Army sergeant before I went KIA. Until then, killed in action was about as high as I was gonna go.

That's the day I became a SOAR sergeant. Just took my career three years of brutal work to catch up with me."

Archie nodded. Nodded as he accepted her story. Nodded as he slid his hand until his palm covered the front bullet scar and his fingertips the rear one. Exactly the position she'd been held in by the SEAL medic aboard that Pave Hawk to keep her from bleeding out before they made it back to base.

"I lay in that hospital for two weeks. On my first day out, I applied for the Green Berets. Inside of six months I was the first woman through Green Platoon after Ms. Legend Beale. Haven't looked back since."

He pulled her forward by that hand wrapped around her scar as if holding her life in her body.

When their lips met, the heat didn't flash like powder. Every other time they kissed, it slammed into her like an ignition circuit on a Hellfire missile.

This time Archie's kiss ran gently over her lips. Instead of pure heat, she felt texture, shape, care. In contact only at their lips and his hand on her waist, a circuit was completed. A circuit that opened a honey-slow flow of warmth.

He pulled away. Just a breath apart. Her heart pounded so fast, she couldn't have shot a target three meters away, never mind 375.

She'd never wanted anything in her life as much as she wanted Archie to kiss her like that again. He slid his other hand along her cheek and into her hair. Unable to raise her own hands from where they rested on his knees, she leaned in for more of that kiss.

A high-pitched, double trill sounded so loudly, they banged foreheads hard.

Even as they scrabbled in their fanny packs, Kee knew two things for certain.

First, their pagers had just announced the end to their vacation.

Second, she'd never forget exactly where they'd left off because she wanted to start up in exactly that same spot.

Chapter 27

"SERGEANT KEE SMITH ANSWERING A PAGE." SHE'D snagged a pay phone at the Castello. She still hadn't completely caught her breath from their run back.

"Location?" The operator's voice was Army impersonal.

"Castello Sonnino, south of Livorno, Italy. On a non-secure phone."

"Understood." The silence stretched for thirty seconds as a keyboard rattled at the other end of the line.

To Archie's raised eyebrows, all she could offer was a shrug. He moved close enough that they could both hear. She could feel his body heat, but how long would it be before she found another chance to do something about it?

"There is a northbound bus that will be stopping your location in one hour and five minutes. Proceed all haste to Livorno. From there," more keys rattling, "you'll have an hour to catch the bullet train to Rome. Tickets will be waiting at the airport."

"I also have contact with Lieutenant Archibald Stevenson."

"Roger that. Same. Confirm?"

Boat? She mouthed at him.

Dad. Archie nodded it would be okay.

Dilya? He asked in turn.

Kee smacked her forehead. Who knew what they were flying into?

Parents? She asked.

Archie waggled a hand, then shook his head. He mimicked signing a piece of paper. Right. Dilya's travel documents required she be in Kee's care.

"Do you confirm?" The voice on the other end, clearly impatient.

"Um, make those tickets for three."

"Everyone else paged has already reported in."

"I have a dependent traveling with me. Check your records."

"Hold… She's a kid."

"She stays with me."

"Your head." On a platter. And his tone told her that he couldn't care less if it were cut off or not.

"Confirmed." Definitely her head.

The line clicked dead. The operator, safe in some Fort Campbell billet, didn't care how much trouble Kee got in. As long as they were moving.

But what else was she supposed to do?

If she was lucky, they were being called back to their same base and Dilya could drop right back into her old routine.

If not… She didn't have time to think about it right now.

Dilya took the sudden uprooting with the same flexible calm she always maintained. Archie's father knew from experience that Archie could be gone on a moment's notice.

It was his mother that Archie worried about. They'd built their first fragile connection and he didn't know what to do about it. Given a couple days, with the start Kee had given him, they might begin to bridge the misunderstandings and hurt feelings that kept them apart. But now instead of days, they had minutes.

He knew he should be doing something about that, but he didn't know what. They'd all rushed out to the boat and gathered their belongings. Now they stood at the Castello's bus stop with a bag of sandwiches, sodas, and a large collection of cookies Kee had thrown together.

They had ten minutes. Maybe less.

He inspected the pretty sailboat anchored out in the cove along with a dozen others. The wind carried the soft sound of the surf up the hill. He'd thought to have time to teach Kee how to sail. Not even three days aboard, not enough time. Never enough time.

Kee swore loudly in Spanish, clearly ready to unleash a stream of profanity but stopping for Dilya's sake. The girl knew so little English, they'd all agreed to be careful not to start her off speaking like an Army grunt. Even Tim and John had bought in.

Kee grabbed both his hand and his mother's. She dragged them five quick steps along the road, away from Dilya and the worried look furrowing his father's brow.

She turned to his mother.

"Betty, it has been a great pleasure meeting you." She gave the woman a hug that was returned tentatively at first, and then, with a sudden strength, his mother wrapped her arms tightly about Kee's neck and held on.

Archie could feel envy for that. Kee grew close to people so easily. They trusted her, and she them, with an ease he had never achieved.

When they parted, his mother nodded. Archie knew

how hard the words were for her, he hoped Kee understood how much his mother had unbent in her presence.

Kee turned to stand toe to toe with him and looked up into his face. He raised a hand to brush her cheek, but she slapped it aside. She'd thrown that internal switch she had, faster than the blink of an eye from lover to Army sergeant. Was lover the right word, or perhaps—

"Okay. Remember, it was you who asked."

"Asked what?" Had he asked anything in the hectic hour they'd just spent rushing to ship and back to shore?

"I grew up on the Street. Capital *S*. It's a place all its own. Daughter of a coke whore and who the hell knows. She sure didn't. She's dead now, I guess. I couldn't find her when I went looking after basic training. I didn't look too hard. Didn't see her much before the Army either."

Archie opened his mouth, closed it again, and looked over Kee's head at his mother. She didn't look surprised, as if she already knew. Just accepting. Perhaps sorrowful.

Kee didn't turn to check on her reaction, her attack had a single point of aim. Him.

He tried to think if he even knew anyone whose mother was dead. Divorced, sure. But dead? And not caring?

"I grew up stealing for food, fighting for a place to sleep, and trusting absolutely no one at any time for any reason." Kee's voice continued like hammer blows battering against him. He fell back a step but she didn't stop. Her words shot out short and sharp as if fired from her minigun in a rapid-fire stream he couldn't dodge or evade.

"I slept with men or women for food. Not for money, though in a way I did. Anna fed both of us. When the hunger gnaws at your belly long enough and deep enough, you don't care anymore. I killed to stay alive. My best and only friend was a whore," Kee reached for the small braid of blond hair, "who died in my arms at eighteen. I killed her murderers in a gunfight, and I don't have a single regret about that. If I could have known beforehand, I'd have killed them first and taken the Murder One charge. It wasn't self-defense. I was alive. They were leaving. It was an execution. But they'd taken down cops. They were on L.A.'s Most Wanted. The judge gave me a choice of prosecution or the Army."

Each phrase so foreign, so alien. From another life.

"This is your mother." She turned to his mother. "This is your son. You two have no idea what a gift you each have in the other. Now get with the goddamn program!" Fury suffused her face, making it dark and more dangerous than he'd ever seen. She stalked away still in full warrior mode past Dilya, past his father. Finally grinding to a halt a dozen yards down the road.

Archie looked at his mother. They stood two steps apart, a chasm that neither had really crossed in as long as Archie could remember.

It always felt like she hadn't been there, but he could remember she had. She'd rarely missed a school event. Was aboard for the maiden voyage of every sailboat he and his father had ever built. She was the one who had taught him Cat's Cradle, Jacob's Ladder, and all the string figures he shared with Dilya.

He'd gone to West Point to impress her, but now he saw that he hadn't needed to. That he had grown to love it as well had been a gift of its own.

He closed his eyes against all those years with so

much distance between them. So far apart. Yet here she stood, right now, living and breathing.

He could hear the sound of the bus as it crested the hill out of Quercianella and put on the brakes at finding their party waiting at the stop in front of the Castello.

He opened his eyes and saw the tears running down his mother's cheeks, felt them on his own.

All these years they hadn't needed words.

They both took a step forward and wrapped their arms around each other.

And they didn't need words now.

Chapter 28

KEE FEIGNED EXHAUSTION ON THE BUS AND THE TRAIN. She couldn't keep it up forever, but it wasn't all a sham. Stepping back into her past had drained her to the core. Keiko Sato was a screwed-up, nasty, vicious little shit she'd left standing at the curb five years ago. Hadn't even bothered to toss her gun in the sewer. Just stood there and watched Anna bleed out. The hole in her forehead didn't bleed much, but it made tending any of the other injuries a waste of time. The cops were a long time coming.

She was better than that girl who'd had no concept of life beyond the streets. She changed her name the day she signed with the Army and no one complained. Kee Smith, the all-American kid from absolutely nowhere. Now she was SOAR. And that was more than she'd ever expected to achieve. A member of Emily Beale's crew, and Kee now knew that meant something. People trusted her. Trusted her not to screw up and get them all killed.

And that was where the convictions rose.

Anna had depended on her. Had called Kee her own personal lifesaver. Kee was always finding little gifts of bright, round Life Savers in her pocket, under her pillow, in her shoe. Anna had been a gentle, dark-eyed, golden-haired beauty. Willowy and fragile against Kee's strength. When a trick tried to rough Anna up, Kee was crouched in the hallway ready to pound the shit out of him.

And she'd died in a random drive-by, not something even Kee could guard against. Even the best guard couldn't stop that, but she'd been the one to fix it. Personal risk was never an issue. On the Street, living past sixteen wasn't all that common. It allowed a certain mental freedom to take on all comers.

The Army offered a different view and a better life expectancy. For one thing, you had to be eighteen to join. It already selected for the survivors. Still Kee'd lost so many squadmates in the 10th Mountain and later in the Green Berets that it was hard to keep track. Usually they lived, if you got to them fast enough. Field medicine and medevac were so good that if you found 'em alive, they usually stayed that way. But no one who'd been in combat deep really counted themselves alive if they were blind or crippled or one-armed. Especially not the guys who'd been hurt.

For now she had a crew and a little girl. And whatever Archie was. She glanced over as covertly as she could, picking up Dilya's cat from the floor where it had slid while the girl slept. Archie stared off into the distance not seeing the outskirts of Rome flitting past their window. He'd kept to himself since they'd left the bus stop.

Had she chased him off? Too much reality for the Boston blue blood? Easy answer of yes. Bastard. Well, it had just been one night in the sack, plus some fooling around on an Italian hilltop. She'd certainly had enough one-night stands in her life. No biggee.

While it proved hard to be surprised, that it hurt like hell shocked her. Kee'd certainly enjoyed his body. She hadn't gone with the long and lean often, but what he could do with it had made her a convert.

And running. There were men who could outrun her, a few. She'd always enjoyed running in unison with a squad, even while wearing full gear and a pack. And there were always other grunts who loved to run. Archie was a step beyond. Their run over the Italian countryside had filled her with a harmony, an ease, a joy that even the sex in the grass hadn't really matched. Their bodies constantly found a state of soundless communication that just flat-out worked for her.

Now... Walking away from a lover had never felt like a knife in the gut. Not before this.

On the flight from Rome to Kabul, he still hadn't come back. Even Dilya was watching him strangely.

"Thousand-yard stare." That look when someone's thoughts were turned so far inward, you could slip a grenade down their pants and they might not notice. Usually happened to forward-deployed grunts who saw one buddy too many wiped off the face of the planet. Archie looked as if Kee'd just been shot dead in front of him. Maybe she had. Gone from a cuddle-some quick bit on the side to way too real. He looked full-on shell-shocked.

That had been one of the things that had perplexed the psychologists at her pretrial assessment. Her best friend had died in her arms. She'd shot the three perps dead in cold blood. And the psychs couldn't figure out why she wasn't in shock.

She could have told them, but they never asked her.

They were measuring how they would react with their own little college backgrounds and their safe little families and their little hopes for the future. Sure. No big surprise. Death would shock the shit out of them.

After the twentieth member of your gang eats it before the age of fifteen, it's no longer a surprise. The surprise is surviving. She and Anna had often talked about their own life expectancies. Certainly neither had thought to hit sixteen, never mind eighteen. They were old for the Street. Anna's time had come. Sure, Kee mourned her, but there was no surprise. No shock. She'd been absolutely clearheaded when she'd gunned down the three assailants. She knew it for the cold-blooded murder of scum who had it coming, not the "momentary insanity" the psychologists put in her file.

She and Anna had held no dreams of adulthood, just as they'd never had a childhood. The Street never let anyone out.

But here Kee was. And she'd made it to the old age of twenty-four. The Army had already extended her life by six more years. Damn good deal even if some raghead deep-sixed her tomorrow.

Well, if Archie couldn't deal with the shit that was her past, to hell with him. Just as well, officer and enlisted had no way to work except in some sailboat dreamworld.

And with that, she slept most of the way to the front.

———

Dilyana waited and watched. The Kee and the String Man had changed twice after leaving on their run. Almost like different people in the same skin.

First, they had come back from their running, all in a hurry. That was fine with her. She'd liked the beach but had worried that The Kee would forget her promise. Dilya knew the chances of finding her parents' killers were small. But other girls might be losing their parents and Dilya worried that The Kee would spend the rest of her life on the boat. She'd promised to kill the killers if she could. They wouldn't be on the sailboat or the beach. Then she saw The Kee packing Dilya's drawings in her bag and knew she hadn't forgotten.

The second change worried her. It had started with all those words The Kee had spilled on Calledbetty and the String Man. The *domla*, the Professor, had held his mother and they both had cried. It had looked like happy crying.

But The Kee hadn't been happy. She had crawled inside herself so deep that Dilyana wondered if she could find her way back out.

At first the *domla* failed to notice, too lost in his own world. On the bus and the train he kept his silence, and neither she nor The Kee broke it. On the plane, he came back to himself. Enough to look at The Kee sleeping. He watched her a long time, a soft smile on his face.

Dilyana knew that look. The Kee raged and fought and struggled, but the *domla* would again teach his lesson in his language of patience and they would be together.

As sleep finally overtook her, Dilya daydreamed of an image. One she couldn't quite see. A dream of three.

Tall, medium, and the last one Dilya-sized.

Chapter 29

THE MILD HEAT OF THE MEDITERRANEAN HAD SPOILED Kee. The desert heat of the soccer-stadium air base hammered against her brain as it cooked the briefing tent.

She looked around the scattered chairs and benches again, trying to fill in the missing pieces, but it wasn't making sense. In an area where the entire company of eighty or so pilots, copilots, and crew could meet, there were six people.

The liaison was there for the C-130 Hercules tankers, which provided midair refueling. She and Archie. Clay, the pilot from one of the transport Pave Hawks, sat on Archie's other side. A couple rows up and over, a decent-looking white chick. A trim brunette who wore the fatigues of a warrior with the looks of the sitcom stunning girl next door. Clearly newly assigned to the forward base, she looked all perky and fresh minted from the factory. Who was she clerking for that she'd gotten stuck out here?

No Beale. No Big John or Crazy Tim. And Major Muscle Henderson wasn't the briefing officer. What the hell?

"Good evening. My name is Colonel Jeff Isaacson." A bird colonel. At Bati. Something bad was up. He stood at parade rest at the front of the tent, facing them as if there weren't six rows of chairs separating him from his reluctant audience. A big man, the way the regular Army

grew them. Bigger than Major Henderson. Not quite Big
John, but nobody was. Arms the size of Archie's legs—

Bad analogy, Kee. She didn't want to think about his
legs or how it felt when she sat across them or—She
almost slapped herself to clear the image.

One thing for sure about the briefing officer. He
wasn't SOAR. He stood wrong. But he had a thick gray-
ing beard that hid much of his face and his hair hung a
month or more past Army. Only folks who could get
away with that were SEALs and Deltas and SOARs.
Something still wasn't right, though he was clearly one
tough son of a bitch.

"Sorry to interrupt your vacations, but we have an
immediate mission. It should be simple and quiet. As
a matter of fact, if it isn't, I'm screwed. That's why I
asked for you SOAR folks."

The Colonel with his regulation stance and his regulation attitude didn't strike her as an operator. For one
thing, she'd never heard a SEAL say so many words in
a row. And D-boys talked even less than SEALs. Maybe
not even Green Beret. This guy must be a Ranger. Or, her
mind slipped over to worst-case scenario, maybe he really was Regular Army. More rank than common sense.

Kee raised her hand.

He gave her a crisp nod. "Sergeant."

"Where's the rest of our crew? Who is manning the
other helicopter?" Helicopters always flew in pairs for
support and for rescue if something went wrong.

She could feel Archie's attention, though the two
of them still hadn't spoken since Italy. So damn petty,
shunning her for her past. If he had to live even half of
her reality for ten lousy minutes, he'd run screaming in

the other direction. *Accept it, Kee. Just as useless as a civilian. He's been fun, but he can't handle you. He's history. Toss him back into the pond.*

Back to the problem at hand.

"This," the Colonel indicated with a nod of his head rather than breaking parade rest enough to wave a hand, "is all we need. There will be on-call support in case of problems, but they aren't to be aware of this mission until absolutely necessary."

Kee scanned the room again. That creeping sensation of something out of place slid up her spine and lodged there, sharp like a knifepoint.

The flight felt wrong.

They'd arrived at sunset, and been in and out of briefing in twelve and a half minutes.

That's when everything started to slip just a little sideways.

Clay Anderson and Archie were in the cockpit of Beale's DAP Hawk. Clay flew a Pave Hawk, and he flew it well. But that was a transport bird, not an assault chopper.

And the new chick, Connie somebody, who looked like she should be on a damn cooking show laughing it up with Rachael chirping Ray, was preflighting the Hawk. Kee shadowed her as she checked fuel, armor, tires, climbed up to open the engine covers and visually inspect for leaks as if everything were normal. More than once she pulled a wrench from a thigh pocket to make sure everything was tight, as if Big John would leave his bird in less than perfect shape.

She poked into every corner of the bird until Kee felt stripped naked just watching her. But for all that, Kee couldn't see that she'd missed anything. She even checked Kee's minigun just fine, but what was this woman doing on a SOAR flight?

No answers. Kee had to scramble at the last second to make sure her own gear stood ready to rock and roll. The woman looked over as Kee checked inside her sniper rifle case. Kee kept the lid only partway open so that Ms. Nosy couldn't see in. Everything shipshape, gleaming in the evening light from the fine sheen of oil she'd wiped on when she'd finally done the cleaning. Kee closed and locked the case. Ms. Nosy didn't ask, merely blinked and looked back to her own gear.

That blink gave her away. She'd been creeping Kee out far more than merely being a woman on the wrong helicopter. Connie Davis, that was the chick's name, reminded her of Anna. If you took her friend, turned her into a brunette, gave her soldier's shoulders and added a few inches of height, you'd have Connie Davis. What Kee'd first thought to be a vacant look, she now recognized as one of intense concentration held behind a facade of the dispassionate observer.

Anna had possessed an immensely clear view of the world, one Kee felt lost without, even to this day. But Anna too had generally kept it to herself. Kee learned to read when Anna was processing and storing something in her neatly ordered mind. And this Connie woman had just done the same thing. Except Anna had been born to die on the streets. Connie Davis clearly came from some ordered and safe world.

It's not as if they could possibly be related, but the

painful reminder of her friend sat across the cargo bay from her as Clay and Archie lifted the DAP Hawk into the night sky. The Colonel sat alone at the back of the cargo bay, clipped to the rear cargo net.

Kee'd seen Dilyana running toward them even as they lifted off. She'd meant to track the girl down before they flew, but Isaacson was in an all-fired rush and she wasn't about to argue with a colonel. They'd grabbed a quick meal together, but she usually tried to leave a hug behind whenever she flew off. She waved, but Dilyana, stumbling to a halt outside the dust cloud of the rotor's downdraft, didn't wave back.

The cold chill spread along Kee's nerves.

Per orders, they flew to a nowhere spot in the southern foothills of the mountains. Two hours into the nothing almost due north, though the action typically lay northwest. There, at the outer slopes of the Hindu Kush, under a desert camo net, sat an old, white Toyota 4x4 pickup. It was scuffed and dented. Looked like a thousand other vehicles kicking around the theater of operations. War liked reliable trucks. Afghan and Pakistan military used Toyotas as often as the Taliban and other insurgents. Perfect ground transport for going in-country. It would blend in anywhere.

But what did Colonel Isaacson need it for? And why had he stashed it way out here?

They hovered a few feet up. Isaacson jumped out, gathered the camo net, and bundled it under a bungee cord in the truck's bed, along with a dozen five-gallon gas cans. He attached the four-point harness to lift points on the chopper, which was already rigged for lifting.

Kee clicked on the intercom. "We're not the heavy

lifters." She whispered her complaint even though Isaacson was still outside the chopper.

"The big Chinooks are both down for scheduled maintenance," Archie reminded her. "We are the only bird in the theater with the M-mod. No one else has the bigger engines to get him over the mountains. I am not all that sure how well we can."

"Great."

Within thirty seconds of arrival, they were lifting the truck off the sand. It came reluctantly, as if unhappy about leaving the solid safety of terra firma.

For the first time since she'd been saved by that long-ago SOAR flight, Kee didn't want to fly either.

—⁂—

Dilyana raced after The Kee. She'd waved from the helicopter, but Dilya had been too late. The wind from the blades had pushed Dilya back in a cloud of sand and dust. By the time she could see, they were gone. No lights, just the outline of their shape against the stars, disappearing over the north wall and already moving fast.

She'd tried running up to the top of the bleachers, but The Kee and the String Man were long gone by the time she stood beside the Ranger sentry. He'd offered her a smile. She forced herself to return it. This one sometimes shared a candy bar with her.

She sat down to wait, watching in the direction they'd gone.

Afraid, she could only wait. Wait and hope they came back.

—⁂—

The first leg, up through the second midair refueling, was all at altitude. Nothing for Kee to do but sit there and wish for more of the Mediterranean sun while freezing at night over the Hindu Kush. To sit there and dream of how Archie had looked at her as they'd sat together on the stone wall that probably dated back to the Romans. To feel his hand holding her life in where she'd been shot in the side three years before. To taste his kiss that—

A clunk and whirr of motor noise sounded through the deck beneath her feet, more felt than heard over the rotor noise. Kee shook herself and looked out the window around the minigun. They'd extended the mid-air refueling probe. It now reached to the edge of the Hawk's rotor sweep. A Hercules tanker flew ahead and slightly above, dragging a long fuel line with a basket on the end. At over a hundred knots, Archie slid the Hawk forward and dead-centered the basket with the probe on his first try. Mated up, the Hawk started sucking down fuel.

Well, Archie was good at mating up. Damned fine in the sack and out in the Italian sun atop that hill. Why did he have to be such a jerk? They'd been so good together. *Shit! Stop it!*

The intercom had been silent for the whole trip. Ms. Connie whoever hadn't said a word, not in briefing, not in preflight, and not now. Clay and Archie hadn't talked more than to double-check status of their flight plan.

Their high elevation, combined with the heavy load, had the bird sucking down fuel like a mad drunk. Two refuels en route.

As soon as this second refueling was complete, they

were supposed to go low. Below radar, but not NOE. Apparently this mission had no need for the chaos of a Nap of Earth routine. Which was a good thing, especially with a ton of pickup truck dangling thirty feet below the Hawk. On this leg of the flight, all their profile called for was to stay down in the valleys and cross the ridges low. Which was good. With this kind of load, they couldn't climb over the truly tall stuff. Probably couldn't even do the mission if not for the DAP Hawk's engine and rotor blade upgrade.

Kee kept her attention out the window once she'd made sure that Ms. Newbie had her hands on her gun and her own attention outside.

She did, but there was nothing going on except frozen wasteland.

The Colonel didn't say a word either, hadn't bothered patching his helmet into the intercom system. All quiet.

Not even a single stray shot from someone suddenly surprised by their overflight. No one hanging out around here to get their jollies. They were way off in the mountains, cruising down valleys that perhaps no man had ever lived in. Slipping up over passes that had never been walked, and so on into the next and the next. They were so far off the edge of the map, there was nothing to see. And who knew how far back their backup flew if something went wrong. Kee definitely didn't want to think about that.

She did her best to watch the refueling tanker dumping a hundred gallons a minute into their tanks without watching the frozen passes and the jagged peaks of the western Karakoram mountains that stretched in every direction below.

Connie stayed focused, but Kee's attention kept slipping. At first, wishing she knew if someone was keeping an eye on Dilya. Second, what was going on here. Third, what the hell was wrong with Archie anyway? Couldn't he see a good thing when he was buried up to his ears between her breasts? What was wrong with that man?

The instant they disconnected from the tanker and it had turned back for friendlier locales, Archie brought the chopper down until they could see the glacier crevasses far too clearly in the moonlight.

As they descended, the Colonel shed his helmet and flight gear to reveal native dress beneath. She watched him from the corner of her eye and saw him stash a weapon she'd never seen outside of training, a Russian Makarov PM handgun. Then he dragged an AK-47 from a kit bag and slung it over his shoulder. He leaned in close to Kee and jabbed a finger at the bag he'd clipped to the cargo net across the rear with all his U.S. Army gear jammed inside.

"Burn it!"

He maintained his glare until she nodded her assent. She'd burn it, once she'd gone through all of his pockets very carefully.

He kicked a fast rope out the cargo bay door and climbed down bare-handed. Even D-boys used gloves, of course, they slid down these ropes to land on the ground, not hand over hand toward a pickup truck spinning lazily back and forth a hundred feet in the air. He'd climbed out while they flew at 150 miles an hour.

Connie snapped out of her seat and latched a monkey harness to the ceiling. Enough leash to move freely about the cabin, she moved beside Kee to stare down at the mad Colonel as he buffeted about in the winds below the chopper.

He slammed brutally into the side of his pickup truck. But rather than losing his hold and falling to his death, he managed to wrap an arm through the open driver's window. He crawled off the rope and into the vehicle.

Then his arm stuck out the window and waved upward. Did so again until Kee pulled up the rope and recoiled it.

The man ranked certifiable.

Archie kept them low enough that she watched carefully to make sure they didn't leave the pickup dangling on some rocky spire. He might not be as hotshot a pilot as Major Beale, but he was still damned good.

An hour later, her gut lurched as they went from 150 miles an hour to zero in just a few seconds.

They didn't land.

They hovered over a road Kee hadn't noticed. It looked more like a meandering goat path. Unused in a long time.

The helicopter slammed upward, rapping her helmet sharply against her minigun.

Mr. Lunatic had pulled a release he must have rigged himself. It dropped the truck the last couple feet to the ground, and the suddenly lightened load had caused the helicopter to rise abruptly.

Kee finally had a good angle on the pickup. There was another man aboard, hidden the whole time. Riding out in the wind for almost seven hours. The Colonel, in native dress, and a narrow-faced man crouched low in the passenger seat.

She glanced over her shoulder and saw Ms. Nosy had

her attention toward Kee's side of the chopper as well. Kee couldn't blame her and signaled her over.

For a moment, the woman left her gun and came to crouch beside Kee and look out at the truck as Archie overflew it one last time before turning for home.

The woman held up two fingers. It looked like a question.

Kee nodded.

The woman twisted her helmeted head to one side as if there were a crick in her neck. So she felt it, too.

Something was not right here.

Dilyana was awakened by the roar of a descending helicopter. It was past dawn, the sun already high enough to shine over the wall and down onto the field. Her dreams had been dark and it took her a moment to shake free of them.

She knew the helicopter the moment her eyes found it.

Dilya raced down the bleachers and almost beat them to their landing place.

The cargo door launched open, and The Kee squatted in the space only Dilya was able to stand up in. Against the rules The Kee had given her, Dilya launched herself aboard and wrapped her arms around The Kee.

She'd been so afraid that she'd never see The Kee again.

Chapter 30

KEE WAS AVOIDING HIM. REALLY AVOIDING HIM.

After a sleepless night, Archie lay on the bench in the back of the supply tent and slammed the weights upward with a grunt, his arms sizzling with muscle burn.

Twenty reps.

She was starting to really piss him off. Not that it didn't make sense. There was no way in God's green army for a lieutenant and a sergeant to get together.

But that didn't stop him feeling like a piece of his life was missing when she wasn't around.

Twenty-five.

Damn her anyway. How had she latched such a hold on him? It wasn't her damn fine body or the amazing things she could do with it. It wasn't her charming personality, at least not when she was in one of her foul or vicious moods, as if you could tell when those were incoming. They appeared out of nowhere and hammered in without warning, leaving wide damage paths that always seemed to include him.

Thirty.

For five more reps all he could think about was the fury that built in him like a tidal wave as the muscle burn expanded into his chest.

Thirty-five.

Forty.

Crap! He slammed the weights back onto the hooks,

not caring in the least that he'd just beaten his personal best into submission by ten reps at this weight. And without a spotter. Even just thinking about the goddamn woman made him stupid.

He sat up on the bench and knocked back half a bottle of water, dumped the other half over his head, then mopped at his face with his wadded-up T-shirt. To hell with her. He didn't need this.

Kicking to his feet, he headed out of the tent into the glare of the morning light. Too wound up to go get breakfast, too pissed that neither Kee nor Dilya would be there. Pumping iron had only wound him tighter, rather than wearing him out as he'd hoped.

A run. Maybe that would help. He dragged on his T-shirt and set off around the track. On his second lap he spotted Kee. It was as if she'd crawled permanently onto his personal radar screen. He looked away. Focused on the dirt loop beaten into the outer edge of the soccer field by bored fliers with nothing better to do between missions.

But even as he ran, he could still see Kee running up and down the bleachers, stair sprints. In this heat. Brutal.

On lap three, he finally noticed that she wasn't alone. She was in D-boy country on the east side of the stadium. No one kept up with Delta operators, but there was Kee, right in the middle of the pack. Down to the dirt, hard spin, sprint up twenty tiers of concrete, tap the top rail, sprint over to the next set of stairs, and back down. A stream of a dozen of the best-trained warriors on the planet and his Kee.

"His" Kee. Another goddamn joke. He ignored her and focused on his laps.

—◦◦◦—

Kee spotted Archie the moment he trotted out of the supplies tent. Saw the way he flexed and worked his arms and neck during his warm-up lap, he'd been pumping iron and doing it hard.

She spun on the dirt and headed up the bleachers behind Jimmy and Stephen. They'd only been at it for ten minutes. She knew the D-boys would be doing it for another hour. No chance she'd match them, but they'd let her in and she'd last as long as she could to say thanks.

Archie swung close as he settled into a run. She'd give anything to run with him once more over the fields. To chase and be chased, to find that harmony that had echoed through her. She had felt then as if she could run on and on and on. As if she could simply take wing and fly forever.

Tap the top rail. Bati town spread out before them, already slowing down as the morning heat rose. The fast pace of morning giving way to the Third World mosey that would pervade until the cooler evening and the opening of the night market. She missed that, too. Holding hands with Archie as they looked at colors, food, and camels.

Sprint along the top tier, and then back down the stairs. At the dirt, turn to sprint back to the base of the first set of stairs.

Archie trotted along the far side of track.

Kee would complete another two laps before he made it around the long curve behind the Chinooks and back to the D-Boys' workout.

Up, tap, along, down.

He was out of sight behind the massive twin-rotor helicopters, but she could still feel him, feel his timing.

So, he didn't want anything to do with her since Italy? Was that her fault? Her past was her past. So what if it freaked him out? She didn't give a goddamn. Not with how he made her feel. The gentle tug on the blond streak etched in her hair. Those brilliant eyes that had always seen her so clearly, until they didn't.

Across, up, tap, along…

And there he was, coming off the long curve and opening out those long legs on the straightaway.

If she just—

She dove down the tiers, passing Jimmy, Stephen, and Dave.

She hit her turn in the dirt at exactly the same moment Archie passed by.

Instead of turning right, she dug left and fell in right beside him.

He startled for a moment, missed a stride.

Then she saw the look on his face she'd never seen before. Rage. Black fury.

Well, she could match that. He wanted to throw away everything they'd had simply because she had a past, let him. She'd show him what it meant to be a soldier.

She kicked out. Drove ahead, hard.

Archie clearly had the same thought. In moments they were both at a dead run, leaning into the wide turns, feet slipping in the loose soil as they dug for traction.

The first two laps they both drove hard. There were moments when Archie pulled ahead, but Kee always found a reserve to pull even, then to edge ahead. But she could never sustain any lead.

By lap five they had both settled into a fast run, hoping to wear the other out.

Eight, ten, twelve, fifteen laps rolled along beneath their pounding feet. And as they did, it shifted. Kee could feel the endorphins lightening her mood. The sheer joy of running beside the man, that rhythm of jousting for position never let up, but on this field of endeavor they were well matched.

Twenty. She couldn't help herself. She laughed aloud for the sheer joy of it. Archie kicked into a hard sprint.

She glanced over, a snapshot of him that she would never forget.

His long body drenched with sweat. His leg muscles etched in the sunlight. His head tipped back ever so slightly, his long hair a banner in the breeze behind him. And on his face a smile of sheer joy. The joy of running, or the joy of running with her?

For two long laps they sprinted. No mere run, but a flat-out, gut-clenching sprint that tore at reserves faster than they could be replaced. Unable to breathe fast enough, not enough air in the world, she pushed ahead anyway. As they roared into the back curve behind the Chinooks, she had three full strides on him, she veered into the back tunnel beneath the bleachers.

Before the end of the tunnel had been blocked by the U.S. Army, it had led under the cool concrete of the tiers of bleachers and opened out into the fields beyond.

Kee reached the back wall two steps ahead of Archie and turned with her back against it as he skidded into her.

No time to breathe. No time to speak. No time to kiss.

He ripped down her gym shorts even as she shoved his off his waist.

Pulling one leg free, she wrapped herself around his hips.

He drove into her so hard it slammed her back against the wall. She pounded her fists against his shoulders as he took her.

She grabbed a hank of his hair and pulled back enough to see his face. No gentle lover, no sweet Archie.

She looked into his eyes and saw only the need, the raging beast of need.

That was fine with her. It was how she liked her men. Needed her men. Knew exactly how to handle that.

Just use each other, that's what she'd always done. Lord knows, it's what men always did.

When he pounded home, when his ragged breathing was shattered by a low moan, her own body released with waves so hard that they rode that sweet edge between heaven and agony.

He'd barely finished, his pounding need no longer pinned her to the wall, and she slid free. She had her shorts back up around her waist before he recovered.

Archie still stood, leaning in, his palms flat against the wall, his shorts forgotten around his thighs.

He'd think everything was fine between them. He'd give her one of those Archie smiles, but Kee knew. She knew that deep down, the truth had finally come out. He couldn't stand to be around someone with her past. He just wanted her body and assumed he could take it whenever he wanted.

And that hurt worse than anything a long line of men had ever done to her. Being gutshot and dying in a god-forsaken Nigerian forgotten cesspit had hurt less.

"Hope the sex was good for you, Lieutenant." Even

as she said it, she felt the cruelty of her words. But she couldn't stop the next sentence.

"Next time you need service, you ain't gonna find it here."

She turned and walked out of the tunnel even as Archie collapsed to the dirt.

She wouldn't cry. She never cried.

But having just knifed Archie in the back, she had to hammer the pain back down with the iron first that had always ruled her life.

Chapter 31

ARCHIE HAD STEWED OVER IT FOR A DAY AND A NIGHT.

How could she get it so wrong? He'd thought they were together. Felt the joy of their run just as in Italy. Had heard her laugh of pure joy, like no other sound on the planet. The release of his worries and fears had driven him mad for her. And he'd taken her, and buried his fears and his hopes deep inside her.

After worrying at it until he was half mad, he knew he had to talk to her. He went hunting for her right after sunrise. To explain that he hadn't been using her, that he missed her. He needed her.

That stopped him so completely in his tracks that he puffed up twin clouds of dust with his feet.

Archibald Jeffrey Stevenson III needed a woman. Here he was, actually out looking for a woman. One particular woman. One feisty, assertive, pain-in-the-ass woman. Well, if he had to be feisty and assertive and a pain in the ass himself to find out what in creation's name was going on, then, by all that's holy, Archibald Jeffrey Stevenson III would be feisty and assertive and a pain in the ass.

"What the hell are you smiling at?"

There she stood, not three steps away. Dripping sweat from yet another workout. Her light clothes clinging to her in such a splendid fashion that he caught himself staring at her body. Those curves he'd only started to explore. The one where neck met collarbone. That perfect one, right above her hip, that fit his palm so well, he'd felt connected and at peace when his hand rested there.

He reached out to brush his knuckles over the curve of her cheek, and she smashed his hand aside, hard enough to really sting. He tried to shake off the pain, but it didn't go away so easily. She'd really caught him. There'd be a bruise on the inside of that wrist.

Archie opened his mouth to apologize, but he'd done too much of that already, and none of it had worked. Perhaps because he didn't know what he'd been apologizing for most of the time.

Now he inspected her critically. She was flexing her feet, shaking out her legs. Her thigh and calf muscles were even more clearly defined than usual. That's when he registered where they were. She was working out in D-boy country again. They'd cobbled together an agility course of tires, old boards, low wires. If it was possible to admire her more than he already did, it had happened.

"What?" Her tone had shifted from irritated to acerbic.

"I miss you." Not what he'd meant to say.

"Your own damn choice." She went to step around him.

He stayed her with a hand on her arm. She looked down at it, as if she were contemplating whether or not to break his bones. He decided to live dangerously and keep it there.

"I hate to keep doing this, but could you explain that, please?" He asked that an awful lot around her and he was getting sick of it. Hell, it was pissing him off.

She jerked her arm free and tried to again pass him by.

He grabbed her wrist and, with a quick flick, pinned

it up behind her back. He'd had bloody damn-it-to-hell enough of her attitude. She bent forward, immobilized.

"Answer a goddamn civil question."

Except she didn't stay that trapped. She placed her free hand in the dust and did a forward somersault so fast he could barely see it. With her hand once again right side up, she broke his grasp and snatched for his wrist.

Archie dodged back and then hopped upward like a kangaroo as a sweep kick threatened to take him out at the knees.

"You're going to have to do better than that, gunner."

"I'm the best you've ever had, flatfoot."

He blocked her double-hand strike as hard as she had his caress.

"And that's a mission plan you won't get to repeat."

He dove, but even his long reach wasn't enough to snag her. Was that what she thought this was about? Sex?

"Don't you ever look ahead, Smith?"

She hooked his foot and before he could recover, she lifted it and twisted hard. To keep his knee intact, he rolled down into the dirt, losing her momentarily as he clamped his eyes and mouth shut against the fine particulate. He caught her foot inches before her heel drove into his solar plexus. With a twist, she was down beside him. They both rolled clear.

"I don't laze around the cockpit while a real woman does the flying and another the gunning."

They circled again. When her back was to the bleachers, Archie saw the D-boy squad ranged behind. They stood in a silent line, water bottles in hand, and watched. He really didn't need an audience right at the moment.

His instant of inattention was ill advised. Kee swept

a kick at one knee and grabbed for the other as he dodged. Only a quick twist that wrenched at his back kept him clear.

"You have no damn idea what I do, gunner."

"It's how little you offer that matters."

That actually got a soft chuckle from some of the Delta boys.

This time she dove. He managed to dodge and grabbed her from behind. His crosshold had her by the throat and across the chest. Except instead of grabbing the tendon in her armpit and gaining leverage to slam her to the ground, he snagged his thumb in her tank top and almost ripped it free. The move had worked well for him in innumerable training sessions, against other men. All Kee's parts weren't in the right places.

They froze for a long moment, his hand trapped against her breast.

Then her elbow shot into his solar plexus so hard that he knew he was down for the count.

Well, he wasn't going down alone. He shifted his grip from breast to upper arm and rolled into her as he fell. She ended up beneath, his shoulder hard in her gut to drive out her air. Neither of them could speak, but she snaked an arm around his neck, caught his chin, and forced him to roll clear if he wanted to keep his head attached to his body.

They staggered upward in unison, kneeling, squat with hands supporting on knees, both crouched in a fighting stance. As they found enough air to move, they began to circle slowly.

"Is that all you see, Kee?" Archie shifted off the ball of his left foot.

"I see what's right in front of me." She filled her voice with disgust as she faded right against his possible next move.

"No, gunner," he spit the word out along with a mouthful of dust, "you only look behind."

She feinted left then right, and made a strike he blocked easily.

"And you have perfect forward vision, pilot?" she spat back.

Actually, Kee knew he probably did. Archie was the strategist. His seat had the wide forward view, as did his mind.

"And that view has made you so goddamn smart?" Kee shot the words to avoid shooting her fists. So goddamn smug. Mr. Upper-Class Officer had all the easy breaks in life. Left her feeling cheap in a way her past never had. She'd earned every inch of what she had and earned it the hard way.

"You're living your life stuck in the past—"

That's when she got position on him. She dodged in, got him in an armlock that would hurt like hell. She wanted to cause him pain. Wanted to hurt him like she'd never wanted to hurt anyone. Worse than she'd wanted to take out Anna's shooters. Worse than she wanted to hurt the Street for taking her father, her mother, and her life.

Archie managed to shift against the pain and dig his long fingers into the nerve cluster on her upper forearm. A wave of agony rocketed up her arm as they tested each other's limits. A street-chick gunner could sure as hell take it if some uptown jerk could.

A chopper came pounding down out of the sky. A wave of dust and dirt obliterated her vision, her hearing, and her sense of smell for anything but the gritty ocher dust of the high desert. A downpour of grit pounded against her until all she could feel was the racking pain in her arm and his shaking against the pain where she drove his arm nearly out of its socket.

Then, impossibly, at the very worst moment of the brownout, he shifted. In the formless, featureless world, Kee knew she was falling, but no longer had any sense of up or down. Unable to compensate, she smashed to the ground with a body-bruising blow. One arm pinned beneath her, the other momentarily numb from the abuse Archie had given it.

Over the roar of the rotor and dust, a voice sounded close to her ear yet impossibly far away.

"Enough of this shit! You and I are through."

Then her arm was free and Archie's weight was off her. By the time the dust settled enough to see, she lay alone, nursing her offended arm.

No one in sight.

Not even a D-boy.

Chapter 32

DILYA SAT ON HER COT AND WATCHED THE KEE SIT ON hers. For two days The Kee had kept to herself. They didn't eat at normal times any more. There was always some reason to eat when the food tent stood empty. The Kee didn't talk to the String Man or kiss him or hold hands or speak to him.

Dilya's attempts to cheer up The Kee didn't work either. She'd brought out the book they were reading, but even the party in the tree didn't help. *Go, Dog. Go!* always made The Kee happy, but not today.

They tried the game of string that the String Man called Cat's Cradle. But by the time they reached the "carpet" figure, Dilya gave up.

And The Kee didn't even notice. Her hands fell life-lessly back into her lap when Dilya took back the string. And The Kee sat on her bed and stared at the ground.

Dilya could feel the knot building in her stomach. She had enough food hidden under her bed to last a week. Maybe more if she was careful. And the four tall water bottles she'd stolen would be heavy, but in a pillow sack she could carry it all.

She didn't want to go. She liked The Kee. She liked the way that grown-ups were nice to her here.

The knot in her stomach grew so tight, she couldn't sit anymore. She rose to walk between the beds, six of them now. One just for her. She walked up and down the tent, trying to think, but her stomach was hungry and afraid. Her father always said when you were afraid was when you had to think the hardest, so she tried, though it made her miss him even more.

Everything had been good until they went to the beach place. She knew there had been a fight on the sailboat, but Calledbetty had made it better and they had returned to the boat. Building in the sand and visiting the castle. Those were the best days since her parents had died.

Dilya turned at the cloth wall of the tent and walked back the other way, The Kee didn't even look up.

The sand by the sea had been so different from the desert. So wet that it stuck together if you were careful and kept it wet, but not too wet. And they had all been happy. She could remember playing with The Kee in the water and riding on the String Man's back. Everyone had been happy.

Happy until the bus came to take them back to the desert.

Was the desert the problem? No, they had been in the desert before.

Was it the strange man who rode the helicopter into the night but didn't come back? He had scared Dilya; she held her stomach. She hadn't seen him up close, but he was bad. She knew it. If only she knew why she knew it. But The Kee and the String Man had come back without him. That was good.

No, the desert wasn't the problem. The problem was the bus. Everything went wrong at the bus.

What could she do? She stumbled to a stop in front of The Kee. What was wrong with her? She'd bet that the String Man could fix it. But they didn't see him anymore. They didn't even fly on the helicopter at night. Worse than strangers. If they passed, he said hello to her but ignored The Kee. Not even another trip into the big city. No adventures in the market.

The Kee looked up and blinked at her. After a long moment, she spoke. Her voice rough, like she'd never used it before.

"Dinner, Dilya. Go. Eat with Archie."

"Go, Dog. Go!" Dilya answered and ran to the door. Now The Kee and the String Man would be together. It would all be okay.

But The Kee didn't follow. She sat on her bunk. Maybe she was hurt. Like when Dilya had been so sick. She'd tell the String Man. He'd make it all better.

She ran back and wrapped her arms around The Kee's neck. The Kee held her tight for a long moment, then let go and sent Dilya on her way.

Dilya would help. She ran from the tent seeking String Man Professor *domla*.

———∿∿∿———

Kee would be fine. If Dilya would rather be with Archie, who could blame her. Kee was realistic enough to know that her own attitude sucked at this moment. No one wanted her anyway. Beale wished she were off the chopper. Archie had said he was done with her and now wouldn't give her the time of day. He'd cheated. He'd shown her how to want more and then taken it back.

"Hard. Isn't it?"

Kee spun to see who spied on her. That new girl stood in a dark corner by her cot.

"How long have you been there?"

Connie Davis answered her with silence. A silence backed up by a steady assessing gaze.

Like yesterday when Kee'd caught Connie rebuilding a section of the DAP Hawk's tail rotor drive. Kee'd lit into her for taking apart something she didn't understand. Kee'd never done one solo, though she probably could, with a manual. The things were tricky.

Woman had let her rant and fume without a single flicker in those hazel eyes until Kee wound down.

"There's a service issue that we uncovered during training at the factory. We'll be getting a notice next week about it. The transfer bearing on the MH-60M upgrade needs replacement every two hundred hours of operation rather than every three hundred as on the MH-60L. This one clocked at 212 at landing this morning. Therefore, I'm replacing it."

Kee had glared at her. Glared at the repair log spread beside the meticulous work cloth where Connie had spread parts with a textbook-like precision. The Kee had sat in the dirt and watched in silence for two full hours, but she couldn't fault the woman's work. If she hadn't been in such a foul mood, she might have asked for details about two techniques she hadn't seen before.

Now, that same bland silence awaited her in her last sanctuary, the women's sleeping quarters. Nowhere safe.

"What was your damned question?" Only way Kee'd be rid of her.

"I've been watching you. You don't strike me as a happy person, at least not since I arrived. I've watched you with the kid. It's not her. I'm thinking it has something to do with that First Lieutenant who planted you in the dirt."

Connie crossed out of her dark corner and stood at the foot of Kee's cot. Those hazel eyes hidden by the shadows. Outside the tent, the sun had dropped below the soccer arena's high seating.

"His mood has been as foul as yours, except he hides it better."

Great. Just what Kee needed. Another reminder that anyone could read her emotions better than she could.

"I'm thinking you two need to talk. One of you is too stubborn, and I'm betting that's you."

"What about him?" Kee bit it off. Too late. She'd already asked. Asked for advice from this weird, mechanic, middle-America android. Apparently unlike Kee, the woman never showed any emotion at all. If she had any. Kee couldn't read her.

Connie tipped her head one way. Then the other. Puzzling at the problem, her eyebrows pulled down into a slight frown. Her feather-cut hair rippling down in soft waves.

"He's… either sad or afraid. Perhaps both."

"He should be afraid." Kee really had to watch her mouth. The image in her mind of pounding her fists against him until he got his act together, or staggered away as a bloody pulp, would definitely get her booted for attacking a superior officer.

"Damn!" She leaned forward to grind at her eyes with the heels of her hand. "I've screwed this up and I don't know what to do. He won't even look at me."

"Not when you're watching. But when you're out running, I've learned to expect no help from him on any repairs."

"What else are you doing to Major Beale's Hawk?"

Again the bland stare.

"Okay. Illegal change of topic." Kee struggled to her feet. "Now what am I supposed to do?"

"Seriously. You might try talking to him."

Kee hated the answer.

Almost as much as she hated that the All-American girl next door, Specialist Connie Davis, was absolutely right.

Chapter 33

"HEY, ARCHIE."

He stumbled to a halt a dozen steps into the evening darkness past the chow tent and looked around for the voice's owner. He'd almost forgotten the sound of it these last days.

"Kee?"

"Up here."

He raised his gaze. He could just make out her shadow halfway up the end-zone seating. Farther away than he'd thought from the sound of her voice, the curved concrete tiers amplifying her soft call to this spot. In another few minutes, she'd be wholly invisible in the dark of the night.

He could feel all the joy of having Dilya once again as a dinner companion drain out of him. He fought the slide into anger with little success. Forcing himself to take a deep breath, which still hurt a little where she'd hit him, he considered his options.

"Please?" Little more than a whisper.

He'd never heard that from her. Not once that he could remember. Her plea tipped the balance, barely. He climbed up the dozen tiers. She sat, leaning forward, her hands clasped, arms resting on her knees. The dark of the moonless night now hid her. The bit of stray camp light caught in her eyes. The faint streak of blond hair showing in the starlight. Otherwise, nothing more than the vague outline of shadow against faded concrete.

A soft night breeze twisted and swirled across the tiered seating. Sometimes it snagged the last aroma of lasagna dinner from the cook tent. Sometimes the kerosene edge of jet fuel. Then it caught the desert warmth of Kee's skin.

"Sit." She patted the concrete beside her. "Please?"

Again that whispered entreaty.

He sat. Not too close. Not sure of her mood.

"I need you to explain something to me."

"I asked first." Archie was sick of explaining himself to her. "But instead you nearly busted my shoulder and smashed me into the dirt."

"I did? Your shoulder? Are you okay?"

He rubbed the spot more from instinct learned over the last three days than from any remaining pain. "I'm fine."

A silence fell between them. Awkward. Drawn out.

Her breathing was ragged, the only sound other than a couple of the guys' laughter as they left the chow tent.

He wanted to reach for her. To hold her. But she had taught him that wasn't something she took to well.

They waited until the loudest sound in the night was the occasional ping of the metal cooling on the nearby Chinook helicopters.

Now there were lights in two or three of the tents, and the brilliant splash of the Milky Way slashing across the sky. If he was patient, he could occasionally see the outline of a sentry posted atop the wall moving across the field of stars.

"You had a question." Kee's voice was rough.

Archie considered for a moment. Considered not

asking and letting her go to hell. That she could think so little of him, that he would ever just use a woman, take advantage of one.

"Why did you pull away from me after Italy?"

"Why did you?"

"What?" they both said in unison.

Archie would have laughed if it didn't hurt his heart so much.

"Damn it, Kee. You gave me back my mother. Then you shut down like a steel blast shield. Why?"

She sputtered for a moment. "I told you who I was. No one knows my past. Not my recruiter, certainly none of my soldiers in the 10th Mountain, not even the interviewers at SOAR induction. No one. And then you wouldn't even speak to me."

Archie closed his mouth and tried to remember the moment. So much had happened so fast. He'd never made love outdoors. And when she'd leaned her head on his shoulder, his heart had been gone. Given. "Sail, line, and anchor," as his father always said.

Their kiss while sitting on the stone wall. His hand wrapped around the tiny mar on her flesh that had almost stolen her life. He'd never held anything so precious.

Then, in those few minutes while the bus stopped and loaded, he and his mother forever changing their relationship for the better. They'd found each other over a bridge he'd never imagined, that Kee had built and crossed so effortlessly. She'd changed his entire past in that moment.

"You, Archie." His mother's voice a whisper as he held her close. "You are the most important thing I have ever done. I love you so much."

They'd never had many words, and hers had changed everything.

Maybe he had been distant from Kee, but not by intent.

"I had to rethink every memory, every event of my life from the new perspective Mother gave me. That you gave us. She is not skilled at speaking her thoughts, but I think she always did her best to constantly show her love. I can remember how exhausted she would be when she joined Dad and me for family events, and yet she did join. She didn't go to bed afterward, she went into her home office. I thought she loved her job more than she loved us." He closed his eyes to picture it and knew one of the many places he'd been wrong.

"I remember the sadness in Dad's eyes each time he watched her go. I held that pain against her as well. But now I know that he didn't hurt for himself, he felt sad for her. For the burden she's chosen to carry. I know that ever since the Iron Curtain collapsed along with the Berlin Wall, the pressure on her has been immense. I half thought she'd be a casualty of 9-11, simply from overwork."

He rubbed his face. How much had he increased his mother's burden with his misguided judgments? That was a painful misdeed he could never repay. Somewhere in the air on the way back to the carrier he'd realized that. But at least he could stop adding to it now. He'd sent her a long letter, which should be in her hands in another day or so. Telling her how sorry he was. How much he appreciated her. How he'd try to be more aware.

"Kee," he breathed the word like a prayer into the night. "You changed my life. You changed my mother's life. It took me a while to absorb that change. But you've given me the most important gift of my life. You gave me back my family."

Chapter 34

KEE STARED DOWN AT THE VAGUE SHADOW OF HER clenched hands. Her guts were churning. She hadn't eaten since this morning, or maybe last night, yet she felt close to puking.

"So, it wasn't me?"

"What do you mean?" Archie sat so close she could feel the heat of his body as a chill swept into the evening air. If the concrete of the stadium bleachers weren't re-radiating the day's heat she'd be downright cold.

"I thought—" Had she just been stupid?

"I thought that you wouldn't want—" She couldn't say it.

He didn't respond. He simply left her the quiet space to get her own shit together as if that was gonna happen anytime soon. Always the perfect gentleman. Even when pissed. Pissed and sore. He remained the best man she'd ever met.

"—wouldn't want someone from the streets. Who'd sold herself and her best friend to survive."

"Is that what all this is about?"

She nodded her head, knowing he couldn't see her, but it was all she could do. Her shoulders ached from hunching for so long. Her hair hung down like a curtain around her lowered head, shutting out all light.

Out of the dark, Archie rested a gentle hand on the

center of her back. Rested it there as gently as the summer breeze on the Italian hilltop.

Rested it there as the shakes took over. Shakes turned to sobs and to the first tears she'd ever cried but the once on the boat. She wept. Each tear a searing pain that scored her cheeks like hot phosphorous tracer tracks.

She hugged her knees to her chest and wrapped her arms around them. She curled tight around the pain shuddering through her body.

Archie held her. Both arms now tight around her. She couldn't even turn to rest her head against his shoulder. All she could do was sob and gasp.

"I. Was." The words ripped out of her gut. "So. Afraid."

"Shh. It's okay." He stroked her hair and she wept harder.

"So. Afraid. You wouldn't." Each word tearing her insides apart as it ripped free. "Want me." The words shook her to the core. They shredded the Kee that she knew and left her adrift. The only thing worse than saying the words was having them out in the world.

She couldn't breathe. Was past the ability to gasp breath. Not even breath to weep.

"Oh, Kee. I could not stay away from you if I tried." A soft laugh. One she felt through his chest pressed against her shoulder. "And I tried. I don't believe that I have ever been as unhappy as these last days without you."

"Re-re-really?" She was such a mess. How could anyone want her?

He squeezed her more tightly. Until her whole body curled against him. But she couldn't ease from her fetal ball.

He kissed her on top of the head. Like a holy

benediction, it washed over her. The sobbing eased. Her throat let go enough that she could breathe, which she did in wracking gulps almost as painful as her weeping. Her muscles let go enough that now she leaned against him rather than simply being clutched by him.

Archie slid a finger beneath her chin to lift her face. She wiped her tears and nose on the sleeve of her shirt.

But he didn't kiss her. He stopped with his mouth so close she could feel his breath. He slid his other hand down, not groping her breast as it brushed by. Down. Down until it rested on her side, just above her hip. Until it wrapped around where she'd been shot, where a hand had held her life in.

Then his lips whispered against hers.

Once again they sat on a stone wall around a sheep pasture. The Italian sunlight warming her skin. His heat scorching her insides. His mouth consuming hers with a feather touch and a deep caring with which no one had ever touched her before.

Kee needed to say a thousand things. But couldn't think of one of them. Her body still ached from her weeping. She had never wept with that soul-wrenching pain too big to let out. Not even at Anna's death. Not ever that she could recall. And she couldn't stop herself around Archie. Somehow he created a safe place for her. A place where that stupid heart out on her sleeve kept showing itself.

How was she supposed to think when a man kissed her like this? And for the first time, a man kissed her knowing her past and who she was. That was something new.

Archie kissed her with the perfect attention he brought to everything he did. His hand on her hip, his lips brushing hers ever so gently.

It made her feel…

She smiled against his lips, almost laughed, though her throat was still rough and it sounded more of a choked gasp.

"What?" Archie pulled back a whisper's length to ask, their lips still brushing.

"There was a moment. A moment I especially wanted to remember. So that I would know where to start. Or to start over. To pick up where we left off."

He nuzzled her neck and breathed in deep and long before exhaling on a sigh. "What moment? What happened?"

"Our pagers went off." Her voice sounded soft and slow, so languid she barely recognized it as her own. She rolled her head back to give him better access to the line of kisses he was placing along her collarbone.

He paused, then offered a low chuckle that erased the last of the chill that had wrapped around her this whole last week. Returning his lips to hers, he whispered a question.

"Kee?" A question that asked nothing and everything.

"Yes!" There was no other answer she could give, wanted to give. The lightness that wrapped around her filled her with a need. Not for sex. A need for a man. For one man. For this man.

No point in protesting, it would be a lie. No point in saying she didn't want and desire, her body was alive with need for his.

She reached back to tug off her shirt and bra with a single move.

Archie stopped her motion with a gentle touch. "No, let me."

But he didn't strip her. He didn't grab or peel or even pinch. Instead he traced her curves with infinite patience. Studied her in the dark like a critical terrain. The lightest trace of a single fingertip along her jawline, down her throat, and across her collarbone sent shivers that reached down her spine. He expanded his research, not attacking her breast but nuzzling the soft side through her shirt.

Kee floated, let all of her nerves calm and focus on the sensations Archie's actions evoked. For the first time in her life, she did nothing. Nothing but lace her fingers deep in his soft hair. Nothing but turn to allow his investigation to travel farther down a particularly good path.

When at long last he removed her clothes, he did so one piece at a time. He traced how each fold shifted across her skin. She lay stretched on her clothes when he took her in his mouth. Slowly, ever so slowly with the patience of a master strategist she was really and truly learning to appreciate, he lifted her pulse rate a beat at a time. Drove her upward on such a smooth-flowing curve that when she broke the surface, all she could feel was surprise and pleasure.

He didn't stop there. He took her higher than she'd ever been, until she floated disembodied in the night, arching against him, release flowing into release.

When at long last he entered her, he filled her so completely, so perfectly that she wept once more. The tears that slid from her eyes didn't burn. Didn't sear.

They healed. They mended and bound the pieces of her heart back together.

And when Archie kissed the tears away, drank in the ocean salt of her happiness, all she could do was float.

Archie drove her on and up until it scorched her body clean. Only then did he let himself go. She'd never felt so alive as the moment he settled onto her, her hands tangled in the luscious hair.

"I love you so much, Kee."

"Keiko." From Archie she wanted to hear it.

"Keiko."

Men always said they loved you after sex, easy to ignore that. But the sound of her real name in his breathless whisper against her ear.

That was something special, something important. And something she'd not easily forget.

Nor his hand which had never stopped holding her side as he'd reveled in her body.

That still held her life as if it were a precious thing.

Chapter 35

"GOOD MORNING."

"Oh, shit!" Kee looked up at Major Emily Beale. The blue eyes hidden by mirrored shades despite the pre-dawn darkness.

She tried to sit up. Really tried. But Archie lay tangled all about her, more or less on her.

Kee thumped his shoulder hard enough to bruise.

He woke up and shook his head, then he offered her that sleepy smile that started first in his eyes.

"You were wonder—" He cut off and furrowed his brow at her, finally noticing her frantic expression, or at least her tension.

He looked over his shoulder.

Then Kee felt his entire body flinch against hers as if he'd just been stung by a giant bee.

"Oh, shit!" He leapt to his feet, taking the blanket with him.

Kee could feel the cold night air slipping over her skin and realized she still lay naked, cushioned only by their clothes. At the last second she hooked the blanket and pulled it against her.

Archie stumbled free of it before finding his feet. He stood stark naked in front of the Major except for one sock.

He tried to salute. Thought better of it. Briefly shot for parade rest before moving his hands forward to cover himself. Then his knees finally gave out and he sat abruptly on the next row of seating. For some reason covered his knees rather than his crotch.

Kee thought about laughing, but instead watched the Major for her reaction. Fraternization could get them both discharged. He was an officer and she an enlisted, he could get court-martialed.

Major Beale stood at ease, turned three-quarters away from them as she scanned the field. The vague silhouettes of the tents, Hawks, and Chinooks barely visible as shadowed outlines.

"Quiet morning." She began descending the tiers of seating back toward the field fading into the blue-black of early morning

As soon as she was out of sight, they scrambled into their clothes without a word. Kee folded the blanket to the smallest bundle she could and tucked it under her arm.

She ran her fingers through her hair, trying to comb it into place.

When she turned to descend, Archie stopped her with a hand on her arm.

He slid a hand up her back and into her hair before kissing her, slowly and thoroughly, damning the growing light.

"Keiko." Again that perfect whisper that slid and wrapped around her spine.

"Archibald."

He cocked his head for a moment, then shook it. "No, that does not work, does it? To you, I am always Archie. Or maybe Professor."

"Whatever you say, Magic Man."

"Ouch!" He laughed, slapped her butt, and they headed for the field.

"Thanks for getting the blanket." Kee did her best to keep it tucked casually out of sight in case they met someone. "I didn't notice you leave to go get it."

"I didn't. You were lying on my clothes anyway. It isn't my habit to prance naked before my fellow officers, despite present evidence to the contrary. I thought you'd tucked it away in the dark."

Kee missed the step off the last riser and would have fallen onto the track if Archie hadn't steadied her.

"The Major?" She mouthed the question silently.

Archie shook his head.

One of the Ranger sentries?

Kee surprised herself to feel the heat rising to her face.

She thought she was long past being embarrassed by sex.

Chapter 36

"WHO'S BEEN MESSING WITH MY HAWK?" JOHN STORMED into the chow tent looking very big and very bad. He waved a logbook over his head. "When I find the mother, I'm gonna crush his head between these two hands."

He held them out like weapons. They were each the size of Kee's head.

He slammed the Hawk's maintenance logbook down on the table.

"This you, Smith?" He didn't even open the pages.

She held up both hands in innocence.

John glared at Archie, then headed over to confront Major Henderson's mechanic. Dusty James had just freshly returned from surfing off Australia with the ocean-bleached hair to prove it.

Kee glanced around and spotted Connie Davis, calm as could be, working her way down the chow line, getting her breakfast.

"John!" Kee called him back.

He ground around in place like an Abrams tank until he faced her, barrel aimed and ready to fire, his eyes burning like a laser-bright guidance system.

"Is anything actually done wrong?"

"How the hell would I know?" He tossed the book back down in front of her and flipped it open. He jabbed a finger down at the pages. "There's three dozen entries, half of them overlapping in a dozen different ways. Fuel

flow systems, nozzle and air flow adjustments, altera-
tions to the IRSS exhaust cowling that I've never seen
before. Is our heat signature masked better, or will the
next SAM missile within a hundred miles ram itself up
our tailpipe just because it can? How the hell would I
know?" He snapped the book shut. "Just tell me who to
kill, Smith. Who?"

"That would be me." Connie Davis stepped over
from the line still carrying her tray. Connie was taller
than Kee by several inches, but the top of her head still
barely reached John's chin. She probably weighed less
than one of his legs. "Every single change was made
according to factory specifications."

She turned her back on John and set her tray at the
table where she'd been eating alone all week. Kee had
finally started feeling bad about that, but she'd been
eating at odd hours to avoid Archie until now. John
stared down at the book in his hand and then at the
woman's back as she unfolded her napkin and set out
her silverware.

Kee had to give Connie points, it took guts to turn
your back on Big John, especially when he looked so
big and so bad.

He turned to Kee, seething with frustration. She could
hear his teeth grinding as he struggled to make sense of
what had happened.

Connie unloaded her tray and set it aside, cut a chunk
of sausage, and paused. Without turning, she spoke, "I
must say, especially for a forward theater of operations,
you have maintained the Black Hawk very well." She
ate her sausage as neatly as could be, clearly done with
the conversation.

John dropped onto the bench near Kee, almost flipping her into the air. He waved the book at her weakly, his expression so woeful that she had to laugh and reach out to pat his shoulder.

Before John could recover, Archie appeared with Dilya dancing by his side. All the life that had been squeezed out of her these last days by Kee's disagreement with Archie now flooded out of her in a single dam-bursting tidal wave. She danced up to John and patted a quick, two-handed drumroll on his knee. He managed a weak laugh and ruffled her hair.

She jumped into Kee's arms and rubbed her nose on Kee's. It tickled, Kee rubbed Dilya's back.

"The Kee and String Man like blan-ket?"

Kee stole a glance at Archie. He positively blanched, first going sheet-white, then beet red. So red, even John cast him a strange look.

Kee laughed and nodded her nose against the girl's. Then she leaned in until her mouth was at Dilyana's ear and whispered.

"Keiko says thank you to Dilyana." Then she pulled back and checked the girl's eyes.

A sharp nod and Kee knew that the girl understood her tryst with Archie and the story of the blanket were as private as their private names. Kee gave her a squeeze and then lifted her up and plopped her on her feet.

"Breakfast!"

Dilya was off like a shot.

She offered Archie her blandest smile.

He shook himself, a little like a wet dog, and followed in the girl's tracks.

John was watching her closely.

"So, John, did you get a lady out dancing with you?" Kee deflected his question, hopefully before it could finish forming in his mind.

He slowly relaxed into a smile, leaned an elbow on the table. "Oh yeah. A couple of 'em actually. But that Jennifer, wow! Almost put my back out trying to keep up with that lady. Two parts serpent the way she could twist around you like—"

"Whoa, Big John! Too many details."

He grinned and then really looked at her. "Any details you wanna be sharing?"

"Not a one I can think of."

With a loud laugh, he slapped her hard enough on the back that she lost half her air, then he headed off for the chow line.

Connie Davis stood looking at her. Had moved up so quietly, John hadn't even noticed her.

"I don't need to be defended. I can take care of myself."

Kee opened her mouth, then closed it, not knowing what to say. The woman was gone before Kee found an answer.

A woman strong enough to stand up to John in a rage certainly didn't need defending. But why didn't Connie even want a helping hand?

Chapter 37

"WHAT DID YOU DO TO MY BIRD, JOHN?" MAJOR Beale's voice came clear over the intercom. They weren't ten minutes into the night's mission.

Kee knew they were probably safe from any hostiles here, but sharpened her attention outside in case they had to put down. Clear field, a couple of goats, they should be okay.

"Wasn't me. What's wrong?" He sounded panicked.

Kee was a good mechanic, but she wasn't a chief. John was chief of the bird and he worried about it a lot. Which was a good thing considering the abuse the Major heaped on the poor thing.

"Nothing. She's found some more guts than I thought she had. Maybe she needed a vacation, too. At least she didn't have to eat so much fish. Mark had me eating trout three meals a day. I didn't know the man was a maniac fisherman when I married him. We'll have to live in the desert if I want to see him after we retire."

Kee looked over at John. His face was positively grim. Connie had better be careful if she didn't want her neck wrung.

"When did you get back, Archie?"

The Major must have enjoyed her vacation more than she was letting on to be so chatty. The 101st had released the Apache helicopters and they were watching those gunships' backsides, so there wasn't anything else going on. But usually they flew silent.

"Four days ago. Maybe five."

"What?"

"Two days out. Three on the boat. Then we were called back for a single mission. No point going anywhere after that."

And no point revisiting the hell that she and Archie had turned those everlasting days into.

"What was the mission? Why weren't we called?" Major Emily Beale did not sound happy.

"You were too far out of position, I suppose."

"And?"

Archie continued as if he didn't hear the venom seething over the headset.

"Clay and I flew. Kee and Connie were at the guns."

"What?" Big John burst out so loud it hurt Kee's ears, and not just through the headphones inside her helmet. He shouted louder than the rotor roar.

"My gun. What did she do to it?" He faced Kee. "What?"

Kee swallowed hard. "She, uh, did tear them down. Did something to the trigger assembly. Mine, too. Feels a little smoother when I—"

With a foul curse he turned back to his minigun and started checking it inch by inch in the faint glow of his night vision.

"It works fine, John. We took it for a run after she did it. It works fine."

He just cursed and kept checking the weapon. Then he froze.

"Wait a sec, Smith. She flew?"

"Specialist Connie Davis. Knew what she was doin'. Kinda pissed me off."

"Major, what's up with that?" Big John managed to sound respectful, barely.

"She's here a couple months ahead of schedule. Third woman into SOAR. Mark told me she was coming, none of us knew when."

"She messed with my bird. She messed with my gun."

Major Beale actually glanced back at Kee between the seats and offered her a smile. She mouthed, "Men."

Kee returned the smile. Not only did she respect the Major, she was starting to like Emily Beale. The woman did retain a sense of humor underneath all that hard-ass officer she wore like armor plating. And she'd been really decent about finding her and Archie all tangled up together.

"So, Archie." The Major's voice sounded so dry that Kee had to mute her microphone to not laugh at John. "What was the mission?"

"Solo. Long flight, too. I was glad for Clay's extra hand. We delivered a colonel in a beat-up Toyota pickup on the north slope of the Hindu Kush."

"The north slope. Solo." All of the humor had been stripped from the Major's voice. "You flew nine hours over bad terrain solo?"

"Eleven hours. Three midair refuels. Two in and one back out. We supposedly had a deep backup that wasn't directly privy to the mission, but I watched. We were definitely solo."

Kee swallowed hard. Helicopters just didn't do that. She'd felt much better thinking someone had their backside on the mission. Now she felt cold for the dangerous chance they'd taken.

"He routed us over valleys I had never seen before," Archie continued. "I do not think anyone ever has. We were way off the edge of the map. Not a single shot fired. We were low and fast, valley-and-pass the whole way."

"Pickup truck?" Big John didn't sound happy.

"Underslung." Kee decided she'd take some of the heat. "Connie checked the load points three times after I did them."

John groaned in pain for his helicopter and patted his hand on the deck in apology.

"The weird thing was, well, there were a lot of weird things. Like I didn't get to see what he had in the truck, but I saw him strap on an AK-47 and hide a Russian Makarov PM handgun when he changed." Kee thought about mentioning how he'd given her the creeps, but that was personal. Those pale, pale eyes of his, almost no color at all.

"The weirdest thing was the man himself. When we were close, he changed into native garb, upper-peasant level. Then climbed down a fast rope with no gloves. We were still two hundred miles out and moving at re-fuel speed when he went down. Why he didn't die is beyond me. He crawled in through the driver's window. He spent the last hour swinging out there in the wind."

Archie chimed in again, "He released a couple feet up. Popped me up a hundred feet without warning when he unloaded. If any radar had been watching, I probably came awfully close to being visible. If he'd waited even five more seconds, I could have dropped him pretty as could be. Probably jarred his spine hard."

"Their spines."

"Their?"

Kee nodded and then realized how much ten days on the ground had spoiled her. No one could see her nod.

"Yes. As you were pulling up and out, we got sideways on him. He had a passenger. I'm guessing native, but hard to really tell through the night goggles."

A silence descended in the helicopter. Only the rotor noise continued, usually a funky backbeat making her want to tap her feet, now just chopping away at the hard silence.

Kee checked out the window. They were still holding a high and back station. She imagined she could see a couple of rocket flares in the far distance, but it was too hard to judge if the Apaches were being allowed to take some of the heat this time. They were far enough out, they could be static across her night vision. She flipped the goggles back, but there was nothing to see tonight. Stars and mountains and a waning crescent moon rising in the east.

"Let me get this straight." The Major's voice sounded perplexed. An unusual tone for her.

"Some unidentified colonel gets Fort Campbell to call back one team. A mixed team at that. You then fly him five hundred miles over the worst terrain on the planet with no backup. No rescue possible. You drop him on the back side of nowhere with someone you didn't even know you carried as a passenger dangling for five hours in an underslung pickup truck."

Again the silence of the pounding blades.

"And don't forget that woman messed with my bird." John still sounded pretty grumpy. In any other situation, it would be cute.

"Noted, John." Again Beale showed her true colors for not taking him down a notch.

Kee would have told him to get the hell over it. The

Major knew how to treat her people. She could learn a lot from the Major.

Beale swiveled in her seat as far as her harness allowed and stared back at Kee.

"Definitely two aboard?"

Kee nodded since the Major was facing her. "Specialist Connie Davis can confirm it, ma'am."

She glanced toward Archie.

Kee couldn't see his response through the back of the seat that separated their positions, but whatever it was, the Major didn't like it. She faced forward, turned to Kee for a moment, then dropped back in her seat facing forward.

"Screw this." There was the distinct click as she keyed the mic. "*Viper*, this is *Vengeance*, come back."

"*Viper* here." Major Mark Henderson's voice sounded clear over the encrypted radio. Kee usually didn't notice the radio traffic from outside the aircraft, operations kept her mind elsewhere. She'd had commanders who kept their radio traffic off the internal intercom, but Beale believed in open communications. Damned decent of her, treating her crew like people.

"There's a situation we need to discuss."

"Fire away."

"At base."

A silence. A silence that stretched until it was painful.

"Now." Beale's voice left no question or doubt.

"Roger that." No hesitation in his response this time. Either Emily Beale had her husband whipped but good, or he was smart enough to trust his wife's instincts. There was a long pause. Either while he thought it over or while he radioed the overhead AWACS for clearance to withdraw. "Proceed. We're thirty-five minutes out."

"Roger. Moving. Out." Beale slammed the bird over hard. If Kee weren't strapped into her seat, she'd have flown out the gunner's window despite the M134 mini-gun that filled most of it. When the g-forces eased up enough, she glanced at John. He shrugged then tipped his head to relieve a crick in his neck. Exactly the same gesture Connie Davis had used.

Kee knew for damn sure that John wouldn't appreciate that bit of information.

Chapter 38

"Describe him." Major Mark Henderson sat at the head of the briefing table. Beale and John sat on one side, Kee, Connie, and Archie down the other. Clay had rotated stateside for his vacation and the refueling liaison was logging some air time on a Hercules mission somewhere to the west.

It was weird to be in the briefing tent in the middle of the night. Usually it was hot and bright with the evening sun, briefing before they flew at night. Now the shadowed space felt unsafe and secret, a single lantern dangling over the table offering spotty light at best.

Everyone else who'd seen him was here. He apparently hadn't eaten in the chow tent, slept in a bunk, or even crapped in a latrine. Should she have questioned his identity? But he had the pull to get Fort Campbell to issue a personnel recall.

Kee dropped a small bundle held together by a man's leather belt on the table.

"Maybe I can do better. He told me to burn this, but I, uh, forgot and left it on the Hawk."

"Forgot?" Emily arched one of those perfect eyebrows at her.

"Well," Kee refused to blush, "I had intended to do a little investigating first, but I was distracted."

Kee unrolled the belt. She started to set it aside, but something made her hesitate. The buckle was very distinctive and she'd seen something like it. She checked front and back of the belt, but saw no unusual markings. Then the prior memory came clear. Hank, who ran the bakery meth shop, showing her his newest toy.

She folded back the tongue hard and pulled on the buckle. It came free, pulled a long thin wire with it. It pulled out to two feet and stopped.

Kee didn't even have to look at it. "Guitar string. High E. Nasty as a garrote. As likely to cut as to choke. Pulled sharply, it will cut the voice box before the victim can protest." She turned the belt for everyone to see. A small white tag hung from the back of the belt leather. "Made in China."

Big John swallowed hard and glanced around the table. Archie also looked pale. The Majors looked angry. Connie watched her intently with those neutral, assessing eyes.

Kee continued her way through pants and shirt, Army issue. The Colonel's birds were still pinned to his collar points. He'd kept his boots, not unusual attire anywhere in the area. A small bundle of papers had been torn a half dozen times and stuffed into one of the shirt's pockets.

Kee sorted them by color and handed them out in little stacks. In moments they were each assembling pieces of the puzzle that had been the Colonel's past.

"James. Evans." Archie shoved a couple pieces together.

"Not Isaacson. He said his name was Isaacson. Jeff Isaacson."

"Is this the right picture?" John turned a set of four pieces torn and twisted across the middle of the face. Despite the raggedness of the tear, there was no question James Evans was their man. No beard in the photo and his haircut strictly Army, but the pale eyes were a definite match. She'd seen this guy somewhere before. Of course, after six years in the Army and SOAR, she'd seen a lot of officers.

"He's a colonel. At least that looks to be true." Major Beale inspected the bits and pieces in front of her.

"Who has some tape?"

Connie set a dispenser on the table at Henderson's request. As always, no wasted motion or comment, but absolutely prepared. Kee half expected her to open a thumbnail like a science-fiction cyborg and dispense the tape directly.

In a couple minutes they had the few papers put together.

"Anything else?" Major Henderson's voice was grim as he gathered up what little they had.

Kee looked around the table. No one really wanted to meet anyone's gaze.

She looked at Connie.

She looked back at Kee with completely expressionless eyes. A bland hazel, with sparkles of green.

With a shiver Kee turned to face the Major.

"He gave me the creeps, sir."

The Major's eyes were nearly as light a blue as the Colonel's, but they were alive with the heart and pride of the man behind them.

"When the Colonel looked at you, there was no one home."

"Anyone else?"

Archie nodded. "I would have to agree with Sergeant Smith's assessment. I would class him as a stone-cold killer. Not Special Forces. He didn't have the skills that any operator would have. Regular Army, but a real hard case, sir."

"Is that it?" Once more he scanned the table.

—⁓—

In the dim light, Dilyana reached out a hand to pull on The Kee's sleeve. The Kee jumped in surprise. Everyone at the table spun to stare at her. Dilya bit her lip and did her best to be brave and not run away. She had listened and watched from the shadows until her curiosity overcame her shyness in front of so many people.

There was no mistaking the big man's curse, and she knew enough of the words to know the Leader Man was not happy that she stood there.

"What is it, Dilya?" The Kee's voice came soft and quiet as it always did.

She held onto The Kee's sleeve for confidence, then pointed with the other hand at the papers the Boss Man had gathered.

The Kee reached out and took them. She spread them out on the table up close.

It was the picture Dilya was interested in. She studied it carefully, twisting it back and forth in the light.

She couldn't tell. Not really. But she knew she was right.

"One dog. Two dog." She held up her fingers, one then another.

The Kee told the others at the table something about *Go, Dog. Go!*

"Two men? One man. Two man."

She didn't know the word, but nodded. It sounded right.

She pointed to the picture she held. "One dog."

Then she pointed as if there was a second picture.

"Two dog *qilmoq* Dilya mother and father dead."

The Kee spun to face her.

"Two dogs." Then she imitated drawing the pictures she'd made on the boat.

The Kee pointed toward the sleeping tent.

Dilya nodded and bolted. She knew where the drawings were, still folded carefully in The Kee's bag.

She was back in moments, and smoothed them out on the table in front of The Kee. Everyone leaned in to look.

The Kee nodded. "The same." She wrapped an arm around Dilya and pulled her in close but didn't turn from looking at the photos.

Dilyana asked her question again, softly, "Kee *qilmoq* dead?"

She'd taken Dog One away. To kill him?

The Kee looked at the picture. Then she cursed.

Dilya didn't know the words, but they sounded nasty.

"No. Kee no make dead."

But she'd promised. The Kee had promised. Promised and lied.

Dilya turned to run, but The Kee grabbed her by both arms. Held her while she struggled until Dilya stopped, knowing she couldn't break free.

The Kee brought her face very close.

"Kee *qilmoq* Dog One and Dog Two dead. Understand? Kee will."

Dilya watched her eyes. Saw the truth there.

She whispered, "The Keiko say?"

"*Ha*. Very *ha*."

That was all Dilya needed to know.

———※———

The picture of Dog Two wasn't a photograph, but it might be enough to identify the man to someone who knew him.

Kee slid the two images across the table to Major Henderson.

"Sir, I would say there is a very good chance this was the passenger in the Toyota pickup. I didn't get a clear look at him, a brief glance in profile only, but it could be."

The Major studied the photo ID and the two drawings for thirty seconds without anyone making a sound.

"Okay, folks. I'm going to wake up some folks at Fort Campbell and find out what is going on here. Emily, it's after 4 a.m. It will be light by the time you get there. I want you to take your crew and Specialist Davis back to where they picked up the truck. See if you can find anything. Do not discuss this with anyone who's not in this room right now. Clear?"

"Clear, sir," they all said in unison.

"Sir?" Connie stopped everyone halfway to their feet. "Davis."

"It is 6:14 p.m. Sunday evening stateside. You won't have to wake them."

Kee wondered if he were biting his lip to keep from laughing at her. Of course, he knew the time at Fort Campbell, all SOAR fliers always did. Had to. And the weather too, in case a family call was routed to them. No matter where you were, you told family you were in Fort Campbell.

"Thank you, Davis."

Chapter 39

IT WAS PAST DAYBREAK BY THE TIME THEY LANDED AT the nameless spot in the desert. A hill and two ridges made a natural bowl hiding its secrets, except from directly above. The ridges were rocky spines, the hill was really just a lump in the local topography compared to the Hindu Kush towering just to the north. A wide goat trail led through the bowl, perhaps wide enough to drive the truck along. The area had accumulated a fine layer of windblown sand deep enough that few plants managed to secure their roots.

For five minutes they walked back and forth across the area.

"It was right here." Kee pointed downward.

Archie looked back and forth between the two ridges, clearly rebuilding their profiles in his mind.

"I would have thought it was a few dozen paces farther east, but you may be right."

Connie Davis nodded her simple agreement with Kee.

John and Major Beale studied the ground carefully around their feet.

"Two more minutes, then we're gone." The Major didn't sound happy. "Doesn't look as if there is anything to learn here."

They paced back and forth over the area where Colonel Isaacson or Evans or whoever the hell he was had parked his pickup truck. And she and Archie had lifted it airborne.

On the verge of giving up, Kee's boot caught on something harder than sand. She kicked at it a couple times to bring it to the surface.

A half-used roll of black duct tape. It was military grade. Super strong for patching anything from an emergency field kit to a shot-up helicopter rotor. She held it up for the others to see.

"Hundred-mile-an-hour tape. He couldn't be caught with anything that would tag him as U.S. Army, so he buried it."

They dug a hole quickly and two feet down they uncovered an M4A1 carbine, an Army-issue KA-BAR knife, and a small notebook.

Kee checked the rifle while Beale glanced through the book.

"He couldn't carry this with him." Kee pulled back the bolt far enough to see that the chamber was empty. She popped the magazine, it was full. Full of cartridges and sand. "It would raise too many questions if someone saw it. That's why he had the AK-47. This looks fine, though I'd rather not fire it until we knock some of the grit out."

The Major slapped the book against her thigh, knocking a spray of sand loose. She reopened the book.

"A lot here I don't understand. Numbers and times, but they don't relate to anything."

Kee and Connie crowded around, but Kee couldn't puzzle it out either. Except for a date, three days away.

Kee slung the M4 over her shoulder and turned back to watch the diggers as the Major flipped one by one through the blank pages that filled most of the book.

The Major swore. Archie and John stopped digging, nothing else had come to light anyway. "What?"

The Major pulled a picture out that had been stuck between the pages.

It showed the two men, they matched the photo and Dilya's drawings. And two women, clearly related, perhaps sisters. They stood side by side, but just as clearly aligned with the two men who flanked them.

Kee studied the photo. Pretty, generously built, smiles for their men, native garb, native coloring. A background of oddly rounded hills, scrub plants, and small trees.

Then she noticed the writing and echoed the Major's curse. Along the bottom were four dates, one positioned directly beneath each person. Below the two women was the date, "30 May 2005."

"What does that mean?" Archie stared over her shoulder. "What are the other two dates? Hey. That's three days from now. Marriage dates? But why would they be different for the men?"

Kee didn't need to wait for the Major to flip to the front of the notebook. The same date.

The two women with the one date in the past, the two men with another in the future. The very near future.

"Oh, shit!"

They all turned to look at her.

"Not marriage. Date of death. Colonel Evans and Dog Two know the date of their own deaths, three days from now."

Chapter 40

"WHAT DO YOU DREAM OF, ARCHIE? FOR THE FUTURE."

Kee sat with Archie and Dilya high in the stadium, just a few rows below the sentries. All the choppers were still huddled about the field except a pair of Little Birds that had gone back to the carrier for their 120-hour service.

The dark had dragged its feet this evening, which was fine with Kee. The sunset had been as spectacular as the stars which now studded the night sky.

They were at a standstill while SOAR command chewed on the information they'd sent, including a copy of the photo, Dilya's drawings, and scans of the scrawled notes in the book.

Sitting together in peace with the helicopters nearby, but almost lost in the dark, she felt safe. Night Stalker to the core.

Dilya sat behind her, light tugs on Kee's scalp as the girl braided her hair. Either by touch, or perhaps the girl possessed built-in night vision. She never failed to find Kee either in the light or dark. The braids would be uncomfortable under her helmet, but Dilya enjoyed doing it so much Kee couldn't bring herself to complain. And each braid was a different style. Sometimes to tease her, Archie would reach over and quietly undo a particularly complex braid. Patient as the sea, Dilya would start again.

"I don't dream. I like flying with Major Beale very much. I like the missions, of course. I like the sense of purpose. But I never looked much beyond the next assignment. Figured if I ever walked away, I'd work with Dad building boats. Maybe take over the business some day."

Kee turned her head enough to see his profile without pulling her hair from Dilya's hands. He leaned his elbows back on the riser behind him and gazed up at the brilliant stars.

Once again, he surprised her. She understood not dreaming when you didn't expect to survive the streets. But was Archie so forthright that he really never thought beyond what came next for himself?

And boats? She could picture him working with his mom more easily than building boats. He was clearly the strategist of the chopper.

"I should say I never used to dream beyond that." In that uncanny way of his, he found her hand unerringly without looking down and laced their fingers together.

Kee could feel her skin tighten, her clothes needing a tug to once again feel right as her body responded to his simplest touch.

He turned to look at her. His eyes invisible except for the slightest sparkle of reflected starlight. But she didn't need to read them for the heat to wash over her face.

"Me?"

He hesitated, then a slow nod. And she could feel that slow, lopsided grin of his, even if she couldn't see it.

Kee looked away. He dreamed of her? No one had ever done that. No one had even pretended.

Sergeant Kee Smith stood alone.

Faced the world in her own way at her own pace. And the Kee Smith she knew only had one pace. Full thrust.

Now an eleven-year-old girl braided her hair and a SOAR officer held her hand and spoke of dreams.

She tried to breathe past the tightness in her chest.

Chapter 41

PRESIDENT PETER MATTHEWS STARED AT THE SCREEN on the Situation Room wall.

"Tell me."

General Brett Rogers, Chairman of the Joint Chiefs of Staff, stood and strode to the screen.

"The more our analysts chew on this one, the worse it looks. It started as a lead at a forward air base south of the Hindu Kush. They kicked it to Fort Campbell, which bumped the problem to SOCCOM. We're now twenty hours in and we know there is trouble, and we think it may be bad. Definitely international, potentially disastrous."

"First slide," he called out to the room whose only other occupant was Daniel Darlington, the President's Chief of Staff. Some orderly hidden in the next room put a picture of a rugged soldier in his fifties up on the room's center screen. A bio ran down one side.

"Colonel James Evans has a long and distinguished career. He goes back to Operation Urgent Fury in Grenada, Desert Storm, every military action in the last thirty years, he's been in it. Always at the front. We've used the man on several high-security missions. He isn't trained Airborne, nor Special Forces."

Peter shared a smile with his Chief of Staff, who looked as at ease here as he had when he'd been Chief Assistant to the ex-First Lady. They both knew Brett had been the Commander of Special Operations Central

Command before being tapped as Chairman of the Joint Chiefs of Staff. He still defended his own, not that it would slow the man for a moment if someone in his former command actually screwed up.

"He tried for SEALs and Spec Ops a couple times each. Frankly, no one wanted him. He was a bit of a wild card. But he has a killer instinct we found useful and he also had a real habit of not ending up dead. Known for taking matters into his own hands a little too often. He even hit the news a couple times. You may remember the forces who wanted to take Baghdad for President Bush Senior. Evans's unit struck almost fifty miles past the Kuwait-Iraq border before we reeled him back in."

Peter hadn't heard of it, but he'd been in junior high school and mostly thinking about girls. Daniel shook his head. Daniel was half a decade younger and had been learning how to add single digit numbers at the time. Peter did his best to nod sagely for the General to continue.

Brett Rogers cleared his throat. "Frankly, Mr. President, we're worried. We've talked to his commander. Evans took an extended leave, hadn't taken any in over three years, now he's been on his own for over a month. No one that we've spoken to has any idea what he's been doing. His personal effects are gone as well. No parents, no siblings, can't find any girlfriends. He just flat disappeared."

"What are his most likely objectives?" Peter had slowly adapted to these Sit Room meetings. Being the youngest President in history didn't make him any less the President. If he asked enough questions, the experienced people in the room gave him all the information he needed to make decisions.

"That's what bothers us. We don't know. But the problem kept getting escalated because it has all the earmarks of a covert operation. Lower-level analysts kept bumping it up, hoping that it would eventually reach someone's level of security clearance. But it didn't." He called out for a map.

Northern Afghanistan popped up on the screen.

"The pilot's report placed him fifty miles short of the Uzbekistan border, but not on any road that we have on any map. We've redone the imaging with a couple of unmanned Global Hawk recon birds we had in the area. Four overflights in the last twelve hours. This is what we have."

Three images came up on the wall, the second two clearly close-ups of the first. A pair of tire tracks appeared, starting from nowhere, descending down the mouth of a widening valley. That's where he must have landed.

The close-up scrolled rapidly along the tire tracks. They disappeared several times, but after a little hunting, they locked back onto them.

The image stopped abruptly enough for Peter to jerk forward in his chair.

"A windstorm wiped the area clean beyond this point. We've searched for white Toyota pickups along this general heading for a hundred miles. Over forty have been located, they are the camels of modern desert warfare. And also the vehicle of choice for any wealthy farmer or opium runner. In the last seven hours we've eliminated about half of the suspect vehicles. We could be chasing a ghost. If he changed vehicles, we'd never know."

Peter stared at the high-altitude close-ups of three

dozen white pickup trucks. Several had an animal tied in the back, sheep or goat. These had red Xs in the corners. A few had a dozen men piled in the back. Either working as a local bus, or a group of insurgents. Two had the clear profile of large machine guns mounted, their black outline clear against the white top of the cab.

Each vehicle without an X had a number in red. A list on a side screen was scrolling through the analysts' comments on each vehicle.

"Boil it down for me, Brett."

"We don't know where he is. We don't know what he's planning. We don't know where he's heading. But we have a general direction. Because it is Colonel Evans and because he used his single strongest covert operations connection to arrange a ride from SOAR to cross the Hindu Kush in a hurry, we know he has a definite target and a timeline that is now only two days away. Until we know more, we're recommending a heightened alert to all embassies and bases throughout the region. And that requires Presidential authorization."

The long-range map came back up. White dots appeared all over the map. Over half had red Xs. Others were far to the east or west of where Colonel James Evans had landed. Even as he watched, red Xs appeared on two of those vehicles and they blinked off the side-screen list.

"If he continued straight out of the valley and due north across the desert…" Daniel leaned forward to stare more closely at the screen. "There's nothing there."

Brett scrolled the screen down. It was too large an area. There were a dozen possibilities. At some point, he'd pick up a road and could go anywhere.

Another pickup disappeared, then two more were added by analysts working away in the Pentagon.

"We need more help." And he knew exactly who to ask.

Chapter 42

"Hey, Em."

"Hello, Mr. President." The video occupying the center of the Sit Room screen showed Major Emily Beale. He'd seen her just a few months ago at her wedding, but he'd forgotten how beautiful she was. She may have been his childhood friend, but the woman took his breath away every time.

"So formal with your Commander-in-Chief?" They had grown up next door to each other, after all.

"My crew is here with me, Sneaker Boy. You want to go a couple rounds in front of them?"

"Hello, Mr. President." Major Mark Henderson leaned in over his wife's shoulder.

"Hi, Mark. How's married life?"

"How are we doing on Colonel James Evans? Something nasty if we're getting a call from you, sir."

"You never were any fun, Mark." For one thing, he'd captured the woman of Peter's dreams. And he'd done it before Peter had been smart enough to figure that out. Actually, Emily Beale had done the choosing, and Peter knew from years of experience, nothing could change the woman's mind once she made it up.

"Nope!" Mark's grin belied the statement. They'd had a particularly memorable bachelor party in the White House involving too many cigars, too much brandy, and an expensive poker game, which Mark had won handily, as you'd expect from a career officer. Peter had been totally outclassed and merely watched the last half of the game and surprised himself at how much he liked Em's fiancé.

"We tracked him out of the valley and forty miles north before losing his tracks to a sandstorm."

"That would put him almost to the Uzbekistan border."

"Right. But we don't know where he's headed or why. Every hint of his past is a dead end. He didn't have one buddy, nothing. A loner. And a damned skilled one. The second man is a dead end so far, but we're still working on it."

Even liking Mark, it was hard to look at the two of them, practically cheek to cheek in front of their camera.

"K2?" a voice sounded from someone on Emily's side.

"Who said that?"

Emily and Mark shifted back a bit, revealing a tall, thin man with a mop of brown hair and a short Asian-American woman by his side.

"First Lieutenant Archibald Stevenson III, sir. We met at the wedding, my mother introduced us."

The son of Betty Stevenson, high recommendation. Personally, the woman scared the crap out of him. Her team's insights into future geopolitical alliances and reconfigurations were downright spooky in their accuracy. And their long-range predictions frequently cost him more than a night's sleep. The long-range stuff occasionally so ugly he mostly prayed for it to happen in someone else's administration.

The Sit Room orderly splashed Stevenson's picture and short bio up on a screen. He'd flown with Emily for almost a decade, an even higher recommendation.

"So, what's K2? I thought that was a mountain in Nepal. He can't be heading there."

"Actually, sir, K2 the mountain is on the border of Pakistan and China about three hundred miles northeast of here." The man didn't even bat an eye at correcting the President. Just as formidable as his mother. "K2 is what they call Karshi-Khanabad air base in Uzbekistan. We were there until 2005 when the Russians and Chinese convinced the government to throw us out."

An image came up on a side screen. It looked like any single-strip airport he'd ever seen.

"Why there? What's the connection?"

"It is the only military asset in the area."

"Did he —" Emily started.

"—Evans serve there?" Daniel finished.

That always bothered Peter. They did that a little too often for his liking. Yes, he wanted a smart man for Chief of Staff. But he was a little too fast sometimes. Peter smiled and remembered his mother's advice from her years as a federal judge. "Surround yourself with people smarter than you and listen to them." Well, between Emily and Daniel, there were two very, very sharp minds working on this.

Colonel Evans's bio was returned to the screen and scrolled down.

"Four years, Em. He served there from the day we took residence in 2001 right up to the shut down on May 29, 2005. Well done, team. Now, why?"

Chapter 43

EMILY LOOKED AT THE PEOPLE GATHERED AROUND her. Mark close behind. Archie and Kee practically attached at the hip. Did they have any idea how obvious they were? She'd have to warn them if any upper-tier officers came around. Had she and Mark been that obvious? Emily almost laughed. No, they'd spent too much time hating each other's guts. Or at least she hated Mark's. He claimed that he'd been besotted from the first moment he saw her but had been careful not to let her catch even a hint. The fact that she'd done the same only made the joke worse.

Big John and Connie hovered to either side like bookends, barely able to stand being in the same tent.

The image on the laptop of K2 bothered her, but she couldn't place her finger on why.

"Could you zoom in to the right end of the airfield?" Archie asked and leaned in.

Emily watched the screen closely. Jets, a lot of jets. Russian jets. Mostly old ones.

"A lot of old MiGs. Couple Yak bombers. And some Sukhoi, a few 27s but mostly the SU-24 Fencers." Of course, Archie was first across the line, even faster than the guys at the White House who were serving the images. Labels started appearing even as the image continued to expand until the angular taxiways filled the screen.

"What are those?" She pointed to the squared-off humps beside the taxiways. Even as she asked, she knew the answer.

"Hardened bunkers. What's tucked away in those?"

More labels began appearing. "This is our latest intelligence." General Brett Rogers's gruff voice sounded clear across the encrypted link to Washington. The Chairman of the Joint Chiefs had offered to wrestle her father for the right to give her away at her wedding. Awfully sweet, and more than a little scary that the leader of the U.S. military thought so highly of her.

"Much of which dates back to 2005," he continued, "when the SCO had the Uzbekistan government kick us out of K2. It was a damned useful base. Would save you boys, er, and gals, a lot of flight time if we could still station you there."

The labels that kept appearing were consistently older aircraft.

"This is all third-gen gear." Archie leaned in for a closer look. "There isn't a single fourth-generation piece of equipment. Some of these are even second-generation fighters. This is like Davis-Monthan Air Force Base where we store our old fighters and bombers outside Tucson. High desert, dry, planes left there to rot. Except they don't rot."

"New or not, I would wager that a lot of it still works." Kee was thinking the same thing she was.

"Hold on. Pan right please." Archie this time. He and Kee were working in some kind of synchronicity. He'd always been tentative. Brilliant, but tentative. With Kee at his side, her old friend spoke with a clarity and confidence Emily hadn't heard outside of actual combat in a decade of flying together. Sergeant Kee Smith had earned her place on Emily's crew but still kept revealing more surprises.

"MiG-29s. That's some serious group of fighters." A MiG-23 scared Emily enough, but her Hawk stood some chance against one. The half-dozen 29s was a different matter.

"Our analysts here are saying they haven't been seen to move in over a decade."

"Pull way back." Now Kee was taking the lead. "More. More. More."

"There!" And Emily saw it. Each white pickup truck trailed a little line of white dots as the analysts tracked them over the countryside. Most went in circles, taking the kids to school, picking up groceries, etc. Some went farther, running sheep to market or insurgents over the border.

A series of four separate tracks stood out. The first was their known one, Colonel Evans's Toyota, the one they wanted. They'd picked up another a dozen miles into Uzbekistan, out in the desert far from any road. The dots weren't connected, they were mapped as separate trucks. But the first two followed the same general line, as did the next two. The latest was on the road system now and headed straight for K2.

"There's our man."

Four images flashed up. A white pickup truck with nothing of note except a small bundle in the rear cargo area.

"That's where he stowed the camouflage net when we picked him up along with a dozen cans of fuel. You can see, he's discarded the cans he's emptied."

Sure enough, the truck bed was emptier with each photo.

Kee snapped her fingers. "The camo net. That's why the line was more broken than you'd expect. They hid under the camo net whenever they stopped."

Kee had proved herself to be an exceptional gunner and rock-steady under fire. But she fought against everything so hard that Emily had been reluctant to trust her. One of the biggest votes in her favor was the little girl. To engender such trust from a child spoke volumes about a person. And her association with Archie spoke volumes as well, though in a different language. Despite a presented attitude of promiscuity, she was proving very loyal to one man.

Kee Smith remained a puzzle to Emily. So rough, never finished high school, but ate up advanced Army training with scores she and Archie had trouble achieving. Trusting no one except herself. No, that wasn't quite right. Once her loyalty was won, Emily was sure Kee Smith would die to protect you. But that loyalty wasn't given without serious proof. Dilya had won that, but even Archie didn't appear to be all the way there yet. Oddly enough, Emily thought maybe she herself had.

The girl now looked at her like an idol, which certainly wasn't how they'd started. She'd caught the reflection of Kee's spiteful salute that first day in the window of her Hawk. She'd almost turned and taken the woman down, but she was so sick of being the only female combatant in SOAR that she decided to wait and see.

"There." Emily followed Kee's pointing finger. She didn't see it at first. Then...

"Two dogs." An elbow stuck out the passenger side window of the third image.

Emily smiled to herself, glad she'd waited.

—∿—

"Can you get to them? Before they get there?" the President asked anxiously.

Emily glanced at Archie while she worked the figures herself. Early morning now. Fourteen hours of daylight in this season. Evans's distance to K2. She shook her head and Archie hesitated, then nodded reluctant agreement.

"Sorry, sir. Even if we flew the first leg in the daylight to strike a couple hundred kilometers inside a supposedly friendly country, we can't beat him to K2. The fact that they actually aren't friendly means we'd have to be that much more careful, which means slower. He'll be there before we could get him, probably even if we left now and flew the whole mission in daylight."

Did she need to explain to the President again about the dangers of daylight flying? There was a reason that SOAR flew their missions under the cover of dark. They were good, damn good. But during daylight maneuvers, all the ground-hugging you could do didn't count much to the overflying fighter jet or the anti-aircraft guns.

SOAR worked because they ruled the night using methods and training no other nation had yet duplicated. Even the other divisions of the U.S. military hadn't managed SOAR's proficiency in the dark. Some day another nation would, and SOAR would have to rethink itself as they had for the thirty years since their founding.

Peter's lack of any military experience prior to becoming Commander-in-Chief worried her at times. He meant well, but he didn't always listen.

"I'll trust your judgment on that one, Em."

Maybe he did listen. Finally.

"So, what do we do?"

"We now know where. Let's work on what and when."

Chapter 44

KEE LOOKED UP AS ARCHIE SET HIS TRAY DOWN ON THE table. He looked hammered. Moving slowly as he climbed over the bench. He didn't even take his food off his tray.

"How is it that you look as perky and stunning as always?" Even his voice sounded tired. And still he complimented her. The man was so sweet.

Kee felt wide awake and completely frustrated.

First, she couldn't get over the fact that she'd talked to the President. The Commander-in-Chief himself. That stupid old line of, "You've come a long way baby," kept rattling through her head. She didn't even know where it came from, something her mother used to say as she shot up, but absolutely true. Six years ago, she'd been a grunt in Army basic training. And she'd just spent hours talking to the President of the United States. Pinching herself hadn't made it go away.

She'd done her best to stay in the background. Archie had really stepped to the fore, often way ahead of the best analysts the Pentagon could throw at the problem. She felt so proud of him she couldn't wipe the grin off her face. And Emily Beale. Kee would never look at the woman the same again. She'd been so at ease with the President. So smooth and cool and unflappable. Everything a woman should be. Kee wanted to be like that some day.

Second, they'd spent hours more studying K2 and Evans's history. Something wasn't making sense. A career officer clearing out all of his belongings and going rogue over a hostile border under his own orders pointed to a disaster in the making.

Was the truck a bomb? But most of the bed had been empty rather than packed with an explosive of any sort. No one could pin down what, where, or when Evans's plan would go. Pin down? They couldn't even come up with a distant whiff of it.

And they'd lost another half a day on their deadline.

They'd discussed infiltrating a squad of Delta Force operators. But to do what? No one knew. And putting a squad that far into unfriendly territory needed more than a guess.

Evans was rushing to a foreign desert air base with reasonable security, stuck out far away from everything. But he wasn't a pilot. Couldn't fly a plane, that anyone knew about. It made her head hurt even thinking about it. Why would he go there?

"I'm stunning because I'm five years younger and much fitter than you are." The latter was a lie, she could attest to that intimately. Archie was immensely fit in so many nice ways.

No rise from him at all. He really must be tired. He could always find a leer for her. They'd been working this for over thirty hours, but she felt wide awake. Awake as if… As if something were out of place and self-preservation was keeping her on her toes until she found the problem. But she didn't have a clue where to look.

Big John slid in looking as tired as Archie. They'd

left Dilya asleep on the conference table with a blanket spread over her. Since there was no way to keep the girl away, they'd let her hang out in the background. Other than a brief introduction to the President as the artist of sketch number two, she'd stayed out of range of the web camera.

The President had been genuinely decent and thanked Dilya. The highest and the lowest meeting each other across ten thousand miles. Kee hadn't been able to speak when his face showed on the screen. But once they were looking at Evans's background and K2, she managed not to think about speaking directly to the Commander-in-Chief and the Chairman of the Joint Chiefs of Staff.

The highest and the lowest…

"Professor, hey, Archie, wake up." He'd almost nodded forward into his soup. She kicked his knee under the table and he jolted upright. John had rested his elbow on the table and his head on his fist, he appeared to be asleep sitting up.

"I may have an idea." She ignored Archie's groan, but he blinked hard and focused on her.

"Evans was stationed out of K2 for four years, so he knows the base well."

"Right."

"He always played the edge before that, hopping around from one war to the next. Then bang, he hits Karshi-Khanabad and sticks."

"Okay." Archie was actually watching her now.

"I was thinking about the lowest and the highest. Dilya speaking to the President. For God sakes, me speaking to the Commander-in-Chief. How's that for bizarre. But never mind. For four years Colonel Evans had some reason to stay put, probably the woman in the photo. Whatever it was, he had to make some interesting contacts in the Uzbekistan military while he was stationed there."

Archie blinked at her like an owl. Once. Twice. Then it hit him and he was wide awake, too.

"The high and the low. The number-two dog, the one he made ride in the truck."

"Mr. Two Dog's the high one. High inside Uzbekistan."

"And either Evans has something on him…"

"Or the other way around."

"Do you want the scary version?" Kee wished she hadn't thought of it.

"Just what I need, a scary version." He shrugged. "I have no clue. Hit me."

"Remember the photo, the two dogs with the two women. Maybe they're in it together?"

For a long second they stared at each other frozen across the table.

Archie spoke first. "And I thought you just had a great body."

She couldn't stop her smile.

"You're awesome, Kee. I love you."

He wasn't saying the words right after sex. They were sitting there in the chow tent. And he said he loved her. She wanted to deny it, cast it away, pretend he was joking. She wanted to hold it close, cherish it, cradle it in her deepest memory forever. Mostly it scared her to death.

Maybe she'd imagined it.

John's head slipped off his fist. He shook himself for a moment, then aimed a wobbly thumbs-up across the table.

"Way to go, Arch." Then he laid his head down on his arm and fell solidly asleep this time.

She hadn't imagined it.

—◦◦◦—

"Sirs. Wake up. We have to call Washington," Kee called into Beale and Henderson's tent. "Wake up!"

After a brief crash, Major Mark "The Viper" Henderson shoved aside the flap of the curtain wearing only underwear. Briefs, not boxers.

Kee did her best not to look down. Every bit of lean that Archie had going for him, the Major embodied in the category of seriously built.

"What in the hell? I've been asleep for…" He looked at his wrist but no watch wrapped there.

"Fourteen minutes." The sour voice of Emily Beale sounded over his shoulder, then she shoved him aside. She wore a light nightie that hid almost nothing and made her legs look even longer than usual.

Kee checked and Archie's eyes were bugging out. She punched his shoulder.

He glanced at her then blushed furiously.

"Sorry to wake you, sirs. But we have to call Washington."

"And why would that be?" Beale leaned against her husband who held onto the tent pole to remain upright.

"We have a lead on the identity of dog number two. And it's bad."

Archie found his voice. "We're betting he's a pilot."

—◦◦◦—

"It checks out. Once they narrowed the field of search, the match wasn't hard." General Rogers pointed at the profile on the Sit Room wall. "There just weren't that many high-ranking military at Karshi-Khanabad during those years. Only five aren't accounted for, four now. We thought they were all dead."

Peter rubbed his eyes trying to focus on them. Being President should mean they let him get enough sleep. That wasn't happening as much as he'd like. Maybe if he issued an Executive Order commanding himself to get more sleep...

Daniel, for once rumpled in his suit and tie askew, pinched the bridge of his nose.

"The second person in the truck, our Dog Two, is General Hamad Arlov," the General continued. "Commander of their Red Hammer fighter-bomber squadron. One hell of a pilot. The Sukhoi SU-24 was his plane, flew the first one the Uzbekistanis ever received. Never flew anything else that we know of. It barely cracks Mach 1, which is good news for us. And it is a two man fighter-bomber, making it a likely choice for the two men. The first catch, Arlov flies it like a magician. The second catch, we still don't know why they're doing this."

Daniel leaned in toward the file picture, where it displayed next to the little girl's sketch and the four-person photograph. No question. Absolutely the same man.

"What's his issue?"

Peter didn't care. Wait. Yes. He did. Colonel Evans's motives had proved a dead end. If they found General Arlov's gripe, maybe they could line it up with Evans's history and figure out what was about to happen. Because there was no question about it, something was about to happen.

"Okay. So, tell me."

"This is the last shot we have of him. It's a BBC News photo of the day our last airplane left K2. There he is in the distant foreground." Rogers drew a circle with a light pen.

"You sure that's him?" One of the voices from Emily's end of the wire.

"Our analysts are sure, I'm going to trust them."

"And this is the last time he was seen?" It was that other woman, Kee Smith.

Cute, too. Damned cute. Peter shook his head trying to focus his exhausted mind on the problem at hand. Of course, the last time he'd been attracted to a large-chested woman he'd ended up married to Katherine. He shuddered at the memory. Focus.

"Last time we have him on any image or sighting."

Or sighting. So, they had a man on the ground at K2. He glanced at the General, who shook his head.

"We kept an agent on the ground there until 2008. It was one of the most boring assignments we've ever given. We moved our agent elsewhere two years ago."

Figured. You couldn't cover every inch of the whole planet, especially not a sleepy desert air base.

Peter put his head down on the table for a moment and tried to concentrate.

"Okay." He looked at the screen. Everyone had their motives. In any negotiation, you just had to unravel who wanted what and why. And the motive was always in the past. People made the mistake of thinking it had to do with the future, but it didn't. A robber didn't rob a bank because he wanted to be rich. He did it because he was sick of being poor.

"First, we have a colonel who liked life at K2 and probably wasn't too happy at being forced to leave for reasons unknown. Second, we have an Uzbekistani general who liked life at K2 and would be very unhappy at losing all his status and perks of being a commander at an air base busy with American military. Third, we have two men and two women. The two women died, if that's what those dates are, the day after the Americans left the K2 air base."

"And he lost far more than his perks." Daniel indicated a side screen. "It looks as if he went from K2 to five years in prison. Well, he's out now. Hard to believe they released him. Maybe he escaped. Maybe Colonel Evans helped him escape."

"So, they married the sisters, who were executed the day after our troops, including Evans, departed. Our guy was thrown out of the country and their guy was thrown into prison. Could someone please tell me who they aren't mad at?"

"Evans and Arlov will be most mad at the people who threw them out, then murdered their wives." Betty's boy again. Smart.

He looked at the General, who was staring at the screen. Then ever so quietly, the upright and proper soldier, the Commander of the Joint Chiefs, former commander of the U.S. Special Forces hung his head. Then he spoke very quietly.

"Oh, shit!"

Chapter 45

"RUSSIA AND CHINA PRESSURED UZBEKISTAN TO PUSH the Americans out of K2."

Archie listened to General Rogers's voice. The small speakers on either side of the laptop took some careful listening when people didn't speak clearly. Despite a lack of sleep, the others were no less attentive. Only Dilyana slept on, her head pillowed on Kee's jacket, curled up on the other end of the table and holding the orange cat he'd given her. She'd named it Sebiya, little girl.

"So these two nutcases are going to K2 to steal a jet and attack Russia and China on their lonesome." Kee was close to the mark.

Almost right. Almost.

Archie looked at her. He could see that she chewed on it as hard as he did. It felt as if their minds were rolling forward in tandem. How could two men, even working together in complete agreement, expect to damage—

Archie whistled in surprise. Loudly enough to stop all conversation.

"Sorry. I just… Sorry." He looked around, everyone was facing him. Even the President's face stared out at him.

"Russia and China didn't do it."

"I just said that they did, young man." The General sounded peeved.

"But they didn't, sir. They had someone else do it for them."

There was a pregnant pause and Kee got there first.

"The SCO."

"Right." He wouldn't have remembered, but he'd overheard his mother and Kee talking about them at lunch on the boat, a couple lifetimes ago. "The Shanghai Cooperation Organization, the largest military alliance on the planet. Uzbekistan let us into K2 before they became the sixth member of the SCO."

"And it took them a few years, but they drove us out. Shortly before Russia and China did those massive cooperative military exercises and Russia began flying her long-range bombers again."

Archie felt sick and sat down in a handy chair. Russia, China, and four of the 'Stans. A third of the world's people and over half its land mass. Toss in the observer nations like India and Pakistan and it was half the world's people. The biggest and one of the newest major political organizations on the planet.

What were these two guys up to? He still couldn't get there.

A hand rested on his shoulder. He knew without looking, by the gentle strength, it was Kee.

"How, Archie? How do you attack something like the SCO? They're half the world."

"No. It's like the UN, but instead of a hundred and seventy-odd members, you have six. You can kill six."

He leaned his cheek on her hand and closed his eyes to picture it. A single jet. A single bomb. And you kill all the heads of state. Hard to get to. Not impossible, but you could. If you could get them all in one place.

Why go to all the trouble of going to K2? Just carry in a briefcase with a bioweapon or a small bomb. It wouldn't be that hard.

The only thing at K2 was old Russian jets. Russian jets inside the Uzbekistan security perimeter. Bingo!

"General." His voice was sharp enough that he saw Dilya startle awake and instantly moderated his tone. "When and where is the next meeting of the SCO's leaders?"

He chewed on his lower lip waiting for the answer. When it came, he didn't like it one bit.

"In two days in Tashkent, Uzbekistan. That's it, the date in the book. They're going to bomb that meeting."

"No, General." He really needed to stop correcting the planet's highest-ranking soldier if he wanted to have a military career. Major Beale gave him a wide-eyed look asking if he were insane. Absolutely.

"Not quite, sir. What they are going to do is bomb the SCO meeting in a Russian jet that will be traced to an Uzbekistani air base."

Again the silence stretched. But it was no longer puzzled silence, now the tension crackled around the room as the truth sank in.

Finally the President spoke. "China will assume Russia did it. Russia will assume the Uzbekistanis were acting on China's orders. They're going to start a war between Russia and China."

—⁓—

"I've got to call the SCO. Warn them."

"Wait, Mr. President." Archie could feel Kee trembling under his hand. He could empathize. World War III could come out of this.

He had to speak up. "You can't."

"Why not!" Not much of a question in his tone.

"What will you tell them? A renegade American colonel has slipped into Uzbekistan, with the aid of United States of America Special Forces SOAR, to steal a jet and kill all your presidents and chairmen? We'd be lucky if they didn't all turn around and attack us. Even if they didn't, it would be a political disaster that the U.S. would not recover from for years."

"Damn it." The President's voice came out as low growl. Then his labored breathing sounded clearly over the microphone. "Damn it! You're right. Learned a lot from your mother."

Archie rocked back on his heels. If his hand hadn't still been on Kee's shoulder, he'd have stumbled backwards.

Was that possible? He still felt as if he'd never spoken with his mother in all of growing up, certainly not about matters such as this. Or had he? He had to grant that he'd always been a better strategist than Emily Beale. And that had bothered him. Now the President had told him why and it made impossible sense. *Later*. *Think about it later*.

Kee patted his hand without turning. She'd know. She'd know how that knowledge slammed into him.

"So, what do we do?" The President didn't sound happy.

"We do it ourselves, sir."

That was his Kee.

"And if you fail?" the President growled back at her.

"If we fail, place the call. But sir…"

"What is it, Smith?"

"We didn't sign up to fail, sir. Night Stalkers don't quit, sir."

Yup! That was his Kee, through and through. How could he help but love this woman?

Chapter 46

"YOU HAVE, THE WEIRDEST, IDEA, OF WHAT, IS RESTFUL."

"We. Can't. Leave. For." Kee gasped out as she rocked her hips on top of him in a way she'd found to make him completely insane. Long, deep motion that almost dragged him free of her each time before she drove him back inside her like a velvet punch. "Six. Hours. This. Best."

He slid his hands up the outside of her T-shirt, catching her nipples tight between his fingers. Again, with that perfect judgment of his, he found the pressure to drive her mad rather than into pain.

"Maybe. Sleep." His voice as fractured as hers.

"Lat, er." She gasped out. She hoped they weren't making the parked helicopter rock too much. It was seven hours until sunset. And—She groaned as Archie pounded up into her with that long, hard release of his. His whole body clenched and shook when it happened. His eyes, she knew without looking, would be squeezed shut. His fingertips dug into her breasts, holding on as he shook with the force of it.

She rocked her hips back and leaned forward to drive him all the way home and found her own release hammering through her. She grabbed the backs of his hands, holding his grip to her so that he wouldn't let go. Couldn't let go. She leaned into those grasping hands as the light pounded through her.

Night Stalkers might live in the dark, but Archie spread a searing light through her every time. One that lit old alleys and filled in dark corners. One that shone through her present and her past with equal ease, shedding warmth and safety wherever it flowed.

A part of her brain kept trying to compare it to something, as if labeling it would make it better. Safer. Better than flying? Cliché. Better than firing a minigun and bringing the wrath of justice upon the heads of those who killed in the name of their God? Sure, but even for her that was a creepy image. She couldn't find it, but she knew it existed somewhere. Some way to describe how he could make her feel.

Both their bodies relaxed in stages, the odd shudder of sudden muscle release rippling through them both as if they were inside the same skin. He lowered her by the hands clenched on her breasts until they lay chest to chest. Until her head tucked under his chin, her ear on his chest, the rapid trip-hammer of his heart slowing even as she rested her ear there.

"Now," she whispered.

"Now, what?" Archie barely managed a mumble.

This time she could smile. His need for a short nap after sex would tick her off if he didn't always wake with such renewed vigor.

"Now, you can sleep."

Archie had managed to slip his hands off her breasts just as their bodies came together. Which was a good thing as it saved him potentially dislocating a shoulder to maintain his hold. They lay on the cargo deck of the

Hawk with the bay doors slid shut. It was hot, midday hot, and he didn't care. He loved the feel of her lying upon him. Thought it was a good thing they hadn't taken the time to get completely undressed. Without shirts, they'd be sticking together at the moment rather than so cozy together he never wanted to move again.

He slid one arm over her back, amazed as always at what a small-waisted woman Kee was. You wouldn't think it of her, with those strong shoulders and bulldozer-strong attitude, but she was quite deliciously trim. His arm reached all the way around to hold her by her far side. He rested his hand over the spot where her life had almost leaked away. He slid his other hand up her back and into her hair, spreading it like a soft wash of silk over his face.

He picked up his head enough to kiss her atop her hair.

She mumbled something against his chest.

"What?" he whispered.

"You didn't say it." Her voice almost a complaint, but closer to sleep than she'd ever been after sex. And he felt wide awake for a change.

Didn't say what? He brushed her hair aside to look down at her as well as he could with her head under his chin, her body sprawled limply on his and still connected in the most delicious way. Which meant he could see a bit of tousled hair, a muscled shoulder, and then across a long valley, that splendid rise of firm buttock that would stand out in any room that didn't already include her chest. He'd never been with such a perfectly proportioned woman. Shocked him speechless every time he looked at her.

He was about to ask what he had failed to enunciate when it clicked. He knew exactly what she meant.

He had told her he loved her after sex. He told her when he was especially proud of her across the chow table. Thankfully Big John appeared to be too tired to remember hearing him say it.

And he'd stopped saying it because not hearing it in return hurt. Hurt more than he'd expected. She could have simply requested that he no longer say it. He would have stopped. Would have stopped laying his heart at her feet far sooner than he had. But now that he had managed to keep his silence, she had reprimanded him.

He looked again at what he could see, tousled hair, shoulder, and hip. Thought of the joy she gave his body and his mind. Thought of the joy she'd taught him about his own mother when she didn't even have one. Whether he spoke it aloud or not, no question remained. For the first time in his life, he didn't just respect a woman, lust for her, like her more than anyone he'd ever liked before. For the first time, he truly loved a woman.

He whispered into her hair, "I love you, Keiko Smith."

"Hmm." She snuggled down more comfortably against his chest. "I can hear you say that through your chest. I love how that sounds."

Then with a deep sigh, she fully relaxed and within moments he knew she slept.

She loved how it sounded?

How it sounded!?

He lay his head back and looked up at the ceiling. At the giant adder painted so that it slid and coiled across the ceiling. It wound upon itself, sliding over service hatches and cable runs, under emergency supplies and extra headsets snapped in place with bungee cords. John and Crazy Tim had started painting it, adding to it a piece at a time when they were a long time between missions. The detail was magnificent. Every scale was edged with a razor-like brightness. Every twist revealed the muscle beneath scale and skin.

Then splitting over the forward center of the cabin into a two-headed beast. Each serpent head driving down the curve of the ceiling toward the two miniguns as if the guns were spitting their death forth from inside the serpent's mouth. Its own taste for vengeance revealed in wide jaws and glistening fangs.

At least John's did. Something had been added over Kee's position. Something new, not a single scuff on the image, no battle scars, no bullet holes punched through. Kee must have made it recently. It took him a few moments to unravel its sense.

A demon. A red-faced, horned demon. With a face revealing stark terror.

She'd drawn a heraldic *serpent vorant*. The medieval shield crest of the snake swallowing the demon whole and alive.

He could feel her sleep through his arms and his chest and his hips. The perfect lassitude of the somnolent. This sweet woman, who had just used his body most splendidly and asked him to tell her that he loved her, was also the most driven warrior he'd ever met, male or female. Most soldiers like her would have done something stupid and gotten themselves, and probably their squadmates, killed but good. What saved her was a very sharp brain.

A street kid who knew about the SCO. An orphan and dropout who had passed every test on her way to SOAR, a height very few climbed, and only two women.

A gunner, a sniper, a killer, with a heart that had adopted Dilya without hesitation and certainly cared for him. Now he understood even if she didn't.

Kee Smith didn't think she deserved love because of her past. On top of that, she believed that she didn't have a heart to give. Of course, she'd never said the words back to him. She might like it, like the sound of it, the feel of it. But she would no more trust her own heart than she'd trust that demon on the ceiling to magically become a good guy.

Well, he was a warrior as well. He had fought and won many battles. If he needed proof of that, he was alive. Where SOAR fought their battles, if you failed, you died. And he wasn't dead. Clear cut and simple, they hadn't gotten him yet.

So, he would keep after her until he convinced her that she had the most wonderful heart he'd ever encountered. He would tell her over and over until she understood, until she knew, until she believed.

Until she felt how wonderful her heart could be. Then once she knew it was there, maybe, if he won the biggest lottery ever, she would give it to him.

He kissed her once more atop her head.

"Love you, Kee."

Chapter 47

AT LEAST THEY WERE UP AND DRESSED BEFORE ANYONE found them. No Major Beale hovering over them.

They were halfway to the chow tent before final briefing when Kee realized she was still holding Archie's hand. Not good. A quick glance showed that they'd walked past a group of red armorers working over Major Henderson's bird, and some grapes were heading over to fuel up the Hawk she'd just screwed Archie in. A couple of the guys were making fist-pump motions at Archie's back.

They stopped as soon as they saw her watching.

She casually dropped Archie's hand and offered a hard fist-pump of her own. That really stopped 'em. Give them a moment or two for that to sink in, and they'd be green with envy.

She returned to his side and, as naturally as she could, fell in step without actually taking his hand. A part of her really wanted to hold hands as they walked. Some soft mushy side she'd never noticed in the first twenty-four years of her life. But she resisted the urge. Messing with the minds of a service crew was one thing. Facing down the Majors in broad daylight, that was another.

"Did you find that strictly necessary?"

Kee glanced up at Archie's profile. She pulled her shades down her nose a little to check his color. Red, brilliantly.

"Hey. Think of all the respect you'll get for having nailed the warrior babe."

His face went several shades darker. Her work here was done. She slapped her shades back into place and didn't try for a second to suppress the grin she could feel spreading wide across her face.

—⁓—

The briefing went off clean.

Kee felt geared up for the mission. Sometimes they looked nasty before you even went in. Those you knew were gonna be ugly. But some felt clean and in the groove; they at least had a chance of not being a complete clusterfuck.

They'd take both DAP Hawks with a ground refuel just before they crossed the border into Uzbekistan without permission. They didn't want to risk border radar detecting a midair refuel.

An E-2C Hawkeye turboprop with its massive, UFO-shaped radome would serve as airborne radar observer and communications. The eye-in-the-sky wouldn't cross out of Afghanistan, but they'd be high enough they could at least watch and report. They probably wouldn't see the jet out of K2, especially if Evans and Arlov stayed close to the ground, but the Hawkeye could see if other nasties were coming their way. Maybe a few jet fighters vectoring in to kill the unwanted helicopters.

No need for D-boys or Rangers on this. It wasn't a ground action. They'd unraveled the rest of the numbers in the notebook once they knew what they were looking for.

Time of K2 local sunrise. They wanted to be seen

leaving K2 air base, clearly seen. That meant earliest liftoff would be fifteen minutes before sunrise, but probably fifteen after. Distance and speed necessary to arrive for the 8 a.m. start-of-conference breakfast meeting. This was the one time all six heads of state could be guaranteed to be in one place.

They wouldn't do anything flashy, no reason for any special report by the K2 air base commander. But a clear trail of evidence if someone went looking. And the countries with their newly murdered heads of state would definitely go looking.

SOAR's mission. Get in place between K2 and Tashkent. There was a hundred mile stretch of pretty much nothing northeast of the Karshi-Khanabad air base. Evans's notebook calculations showed that he'd be flying a straight path. No reason not to. To do anything else would actually draw attention from the Uzbekistan Air Force, attention Evans and Arlov wouldn't want once they were airborne.

So, the two DAP Hawks would wait out there, well below radar cover, and take out the jet without anyone the wiser. You could pretty much guarantee that General Arlov would want to keep a low profile as well. If he went high, he'd be on radar. After takeoff, he didn't want to be found again until after they were done.

The same reason the U.S. couldn't send in jets of their own. Too obvious. Too easily spotted. And no one could know the U.S. Armed Forces were there inside a friendly foreign country.

Once they nailed him, before anyone saw them, they'd beat it back south.

If someone spotted them, they'd run for the

Karakoram mountain range and wind their way home through Tajikistan. Not the best choice, but the mountains were nearly impenetrable, so that should work well for cover.

But if they weren't careful, they'd have a chance of seeing K2 the mountain as well as K2 the air base. If that happened, they'd be in way over their heads. There were some places helicopters were never meant to go. When the air stretched too thin to breathe, rotor-craft died too, they couldn't find the air to generate enough lift to stay aloft.

That was the other reason the AWACS would be up and watching for them. First, if they failed, it could shout the alarm to the President to call the Uzbekistan government about their rogue Russian jet. Second, if they succeeded but had to retreat into the mountains, the combat search and rescue guys would know where to look for you. And if the CSAR guys had even a fair guess, they'd find you. They were awesome.

She and John took four parkas and some other emergency gear and strapped it all to the rear cargo net. Crazy Tim and Dusty James were doing the same in Henderson's bird. They were stocking even more gear. Connie Davis would be riding in their bird in case her intel could help. She was the only one other than Kee who'd actually seen General Arlov.

"Sweaty work," Kee offered as she tied them down.

"Yup!" Big John dumped his load and waved his arms around to get some air moving across where the parkas had insulated his big arms while they carried them. "Seems weird to be doin' this in the desert sun."

"Good thing we won't need them."

Big John grimaced. She didn't like the look. John didn't strike her as a worrier.

"Yeah. Good thing." His voice low, his eyes focused too hard on the strap he snapped over the pile.

Now she felt a shiver. One that she didn't like at all.

She'd felt so positive at the briefing, or had that just been the afterglow of sex with Archie? She'd never had a man before who clouded her judgment about a mission.

"Are you coming with us, Sergeant?"

"Yes, ma'am. Sorry, ma'am." Kee climbed aboard and moved to her seat. In moments they were above the camp in the afternoon light and rising quickly. She stared at the ground again, but could spot no sign of a little girl running towards the chopper to wave good-bye as she always did. She'd checked the cots twice, the chow line three times, even checked with the guards at the gate. Nothing. Nowhere.

Dilya had probably found a cozy spot to study *Winnie-the-Pooh* and fallen asleep. They were down most of the third page, word by painful word, but Dilya never forgot anything she learned. Kee felt guilty for not doing the same, for not learning more Uzbek, but first the interrupted holiday, then this mission. She had to smile. Lieutenant Archibald Jeffrey Stevenson III also accounted for some of her distraction. In very, very pleasant ways.

She shifted her eyes out over the town where she was supposed to be watching. Dilya had survived alone in the Hindu Kush, she'd be fine for another night at the air base.

"Does this area seem familiar?" Kee didn't know she'd asked the question aloud until she heard it over her own headset. But it did. They'd been aloft for only two hours. She scanned the rugged hills and winding valleys. It looked exactly like every other lousy part of central Afghanistan, but it felt familiar anyway. Brutal country, almost impossible to cross without a helicopter. It looked even nastier in daylight.

"Nothing particular." Beale's voice sounded disinterested. She'd probably flown over this section dozens of times this last year.

Kee glanced over her shoulder, Big John shrugged at her.

"There," Archie called out. "Ten o'clock, three hundred meters."

Kee leaned out to check. A burned-out chassis. A dead Jeep. Just visible in the failing light. Her first flight, where they'd almost been knocked down by an RPG and she'd first proven herself as gunner.

"Roger, that's it."

Full circle, Kee. This is where you started on this bird. Less than four weeks ago.

"It's where we found Dilya." Archie's voice softened at the mention of the girl. He was so patient with her. He'd learned more of her language than Kee had, but he'd used it to entertain her. To talk about string figures and food, about trips to the town market and funny stories of impossible beasts.

Kee watched the spot as it slid by below them.

Dilya had lain right there on that flat spot of an

impossibly remote hilltop. Starving to death but still walking, crawling toward food.

"Oh, damn." This time she kept the whisper to herself. "Excuse me, sir? How far are we from the site where we picked up Evans's truck?"

"Ten minutes, perhaps fifteen flying time."

Dilya had recognized Colonel Evans. Seen General Arlov clearly enough to draw his face. That meant she'd been close. Close enough to be kneeling beside her parents when they'd been executed. Executed for stumbling upon Evans and Arlov's hidden Toyota. Maybe seen it and come begging for help.

But they'd spared the child. Left her to wander an orphan over the brutal terrain until she'd stumbled on the fateful Jeep.

Spared the child.

"Major, could I see that photo again?"

She handed it back to Kee.

Kee angled it to catch the setting sun. Not enough light, she pulled a flashlight out of her thigh pouch. She turned the photo to one side and the other as if she could get some perspective on it. It was hard to tell through the loose native cloth, but there was a shadow. A shadow on both women.

They were pregnant. When the women had been killed, they'd taken Evans and Arlov's unborn children to the grave with them.

Evans and Arlov had chosen the future day of their deaths, the day they would unleash war on the SCO for driving them away and then killing their wives, one for marrying a foreign officer and the other for marrying someone suddenly labeled a traitor for having worked with them.

No, they hadn't just killed the men's wives.

They'd killed the women the men loved as well as their unborn children.

If someone killed Archie and Dilya, Kee wouldn't hesitate for a second to start a world war as long as it rained retribution down on the heads of the guilty.

How would she feel if someone executed Archie the day after they threw her out of SOAR not for screwing up, but because someone else, someone far away, made a decision?

Pretty damn pissed.

Suicidal enough to bomb a major city. Sure. But Evans and Arlov would want to be sure. Sure enough to play kamikaze with a Russian jet.

Chapter 48

FOUR HOURS LATER, NEARLY THE STROKE OF MIDNIGHT, both Hawks arrived at the exact coordinates where they'd dropped Evans's truck.

One of the big twin-rotor Chinooks waited for them. Beale and Henderson set down their DAP Hawks to either side. Before they were even off the birds, two crews poured out of the Chinook. In moments they'd set up grounding cables and refueling lines to both Hawks. Then they started checking all the weapons despite the fact that not a single shot had been fired.

The Chinook would pull back and wait to see if they needed fuel on the way back out. They shouldn't. They'd be okay with a midair refueling at that point. Assuming everything went as planned.

The two crews wandered about to stretch their legs, an unusual luxury while on a long mission.

On the rough earth track lay a rope harness. The harness that had tied Evans and Arlov's Toyota to the Black Hawk for their lift over the mountains. The rope's ends were taped off with black duct tape to keep them from unraveling, which explained the roll of tape Kee had found buried in the sand. Four metal hooks dangled at the ends. Nothing else, though they scouted the area for several minutes using the floodlights shining out from the Chinook.

Evans and Arlov had hit the ground running, literally.

Kee wandered up the ramp and into the belly of the Chinook. The high whirr of fuel pumps filled the helicopter. The massive fuel bladder tied down to the deck occupied much of the space. Ammo cases lined the walls for the miniguns and the Vulcan cannon. A rack of Stingers, air-to-air missiles, had been stocked for this mission. They'd switched the armament on the DAP Hawks's pylons over to mostly missiles that morning.

"Is this what you're looking for?"

She turned to face the crewman who'd come up behind her. He held a small box out to her. Kee held out her hand and he dropped it into her palm even as she recognized it.

"M118LRs." A box of the cartridges for her sniper rifle. She hadn't been looking for them. Not really. But now that she held them, she knew that's why she'd wandered aboard. There wouldn't be any call for her rifle on this mission. Besides, she'd never use up the twenty-five rounds she had in her case. Her record had been seven rounds on a single assignment, but having ten more made her feel better anyway. As if she just scratched an itch.

"Brought them for you special, ma'am." The same guy who'd gotten them for her on the ground.

"Kee."

"Robert."

She knocked a fist lightly against his shoulder. He deserved a kiss on the cheek, but their helmets made that impossible.

"Thanks a lot, Robert."

He grinned down at her. "We aim to please. You all set on 5.56 and .45?"

She tapped the pockets on her vest for the spare magazines for her SCAR rifle and her handgun.

"Yeah, I'm good."

"You are. Go get 'em."

"Thanks, we will." She wandered back down the ramp and spotted the two Majors conferring with the Captain of the Chinook.

She watched them, picked out of the darkness by the Chinook's soft work lights. Beale and Henderson were so comfortable together, at ease beyond any mere experience of flying together could explain. They were in tune.

Did she and Archie look like that to the others? Look as if they belonged together? Hard to imagine. Even if she could imagine it, was it something she was willing to risk?

Kee turned away to watch the refueling grapes rolling up the hoses.

Six years, ever since Anna's death, she'd avoided all human connection. Too much risk of too much pain. And in all that time she hadn't missed it for a single minute. She'd been enough, on her own. Now, she missed Archie merely because he wasn't beside her. Needy? Really sad.

Kee stood taller. She wasn't going to be needy. Kee Smith was just fine by herself. She didn't need…

"Hey, beautiful."

He stole her breath away. He'd come up beside her in his avenging angel mode. Flight suit with armored vest, a SCAR carbine hanging comfortably from his chest, his helmet strapped on and night-vision goggles flipped up out of the way. How could a man make her feel so safe simply by standing beside her?

She didn't say anything. All she did was lean over until they brushed shoulder to shoulder. They didn't need the words at all.

"I love you, Kee."

Of course, there wasn't enough breath left in her body to say any words, even if she had them in her.

"Would you two get a room?" Big Bad John stood close behind them. Then he lowered his voice. "And get it somewhere that you aren't gonna be slapped with Paragraph 14 of the Personnel Policy."

They jerked apart at that.

"C'mon. We're outta here."

They all headed to the chopper, splitting up to climb in through their various doors.

The long-range cartridges were still heavy in her hand. She slid them into a thigh pocket of her flight suit.

With each passing minute, she liked this mission less.

The Afghanistan-Uzbekistan border slid by twenty feet below their wheels with no mishap. Right on schedule, they weren't pushing it. At 150 knots, they were cruising nicely in a country where they absolutely didn't belong.

For ten miles everything was normal. Kee sitting on her seat, keeping an eye on the landscape around. The next moment the bird rattled with gunfire, but nothing showed in her goggles. It must be on Big John's side. She flipped on her gun and the barrels spun up. Safety off and she was ready for a target.

"We're hit!" Henderson's call. "We overflew an AA battery."

There'd been no intelligence of an anti-aircraft

battery along their route, but since you could move one around on the back of a heavy truck, that didn't mean much.

"Got it. Firing," Archie called. The Hawk slewed sideways.

Kee blinked her eyes shut to avoid being blinded by the glare. Even so she could see the bright streaks of two FFAR missiles through her eyelids. She opened them in time to see the 30 mm cannon on John's side light off. Archie was hammering the site.

Still, rounds were pounding against their bird. Then, as if a switch had been thrown, they stopped. A moment later the roar of the shock wave hit them, slapping them aside. She could feel the heat wash over them.

They'd been flying close to the ground, only a few hundred meters behind Henderson's Hawk. No time to slow down or evade. Barely time to react.

But Archie had. He'd hammered the site even as they flew a dozen feet over the AA guns. His rockets had flown true, and the battery was blown. Blown up, right into their path. She listened, but heard no faltering in the engines. So they hadn't sucked up any shrapnel along with all that heat and flame.

Beale circled hard, exposing Kee's side to the site.

"Steel!"

She opened fire immediately. Even though she couldn't see anyone standing clear, she wasn't taking chances. She raked the stream of fire back and forth over the truck and the twinned machine guns burning on the bed. A man on fire ran for the desert and she took him down as well.

Five full seconds she laid in. Nothing else exploded,

no one else moved. Archie had nailed them, and nailed them hard.

She stopped her fire and studied the area. Nothing and no one.

"Looks clean," Kee called. "Have John double-check."

Beale did one of her gut-wrench swoops, and Kee could see nothing but the black of desert.

"Confirm, no movement," Big John called. "I—"

"This is *Viper*." Henderson's voice was completely steady. "We're going down."

Kee could feel their own helicopter flinch as Major Beale's perfectly steady hands twitched.

In seconds they were racing ahead once more. Kee leaned out to try and see ahead. A mile past the AA battery, she saw the other DAP Hawk. They were descending rapidly. A crash with a fresh load of fuel and a full load of weaponry. Not good.

Beale must have had the same thought as she jerked them back into a hover, practically standing them on their tail to avoid overrunning The Viper's bird. If there were an explosion on landing, they would not want to be at ground zero. All they could do was watch.

Even in the dark of the night, Kee could see the black cloud billowing out of the exhaust, filled with sparks from a critical hit.

The flight was erratic, but controlled. A few feet up, the nose flared hard, stalling them barely a meter above the desert. In three more seconds, they were down, rocking hard on their shocks, but down.

"We're down. Hold at guard station." Henderson's voice sounded absolutely calm.

Kee glanced over and saw Beale hang her head for a moment before acknowledging.

They set up a circling perimeter, about a quarter mile from the downed Hawk. Kee faced into the center, looking at the downed Hawk. She flipped down her night-vision binoculars and saw four people climb out of the bird. Then two of them turned back to pull out the fifth member of the crew.

"Dusty took a couple rounds. He's conscious, but bleeding. Tim, help me check him over. Richardson, Davis, check the bird." Henderson had left the comm open.

For several minutes Kee's Hawk continued its slow circle. The AWACS, their eye-in-the-sky still thirty miles back inside Afghanistan, reported that the air remained clear, no enemy aircraft inbound. Maybe they'd taken out the anti-aircraft gunners before they were able to report any problem. They were certainly far enough away from everything. They'd hidden themselves well, dug into the backside of a low rise. Almost invisible until you were on top of them. If no one missed them for another four hours, everything should be okay.

"Okay, Dusty is stable, but I've had to dope him. What about my bird?"

It was Connie Davis who answered. "I can fix the hydraulics they nailed, that's pretty easy. It spilled fluid into the exhaust, so all the smoke didn't mean much. That's not the problem."

Kee watched as one figure led the other three around forward. That had to be Connie.

"Avionics, fire control, FLIR, all gone. If you try to fly Nap of Earth, as this mission calls for, you'll be flying blind. And even if you could, once you got there, you couldn't fire anything. I can't fix this. They smithereened a quarter of a million dollars of electronics. I can get us flying in thirty minutes, but we can't fight off an angry mosquito without replacing half the panel. Even the redundant systems are all shot up."

Kee pictured the line of fire that had hit Henderson's Black Hawk. Firing up from below, rounds passed through the control panel. Enough rounds to wipe out all of those systems. More rounds passing through and punching up into the engines, hard enough to part the hydraulics lines. In those few seconds, rounds slashing everywhere through the forward compartment, big rounds, at least .50cal, probably bigger to punch through the chopper's armor. That it took out that much equipment and missed both pilots ranked nothing short of a modern miracle.

She leaned over and could just touch Major Beale's shoulder.

Emily Beale grabbed her hand, squeezed it hard, and held for the length of three heartbeats, then she nodded her thanks and released Kee's hand. All without turning. No matter how strong she appeared, by all odds her husband should dead down on the sand at this very moment. And they all knew it.

Kee reached for the wryest voice she could manage.

"You know he's going to become even more insufferable."

Emily's head turned sharply at that to face her.

"I mean this is bound to become another legend in the name of Major Mark 'The Viper' Henderson. The man who flew between the bullets, a hundred holes puncturing his pilot's seat."

Emily glared a moment longer then burst out laughing. She pushed her night-vision goggles up and mopped at her eyes.

"Oh, God. You are so right." She aimed that radiant smile of hers at Kee while she laughed and wept. "You are so right."

"*Vengeance*," Mark called their bird.

"Here, *Viper*." Beale's voice was rock-steady as she replied.

"We're safe, but unable to proceed. You must continue to target."

The Major rocked back in her seat. She looked right, then left, as if hunting for another answer. Any other answer. But they all knew that Henderson was right.

"Should I pick up Davis?"

"Negative. With Dusty doped up, I need her to get me back in the air. Smith has seen the target, that's all you need. All we've got."

"Roger."

Beale didn't hesitate. She turned the bird, aimed the nose down, and yanked up on the collective, hurling them to the northwest.

"And *Vengeance*?"

"Yes, *Viper*?"

"Make damn sure you come back in one piece."

"Yes, dear."

Kee turned to look outside. Major Beale's voice had gone soft and whispery. She'd heard the Major sound tough, sound amused, even sound gentle when she talked to Dilya. She'd never heard this. Never heard the sound of a woman so in love.

She wanted to discount it. As if she were some woman

in one of those long-dress shows on late-night TV. But it wasn't. It came from the first woman of SOAR.

Glancing forward for a quick peek at Emily revealed no change in her expression. The Major sat in quarter profile, flying a DAP Hawk, attention on the heads-up display, flying $40 million of Battle Hawk two dozen feet over hostile territory.

Kee turned and glanced toward the back of the chopper. She saw something move across her night vision. But it was inside the helicopter.

The pile of coats she and John had secured to the cargo net shifted.

Dilyana stuck her head out and looked at Kee.

Kee couldn't hear her, but she could read the words on her lips.

"Safe now?"

Chapter 49

"I DON'T KNOW HOW SHE GOT HERE, BUT WE CAN'T take her with us." Kee wrapped one of the coats properly around Dilya. She was partly a Popsicle from huddling so long under the pile of coats on the steel deck. Kee zipped it and patted down all the Velcro closures. She opened the front for a moment, stuffed in the small orange cat Dilya was never without, and resealed the coat again. It was long enough that, with her legs tucked up, the girl disappeared completely inside it. Kee pulled the furred hood up, and it flopped down over Dilya's face. She pushed it into place until just the elfin face popped out.

With a quick flip of a strap, she secured the girl and the coat once more to the cargo net.

"And what would you suggest, Sergeant Smith?"

Kee blinked rapidly as her mind struggled to kick into gear.

"We could—" *turn back and leave Dilya with the others*. Not an option. They were already fifteen minutes behind schedule. They'd planned to be on station an hour early, now it would be a mere forty-five minutes. She could hear the turbines running higher, trying to make up the lost time. Going faster made them louder and more detectable. A calculated risk.

If Evans and Arlov decided to leave earlier than planned, they risked missing them. The one hour of leeway had been a gamble between the baddies leaving early, or the good guys on site for too long and being discovered. They couldn't afford another half hour that the return trip to *Viper* would take.

"What if—" No. Landing and leaving Dilya wouldn't work. There'd be no guarantee they could stop and fetch her on the return flight. If they were on the run or had to leave by a different route, she'd once again be an orphan lost in the high-mountain desert. At least she'd be back in her own country, but it was a country she didn't know or even really belong in anymore. The first time she spoke in English, who knew what would happen to her.

Kee made sure Dilya understood that the strap had to stay around her waist, then rested her hand on the girl's head.

"Please, keep her safe." Kee didn't know where she sent the prayer, but she felt better for doing so. She kissed the girl on her forehead, receiving a nose full of furry parka hood, then returned to her seat by her minigun.

When she was clipped back in and had her hands back on her gun, she responded.

"She's a Night Stalker now, ma'am. And Night Stalkers Don't Quit."

"NSDQ," Archie and Beale murmured.

"Damn straight!" Big John echoed softly.

———～～～———

They were less than half an hour from position. Archie sat and watched the desert rolling by. They'd chosen their route carefully, they had flown over no towns at all and very few dwellings. Occasionally a road would flash by beneath them, the only interruption of the rolling landscape.

A couple of times he turned to check on Dilya, she'd waved back cheerily enough for a kid strapped down in a helicopter jerking and twisting to stay no more than twenty feet above the rolling terrain. This area of Uzbekistan was more arid than western Pakistan. Scrub trees were often miles apart because the land couldn't support more growth except where irrigated.

"Major, I've been thinking."

"Am I going to like this?" She rolled them to the right to edge around the base of a hill. He waited until it had flashed by and they'd once again settled on their original course.

"No."

Emily sighed. "Why am I not surprised. Okay, Arch, what are they going to do?"

Her question surprised him a little. As if he had some magic crystal ball of tactics and strategy that no one else possessed. With the perspective that Kee had given him, reinforced by the President's comment, maybe his theory wasn't as completely outrageous as it sounded. The next problem simply felt… obvious.

"With only one helicopter, we've lost more than half our chances of catching him in the air. We could spot him, but we are in a slower craft. Our plan depended upon two layers of attack and the ability to herd him from one of us toward the other. We can't do that solo."

"I knew I wasn't going to like this. So, what are we going to do?"

Archie hesitated. He didn't like his own conclusion in the slightest.

Kee spoke. "We take them out while they're still on the ground."

She was absolutely right, and it confirmed his worst fear. Kee thought with her gut and her survival instinct, supplementing his own mental calculations in a synergistic way that would have fired up his body under any other conditions.

"You're saying." Major Beale rolled the words around slowly, as if she'd just bitten into something nasty. "That we need to attack an armed air base in less than two hours? No matter how sleepy, they aren't dead. And we are supposed to make it look like an accident. The whole point is that the U.S. Armed Forces has not just staged an invasion on friendly soil. That would be even worse than the President calling to warn them. Any bright suggestions on how we do that and then slip away in broad daylight in a U.S. Army Sikorsky MH-60M Direct Action Penetrator Black Hawk?" Emily sounded pissed by the time she finished.

The silence stretched out. Archie hated his answer to this question even worse than the one before it. He decided to sneak up on his answer.

"We think Evans and Arlov will be taking off shortly after dawn, the notebook confirms that with the note about the local time of sunrise. They want everyone to absolutely know that their jet came from K2 and that it is Russian. It also has the schedule of today's events with the 8 a.m. breakfast meeting circled. Everyone will be there, all of the countries' leaders, advisors, the media. It's the splashiest event, the only one they can guarantee no one will skip."

"I know all this." Emily didn't sound happy. She

jinked hard left to slip between a line of trees and a low building.

Archie pulled up a satellite map of K2. He scanned around for a minute before he found what he was looking for.

"Here." He punched in the GPS coordinates on the nav computer. "We want to go there. Five miles southeast of the runway. Nothing there but farmers' fields. Come in low and quiet. There is a single house and a grove of trees. We park in the trees and secure the house. After we're done, we can lie low there until dark and fly back tonight."

Again the silence. Archie held his breath. He knew he was asking too much, but it was nothing compared to what he'd be asking others to give.

Emily swore, then corrected her course to the west, placing the house dead ahead and ten minutes out.

"And what, Mister Genius, do we do after we land there?"

"After we land…" Kee responded.

Archie knew she would see it.

"I go crawling across the landscape with my rifle and shoot down a jet before it can take off."

Chapter 50

EMILY CIRCLED THEM AROUND THE BACK OF THE GROVE of trees. She hated this. Far too many things could go wrong, already had gone wrong.

A downed jet in the middle of the desert could be written off as an accident. One parked on the tarmac with two head-shot pilots aboard couldn't be so easily ignored. The heat that would land on them would be horrendous. Any attempt to fly home, day or night, was going to be ugly beyond imagining.

She'd had Archie bounce a call to the Hawkeye observer. He'd explained their plan briefly. And all she'd gotten back was, "Abort at pilot's discretion."

Completely useless. If she aborted now, she'd hit daylight an hour and a half before she hit the border. So, they'd have an international incident, right before these two goons started the next world war.

Lousy option.

She slid over the tops of the trees and found a hole to settle into. Trees blocked the view on three sides. A barn blocked the view straight ahead. Off to the right, through a gap in the trees, what had appeared to be a small house on the aerial photo was actually three hovels.

What they needed was a squad of D-boys. What they had were four Night Stalkers and a little girl.

Emily cycled down the engine quickly. She'd debated about keeping it hot and ready to go, but they needed to hear. And they didn't want to attract more attention than they already had.

Kee, Big John, and Archie spilled out the doors and moved toward the hovels, rifles at the ready. Less than one more hour of dark. They had to secure the helicopter and then move Kee five miles northwest to the airstrip.

Emily dropped to the ground and hurried to catch up with them. They were moving ahead in two-by-two formation. Archie and Kee rushing ahead, then squatting with weapons raised. She and John rushed by and did the same behind minimal cover.

In two minutes they'd surrounded the first building. In thirty seconds more they'd confirmed the three small rooms were empty and moved to the next.

At the next, she could smell last night's cooking. A sharp tang of a curry still lingered in the still air. At a window, Archie popped his head up for a moment then ducked back down. He held up four fingers and pointed where they were, huddled in a corner. The night wasn't cold, they were probably awake and afraid. The Hawk was quiet for what it was but still made a huge racket on a quiet country night. That fear could work to their advantage, getting everyone to hide in the same place.

Emily pointed at Big John, then made a slashing motion toward the third building. The moment he moved, the sharp crack of a bullet passed by her head.

"Close. Damn close," one part of her mind thought. The other part dived and rolled behind a water trough.

John hit the dirt, but his roll showed he hadn't been hit.

Kee knelt with her rifle pointed back in the direction of fire. Even as Emily looked over, a spray of muzzle-blast shimmered forth from the point of her barrel. The loud crack was followed by a very abrupt and brief scream.

"Go! Go! Go!" Emily shouted. They rolled into the house as one. Emily and John securing the startled family, a boy, two women, and a couple girls, who were indeed huddled together in one corner cowering. Kee's attention remained out the door, she knelt in a marksman's squat, her rifle still aimed and ready. Her position mostly shielded by the doorjamb.

Big John checked the back two rooms. Everyone was in here.

Everyone except Archie.

Archie leaned against the wall below the window and did his best not to breathe, because the whole breathing thing didn't feel good at all. Not in the least. Nope. He'd just lie here for a while. Maybe it was just shock. He'd been shot a couple of times before. The armor in his flight suit had always deflected it. Afterward you were numb and sore from the impact.

When Kee had wrenched his shoulder, that had hurt, too.

This hurt worse.

He really wished Kee were here. She'd know what to do.

A face loomed up out of the dark in front of him.

She couldn't hide from him that easily. Helmet, safety goggles, chin strap, flight suit, and enough gear to hide Helen of Troy couldn't hide his gal.

"Hi, Helen."

"Who the hell is Helen?" She knelt and began poking him.

"You are. My own personal Helen of Troy."

"Can you move?"

"Don't know. That was seriously loud, Helen. Wow!"

"I have to move you."

Before he could protest, she had him by the harness and was dragging him around the corner and into the house.

"Where are you hit? Where?"

Suddenly two lights were dancing over him. His vision was clearing, until someone shone a light in his eyes.

"Ow! Cut that out!"

Emily whistled low. "Look!"

Both lights focused on his face.

"Ow! I—" One of them knelt on his chest. Hard.

"Be still!" Kee. Of course. His own personal mistress of pain.

She unclipped his helmet and slid it free. She tipped his head to the side.

"Hey, Emily?" Her voice, he couldn't read his condition in her voice.

"What? Am I hit? How bad? Is there an entry wound?"

Kee clapped a hand over his mouth as she drawled, "Emily, you got a Band-Aid on you?"

The Major opened a pouch on the front of her vest and handed one over with a tube of salve. The salve was cool on his temple, though it stung like a son of a bitch.

Then Kee taped it.

He sat up as Kee dropped back onto her butt. "How bad?"

Emily handed him his helmet.

It took a moment, but he found the bullet's path. A deep crease through the foam alongside his temple, a tiny tear in the fabric. He ran a hand across the back of the helmet and found a distinct bump where the bullet had lodged.

He laughed. It was half a choke, but he laughed. So did the others, though they were all shaky. They sounded almost as relieved as he did.

Then Kee went white as a sheet, turned for the corner and barfed her guts out.

Archie looked around the main room of the little building. A single chair, father's place of honor, probably. A low table. A few belongings and a dirt floor. A woman and three children crouched in the corner whimpering with fear. He would too if he were sitting at the wrong end of Major Beale's carbine.

"Where's Dilya?"

"Waiting at the chopper or I'll skin her alive." Kee'd found her voice, though she didn't move from where she'd been sick.

Archie looked to the door as Dilya slipped in from the dark night and stood in the shadows. Had she seen him shot? A new nightmare for her, or just another body in her world filled with death? Maybe he'd rather not know.

John came in right behind her hauling a thin man by one arm. A battered Russian SKS rifle with a shattered stock in his other hand.

He flung the man toward the cowering family. He fell to the dirt floor even as the family gathered him in. He nursed a hand that the older woman started binding in a bit of rag. John brushed her aside and opened his med kit to tend the man's wound.

"You shot him in the rifle, Kee. I think you dislocated two of his fingers because he tried to hold on too tight. Good thing he had it across his chest or you'd have drilled him in the heart. How do you do that kinda shit?"

"We're running out of time here, folks." Major Beale had her rifle casually aimed toward the cowering family to cover John. "So, what's the plan, Lieutenant?" She had to raise her voice to be heard over the whimpering of the family.

Archie didn't have much of a plan. Well, no plan at all really. If his head would just stop ringing, maybe he could come up with one. Until then, they'd do what came next and he'd keep hoping he didn't run out of next steps.

"Kee, go get your sniper's rifle from the chopper. John, Major, check the third building. Dilya."

Kee spun to face the girl. Then she blanched white, and leaned back hard against the wall. She probably would have gone to the ground without the support of her flight suit.

"Come here, girl." Archie waved her over.

"You talk?" And he pointed to the family whose worried tones were reaching clamorous in the small space.

At her first words, they went quiet. The eldest woman answered her quietly as the rest of the crew slipped back into the night. The father, recovering from his shock, took over the conversation. He and Dilya back-and-forthed a couple of times in a rolling lilt of Uzbek that picked up to normal conversation speed in moments.

"The Kee make father ouch. All dogs here."

The man spoke some more.

"Father tell me story."

"Story?" he asked as much to fill the time as from any understanding. He really needed to think of a plan.

"Story. Like I tell to Winnie-ther-Pooh. Him that kind of bear."

Archie looked up at her, but her face looked absolutely serious in the dim spill of the flashlight he had laid on the floor.

Kee must be teaching her English from *Winnie-the-Pooh*. He wondered how far they'd gotten.

"What story?"

"Father know only one reason to make buzzing noise."

Buzzing noise. Bees. Bees had made buzzing noise for Winnie. Bees or helicopters.

"What did father know about buzzing noise?"

"Bad men. Uzbek men."

Government men. Great. The father had shot Archie and then nearly been killed by Kee because he thought they were government oppressors.

"Tell them to be quiet and relax."

"Quiet. Relax." Dilya said the words slowly, trying on the sounds, her hands fluttered before her as if testing the shape of them. Clearly she didn't know what they meant.

Major Beale ducked back through the door with Big John close behind. "House and trench are clear, how's the patient?"

"The man thought we were Uzbekistani raiders. Trying to defend his family."

"How do you know that?"

"Dilya talked to them. Now let me think."

He checked his watch. Not enough time. Even at a run.

"We really need a car or truck."

"There's one in the barn."

"Excellent. Major, you and Dilya keep an eye on the family and an ear on the radio. If we scream, you may need to come and get us. And if we don't scream…" He didn't finish the sentence and Emily's nod was tight, as if her neck wasn't working quite right.

She nodded her understanding and her face made her thoughts easy to read. If they cried for help in daylight, Emily would come, but they'd all be dead before nightfall if not inside the hour. If they didn't call, the results might well be the same.

"John, go see if you can start the truck. Then get a camouflage net over the Hawk as well as you can. You need to be back here, inside this house before sunrise. Clear?"

He nodded and headed out the door.

Kee entered even as John left. This time, her Heckler and Koch sniper rifle hung over her shoulder. Her carbine still dangled from her hand.

"Come on, Kee. We've got to scramble."

She knelt down and hugged Dilya close for a moment then pointed to Dilya, to the Major, and then emphatically at the ground.

Dilya nodded understanding.

Didn't mean that Archie wouldn't be watching carefully to make sure they didn't acquire a Dilya-sized shadow. He scrubbed a hand over the girl's head and ruffled her hair enough to completely hide her face. Kee brushed it aside.

"Kee *qilmoq* dogs dead. Good?" Kee was asking the girl's permission. She was so good with children. She'd be a natural mother one day. That would probably shock her to know, but he didn't doubt it for a second. Assuming they got out of this one.

Archie could read the grim set of the girl's jaw as she thought about her answer. He had to turn away. So young, yet she'd learned to kill, or at least thirst for it.

His gaze landed on a large wooden chest. Flipping up the lid, he unearthed a pile of clothes. The father started to protest, but then eyed the Major's carbine that had swung to aim right between his eyes. He settled quickly enough.

The men's shirt would never fit over his vest, but the loose *hajib* went on easily enough. He and Kee had to dump their helmets to pull on scarves, but they were able to keep most of their gear hidden. Maybe they could just stroll back to the hut in broad daylight.

Emily was grinning at him dressed up as an Arab woman. She controlled her expression quickly, then offered him a salute.

He returned it, hoping it wasn't the last time he ever saw her. Her face sobered as she clearly had the same thought.

He and Kee turned for the door as he heard a truck roar to life in the barn.

"You're driving." Archie closed his eyes for a moment and took a deep breath. His temple throbbed to remind him how close he had just come to dying.

"I have a headache."

Dilya grabbed The Kee's sleeve before she could leave. She had never seen The Kee kill before. But she had been in the dark, a dozen paces behind and listening when the father had shot the String Man. Only Dilya had seen him fall.

She'd opened her mouth to scream and then remembered. Her mother had screamed when the two Dogs shot her father. They'd struck her, shouted at her, but she wouldn't stop. They had shot her to make her silent.

The Kee had turned so fast. The Kee had shot so fast. Dilya hadn't had time to blink between the String Man being hit and The Kee shooting the father.

The family who knelt and shook in fear beside her had almost lost their father. If The Kee had, would they now hate The Kee? Hate her the way she hated Dog One and Dog Two?

Maybe. But the father had shot at the String Man with a gun. Her own parents had had no guns. No food. No water.

She tugged once more on Kee's sleeve until she knelt again.

"Dilyana say Good."

The Kee nodded. Clear-eyed. Nodded. Then rose and walked into the night.

Dilyana would wait. The Kee always came back. She hoped. She didn't want to live with this family that shot people in the dark.

Chapter 51

IN THE BARN THEY FOUND AN OLD RUSSIAN TRUCK, John under the hood. Even as they inspected it, the engine settled, ran smoother. A flatbed good for hauling hay, no doors or windshield, but the tires were wide and had large if worn tread. Should be okay on the sandy soil.

Now they were in business. Kee handed Archie her H&K sniper rifle, which he propped between his knees as Kee shoved the truck into gear. John dropped the hood and sprinted off to cover the helicopter with a camouflage net.

"We have half an hour to first light. Absolute maximum of an hour until they fly."

He was talking to her but she had to concentrate to make sense of the words. He'd been a half inch from death. Less. *Focus, Kee, goddamn it. Focus.*

She got the old truck rolling and turned it down the track along the narrow tree line that wandered north and west. Must be a stream running along here whenever they received any rain.

She held her breath as she decided to risk second gear. It was rough, clearly little used, but it ground into place. The truck picked up speed from a fast trot to a solid run.

"So, Kee. How do you want to play this?" The trees ran out. In the dim headlights, she could still make out the streambed, so she followed that.

Nothing. She searched her head, but all she could see was Archie lying against the outside wall of the hut, clearly injured.

"It's pretty flat out here." Archie's words were slowly coming into focus. "I've taken SERE, but I never took the sniper course. How do you hide on flat terrain?"

Kee looked up and out where the windshield was supposed to be, squinting at the landscape.

They crossed a dirt road. Kee was about to turn onto it when Archie spoke.

"Don't. There's another line of trees ahead. We'll run north along that."

Kee shifted back down to first as they crawled over the rough field. When they hit the tree line, which was actually a sandy ditch with tall bushes, they turned right.

"Cross it where you can. We need to be on the other side before we hit the irrigation channel."

The truck wallowed but made it through.

Kee knew that Archie had only about fifteen seconds to memorize the map back at the Hawk. She'd had about the same when she went back for her weapon. She'd seen the layout and the distance to the airfield. It was all a blur. Archie had seen a tactical landscape to be crossed. She'd only seen the vast expanse of flat all around the runway. How was she to get close enough for the kill shot?

"At the channel, about five hundred meters, turn left."

His voice. She'd just focus on his voice. Keep listening to that.

"Hurry."

She spared a glance at the night sky. Still dark, but the fainter stars were disappearing.

She took the left and continued. Rough or not, she put it in second and stayed there. Thankfully there was a trail along the channel. More a wide goat path than a road, but the truck tackled it gamely enough. They were moving faster than a dead run. Not much, but enough to matter.

"In another mile, you'll run into a cross ditch. Drive down into it."

The edge was so abrupt that Kee almost went down into it unintentionally. Only by standing on the brakes and stalling the engine did she manage to stay out of it.

"We won't get out of that."

"Do it. Then turn left at the bottom."

"But…" Kee checked the compass in her head. "Left is away from the airfield."

"I know. Do it."

She took a deep breath. They were now operating within Archie's specialty, not her own. She hated the out-of-control feeling, but you had to trust your team.

The engine fired off very reluctantly, she nudged the truck over the edge and down the steep bank. It was deeper than it looked, turning left trickier than it sounded. By what miracle she avoided rolling the truck, she didn't know, but it stayed upright.

They rode in silence for another hundred yards.

"Kill it."

Kee stopped the truck. "If I shut off the engine, it doesn't sound as if it will restart."

"Don't worry. We won't need it again."

Kee looked out the side where the truck doors should have been. Only a few feet to either side rose the banks of the ditch. The truck would be well hidden from the fields above. It was aimed away from the air base and had been driven that direction. So if someone did find it, they'd look south, not north toward the air base. Smart.

"How are we getting home? Never mind." If they were alive, they were walking. Four, maybe five miles back up the irrigation channel. They'd only used the truck because they were out of time.

"Let's go." Kee was speaking to herself. Archie had already jumped out of the truck. Kee checked that they'd left no clues behind and jumped down herself.

He was already trotting up the ditch. Kee recognized the pace, not the fastest, but a steady mile-eater that you could run for hours if need be. She fell in behind Archie wondering at that. Time was essential. Why not a full run?

Another piece of her training clicked in. Even more essential than time would be getting Kee into position and still physiologically able to fire. That's why the fast jog-trot.

In a mile, they turned left and followed a hedgerow.

Her nerves were sparking. She unslung her SCAR rifle and kept checking behind them. No one. Not even a rooster yet, though a faint lightness now sketched the entire horizon in that shimmer of predawn light.

Archie stopped so abruptly that Kee almost ran into his back.

"What?" She had to gasp it out between breaths.

Archie squatted and pointed, barely breathing hard. She had to get control of herself. She was breathing wrong, running wrong.

Ahead of them lay Karshi-Khanabad Air Base. No runway lights, all silhouette and shadow. A long strip of runway. On the far side, the rounded mounds of the hardened hangars rose almost like Hobbit hills. As her eyes adjusted, she made out the smaller shapes. Dozens, maybe hundreds of jet fighters were parked along the taxiways.

And she'd suggested shooting down one in the air? Why had anyone listened to her? If they'd followed the original plan and done that, they'd have faced a hundred fighters so fast they'd have died on the spot. Even if *Viper* were still with them.

Kee swallowed hard.

At the last report Major Henderson was safely south of the border and limping his way home. Her own chances were feeling less certain with each moment.

Chapter 52

KEE FOCUSED ON THE TERRAIN AHEAD AND DIDN'T LIKE what she saw. Not one bit. This sucked on so many levels.

Closing her eyes, she clamped her teeth down on the side of her tongue. The pain brought clarity and focus even as it brought the taste of blood. She'd been clamping down since the moment she'd seen Archie leaning against the wall calling her Helen of Troy through a haze of shock. She knew her nerves were shot, and now it was all up to her.

Focus, damn it. She pulled her rifle off Archie's shoulder and removed the caps from the scope. She'd mounted the day scope when she'd grabbed the rifle. There was just enough light to see.

They were atop a nice rise, well hidden but much too far from the airfield. The hedgerow they'd been following curved away to the left. Where she'd expected to see another irrigation ditch, she saw a wall. The satellite photo had shown a geometric line, just like the ditches. And she hadn't had time to inspect it more carefully. A dozen feet high and nearly as wide, built of concrete and stone. She followed the wall with her scope, a lone guard tower stood almost a mile away.

"That's where I'd like to be."

Archie unslung his own rifle and used his much-lower-power scope.

"I see buildings beyond it. Would be very tricky."

Kee smiled to herself. The Lieutenant had just told her very tactfully that it was a fast way to commit suicide.

"How about there?"

Kee glanced to the side to see where Archie's scope was aimed. She swung her own rifle until she spotted it.

A small shack, very isolated. Maybe two-thirds of the way from their position to the airfield. She didn't like the angle, or that it was almost a thousand yards on the other side of the wall across a low field, young wheat perhaps, but she didn't see any other options.

"Let's go."

This time she ran, ran hard. And found the groove. They covered the distance to the wall fast. As she hoped, the wall was older and needed work. In moments they were both up and over, digging boots and fingers into crumbling cracks in the concrete.

They sprinted for the shack, staying as low as they could. No windows on the side they approached from. They lay their backs against the wooden frame. Kee re-slung her rifle and pulled out a knife and her handgun. Quiet. They had to do this quietly.

Archie did the same. Then they traded a nod and peeled off around opposite sides. No windows.

They met at the door. She didn't waste time trying the handle, simply laid a shoulder into it and the wood gave way with a puff of dry-rot dust.

The tiny room was filled with racks of equipment, and two men. She jammed her knife under the first one's chin even as his hands grabbed for the rifle leaning nearby, the point driving up and back.

She heard a muffled shot as Archie took down the other.

But Archie was holding his knife.

He looked at her strangely.

"You okay?"

He nodded. "You?"

"Fine." She inspected the room.

Racks of electronics right out of a '50s mad-scientist movie. Not powered up, maybe the end of the shift. No one likely to check on them any time soon.

She looked back out the door and liked it less. The runway was awfully far away. The night breeze, which had been from the east, continued. So Evans and Arlov would be starting their roll at the far end of the runway and coming toward her. They'd be rotating for takeoff a mile away. At that distance, she needed a .50cal Barrett, not her H&K.

Archie watched her.

Kee could look all she wanted, but the answer would be the same. She shook her head.

He ran out the door without even a nod of acknowledgment. If Kee said no, then it was no. She followed, trusting to whatever next step he saw that no one else could.

Wide open. They were running in the wide open. She didn't need to squint to make out all of the planes. The guard tower that stood west along the wall now towered barely half a mile distant, etched clear against the predawn pink of the sky. The last of the stars had gone, and still they ran.

He dodged and weaved for no reason she could see, better to run straight line, but she followed and did the same.

Then Archie disappeared and Kee dove to the ground. Crawling forward, she spotted the end of a drainage ditch. Archie lay in the bottom of it, barely four feet down.

Kee took her knife and began harvesting the young wheat all around her. She tossed it down in large handfuls. When her nerves could stand it no longer, she rolled over the edge and landed hard against Archie.

His grunt of pain was out of all proportion to the hit.

He began scooping dirt on her. Kee squeezed her eyes shut and did her best not to sneeze. Now she was the same color as the trench. Good thinking. They'd use the wheat as additional cover when it was full daylight.

When the dirt shower stopped, she pointed up the side of the ditch. They popped their heads up and over the edge. It was a good position. From here she had a decent line on most of the runway. She tried not to glance over her shoulder and see how good a view the guard tower had of them.

She couldn't resist. Actually, it wasn't bad. Whoever dug the ditch had left more dirt on the southern bank. They were fairly well hidden. Fairly. She pointed.

But Archie wasn't beside her. He was back in the bottom of the ditch holding his arm with a hand, with a very red hand.

She slid down beside him.

"Are you hurt?" Stupid question. She pulled out a switchblade and flicked it open. In moments she'd cut back the *hajib* and exposed his flight suit. More red. In seconds she was down through that as well.

"Archie, you've really got to stop getting shot. It's not good for you."

"Noticed. That. Mysel—Ow! Shit!" A whispered hiss. "That hurts!"

She found the entry hole. Very little blood there, as it was naturally clamped by his arm held tight against his body.

"He got me. Under the arm. Feelsh wrong."

Kee didn't like the sudden slur in his voice. She shifted his arm. He went sheet white and clamped his teeth on a groan.

"It feelsh more than wrong." She imitated his slur trying to make something that scared her so much at least a little bit funny.

She found the bullet lying against the back of his shoulder. It had punched through, and been trapped against him by his body armor. Dozens of tiny white shards of bone were scattered through the bloody mess. The fact that there was no pumping blood was the only good thing about the whole situation.

She yanked her medical kit free and opened it. She pulled out a field ampule of morphine.

"No." Archie caught her wrist. "Not yet. I need to think still."

"Well, this is gonna hurt like a bitch."

"Just do it. You know. You love. Causing me pain."

Kee scrambled to the edge of the ditch and scanned the airfield quickly. No activity, but she didn't dare look at the sky. It was plenty bright enough to see what she was doing without a flashlight. Time was running very short. If it was going to hurt him, better to do it fast.

She used tweezers to pick out most of the bone shards, rinsed the holes with antiseptic, and hit them with a little glue to close the wounds. Then she slid a rolled bandage up between his arm and body and tied it tight over the top. A quick flip with a triangular bandage and she had him in a sling. Then she pulled out her Vetrap and began binding his arm, sling and all, to his body. He looked near to passing out. She asked him a question to keep him conscious.

"What about the two bodies we left back there?"

He flopped his head until he faced in the direction of the hut, though it remained hidden from view. He blinked rapidly a few times as she continued wrapping his arm.

"Maybe we could pretend that Evans and Arlov did that. It will be the least of today's mysteries we leave behind if this all works."

"And what are the chances of that?" Kee didn't actually want an answer to that question, but she wanted to keep his attention. If she lost him right now, she didn't know what she'd do. He'd battered down most of her defenses, defenses that had served her well for six years, and she'd need time to put them back in place. If she could even resurrect them after the holes he'd punched through them.

Archie clearly struggled to concentrate, but his guess was as bad as hers and she could see him trying to hide his thoughts. Their chances were lousy, really lousy.

When she finished, he nodded, sweat streaming down his face. He pointed to the south edge of the trench and the stalks of wheat scattered about them.

She didn't even have to be told. They remained in sync. Kee grabbed a handful of the wheat. Crawling up the south side, she reached a hand over the edge and began planting the stalks upright in the soil. Another dozen inches of shield. In moments, a line of waving stalks blurred the sightlines of the guard tower.

Kee returned her attention to the field. Still no plane on the runway. They weren't too late. So many jets were parked here, dozens, maybe hundreds sat along the taxiways. It was hard to decide where to look. Tires. She tried to identify the ones with flat tires so that she could discount them. Even through her scope, the heat shimmer already rising off the runway and the flat angle of sight made that impossible to see. Besides, the dozens of dome-shaped hangers could be hiding anything.

The hardened hangars. Once more she slid out the photo of the two happy couples, the two pregnant women. The oddly shaped hills in the background hadn't been hills. They were the hardened hangars, dirt mounded over each structure to protect it from gunfire and smaller bombs. Scrub trees growing on them to stabilize the soil. The four of them had stood right on K2 air base for the photo. She propped it in the face of the trench. No doubt about it, her two dogs were here somewhere.

The heart of the base lay at the west end of the field and the town of Khanabad to the north. Now she just needed two crazy pilots and their plane.

She checked her watch. One hour until the start of the breakfast meeting in Tashkent. Three hundred miles away, dignitaries, presidents, and premiers would all be rolling out of bed and showering, having no idea they could well be starting the last hour of their lives.

"Is that them?" Archie had crawled up beside her one-handed, with his rifle scope clutched in his fist. His attention was directed far to the west end of the field.

Kee swung her rifle, not too fast. She didn't want to draw attention.

There. Two men climbing up ladders on either side

of a massive jet. Damn, the thing was huge. How was she supposed to take that down? It stood as tall as a two-story building. Its swept-back wings were longer than the Black Hawk's rotor span.

"She looks a hundred feet long."

"Only seventy-four," Archie replied between gasps of breath.

"Oh. That makes me feel so much better." She wanted to check him. She wanted to drag him to the nearest hospital, Uzbekistani or otherwise. She wanted to shout and cry. None of which would help her find the calm zone necessary for a hard sniper shot. Hard? Hell! Impossible was more like it.

"Can't you get them now?"

Kee gauged the seventy-four feet along the horizontal crosshair.

"Not a chance. Over two thousand meters. We need to be under twelve hundred. If I want any real chance, under a thousand."

"And less would be better."

"And less would be better," Kee agreed.

"Too bad we didn't bring along the 30 mm cannon."

"Too bad." It weighed more than Kee did, and that was without the ammo or the electrical supply to run it.

Kee watched the two helmeted men working over the plane. A couple of ground crew helped them. Probably with no idea they were helping prepare for the cataclysmic attack. Either they had men on the inside, or they'd presented very convincing credentials. Just as Evans had pulled strings for the free ride from SOAR. It made sense that Arlov would have those connections after four years as the base commander. Able to pull in favors from a few other people who'd hated his fall from good fortune.

They appeared so calm from this distance as they inspected the bombs being underslung. The calm of knowing that they were so close to their goal. Certain death was the accepted end for these men. Perhaps it was a relief, knowing they'd soon be joining their wives. If Archie died, Kee couldn't exactly see immolating herself. If she lost Archie and Dilya in the same instant, she might be pissed enough at the world to do it anyway.

Kee knew to stop watching. She couldn't stay on scope, fully alert for more than fifteen minutes. Snipers were trained to lie low for hours, days if necessary. But they were also trained that once the scope came to their eye, they were on full alert. Her body had been taught over and over what to expect when she finally sighted her weapon. That's why it was best to have a spotter. Someone to keep out a detailed eye until she was ready to shoot. Then someone to watch her back while she did. Her absolute concentration on her target would allow an elephant to trip on her before she noticed him.

She slouched in the bottom of the ditch and drank some water. They would be ten minutes at least. She couldn't trust Archie's ability to spot for her now, so she'd have to risk a longer alert.

Once more she stared at the photo perched on the ditch wall. She could remember most of the faces she'd ever taken down as a sniper, but she'd never before had a picture to study at length. Normally her assignments were in the heat of combat, like clearing the machine gun nest above Naopari. Unlike the Hostage Rescue Team or Black Ops, she rarely hunted an individual.

Long ago, these two men had wives. Children on the way.

She closed her eyes and pictured once more Archie and Dilya. But this time she saw them dead. Splattered on the floor of that tiny three-room farmhouse in the Uzbekistan desert.

"They're still checking their systems. The fuel truck just drove up."

But Archie was here, here beside her.

"They never had a chance."

"A chance for what?" Archie slid down beside her. "That should keep them busy for a few minutes."

Kee handed him the photo and the half-full bottle of water. He studied it while he drank. That thoughtful face frowning suddenly.

"They were pregnant."

Kee nodded. "They never had their family. It was taken from them. And now I'm supposed to..." She couldn't say it. If it were her, she'd bomb the living hell out of the SCO.

"Did you notice the markings on the jet?"

Kee shook her head.

"Uzbekistan. They aren't trying to start a world war with a Russian jet as we'd guessed. Russian design, yes, but Uzbek military. If the Uzbek military is seen killing the leaders of the organization's members, the other five members of the SCO will shred Uzbekistan. Dismantle it one piece at a time until nothing is left. Until Afghanistan looks like a luxury vacation spot. It will never again be a legitimate country with its own government. Evans and Arlov are very smart. Their vengeance is very, very targeted. They are using the SCO to get back at the Uzbekistan government who decided to kill their pregnant wives."

"We should let them." Kee couldn't believe the words even as she spoke them, but it was true. It was right.

"Kee."

Here it comes. The order from First Lieutenant Archibald Stevenson III. The command to honor country and flag. The command of the military.

And from his perspective, he'd be right.

Chapter 53

"IT CHANGES EVERYTHING, DOESN'T IT?"

Of course Archie wouldn't hit her with the expected. But he was right. Kee kicked at the ditch wall.

It did change everything. And that was the problem. She understood herself as Sergeant Kee Smith. She understood the woman who had climbed from the streets to SOAR. Even, as much as she hated to admit it, she understood the girl who grew up fighting for survival on the streets, becoming hard and self-sufficient.

The woman who curled up with the same man night after night was a mystery. One who enjoyed every second that a little girl clung to her side. One who begged to be told she was loved. That woman had come from another planet.

"Alien abduction."

"What?" he said with a laugh.

A soft, friendly sound that surprised Kee. She couldn't bring herself to explain it.

"Okay, Sergeant Smith." But it wasn't the Lieutenant speaking, it was still Archie. "It is up to you. I couldn't make that shot, even if my arm didn't have a perforation running clear through it and hurt so much it keeps making my eyes cross. Yes, Evans and Arlov were shafted. A lousy, undeserved deal. And yes, Washington and the President's orders are very far away. We're the team on the spot, and you're the one with the ability. So, here's my question to you, it's the same one I ask myself each time I fly. If you let them go, let them continue the killing in the name of revenge, is that something you can live with?"

Kee pictured Archie's face if she didn't at least try for the shot. He'd be furious.

"They killed Dilya's parents, and their plan will kill many, many more."

That hurt her heart so badly she was half afraid it would stop beating.

"Either way," he continued, "you will feel awful for them, family is so important to you. But if you let them kill more families, I question if you are strong enough to live with that."

He knew her so well. She had killed Anna's killers. Immediate blood satisfaction. Instant vengeance. She still believed she'd had been right to do it. And the killing had stopped there. If she'd instead hunted them and their families, she'd have sparked a turf war that might have taken down dozens. Here it would be millions. The killing had to stop somewhere.

He must have read her face for he nodded. "Just because the choice sucks doesn't make it wrong."

Chapter 54

KEE AND ARCHIE CRAWLED BACK TO THE UPPER EDGE of the ditch. She checked on Dog One and Dog Two in the scope. The fuel truck had pulled away. They were climbing the ladders on either side of the plane. They sat side by side in their jet. A pair of crewmen pulled the ladders away.

That cockpit worried her. She'd be trying to penetrate the canopy at an awfully long distance. The bullets might be so spent by the time they reached the jet that they'd bounce off the glass rather than punch through. But she had an image in her head and hoped that the desert heat was on her side.

The area behind the jet shimmered as they started the engines. A wave of heat ripples rolled back from the jet's twin exhaust cowlings. In moments they were rolling toward the far end of the runway.

And they were rolling with the canopy hinged up. Now the question came. How long would they leave it up? Closed, the heat would pummel the men until they were moving at flight speed. She was banking on them leaving it open as long as possible, closing it only as they took off.

They taxied to the far end of the runway and paused at the edge though no one else was around. Probably requesting clearance from the control tower. Making very certain they were seen, but that they didn't set off any alarms. They needed to fly almost an hour to cross the five hundred kilometers to Tashkent without being suspected or intercepted.

Kee double-checked the seating of the twenty-round magazine in the rifle. She ran the bolt closed by hand to keep it silent. She propped the spare five-round magazine beside the gun just in case. She checked the flash suppressor. At least it would shroud any muzzle flash and bang. The supersonic crack of the bullet itself... Well, hopefully it would be lost in the jet's engine noise. With a flick, she swung down the bipod beneath the barrel but didn't rest on it yet.

"Here we go," Archie whispered.

Kee spared him a glance and saw that he was watching the guard tower intently through his scope, rather than the jet. Exactly as he should. Kee turned back to her target, but kept listening.

"There's no patrol along the inside of the wall. I see one guy asleep inside the tower in his chair. There's another walking slowly around the balcony outside the upper story of the tower."

Kee concentrated on the jet; they were moving into position now. Three thousand meters. In the stillness of the morning air, the windup of the jet's engines reverberated across the field. A secondary echo sounded as a reflection off the perimeter wall.

"Rolling," she called to Archie. Safety off, she held the impossibly tiny dots of the two helmeted figures in her sights.

"The outside guard has stopped on the far side of the tower to watch. Maybe he won't hear us from there."

Kee couldn't worry about that now. She was in the

zone. Noise faded. The jet's whine, which would be getting louder as it approached, faded in her head. The only sound she heard was the beating of her own heart. Steady, unwavering, one second apart. She could see the scope crosshairs pop up ever so slightly with each beat of her heart.

She knew where her shot would have to be. Where they would cross into range. She only hoped the canopy was still open when they arrived.

Lowering her lead hand, she planted the bipod solidly on the soil and clicked the scope down for maximum range. Eleven hundred meters, theoretically possible.

The jet required a long takeoff roll. This was no American Hornet, but still they were gaining speed quickly. The canopy started coming down, slowly closing from the rear like a giant clamshell.

They were almost beside her now. Moving nearly a hundred miles an hour and still accelerating. Her mind calculated how far to lead them, and her hands instinctively shifted to compensate for the answer.

Through her scope she could see the face of the nearer one clearly. Colonel James Evans sat with his head up, looking directly down the runway. Picturing the last moment of his life, as they killed the SCO cabinet.

On the backside of the heartbeat, Kee fired. At this range, the round would take a second and a half to reach the plane.

On the next heartbeat she shifted her aim, and with the next beat she fired at the second pilot. Then she swung farther ahead of them and began dropping a round per heartbeat. Up. Down. Slightly ahead. Slightly behind. Trying to set up a cloud of lead for them to run into, but she knew it wasn't needed. She'd done it solid the first time.

Evans's head whipped sideways as the round caught him in the helmet.

Arlov turned to look just as his round came in and caught him in the face. Not centered, but Kee wasn't complaining. The jet veered as Arlov collapsed.

Evans wasn't dead. He clutched for the control and steadied the plane.

Then he caught up with one of the other rounds Kee had placed in his path. This one hit him in the neck and he collapsed on Arlov just as the canopy slid shut. She could see a couple of the later rounds bouncing off the canopy's glass.

The jet continued to roar ahead at full throttle with no guiding hand. But she couldn't trust it. If the jet merely ran off the runway and bogged down in the sand, too many people would recognize Evans from five years before. For this whole plan to work, no American could be found here. The rounds of NATO 7.62 mm ammunition she'd fired had to disappear, not appear in some autopsy. This had to simply be an unexplained accident.

She fired her last three rounds at the bombs hanging under the wing. Barely conscious of the motion, she dropped the magazine into the dirt and rammed the five-round mag into the gun. Even as she did, she could see the earlier rounds bouncing off the bomb casings.

"Archie. My left thigh pouch. Ten more rounds. Reload."

Kee could feel the probing fingers along her side as she unloaded five more rounds into the bombs. The jet was past them now, the shots were becoming longer again. Less powerful.

She dropped that magazine and he slapped the re-filled mag into her open palm. How far had he strained himself to do that? Kee couldn't spare the time to ask. She rammed the magazine home and pulled the bolt to load the first round into the chamber.

Still no joy. No hit on the munitions that mattered.

"Aim for the rocket motors." Archie's voice sounded soft. Strained. But his brain still worked.

The jet would be starting to fly now if there'd been anyone at the controls. It was nearing the end of the run-way. From her rearward angle on the massive jet, she could see the target Archie had picked out.

Kee didn't aim at the bombs, but at the drive motor of one of the missiles. She emptied the magazine, shooting on the down stroke and the up stroke of her heartbeat. The third round did it, but she kept firing. She was re-leasing round eight when number three struck. She sent the last two on their way and her magazine was empty, but it no longer mattered.

The fuel for the missile's drive motor exploded. In a cascade reaction, the missile went off, which triggered the bombs. They in turn blew off the wing, and a thun-dercloud of fire rolled upward as the wing tanks of jet fuel were breached.

She slid back, even as she fired the last round, down into the ditch. Archie wasn't lying beside her. She grabbed his boot and dragged him down to the bottom of the ditch with her.

The ground shock hit them first, a basso thump that filled the ditch with dust so thick Kee could barely breathe. She covered her face with the long cotton sleeve of her native garb.

Then the sharp "Krump!" of the plane's explosion. Seconds later a heat wave led a wall of dust over the trench and Kee half feared they'd catch on fire themselves. Her exposed hands stung with the sudden heat. But the wave rolled over them and departed for the perimeter wall as quickly as it had arrived.

When she dared uncover her face and open her eyes, Archie still lay at the bottom of the trench. She crawled up the south side of the trench. Her shield of fake wheat was gone. Scorched back to the earth. Thankfully, there were no fires on the fields, the crops hadn't dried out for harvest yet.

Kee swung her rifle over, then, remembering the ammunition was gone, tossed it aside and fished for the SCAR carbine. In the shock and dirt it took her a moment to find it and bring it to bear. She had to blow on the scope twice to clear it enough to use.

The blast had blown all the glass out of the tower windows. Both men up and moving, but pointing at the jet, not at her ditch. Not reaching for their guns. Okay. They hadn't been seen.

A glance in the other direction attested to the complete destruction of the jet. Bits of metal were scattered for hundreds of yards, none bigger than her hand. And a tornado of burning jet fuel swirled skyward from what little was left of the jet.

She slid back to the bottom of the trench.

"Hey." Kee held up a dust-caked hand and inspected both sides. "I can barely see us."

Archie didn't answer.

She rolled him quickly onto his back, a puff of dust by his nostrils affirmed he was breathing even before she bent down to listen.

His eyes fluttered open. "How'd we do, Helen?"

Helen. Damn the man. "We done good. Quiet now."

He tried to sit up, leaned on his bad elbow and groaned.

"Sorry about this, Archie." She dug around until she found the med kit. Pulling out the morphine ampule, she snapped off the cap and jammed it against his bare arm, just below the shoulder. In minutes, he settled into quiet sleep.

She retrieved their weapons and settled in to wait.

Chapter 55

"So I collected the spent rounds to avoid any evidence, covered ourselves with wheat, and waited out the daylight." Kee knelt beside Archie and watched John redo his bandaging. Archie lay still on the dirt floor of the hut, but his color was good under the flashlight's beam. It had been a long, brutal walk back, but they'd managed. She'd had to rig a rope from their three rifle straps to get him over the wall.

Beale wanted to come fetch them when they radioed in, but Archie had mumbled that he'd rather walk. Didn't dare the risk of flying so close to the still humming air base.

"This is one ugly field dressing, Smith." But there was good humor in it. Good enough, it had kept the blood in and the arm immobile.

The saline drip feeding into his arm would help more.

John poured some antiseptic over the wounds and began rewrapping it.

Kee kept to herself how she'd spent those fourteen hours of daylight hiding in the ditch. Holding Archie's hand as they lay in the middle of a hostile air base they'd just attacked. Because it appeared to be an accident, only a few patrols had come near them. And the only soldier to even glance into the dry irrigation ditch in the middle of the airfield didn't see them lying there beneath the wheat and dust. In between, she'd fought off the hysteria of fear that she might have to go through life without Archie.

Their childhoods had been so different. Yet they'd both ended up in the same ditch, skin shaded to the same color with layers of desert dust that still clung to them.

Now, kneeling on the dirt floor of the hut, Kee looked down at the unconscious Archie and wondered how slow she'd been to really see him. How many times had the man said he'd loved her? She hadn't kept count at first, then she'd tried to but failed. Her mind couldn't stay in a "keeping tally sheets" mode when they were together.

Kee now truly understood how strong a woman Emily Beale was. Her man was down, and still she'd flown. She caught the Major watching her. Yes, her man was hit and she'd still done the job.

A brief nod. A nod and a smile. That warm smile. Not the one she'd offered Dilya, nor the sappy sweet one she sometimes aimed at her husband. It was the warm smile of a friend. Of an equal. They were all in this and Kee had proven her place on the team.

"Well." Big John tucked in the tail end of the bandage. "That was one heck of a thump you set off. It shook the walls here, we were showered in decades of dust and crap." John wasn't joking. He, the Major, and Dilya were gray with bits of an ancient Uzbekistan hut still, though they had clearly washed their faces and hands.

Kee held the hand on Archie's uninjured side and watched him breathe. Dilya leaned against Kee's back, with her chin resting on Kee's shoulder. The girl's arms clasped loosely around her neck, as they both looked down at him.

"I gave him another half dose of the painkiller,"

Big John told her. "If he's too wakeful, we'll hit him with more."

"Good. That's good." Kee watched him sleeping. She had never so enjoyed watching a man sleep. Though this wasn't the contented nap after sex, it was another side of the same man. Calm. At peace with himself. At peace with his choices.

And he'd made it clear, she was one of his choices.

"Kee."

"Yes, Emily?"

John startled and looked at her then the Major.

"Could you two translate for me? John, go to the chopper. Bring back a portable stretcher and all of the Uzbekistani *som* from the bug-out bag."

"All of it?"

"Yes, we're going to buy a truck."

It had taken some work, but Kee managed to translate Emily's messages through Dilya to the family.

"Best for you if you don't mention you saw us. Sorry about the truck." And Kee sketched a map in the dirt floor showing where to find it. Maybe they could salvage it. If not, there'd been two thousand dollars worth of *som*, enough for a new truck or at least a couple of years' income.

The man, still flexing his injured hand, though John had reset the dislocated fingers, moved slowly to retrieve his shattered gun. They all watched him closely, but he held it sideways and gave it to the Major to take away. She nodded solemnly as she took it.

They took their final leave and turned for the

helicopter when she noticed that Dilya no longer shadowed her side. She trotted back to the main house, now
lit by a single candle. Her throat closed in panic. Panic
of what?

Her eyes stung as she imagined Dilya choosing to stay
with her own people. A family who spoke her language.

Dilya knelt before the smallest child, a girl of barely
five. The child looked back at her wide-eyed, her features could well have been Dilya's half a lifetime ago.
Were they kin or merely the same race? There was no
way to ever know.

Dilya reached inside her coat and pulled out Archie's
cat. She held it close for a long moment, then slipped it
into the little girl's hands.

"*Sebiya*." Dilya told the girl her cat's name.

"Young girl. Little sister." Kee translated in her head
as she faded back into the night, to give Dilya the privacy of her gift.

When Dilya joined her a moment later outside the
door, Kee made certain to give her a tight hug and a
kiss on the head. They ran hand in hand to catch up
with the others.

Near midnight, they were aloft, twenty feet above the
ground, and moving fast. Major Beale flew alone while
Kee and Big John sat at the miniguns.

At the border, they picked up an escort of Major
Henderson and the Chinook. Henderson had limped
home, loaded into Clay's bird, and turned right back
around to be there waiting for them. He'd been flying twenty of the last thirty hours and had five more
to go.

Kee glanced forward, wondering whether to ask

permission to sit with Archie. Even as she decided not to push her new friendship, Emily turned and mouthed one word at her.

"Go."

She went.

Chapter 56

KEE PEELED HER HELMET AND MOVED TO CHECK THE three parkas wrapped over and around Archie. He was still all tucked in and sleeping.

Dilyana sat bundled in her parka against the cold desert night with her two hands wrapped around Archie's good hand, the only exposed part of him other than his face. The bandage had showed no additional sign of bleeding after they moved him, so they'd decided it was safe to cover it and keep him warm rather than keep it exposed so that they could monitor the wound.

Kee slipped in behind her, so that Dilyana ended up sitting in her lap. She wrapped one arm around the girl's waist and rested her other hand over Dilya and Archie's.

"The Kee did win?" Dilya had to shout a little for Kee to hear her.

"Yes. The Kee did win."

"Good?"

Kee knew the question behind the words. Had she killed the men who had killed Dilya's parents? Against all chance she had. Killed them, and saved the future existence of the SCO and the Uzbekistan nation with no one the wiser. But Dilya wouldn't know about or understand that. Wouldn't understand the two women who had died alone. Or the effect their love would have years later on the choices made by their two men.

In that photo, once again safely tucked in Kee's

pocket, they had been in love. Been happy together. The four of them, they'd had family and been happy. Then very sad. And now dead.

She nodded. The word "good" no longer right, but she'd done the job.

Dilya watched her face for a long moment, then she too nodded. Sad and quiet. She leaned her head against Kee's shoulder.

Maybe the girl somehow understood. Understood that the price had been paid, but that price ran terribly high.

Now they had to think ahead. What to do with the girl? No parents. No way to find any other family. She was as much an orphan as Kee. As alone in the world.

Except she wasn't.

Kee had only thought of herself alone.

She glanced forward. Big John watched intently over his gun despite the flying escort to either side. Kee could just see Emily's shoulder as her commanding officer flew them home, alone in the cockpit, but her husband flying close by her side.

Home.

Kee had called the Army home for a long time. Before that, she had never used the word, it only served to make her uncomfortable. But in the armed services it was one of those standard greeting questions. "Where've you served? What units? Where's home?" Replying "the Army" to the last, offered with a wry laugh, got you past that hurdle.

But home meant more now. It included this crew. It included Emily and Big John. And it included Archie and a little girl.

"Dilyana?"

The girl lifted her head and faced her.

"If Dilyana want, have Kee for mother, Archie for father."

The girl's eyes went wide, then she wrapped her arms so tightly around Kee's neck she could barely breathe. And, apparently not trusting words, nodded her head fiercely against Kee's shoulder.

Kee felt the slightest squeeze on her hand, where she still held Archie's.

She squeezed back, hoping it was more than a reflex response. His hold grew stronger, she hadn't imagined it.

Looking over, she met his half-lidded gaze.

"Hey there, Helen."

"Hey yourself, Magic Man."

His gaze traveled for a moment to the girl snuggled against her. Then returned to hers.

"Did I hear correctly?"

"What?"

His smile broadened, started in that funny way of his. Finally that lopsided grin that swept her away.

"Did you just propose to me?"

Kee blinked. Hard. Had she? She'd offered herself as stepmother and Archie as stepfather to a girl who had accepted. A promise made.

She'd pictured them each caring for Dilyana and raising her, but she hadn't pictured it as "family." As man and woman. As husband and wife.

Archie had already made his choice clear. He'd chosen her.

Now it was up to her to make her choice. Maybe she hadn't meant to propose to him. But now that she had, the picture came loud and clear, five by five.

"Damn straight, Night Stalker! And, no, you don't get a choice. Your answer is yes."

He held her hand more tightly as he headed back to sleep.

"Good. That's my Kee."

"I love you, Archie."

He nodded vaguely as the drugs took him back under.

Damn the man, he'd better remember that she'd finally said it. For the first time in her life had said the words.

Then Kee smiled and kissed Dilya on top of the head.

Kee would have plenty of opportunity to remind him.

After all, she now knew exactly how to describe how he made her heart feel. How he made her feel.

Loved.

Chapter 57

KEE SPUN THE WHEEL EASILY AND THE SAILBOAT swung its bow up into the wind. Just as they lost all headway, Archie let the anchor loose. It plunged down into the crystalline waters with a splash. They drifted back until he snubbed it off, setting the anchor in the sandy bottom and stopping the boat's drift.

In moments they had the sails furled, each working down either side of the boom, and the boat rested easily off the beach.

The beach. That same beach they had run on a lifetime ago. A lifetime because surely Kee had been a different person her last time here.

"How's your shoulder?" Kee inspected the scars, the ugly jags made by the bullet and the neat surgical lines. They stood out white against the fine tan he'd cultivated on medical leave. Wearing nothing but swim trunks revealed the serious work he'd done to keep fit. Even the Roman gods who'd ruled over these cliffs and sea couldn't have looked this good.

"Will you stop asking me that?" But Archie rolled the shoulder easily, revealing good muscle definition around the joint replacement. He'd never be a hundred percent, not enough to fly forward combat again, but he'd worked through the pain of physical therapy and it wouldn't be a disability in any other situation.

"Have you decided what you're going to do?"

He closed his eyes and faced into the wind, so that it rippled his hair back. The man was so damn handsome, Kee still kept being surprised every time she woke next to him or saw the diamond ring she mostly wore strung with her dog tags.

His hand slid around her waist and pulled her in close.

"I'm going to take the Majors' offer."

"Good." It was right. Hard to think of Archie not in the copilot's seat, but moving into the AMC role, well, no one could be better than her Archie. Air Mission Commander planned and ran multi-aircraft missions. Fifth Battalion, 3rd Company needed one. Needed his strategic genius combined with his intimate knowledge of the team. It was perfect.

"It will also let me give Dilya some security." He didn't finish the sentence, no SOAR flier would. Dilya would still have a parent if Kee were ever shot down. He, at least, would be on the ground or safe in the background aboard a command chopper. Their girl would never be without a parent again.

"Assuming," Kee drawled out, "your parents let us have her back after this." Steve and Calledbetty had been ecstatic at the chance to spoil the girl rotten while Kee and Archie took a delayed honeymoon.

She leaned in and kissed Archie on the scar.

He pulled her around until they were tucked together, the deck rolling gently beneath their feet.

"I have this crazy idea."

"Hmm…" Kee laid her ear against his chest to listen to his heart as he spoke.

"There's this grassy hilltop I know about. It's a bit of ways. But if we run…"

She looked up into the sky-blue eyes that always inspected her with such wonder. With such love.

"Seems I remember a place like that." She considered how her body was humming already from holding her husband close. Her husband.

"There's also a very nice bed much closer by." She tapped a bare foot on the decking.

In an easy motion, belying any injury, he swept her into his arms and headed for the hatchway.

READ ON FOR AN EXCERPT FROM THE FIRST BOOK IN
THE NIGHT STALKERS SERIES

THE *Night* IS MINE

AVAILABLE NOW FROM SOURCEBOOKS CASABLANCA

Chapter 1

THE CNN FILM CREW HAD MADE IT FUN. BUT NOW...

The laptop stood balanced on a couple of empty, dull green ammo cases for the minigun. Sweaty pilots and crew stood gathered around the computer, waiting for the network to roll the clip.

Captain Emily Beale and her team rushed into the tent from the Black Hawk helicopter landing area, still in their hot, sticky flight gear, helmets clutched under their arms. Just past dawn here, late-evening news back home.

A dozen guys who hadn't been lucky enough to fly that night packed the already baking tent. They wore shorts and army green, sleeveless tees revealing a wide variety of arm tattoos. Some with girls' names, some snakes, some helicopters, all with feathered wings. The men squatted on the dirt and sand that passed for a floor, perched on benches, or stood, feet wide, with arms crossed over muscled chests.

The observation jolted Emily a moment before she shrugged it back into her mind's dustiest footlocker. Just another reminder that the entire female roster of this forward deployment included only one name—her own.

Brion Carlson came on and flashed his famous scowl, cuing his multimillion-person audience that the next clip would be fun, not war-torn hell, not drowned mother of twins, not car pileup at eleven.

Emily's free hand rested on the M9 Beretta sidearm

in her holster. Tempting. A couple of 9 mm rounds through the screen might cheer her up significantly. But then they'd all know how she felt. Be hard to laugh it off after that level of mayhem. She knew hundreds of ways to kill a person but how do you kill a newscast? Shooting a laptop didn't meet the ultimate criteria for complete suppression. She scanned the intent faces of her flightmates. Still, a bit of localized destruction held its temptations.

She'd only been in the company for two months. The first week or so, she'd been a total outsider. But as she'd proved herself on mission after mission, she'd gained acceptance, grudging at first, then not. Now, on the precarious cusp of true welcome, this.

"Hot from the fighting front, at an undisclosed location in Southwest Asia, CNN caught up with Black Hawk pilot Captain Emily Beale as she cooks up a storm for her flight crew. She's the first, and so far the only, female pilot to qualify to fly helicopters for SOAR, the elite 160th Airwing."

"Air regiment," Big John called out. Someone shushed him.

"With the Night Stalkers, as the Special Operations Aviation Regiment call themselves—"

"Damn straight," John answered and then turned to scowl at whoever had been foolish enough to try and shush him before.

"—she flies, literally, where no woman has flown before."

The clip rolled. A close-up of steak sizzling on a surface so black that it didn't reflect the scorching, midday sun. Odd place to start, but what the hell. The Black

Hawk's nose cone covering the terrain-following radar assembly really had been plenty hot to sear a steak. And the meat had tasted damn good. A humorous opening. So far she could live with this.

Then the camera pulled back.

First the nose of her chopper, which was kind of cool. Made a nice surprise for the average viewer.

Then the camera swung toward the person wielding the cooking tongs.

She groaned. Silently. But, damn! She'd given them loads of footage why she flew had answered a thousand probing questions about a woman in a man's world and this is how they started?

Ray Bans. Blond hair running loose over her shoulders. A trick only Special Forces, SEALs, and SOAR pilots could get away with in all the U.S. military. The elite fighting teams were supposed to wear nonmilitary hair, even mustaches and beards, to blend in wherever they were inserted. SOAR pilots usually did the close-cropped military thing, but not her company. She liked the sound of that, her company. No longer the newbie on the outside looking in.

The laptop image scanned down her body as if she were a model for *Playboy* or *Hustler*. This was not what she'd signed up for. At least it would be uphill from here.

She'd made it into the Black Adders, the nastiest and toughest company that SOAR had ever fielded. They belonged to the 5th Battalion, which was the nastiest and toughest battalion, no matter what the other four claimed. That's why the 3rd Black Hawk Company of the 5th Battalion of the 160th Special Operations Aviation Regiment (Airborne) wore their hair long. It made them more like their customers, the Special Forces operations specialists they transported to and from battle. Of course, none of them minded the added bonus of being able to thumb their noses at the establishment they'd give their lives to defend.

The camera continued its slow scan down her body. Army-green tank top. Running shorts and army boots. Standard desert camp gear. She was soaked in sweat, and the clothes clung to her like Saran Wrap. A point the cameraman had made the most of, both on his pan down and back up.

But this wasn't who she was. It wasn't the point of the interview. She flew the most lethal helicopter ever devised by man, and they were turning her into a porn star. Her grip on her still-holstered M9 sidearm grew painful, but she couldn't ease off.

"Em-i-ly!" "Whoo-hoo, Captain!" "Now that's what we're talking about!" The catcalls in the tent overrode the voice-over. Attracted attention from outside the tent. More air jocks drifted in to see what was up. Is that how they thought of her every day? To react would only admit her intimidation. And that door wouldn't be opened for anybody.

She should've shot the stupid screen while she had the chance.

Even on the tiny laptop you could see good muscle definition right at her fighting weight. Not bodybuilder, though she lifted enough weights. Still, she wasn't particularly happy with how she looked. She'd never met a woman who didn't feel that way.

Did guys feel like that? This crowd seemed pretty pleased every time the camera caught one of them. A lot of macho shoulder punching, hard enough to bruise, each time one of them made national television.

The next clip showed her pulling out an emergency foil blanket, good for reflecting away the worst of the sun if you were smacked down in middle of sand dune nowhere. She'd demo-ed how to use one to hide from the sun, even digging it into the sand before disappearing beneath.

But in the next instant, she knew this broadcast didn't go there. Instead they went with her quick origami moment to create a decent solar oven from the foil. Taken her a while to figure that one out back when she flew for the 101st. They jumped to a finished loaf of sourdough bread, from some starter she'd had smuggled in. Not bad. She could live with this. Somehow.

And then the next image rolled.

Not a helicopter or flight suit in sight. How long was this stupid clip anyway? They'd dogged her heels for a full day and this was the best they could do?

Back to the solar oven. The soufflé. They wouldn't. They couldn't. They did.

A whole circle of broad-shouldered, badass flyboys standing around her with their arms crossed over bare, serious-workout chests. A solid wall of shirtless, obviously posed male flesh she'd hadn't even noticed the news crew setting up. Her tiny image on the screen lifted the chocolate soufflé from the makeshift oven. Perfect. And the desert was so frigging hot that the soufflé didn't start its inevitable collapse from cooling until after the camera moved on. The round of applause had tickled her at the time. But on the squidgy, little piece-of-crap laptop, it just made her look like a half-naked Suzy Homemaker in shades.

"Flying into battle, you know her well-fed crew will follow Captain Emily Beale anywhere because she's the hottest chef flying." In the parting shot, a helmeted pilot, visible only as a silvered visor and blue-black helmet, lifted off in a swirl of dust.

Her helmet was purple with a gold-winged flying horse on the side, and everyone in the tent knew it. It remained clamped under her arm at this moment in case they wanted to double-check. She'd had no missions the day the film crew was in camp so they'd shot that dweeb Bronson, of all useless jerks.

That couldn't be the end of the clip. But the wrap shot was perfect, the camera following Bronson high into the achingly blue sky.

All those interviews about her pride as the first woman serving in a man's world.

Not one word made it in.

Descriptions of nasty but unclassified missions that she had been authorized to discuss.

All cut.

Actually, they hadn't used a single word. She'd never spoken. Just cooked and been ogled.

And finally, to drive the hammer home, they'd used Bronson in his transport bird, not her heavy, in-your-face, DAP Hawk for the closer. When you wanted a joy ride, you called Bronson. When you wanted it done, you loaded up her MH-60L Direct Action Penetrator Black Hawk.

They had to include at least one—

"In New York's Bryant Park today…" The laughter drowned out the parade of anorexic women who probably couldn't shoot a lousy .22 without getting knocked on their narrow butts.

She pulled her pistol and let fly at the laptop. The first shot shattered the screen and flipped it off the empty ammo case. The second spun it in midair, and the third punched the computer into the sand.

A dozen guys inspected the smoldering laptop in the ear-ringing silence and then Emily's face as she reholstered the sidearm. A little more mayhem than she'd intended, but she was a pilot first, dammit.

Then, as if on cue, several of the guys fist-pumped the air simultaneously.

"Sexiest chef flying, Captain!" "They got that right!" "Whoo-hoo!"

"Well, your next thousand meals are gonna be damned MREs." She shouted to be heard over the rabble.

They hooted and applauded in reply.

"Cold egg burritos!" The very worst of the Meals Ready-to-Eat menu.

"Ooo!" "We're so scared." "Show us how to make an oven." "Sexiest chef!"

She opened her mouth to offer a few uncouth words about how much they'd enjoyed watching their own lame selves—

"'Tenshun!" The deep voice sliced through the chatter like the rear rotor of her Black Hawk through a stick of softened butter. A voice that had sent a shiver down her spine ever since she'd first heard it two months before.

They all snapped to their feet as if they'd been electrocuted. Some part of the laptop still functioned, Carlson's voice sounded into the sudden silence. "At a recent concert, the Rolling Stones—"

A booted foot smashed down and delivered the coup de grâce to the wounded machine.

Major Mark "The Viper" Henderson stood two paces inside the rolled-back flap of the tent, one foot still buried in the machine. Six feet of cliché soldier. Broad shoulders, raw muscle, and the most dangerous-looking man Emily had ever met. His straight black hair fell to his squared-off jawline. His face clean shaven, eyes hidden by mirrored Ray-Bans. Rumor had it they were implanted and the major no longer needed eyes.

After two months, she couldn't say otherwise. He always wore the shades when he wasn't wearing a helmet for a night mission.

Even the first time they'd met, as purported civilians at Washington state's Sea-Tac Airport, he had worn them. Coming out of security, newly assigned to the 5th Battalion, she'd known instantly who waited for her. She doubted another person in the crowded airport would recognize him as a soldier; they'd both been trained to blend in. But she'd recognized Major Mark Henderson as if some part of her body had known him for years.

In the tent, he swiveled his head once, the sunglasses surveying the crowd. Every man jack of them knew the major had memorized exactly who was there, what they'd said, what they were about to say—and probably knew what they'd been thinking the moment they exited their mothers' wombs. If they weren't careful, he'd start telling them what they would be thinking about during their last moment on Earth, and none of them, not even Crazy Tim, wanted to run head-on into that level of mind-blower.

"There will be no gender-based commentary in this unit. Understood?"

"Sir! Yes, Sir!" Rang out so loudly it would've hurt Emily's ears if she hadn't been shouting herself.

Chapter 2

"Captain." Major Henderson turned, the laptop's plastic shell crumbling beneath his heel with a low moan, and stepped back out of the tent into the driving sun with no sign that he would ever break a sweat.

Emily tossed her helmet to Big Bad John, her crew chief from Kentucky coal mine country. The nickname had been inevitable. Six foot four and powerfully muscled. She hustled after the major, out of the tent and across the sandy landing field.

The most common theory placed Major Henderson's mother as part snake and his father as pure viper. The very fastest, most dangerous viper, everyone added quickly. There were even debates on exactly what breed that would be.

Others claimed that he hadn't been born but rather hatched.

But she'd flown with him the first two weeks before being given her own bird, and she'd seen the two small pictures he tucked in his window every flight. Once, when he'd been out of the bird, she'd leaned in to inspect them more closely.

One a young boy wearing mirrored shades, just like his highly decorated SEAL commander father who had Mark tucked under his arm.

And the other, much more recent of Mark and his parents, all mounted on some seriously large and majestic horses, and all three wore mirrored shades. He and his father could be copies of each other, except Mark was darker, his features more sharply defined. She could see where Mark had gotten that and his straight, dark hair. His mother was a tall woman with strong Native American features and a cascade of black hair that flowed past her shoulders almost to her waist. Above them arched a carved sign that looked quite new and proclaimed: "Henderson Ranch, Highfalls, MT." They were as stunning specimens of the human race as their mounts were of the equine.

Outsiders teased their company about being the Black Adders because their company so fixated on The Viper's nickname. Henderson's pilots took it as a compliment and painted winged, striking adders on their helos, all sporting Rowan Atkinson's Mr. Bean smile. About half the winged tattoos worn by the pilots in the tent depicted striking adders, though only Crazy Tim, to no one's surprise, had placed the classic, beak-nosed Mr. Bean face permanently on his skin.

Major Henderson wasn't just the commander of the 3rd Hawk Company of the 5th Battalion SOAR. He was also the most decorated, toughest son of a bitch in the 160th Air Regiment. And, despite her first impression at the airport, he wasn't much nicer on the ground. But he had the only thing that really mattered in covert helicopter operations. He was the best.

Only the most exceptional fliers were invited to interview week at the 160th. Only the toughest survived it with a residual shred of ego intact. And of the few who made it through the pearly gates of the back lot of Fort Campbell, Kentucky, over half flunked out of the eight months of initial training. Never mind the year and a half of advanced training after you'd made the grade. Only the most terrifyingly qualified of those who survived made command.

Stories of Major Mark Henderson abounded on all sides. One told that he'd taken on a battalion of the Republican Guard during Operation Iraqi Freedom, with only his bird and his wingman's, and won.

Emily had assumed that they were just telling the newbie tall tales. But the crew stuck to the tale of two lonely choppers, totaling eight men, against five hundred troops armed with the very best the Iraqis could buy from Russia. Around Major Mark Henderson, it almost seemed possible.

Another told of the time he'd been smashed down a hundred miles behind unfriendly lines and decided to use his time awaiting rescue to blow up a few military targets. He and his three-man crew had done it running from hidey-hole to hidey-hole with a jury-rigged, four-hundred-pound, nineteen-round rocket pod torn off his chopper in the crash. His actions supposedly opened a whole section of the battlefront for easy access.

And those were before you got into the real whoppers. Tall tales edged well past surreal, one of which Emily knew from personal experience to be completely accurate. And to this day she counted herself lucky to be alive after that mission.

She caught up with Major Henderson around the midfield line. Their base camp was an old soccer stadium. Tier upon tier of concrete benches coated in flaking whitewash ringed the field. Too arid to sustain grass, the field now sprouted with a dozen-odd helicopters of varying sizes and capabilities.

Black Hawks, the hammer force, ranged down near the enemy's goal line.

A flock of Little Birds sprouted about midfield ready to deliver clusters of four Special Forces operators to almost anywhere that they were needed fast. The birds were so small that the soldiers didn't even sit in them, but rather on fold-down benches to either side. A short step to ground or a thirty-meter fast rope into a zone too hot to land.

A pair of massive, twin-rotor Chinooks, half-hidden in heat haze and thermal shimmer, lurked around the home team's goal. The playing field was owned and operated by a well-oiled, three-company mash-up of the 1st and 5th SOAR battalions.

Sentries from the 75th Rangers were perched along the topmost row of the stadium looking outward. Dust rose from every footstep and hung in the still, breathless air for hours.

She matched her stride to his. It was always nice, those quiet moments when they walked side by side. Some kind of harmony like that very first day. She'd come through the gate, bag over her shoulder, and he hadn't even nodded or smiled. Just pivoted easily on his heel and landed in perfect synch with her as they headed toward parking.

The major continued to move steadily across the dusty field toward his small command center set up by the barricaded entrance tunnel at the home team end. Why had he interfered in the tent? She could have laughed it off. Could have. Wouldn't have. Maybe the major had been right to shut down the guys' teasing, but now there'd be an even bigger wall of separation to knock down, as if being a female pilot in a combat zone wasn't three strikes already.

They reached the end of the field together, like a couple out enjoying a quiet stroll. She shook her head to shed the bizarre image. Not with her commanding officer, and certainly not with a man as nasty and dangerous as The Viper.

He stepped onto the sizzling earth of the running track that surrounded the field. They were in Chinook country now. The Black Hawks and Little Birds were but vague suggestions in the morning's heat shimmer. Down here at the command end, the pair of monstrous Chinook workhorses squatted, their twin rotors sagging like the feathers of an improbably ugly ostrich. These birds looked far too big to fly, yet they could move an entire platoon of fifty guys and their gear, or a half platoon along with their ATVs, motorcycles, and rubber boats.

"I'm sorry, sir. I know I shouldn't have discharged a firearm in camp. I'll replace the computer, but I'm a pilot and those news guys didn't…"

He stopped and turned to look at her. Not a word.

"I just…" She looked very small and insignificant in his mirrored shades. Twice.

"Captain?" His voice flat and neutral.

"I… Dammit! I'm a pilot, sir. They had no right. No bloody, blasted stupid right to do that to me. I—"

"Don't care."

Her tiny, twinned reflection dropped her jaw.

Then Major Mark Henderson did the strangest thing.

He reached up a meat cleaver-sized hand and pulled his glasses down his nose. Now she knew she was screwed. She'd never be able to joke with the guys again about the major not having eyes.

Steel gray. As hard as his body. The most dangerous-looking viper she'd ever seen.

Then he smiled. She almost fell as she dropped back a step. The smile reached his eyes and turned them the soft, inviting gray of a summer sunrise.

"Do you think I give one good goddamn about a lousy piece of hardware or about what CNN thinks? In my command, only one thing matters: are you the best flying? Period." His voice was firm, but soft and friendly. Almost teasing.

Then he shoved his glasses back in place, and the smile clicked off in the same motion. He turned back for the tent.

She tried to follow. Really she did. But two thoughts rooted her in place.

First, had The Viper really just smiled at her? Been pleasant? It would prove he was human, which didn't seem much more likely than him pulling down his sunglasses.

Second, her body felt weak and ravished by his simple gaze, though it had not raked over her like the news camera. Those gray eyes, especially when he smiled... What would she have to do to have them look at her like that again?

It still pissed her off a bit. How would he like to be called the sexiest major flying?

She got her feet moving again.

He'd probably love it—he was a guy, after all.

About the Author

M.L. Buchman began writing novels on July 22, 1993, while on a plane from Korea to ride a bicycle across the Australian Outback. M.L. has been a substitute instructor for University of Washington's Certificate in Commercial Fiction program and spoken at dozens of conferences including RWA national and BookExpo. Past lives include: renovating a fifty-foot sailboat, fifteen years in corporate computer systems design, bicycling solo around the world, developing maps for a national franchise, and designing roof trusses, in roughly that order. M.L. and family live on an island in the Pacific Northwest in a solar-powered home of their own design.

"To Champion the Human Spirit, Celebrate the Power of Joy, and Revel in the Wonder of Love."
www.mlbuchman.com

Cover Me

by Catherine Mann

—〰—

It should have been a simple mission…

Pararescueman Wade Rocha fast ropes from the back of a helicopter into a blizzard to save a climber stranded on an Aleutian Island, but Sunny Foster insists she can take care of herself just fine…

But when it comes to passion, nothing is ever simple…

With the snowstorm kicking into overdrive, Sunny and Wade hunker down in a cave and barely resist the urge to keep each other warm…until they discover the frozen remains of a horrific crime…

Unable to trust the local police force, Sunny and Wade investigate, while their irresistible passion for each other gets them more and more dangerously entangled…

—〰—

Praise for Catherine Mann:

"Catherine Mann weaves deep emotion with intense suspense for an all-night read." —#1 *New York Times* bestseller Sherrilyn Kenyon

For more Catherine Mann, visit:

www.sourcebooks.com

Under Fire

by Catherine Mann

—⁓—

No holds barred, in love or war...

A decorated hero, pararescueman Liam McCabe lives to serve. Six months ago, he and Rachel Flores met in the horrific aftermath of an earthquake in the Bahamas. They were tempted by an explosive attraction, but then they parted ways. Still, Liam has thought about Rachel every day—and night—since.

Now, after ignoring all his phone calls for six months, Rachel has turned up on base with a wild story about a high-ranking military traitor. She claims no one but Liam can help her—and she won't trust anyone else.

With nothing but her word and the testimony of a discharged military cop to go on, Liam would be insane to risk his career—even his life—to help this woman who left him in the dust.

—⁓—

"Absolutely wonderful, a thrilling ride of ups and downs that will have readers hanging onto the edge of their seats."—*RT Book Reviews* Top Pick of the Month, 4½ stars

"Wild rides, pulse-pounding danger, gripping suspense, and simmering, sizzling, spiraling passion."—*Long and Short Reviews*

For more Catherine Mann, visit:

www.sourcebooks.com

Hot Zone

by Catherine Mann

—◦◦◦—

He'll take any mission, the riskier the better…

The haunted eyes of pararescueman Hugh Franco should have been her first clue that deep pain roiled beneath the surface. But if Amelia couldn't see the damage, how could she be expected to know he'd break her heart?

She'll prove to be his biggest risk yet…

Amelia Bailey's not the kind of girl who usually needs rescuing…but these are anything but usual circumstances.

—◦◦◦—

Praise for Catherine Mann:

"Nobody writes military romance like Catherine Mann!"
—Suzanne Brockmann, *New York Times*
bestselling author of *Tall, Dark and Deadly*

"A powerful, passionate read not to be missed!"
—Lori Foster, *New York Times* bestselling
author of *When You Dare*

For more Catherine Mann, visit:

www.sourcebooks.com